MW01121713

All the Clouds'll Roll Away

All the Clouds'll Roll Away

Book III

DREAMS TO LIFE

Taylor Morris

GAP MOUNTAIN PRESS
Jaffrey, NH

Copyright © 2009 Taylor Morris
Published by Gap Mountain Press
All rights reserved, including the right to reproduce this
book or portions thereof in any form whatsoever.
For information address Gap Mountain Press,
48 Bullard Road, Jaffrey, NH 03452
Printed in the United States of America

ISBN 978-0-9795603-2-3

Designed by Sally Nichols
Set in Goudy Old Style by Mullein Graphics
Printed and bound by Odyssey Press, Inc.

This book is a work of fiction. Names, characters, places and incidents are
products of the author's imagination or are used fictitiously. Any resemblance
to actual events or locales or persons living or dead is entirely coincidental.

for all of my children

Contents

Book III

DREAMS TO LIFE

Chapter 1

The air was new. The world was new. We had been transformed from caterpillar to butterfly. We had our wings, our bars, our uniforms which proved it and yet we were still so close to caterpillars that we felt like crawling.

"Ahhh, yes, uhh, lieutenant, sir, ummm, what can I get for you?"

"Just hand me some shades, those wings are blinding me."

The five of us: me, Hebert, Tony, RM and Dubya D slept late, ate at the O'Club, the Officers' Club, went everywhere together, reminded of the transformation by looking at each others' wings and bars, and for the first time in a year and a half had no duties. Our orders were to await further orders.

We had filled out forms asking which 'theatre' of the war we preferred—European, China-Burma-India (CBI), or South Pacific—when all the time they knew. There were no navy or marine flyers in Europe so there'd be no meeting with Von Richthofen's son. We were headed in the other direction.

For three days we read the papers and watched the war rocketing past us. Better to be told; 'Alright, line up, six consecutive hikes, one hundred miles a day.' Instead, nothing.

British, Canadians and Americans were in Italy; the American Seventh and Eighth armies were moving "up the boot."

General George Patton visited a hospital in Sicily and slapped two soldiers for malingering. Way off in Florida we argued about it. Patton, to me, was my cruel uncle up in north Louisiana with the glittering eyes. I stayed out of it but RM was livid, and accused Patton (and Tony) of stupidity and more.

"Well, I'm *glad* he did it!" Tony said, jeering at RM.

"Tony! The guy he slapped had malaria!" RM told him.

"Yeahhhh," Tony answered with a slur, "a lot of guys *say* they're 'sick' and get out of—"

"Mannnn, what are you trying to say??" RM was red in the face, waving his spider-like arms as if his own brother had been slapped. *"During a war people don't get sick? No more malaria during a war?? Tony I worry about you!"*

I knew RM was right and yet I stayed out of it. The tough, stern father-figure, the world-famous general, the hero, tough as nails. And something about it I hated. Dreamed of in fear.

"Awright, Tony, listen to this." RM read from the newspaper, "'*I won't have those cowardly bastards hanging around our hospitals. We'll probably have to shoot them sometime anyway, or we'll raise a breed of morons.*' That's General Patton!"

"Listen, RM! I *AGREE WITH HIM!*" Tony screamed, full of rage and something else. During the time the five of us had flown together we were forced to cooperate. Now there was no need for it. A kind of truth was coming out, things held in check while we went through.

"Hitler, my good man, couldn't have put it better. Now, if you agree with Patton, I'll say it again. That's Hitler talking. *In an American uniform . . .* So, I *worry* about you, Tony."

"Yeahh, well, I worry about YOU, RM."

Neither one was 'worried', but it was plain they hated one another.

Dubya D walked up to our table, just split seconds before the two started swinging, or before I'd have to separate them, with the only news that could have stopped it.

"The fuckin' orders are in. You can pick them up at the administration building!"

"WHAT?? WHAT'D YOU GET???"

"Dive-bombers . . . Naval Air Station Deland, Florida."

The drive over was agony. Our choices were carrier duty, or multi-engines. Multi-engines meant Patrol Bombers: "Take-off at ninety, land at ninety, yeah, and live to be ninety."

The multi-engine boys were looking for jobs after the war. "There *is* no after-the-war-for-a-fighter-pilot!" Those words fit *us* and, still, carrier duty was fighters, dive-bombers, or torpedo-bombers. Over those three we had *no* choice.

Slow, lumbering torpedo bombers were the worst. Over and over we had heard of the famous Torpedo Squadron Eight, the whole squadron gone to their deaths in a few minutes. Ducks sitting on water, making their torpedo runs at a hundred and twenty knots, straight ahead. So, it wasn't only risk and not just 'Gangway, fighter pilot!' It was knights on horseback, blazing speed and one person to a plane, no one else to worry about. Jam that throttle forward and get out of the way. It was the marine urging his men, "Come on, you wanta live forever?" It was the Corsair, fastest in the world and most beautiful; the inverted gull-winged widow-maker.

We raced to our fates.

Tony was first in line. "Fighters! Jacksonville! Corsairs! Hot damn! . . . Hot damn! . . . Hot damn!" He was jumping up and down, like a little kid on Christmas morning.

RM, dive-bombers! Naval Air station Deland, Florida!

Evan. Dive-bombers! Deland. He stood apart, reading it to make sure. I felt sick.

Tony was still yelling when I opened my orders. And dying not to read "Dive-bombers, N.A.S. Deland!"

I was dead in the water, watching life go on around me.

Had they just grabbed handfuls? Of one or the other?

The dream was over. RM tried to cheer me up, and old Dubya D, "At least we're all in it together."

Anyone but them I would have killed.

RM was trying to catch my eye, "Hey, man, we'll fly the *shit* out of that SBD. Hey! At least we didn't get Torpedo Bombers."

Evan, too, fellow webfoot, was going to Deland. And Evan was a great pilot . . . also.

Dubya D and RM lugged me over to the Officer's Club. Evan had dropped out at some point. Tony was gone. They were giggling about our new uniforms. Everyone in the place had to know we were as green as spring. New knights with shining wings. RM covered his eyes whenever we walked up to him. "Oooh man, oww, I need some shades," he blinked and squinted, arms out to fend us off.

They ordered drinks. RM ordered for me. They got cigars. RM handed me one.

Douglas Dauntless. Slow and dependable. On a strike dive-bombers dove straight down, torpedo bombers right on the water. They didn't talk about fighters, the glory hounds, the ones who flew protection for the slower more vulnerable planes. And the dream? What about the dream?

"WILLY, WHAT THE FUCK IS WRONG WITH YOU??"

As if I had been slapped awake, I looked up at RM's red yelling face.

"The god damn world hasn't come to an end! The war isn't over, if that's what you're worried about. Big fuckin' deal if Tony has fighters. So, he's not as good as you are, so what? A big fist reached into the barrel and came up with DIVE-BOMBERS. And Tony slipped out of the fist and came up in the next fist for fighters. So, God damn it, what are ya gonna do about it? Sulk for the rest of your life? Bullshit! 'Hundred and fifty torpedo bombers?' Here you go, boss!' One of the instructors told us, 'Sometimes it's a whole gang of fighters. Then it's the other.' But what the fuck are you gonna do about it???? Sulk all day? All week? Man we got six days before reporting. You can go to New Orleans. You can go see *Leyla!* Didya think of *that?* Now, you wanta know what we should do right now? *WAITER?? ANOTHER ROUND!!"*

It was certainly and easily the most sensible thing we had thought of all day. They had even paid us. I looked down at my wings. Yes, mine. And sloe gin fizzes? Sure, and another!

RM found a juke box and we heard Nat King Cole's "I Can't See For Lookin'" and Louis Jordan's "Ain't Nobody Here But Us Chickens." RM the great jazz lover and dancer wanted me to meet his sister who was also a great dancer. Yeah, he'd get her down to Deland in a few weeks. He was a jazz buff and spoke of the greats: Ziggy Elman, Satchmo's horn, Trummy Young, Bix, Cootie Williams, Billy Strayhorn, Roy Eldredge. Then, just as I was set to pop those Sloe gins all afternoon I realized that Evan had been gone quite a while. I knew what he was doing. He had heard the news, checked off the base and was heading for home.

Who needs dive-bombers? Only that's what we got. And the world careened on.

"RM, thanks. I was. . . . You're right."

"Man. . . . " RM said, full of understanding. "It's not *right*, it's what we got! We'll go down there to DeeeLand, wherever it is . . . and we'll . . . well, we'll see."

RM was . . . what was he? My older brother? Well, he'd actually pulled me up out of it.

Dubya D lived way up in New Jersey and might not get home. He didn't know what to do. We shook hands and almost embraced although that was not in our code. I thought of his 'wheels-up' landing and his three-day duty pulling those wheels. The SNJ has a horn hooked to the throttle. When the throttle comes back the horn goes off if the wheels aren't down: 'Cadet, didn't you hear the tower telling you not to land? That your wheels were up?' 'No, I couldn't hear the tower because that damn' horn was going off in my ear!'

How could I have come so close to them in so short a time?

"Well," said Dubya D, "I might go with RM to Montgomery or I might just hang around here a few days; swim and lie in the sun. I just talked to my mother . . . she was thinking of coming down for a day or so, here, to Pensacola."

"Your mother???" RM said in total amazement, "Dubya D's don't have *mothers!*"

When Dubya D. put out an effort his tongue wrapped itself halfway around his chin. "Get up!" he said. RM was up dancing and sparring around, mouthing some jive talk, up on his toes, down in a crouch, biff, pow! Ducking, dodging imaginary blows, "Fuck wiff *me*, boy, you got as much chance's tryin' a san'paper a lion's asshole in a telephone booth. . . . Come on!"

I had to go. Already I might have missed Evan.

"Alright! See you guys in DEEEELAND. Where the dive-bombers play—"

"We'll fly the SHIT outa them Dauntlesses!"

"We'll be fighter dive-bombers!!"

"AWWREEETT!!!"

"What about Claire, RM?"

"Heyy, I might even get married to the girl."

"Awreet avowtayyy!"

Now, if that Cajun bastard hasn't left yet. Evan had his very own way of doing things. There's the right way, the wrong way, the navy way . . . and the Cajun's way.

The thought of Evan did pull me up that last necessary inch. Evan was as good a flyer as anyone and it hadn't killed *him*.

I raced into our room. His side of the room was bare.

Back to the parking lot for the mad sonofabitch.

Back to the barracks, around the corner, and here came the green hornet himself. I flagged him down and, well, he'd have been off by now but for a "consarned belt" he forgot.

Evan gave me ten minutes by HIS watch to get my crap together. Evan, good Catholic boy, said "consarned" and "crap" but he'd steal high octane aviation gas for his car and he would, really, have gone to fly for Germany "or SOMEbody" if they had washed him out of the flight program. I liked him for that. I almost loved him for that.

I failed his test by one minute but he waited, against his better judgment, and then we were *off* to "straighten out a few curves between here and New Orleans."

I had the newspaper which RM had been reading, determined to catch up on the news. We were through Pensacola and kissed it goodbye. At last I was feeling a lift, even gleeful as if we had stolen some wings from those admirals and were sneaking out of town with the goods.

Evan went to mass every day and didn't want to discuss it. He didn't curse and hadn't much use for women, or said he didn't. "Well, ah got a kind of a girlfriend, if you wanna call it that," chuckle, giggle, "back home, you know, but I can take it or leave it, mostly leave it," chuckle, "because I sure ain't been 'takin' too danged much, here lately."

We were zipping along about seventy-five partly because Evan had "obtained" some high-octane aviation gas from a mechanic who drove one of the gas trucks on the base.

"I just drove my car out there last night, he stuck the hose in my tank and that's it."

Then he was chuckling, that interrupted crazy-kid laugh.

We sailed past Mobile and drove on, and since he didn't know anything about the war he was going into, I read the papers out loud to him. Evan kept up a rolling critique: newspapers were full of lies and what the heck was I reading that crap for? Then I discovered, about two hours later, that we were going through Panther Burn, Mississippi, through Bogue Chitto, Rolling Fork, and Nitta Yuma.

"Evan, do you have any idea where the hell we are? Nitta Yuma? Panther Burn? You just flunked your navigation course. Give me the wheel, and those new wings, too!"

"Well . . . you and that consarned paper got me so danged mixed up that. . . . All that crap about the Russians and Kharkov! Why I bet you don't know the first thing about *Kharkov*—"

"I don't know anything about Panther Burn, Mississippi, either, except that it's way off our course."

"Yeah, well . . . "

"Evan, don't you read anything but the funnies? Do you know we've practically destroyed Hamburg? Forty thousand homes destroyed! Five hundred and eighty factories . . . a raid on the oilfields of Romania? A guy from *Kansas* flying a B-24 over Romania? Hell, I didn't even know there *was* oil in Romania . . . "

"See?" Hebert yelled, "You're as ignorant as I am."

"Yeah, but you don't even *want* to know."

"Hey, we're two boys from Louisiana, flying a green Ford over Mississippi!" Evan shouted and laughed, cutting those corners.

"Yeahh, flying *low*."

"Put that consarned paper up, will you? Help me watch out for the law."

He was doing eighty to make up for lost time.

"Did you know that we lost more than forty B-24's over Romania? Out of one hundred and eighty?"

"I couldn't care less about those . . . those garbage wagons. I swear if they told me to fly one of those big garbage cans, geeeee, I just wouldn't do it."

We were stopped in Big Junction, Mississippi, not far from Nitta Yuma, for going, the big fat, tobacco-chewing sheriff said, for going, wellll, he didn't know how fast, but he'd had to do ninety-five afore he could ketch up to us. So he reckoned we'uz doin' eighty-five anyhow, but he'd book us fer seventy cause we wuz sarvissmin (service-men?). I don't know if we could have understood him anyhow, but with a plug of tobacco in the side of his face that looked like a swelled-up jaw-tooth as he tried to explain how nice (spit) he was bein', then with a big stub of a pencil in his old lean-to shack-office scratching across the grain of wood, multiplied four times the number of miles we'uz over the speed and he come up with a fifty dollar charge which he would reduce to just thirty or else we could go on over to the jailhouse.

"You wanna just go on over to the jailhouse?" I asked Evan who was still amazed by this sudden turn of events.

"Are you crazy?" He was grinning and running some cowboy action films through his mad young mind while Mr. swelled-up jaw-tooth just reared back and put one huge ham of a hand, a hog-skinning, tree-wrestling, tit-squeezing hand back on his old hip holster gun and we decided to chip in and pay the man off.

To prove it was all on the up and up, he gave us the little squinched up piece of big-lined paper such as kids use in the second grade with his pencil scratchings on it. We should have framed it but I'm afraid it was lost, ripped up and torn into tiny pieces and out the window on the seventy-five mile an hour winds blowing past us.

What did it mean to us? Nothing if we'd gotten fighters. Less as dive-bombers. We had been injected, inoculated against this, and if there were some way we could have tied that fat old bastard up—strong as he might be—we'd have done it even if he had our license number because we'd be overseas soon enough, and then? Well, there's-no-after-the-war-for-fighter/dive-bomber-pilots. Even for a lot of B-24 pilots.

Chapter 2

Mamoo was down the steps of the house when we honked, yelling, delirious, with Brucie right behind her, and here came Sally, wiping hands on apron knowing she'd be last in this line but advancing on it.

Evan stood for a moment, not sure exactly where he fit in or which way to turn—warrior, hero—head down and eyeing Brucie.

Mamoo flung herself into my arms, "Ohh my darling boyyy soooo happy so happpeeeeee I am!"

Evan and I were both dressed in our gabardines and, although unnecessary, we had wings on our gabardine shirts as well as on our jackets.

Brucie was giving me a big hug and "so exciting!" and Sally too, "Ooh mah boyyy, but don't you looks pretteeee, but don't he miz Aphra?"

"Gorgeous . . . just gorgeous . . . and this is?"

"Mamoo, this is Evan Hebert, who graduated with me, my roommate, he's from Lake Charles and Evan, this is my sister, Brucie . . . and Sally, this is my good friend . . ."

Inside and beyond it all I was laughing at Evan because I could tell he was struck by Brucie, even though she had her hair up for a date or dance. It was the custom in New Orleans for girls to wear their hair up for the entire afternoon before a date. If her date were to see her during the day with "hair up" she screeched like a bride when the groom sees her before the wedding.

Second Lieutenant Evan Hebert deigned to come upstairs to say hello although he had sworn he would drop me off and straighten some more curves from here to Lake Charles. Now Evan was ready to make room in his very ordered though mad life for something new.

"Why don't you stay over and go to Lake Charles tomorrow?"

"What?" he yelled. "That'll leave me . . . gosh . . . that'll leave me . . . Say, do you realize how far Deland is? That place is heck and gone down the east coast of Florida."

Still, Evan was sitting there, figuring it out, and actually deciding what he would do.

Mamoo interrupted and told us we had some sandwiches and that they were "all ready to sit down to, right now."

"Miz Aphra—" Sally began, then in a stage whisper, "ah don' know *what* sangwiches lessen she done MADE some."

Then Brucie and Sally were whispering and they would make it right, and then Mamoo discovered that the sandwiches hadn't been made, as if against her direct orders to the contrary, and she and Sally were at it. Brucie was embarrassed both for Evan's being there to hear it and because her hair was UP, but when she apologized to him with her special appeal, her very special kindness, well, that young man was almost physically bowled over and, "Shucks, well, but she shouldn't have . . . I didn't expect a thing and she certainly—"

Then Brucie was cautioning my mother, and I think for the first time it became clear to me about my mother and her wishes: oh she wished for the whole world, for it all to be right, and it should have been, for there to be platters of dainty and delicious sandwiches to be brought out to the visitors, no, the conquering heroes, home from the wars and for that not to be part of the actuality was so distressing it made her want to exit—just leave the world. In half an hour she decided that it had been her strictest orders that those sandwiches were to be ready the instant, well, whenever "they" came home.

"And Sally, you knew, you *knew* that they would be coming—"

"Miz Aphra, I didn't know no such of a thing! How I'm s'poze ta know when Will be home? How *ahm* to know *dat?* Glad as I *be*—"

"Well, Sally, I told you this morning they would be home—"

"What *I* am?" she began to laugh a little, "Ahm ah mind reader?"

"Sally, I don't even think you're glad he's home—"

"W'Y MIZ APHRAAA!"

Most of it we could hear from the kitchen, especially Sally, who did not have any low-volume control, in fact her whispering was anyone else's parade ground shout.

I told Evan that maybe Sally should have been a drill sergeant at pre-flight and he fell over at that, but in addition feeling a hundred different things.

Evan, struck, immediately and deeply, would probably have been willing to lay down his life for Brucie. I knew it but she would never have dreamed such a thing. Only instead of talking about her he was apologizing for any trouble he might be causing.

"Shucks, I could just as well have gone on my way, but . . . "

Don't flatter yourself, I thought, this is a minor skirmish in a life-battle. Brucie had jumped up and run into the kitchen and suddenly there was silence on the battlefield. My mother came in with a bowl of fruit and a tray and plates, knives and napkins.

"Now! Let me have a good look at you! At you *both*!"

And she gazed with those dancing blue eyes that she gazed through and cast a veil of kindness, of love, over the world.

Long ago she had deplored the war, the whole war, deplored the young men going and the slaughter and said it without distinction as to boundaries and nationalities. Beyond that, she was against killing, all killing, well, not *all*—someone would have to kill the pigs, chickens, cows and so forth—but beyond the killing, she was not political in any sense of the word.

I asked Brucie to come out for a moment to talk, and excused ourselves leaving Mamoo with Evan. I still hadn't called anyone and didn't know how it would work out but I asked Brucie if she would go out with Evan tonight and she just couldn't. It was reservations for supper, a naval ensign she had met at the Junior League dances of the New Orleans something-or-other, and after supper they were going to a dance at the Country Club, she *couldn't* break the date, one of her friends—blind date, reservations. Could we do it tomorrow night?

I told her that Evan was really struck but I don't think Brucie understood what I was saying, or understood Evan. "How about tomorrow?" she said.

I went back to the room to find Evan explaining something to my mother; air speed and ground speed, about which she knew nothing, of course, but there she was—spellbound. I had to laugh, not that she was doing anything unkind. Although it meant nothing to her she was listening and looking interested and, my dear boy, well, after all, what do you want me to do?

And once I had explained to her, "Mamoo, I'd like for you to be *really* interested."

"But I *am*."

Only 'interested,' to her, was synonymous with *acting* interested and she hardly made the distinction any longer.

"My darling, what if I don't really *understand* what is being spoken about?"

"Well, then, ask a question."

"But my darling boy," she had said, sizing me up anew, "perhaps I am not *that* interested."

So, here she sat, poised and gazing out at the young lieutenant who explained ground speed, airspeed, join-ups, and air-sleeve gunnery. And despite my own feelings about New Orleans hypocrisy, Evan was earnestly explaining in great detail. Evan was interested in explaining even if she wasn't interested in understanding. And as long as she sat there making some of the right noises, and she was certainly a master at that, then God was in his heaven, or a New Orleans listening post.

So, I had asked Brucie's hand for Evan and been postponed, if not refused, and the sandwiches came out: cucumber, egg salad with finely sliced onions, and the peppery red pepper that I never saw anywhere else. And then in tall glasses bound in napkins the iced coffee so cold it was smoking, iced coffee with the glass-bottomed silver coasters.

When we saw him off, Evan came as close as any time in his life to asking a young woman to go out with him. He faced Brucie more than he faced me, and told/asked/announced that next time he was in town maybe we could all do something together, "Me and you, and your brother, of course . . . the so-and-so—" Evan cocked back his fist toward me. He thanked my mother, with some pain, then he was in his car and off. We watched and heard it to the corner, and then silence.

"You're home," Mamoo said.

Pensacola was done with; I was an officer and pilot in the Marine Corps.

We walked up the stairs, arm in arm. And I was thinking that maybe this was it. I'd spend time right here, sleep and catch up, see the aunts, Brucie, Mamoo. Up the steps into the apartment.

How she remade an ordinary apartment into something more. The *lit-de-repos*, the mermaid lamps, baby grand piano, the gladiola vase, fresh flowers on the table, the beautiful mother-of-pearl and wood inlaid cabinet from Audubon Place. But it was not things alone; there was balance, a graciousness, a harmony to the arrangement. She had known great wealth, was welcomed in any home, no matter what *our* present surroundings (Her Majesty in an apartment), and the ridiculous argument about the sandwiches was only her wish, among a thousand others, that she might have known, to the instant, when we'd arrive. In that case, everything would have been delicious *and* fashioned not five minutes too soon.

Sally was hovering in the background, just barely. I welcomed it but it irritated my mother. "Sally, would you mind doing those dishes?"

I had a strange feeling, as if the underside, the joshing, laughing side of me, was being sent away in dishonor.

My mother rolled her eyes after Sally and turned to me about when I would have a chance to *stay* home and have a good *long* visit. "You seem, always, to turn right around and be gone again."

"How about *this* time? I'm off for six days and there's not time to get up to Boston and back, to see Leyla, so I'll stay home and see you and the aunts and Brucie and Pearse, Okay?"

The talk made me weary. My fellow flyers were now my family. Almost more than my lifelong friends. Evan and I, RM . . . Dubya D., even Tony. And where had he gone?

Funny that RM suggested seeing Leyla.

My heart lurched when I thought of her. Only her message was the same as my mother's. When are we going to have some time? Some real time?

"You knew Bobby Guerdon, Will, didn't you?"

Mamoo was patting my hand, wanting to keep in touch and still waiting for answers to six questions. News from New Orleans was like news from a foreign country, farther from me than the South Pacific, than Africa.

" . . . it seems that he was killed in flight . . . in flight *training!*" she said, as if that might be impossible for me to believe.

What good to tell her seven cadets had been killed at Pensacola while I was there; mid-air collisions, formation crossovers, unexplained accidents, two "lost" on a night navigation flight.

"Yes, I did hear about Bobby G. He was an OBD. A year or two ahead of me."

"It just never occurred to me that people were killed in training. But I suppose it does happen . . . " She looked over and waited, "I knew the Guerdons. I knew his mother very well and his father, to some degree . . . and, oh my darling, you did hear about Bootchie?"

I felt the blood rush to my face. It was all in the word 'hear' and it meant only one thing. It was as if I had taken a great breath and was exploding with it. She paused.

"Oh my darling . . . I thought I'd *told* you."

Her face told me the rest, but I sat for the full portrait of grief.

"Well, Bootchie . . . " I could feel my face puffing, filling.

". . . . An automobile accident, near Chicago. I'm so terribly sorry, my darling, but so much has been happening."

How to accept something totally unbelievable. I saw him in a hundred scenes. And I found myself hating her, blaming her; ridiculous and still blaming her.

"Yes, it seems he had just become engaged to a girl, to a young woman up in Chicago where he was stationed. You knew he was going through the Naval Air Corps, just as you are, or were, and, I believe he skidded and hit a tree. It happened just a month ago. I can't believe I haven't told you this."

She was very pained and I knew it.

"No, I hadn't heard." Leyla, Leyla, she too was up there and suddenly it was as if death had come between us.

"But, my darling, I don't want to talk about this, these things, so terrible and so sad, I know."

She came back again to her talk of the long leave, a long leave before going overseas. And I assured her I would get one, although that was only a promise and who knew about their promises. All of which I was beginning to understand. Like the questionnaires about where, exactly where in the wide world, would we like to go to serve our country, checking off let's see; Europe, then Africa, China-Burma, or the Pacific—the South Seas, very much a call to my blood.

"New Orleans is so changed now," my mother said sweetly, tragically, "with the war. Uniforms everywhere. Strange faces. Ration cards. I know all of that is necessary for—"

"Mamoo, *Hamburg* is changed! *Hamburg! Hamburg* is very different now. *Hamburg* is totally changed. New Orleans is *exactly* the same!" In a way I was punishing her for Bootchie.

"But, Will—"

"*What?*"

"Such *vehemence*—about Hamburg? Why the anger all of a sudden, for a German city?" She said it uncertainly, as if she weren't quite sure of the facts. After a pause, which I didn't fill in because I, too, didn't quite know how I felt or why the destruction of Hamburg had affected me so much. It was tied up with Bootchie, with dive-bombers, and the whole . . . the whole unmanageable—

"Which reminds me, my dear, the news from Berthe Cameron is that young Bob Cameron is missing. He was flying over Germany."

"Bob? Wonderful? He went into the air force three months after I did!"

"Yes, as a matter of fact. They got the news in August. He had not been overseas for long. But, my dear, I'm just so sick over it. Berthe, his mother, has been calling Washington daily because, well, many times they, umm, they jump out, umm in parachutes. And are taken prisoner. Well, that is her hope. But can you imagine what they're going through in that household?"

I held her hand. She patted mine and I could see my young beautiful and very privileged mother sitting on the steps of the mansion at Audubon Place with my father, in his uniform of the quartermaster corps ("the flaming pisspots" we called the quartermasters at A & M), and those "weak" eyes behind the spectacles, which had kept him from some more dramatic way of serving the country in "the Great War," as they called it.

"Remember, my boysie, those picnics? And the games? And badminton in the backyard at 6031? Oh how hard you used to play, as if you were already at war, and sometimes . . . "

The voice might have been much longer ago, when she sang to me, or rubbed my head after putting Vicks on my chest, the voice so reassuring, all a part of the long healing when one has been shot through the heart. I jumped up, wounded anew at how she had lulled me to sleep for these minutes.

"Oh! Jack called—"

"Jack? Why didn't you tell me?"

To the phone, as if it was my battle station and I was reporting for duty. Who would be home? And what had happened to Tony? I called his number and Mrs. DeLisle informed me that he had gotten fighters, "Which was exactly what he always wanted."

Oh, shut up! I wanted to yell at the squawky voice.

Once, playing football in the Carr's yard, Tony's mother was walking up with some groceries and somebody ran into her, sent her sprawling, and we all glimpsed her motherly thighs up to her hips, stockings rolled halfway between her knees and the very ends of her legs, now the squawky voice ran on, "Well, Tony has decided that such a short time, well, he decided to go on to Jacksonville and report in early."

Ohh, that bastard. I didn't hate him quite, but what had I done? Beat the instructor! Missed a briefing! Or was it only that long hand, reaching into the barrel of new pilots?

I called Jack's house. His mother was "distressed" (just as Mamoo used the word). She was "distressed" and he would be too, to realize we had just missed each other. He had left for New York on Wednesday, emergency leave before being sent overseas, probably to Italy, since he had been studying Italian at the Army's Language School.

I called Harmless Jaroo, gone. Wonderful Bob? I kept shaking my head about it. Billy Fitz? Kansas City, going through E-base, said Mrs. Fitzgerald who was going to call Billy and tell him about my wings, she said. In between phone calls, Sally was signaling to me to come out to the kitchen. My mother, in her cheeriest tones, called to me, "And don't make any plans for tomorrow night, Tatie and Uncle Willie are having a party. Just family. And we'll all have to go."

"Okay!" It popped out of me without the least revolt. Fine. Maybe I would at last have the ideal leave, family, Mamoo, Sally, and the aunts.

"Psssst, mah boy," Sally, under her breath, smiling like a big pirate, motioning for me to go out to the kitchen. I made one last call to the Moonfixer, certain he was still in med school. Mrs. Mooney would give him the message. She congratulated me on my wings and I wondered how much she knew about our magazines, which they "detested," trips to the river, breaking streetlights, swimming the river, bike trips way beyond anything they allowed.

New Orleans is changed? No bombs. No burning houses. Same avenue, same oak trees spreading. Was I only the defender of those oak trees across whole streets, defender of the right of my people to play cards on screened porches in the Garden District under a green shade so deep that not even the night's darkness could pierce it; to play and drink under overhead fans and orange-shaded lights behind ferns and palms, elephant ears and banana leaves—so, did it mean bombing Hamburg in order to be able to come back to all this?

Well, tomorrow night we'd gather at the Garden District home of the Douglases, Uncle Willie and Tatie's place on Second Street. Cut glass, chandeliers, deep porches, plants and gardens, sleeping porches, servants, all of it.

While waiting for supper and for the Fixer's call I watched Sally fill the big kettle with such confidence. Up to the very top with onions, green peppers, a few carrots, garlic, red beans, oil, ham hock, just topped off, from nothing to something delicious. She filled the pan to the top, set the gas just right, walked off knowing that in three hours there'd be a dish people marveled over.

"Yeah, Sally, but how *much* of that chili powder?"

"Hummmph, mah boy, Sally knows."

"Okay, Sally knows, but how much . . . exactly how much?"

"Just a smidgeonit, mah boy."

"Yeah, well, what the hell is a 'smidgeonit'?"

She fell to the side like she'd been shot, threw back her head, the laugh sailed through the ceiling, the attic, the roof to the skies.

"Ha, mah boy, but you makes this old gal laugh . . . SOME."

In between those silent side-shaking sessions she would recover and then SCREAM. Silent laughter again. Another whoop of a scream and maybe she'd recover but only to laugh about it just as hard later.

I told Sally about crazy Evan and how he was ready to go fly for the Germans if they washed him out of the American flight program.

Sally did a quick stomp-shuffle with her feet, "But, Wi-ulll! For them bad GER-MANS!?"

"That's what he said, Sal. But you see that's what I'm saying about him. Evan's a little—" I whistled and wound my finger around my head, not admitting that both of us agreed, oh, that Focke-Wulfe 190 was a honey of a plane.

"Ummm UMMMMMM," she groaned. "He do DAT! Hmmmmmmph— dey liable to put him UNDAH de jail."

"What? Did you say *under*??"

"Das right. Das what dey do be's you doin' DAT. DEY PUT YOU UN-DAH . . . DAS RIGHT. . . . *UNDAH* DE JAIL."

"Ohhhh, Sally, you kill me."

She turned that great head up and screeched to the skies. 'SO BAD . . . DEY PUT YOU *UNDAH*, MAH BOY! YOWZAHH!"

Chapter 3

⌒

"It's a mighty tough titty
But the milk is so doggone sweet!"

The great black singer "Little" Jimmy Rushing, a two-hundred-fifty-pound bowling ball, teeth gleaming, bent over and growled out the chorus of his song.

I was home again. The crazy bluesy humor was pure New Orleans.

We drank beer at *The Famous Door*, which hangs out over Bourbon Street, the Moonfixer and I, the only Corpuscles left at home—this we had to pass on to the others, wherever they were tonight—a drum roll, blare of trumpets, pause, and that gravelly voice, soon enough joined by everyone in the place:

" . . . *a mighty tough titty, but the milk is so doggone sweet!*"

We screamed—the roomful of sailors, soldiers, marines, enlisted and officers. He sang, we laughed and screamed it out.

There was a feeling in us, over us, over New Orleans, perhaps over the country: seamen off of boats on submarine duty, seamen and officers off of American battleships, Free French and British sailors and officers from de-stroyers, cruisers, carriers: French, Belgian, Polish flyers in from Texas and

Mississippi airfields, American G.I.s and officers, paratroopers with their big heavy boots, all strangers to each other—different uniforms, different services, different countries—officers and enlisted elbow to elbow in one of fifty French Quarter dives; this was occupied New Orleans, raw and jazzy, breaking down barriers, doing what people came to New Orleans for, what the city does best: celebrate, party, play pretty for the people. "The city that care forgot" and even we felt the strangeness, the newness, the war come home, and New Orleans still being itself, in war and out the other side.

A long skinny black woman walked on stage, took the mike out of Jimmy Rushing's hand and, with the band behind her, growled back at him:

"I'M GONNA TAKE MY RAZOR! . . . AN' CUT YO' LATE HOURS!"

The place went berserk while "Little" Jimmy crouched down in fear and trembling.

We walked off still laughing, over to Pat O'Brien's, me in my new gabardines with wings, the Fixer in his whites, picked up two lovelies fearful of going into Pat O'Brien's by themselves: Carola and GiGi from Jackson, Mississippi. We got a table for four and I decided on one of those big hurricanes, the kind RM was so angry about that long-ago Mobile night. Young Gi-Gi was having a pink champagne cocktail. The Fixer and I had been drinking beer and were still laughing about that chorus with everyone screaming out the words. In fact I couldn't stop saying it, growling out my own imitation.

Then Gi-Gi it was, with her little champagne glass held between two fingers, so correct and ladylike, telling me not to use that expression again. She wasn't asking, she was telling me. Did she tell me two times? Three?

Pat O'Brien's was very crowded, and one of the last places where civilians were still in the majority. It had a huge patio, flagstones, wrought-iron tables, and comfortable metal chairs with bendy, springy seats. Along the brick walls were ivy, flowering shrubs, and dimly lit old-fashioned street lamps. In the center was a large fountain with ferns placed around it.

"I told you," said that little northern Mississippi Gi-Gi, "if you use that expression one more time," she said, with a chill in her voice, "I'll throw this drink in your face."

Was that an invitation? I couldn't get over it, lost as I was in that earthy, pithy bit of wisdom. "You mean, 'It's a mighty tough titty—'?"

Before I could finish I was blinking champagne out of my eyes and it was running down my face.

Without a thought, I emptied my whole hurricane all over her: ice, juice, water, rum, and parasol. The Moonfixer was stunned, grabbed me by the arm and hustled us out of there.

Everything was extraordinarily clear. She threw at me, I threw at her. What could be simpler?

"Will, for Christ's sake—"

"Now, listen. Just a second. Did she throw first—?"

"Will! She threw an eyedropper at you and you threw a bucketful at her!"

We drove to my house and parked and sat talking.

Suddenly it was calmed down and strange. Bootchie gone. Wonderful gone. The Fixer had been talking about Wonderful and a certain night, just before Wonderful Bob joined the Air Force.

"Remember, the night we sloshed Sabu's kitchen with soap and water, sliding and fighting on the floor and Wonderful got hurt, remember? All of us trying to stop laughing, to the Emergency ward, and how to explain, 'Well, doc, see, we were playing this game—' and Bob got hurt . . . Wonderful, yeah, a cut on the forehead . . . all of us trying to stop laughing, to the Emergency. . . . Stop laughing, it coulda been serious, yeah, man, really bloody . . . 'Shut up,' he says, 'you fuckin' jerks it's *my* head and *my* blood so even a little scratch is serious.' Three stitches and a story . . . Give Wonderful a hanky."

First day and we were sunk deep in New Orleans. And laughing over Wonderful Bob, a kind of laughter like crying and because of memories so vivid—swimming the river together, crazy visit to the Emergency Ward—couldn't, absolutely could not believe, that he had disappeared into the European night skies.

The Moonfixer had seen me at some of the worst moments of my life—when I ran from those bullies in the park, when those other guys had pinned us up against the fence. And tonight I wanted to ask about it. About us, the Corpuscles . . . life . . . but I couldn't get the question.

"Remember the big funeral parlor on St. Charles? Getting in line to see the dead body of the guy none of us knew?"

My mood had turned, and I wanted to talk about something else and couldn't get it out.

"—hitching rides up St. Charles in the winter when the drivers' windows were up . . . 'Kiss my ass uptown'?"

"Turning off Joelle's house lights on the way to the Prytania? . . . The logs on the river . . . and that snake?"

Shep was now in India. Sweet Sid in England, Cacksy Jack in Italy, after his emergency leave home. JoJo in Key West, headed "out there" in amphibious landing craft. OSTOYC the Mouse was already in the Pacific. Christian "Nappy" Smith in Russia, testing P-39s before turning them over to the Russians. And Bob . . . Wonderful Bob.

"Yeahhhhhhh—"

"You think there's any chance he bailed out?"

"Ahh, Will . . . the chances are . . . if they don't hear in a week or two. For Wonderful it's been three weeks."

"Damn, that chills me . . . and Nasty Bat, I have to make myself go down there."

"I know."

Silence.

"Fixer, ooooold buddy . . . what's it all for?"

"What?? What do you mean?" His voice sounded a little panicky at my question.

"I just sometimes wonder about it . . . " I hadn't meant to get into this but it was something that popped out, hidden back there under rocks and debris.

"What . . . what do you mean?"

I had my wings, my bars. Lieutenant in the marines. "I don't know, exactly. I mean . . . I mean, sometimes I wonder, what are we all after?"

The 'Fixer seemed to hunch up before answering, "I don't know exactly. . . . You mean the purpose of it all?"

"Yeahhh, *all* of it. I mean all of my life I've wanted to fly. Waited for a war. Now I'm a flyer and it looks like the war, the thing I've waited for all my life—"

"I guess . . . you mean . . . like being a doctor. I always wanted it, you know. Since we were kids."

"Yes, and now?"

"Another six months and I'll have it."

"Well, that's what I mean. You want . . . and then you *get*. And then. . . ?"

"It's not what it's cracked up to be?"

"No, it's not that. I love it . . . I love flying. But . . . "

"And the war? You still hell-bent for it?"

"Yes . . . that's not it either. I just . . . wonder about after, after all this . . . I mean, tonight, in the French Quarter, New Orleans . . . like an occupied city. Polish seamen! . . . People from all over the world. And after the war? What then? I mean . . . *after.* What will it mean . . . How'll it be?"

"I don't know," he said. "Practice medicine, for me . . . get married, I guess . . . have kids."

"And . . . that's it? I mean . . .that's my question. What's it all for? *All* . . . ?"

"God, Will . . . I mean . . . "

"What I mean . . . what I'm trying to say is . . . I mean, right now . . . it's coming to a peak, and—"

"You mean after . . . the war? All the excitement?"

"Yes . . . yes, what'll happen? Right now it's building, building and, then? After the war? . . . You know what I'm saying? See? I mean, after we get drunk a few thousand times, fly the fastest airplanes, become an Ace, after the ticker tape parade . . . well, after all that? Come home? Get married. Have kids? And . . . and work-at-something-you-really-like?"

"Pheww, Will, slow down. . . . You're twenty years old . . . you've got some changes to go through . . . we all do."

"I guess . . . only, we're going up, now, higher and higher, up and up and—"

"And what . . . you'll change, you'll go through some changes."

"I can't see it . . . And . . . I don't think . . . I'll get through 'em."

We were silenced for a while, and I knew I had gone outside of our bounds, as if I had made a touchdown at White Corpuscle field and kept on running, through the crepe myrtles, across the street, on and on.

After Memphis I had cornered crazy Jack and we had talked about his grand theory that everybody wants to do it with everybody else.

"Ohh, Will-lee, what's the real question?" he said in his sing-song way.

"Well, for one thing, I can think of lots of women I wouldn't want to do it with."

"'Yeah, but you can also think of a lot more you'd love to do it with, right?"

"That doesn't answer the question. You said 'everybody—"

"Listen, Willy . . . what do you want? Okay . . ." and Cacksy Jack started laughing, "There's some syphilitic old whore in Calcutta I don't want to do it with . . . okay?"

"So, then—"

"Jesus, Willy, what do you want me to say? That men and women *probably* want to do it with more people than they'll ever get around to? That's—"

"I just want to—"

"—to say *nothing*!"

"—get it clear, what you said—"

Jack started giggling in his insane way, "Ohhhhhh, the kid wants to get it allllll cleared up . . . oh ho, allll clearsy dupsy."

"You're an idiot. You just want to *astound* people!"

"Nooo . . . I believe it."

"Would you fuck one of your sisters?"

"Oh, wouldn't I, though?" He giggled, "Sure," he cocked his head over, as if considering it, " . . . if they'd let me."

"I don't believe you."

"Man, I'd get in there and hump away like mad. Any one of 'em."

Between his madness, and his insane laugh I had no idea what to believe. But, in a way, with Jack, it didn't matter. No . . . that *was* Jack.

I had started something with the Moonfixer and then gone off on my own about Jack and his theories. We never got any farther, the Moonfixer and I.

"Yeah, well, Willy Boy, Willy the fly-boy," the Fixer broke in on my thoughts, "I've got that exam tomorrow, so—"

"Yeah!"

I got out and walked up the stairs, wondering about Pearse and what he'd say about my wings and bars and about Wonderful, my tattoo-brother. And Bootchie. Old Booch. In cold Chicago, up against a tree. I looked at the stars. No mercy up there. Booch and Wonderful, and how I hated to hear it from my mother, hearing it while she was there in front of me. And Bob, lost in one of those moving night battles thousands of feet over Europe.

The day my mother was married for the second time, Felix's father, the red-faced drunk pirate, who, I found out that day from Arthe, had proposed to Mamoo years earlier, asked her to wait for him till he got back from "the Great War," bending down to me, losing balance, telling me if only my mother had said yes then Felix could have been my brother. The same time telling me, "Get out. . . . As soon as you can, get out of New Orleans, before it's too late . . . don't f'God's sake grow up, join the Boston Club, Mardi Gras, get old and drunk like me . . . " a little later escorted out of the wedding party after warning me again, "New Orleans' a disease," he kept saying, "Get out as soon as you can." Someone I didn't know took him by the arm, and ushered him out to a waiting Checker cab.

The house was quiet but the smell told me Pearse was home. I didn't love him for his 'beautiful cannon fodder' talk, but I'd blow up the ammo dump and come back alive. All hell breaking loose but home free, yeah safe by a red cunt hair, as my old carpenter boss would have put it. Yeah, come back to Leyla, and make seven children.

Mrs. Campbell, calling Washington every day—worse than being killed is not knowing for sure. Only why was I so angry with Her about it? Always connected with Him, my father, and the other news just like it. And didn't know, would never know, what it did to me—opening vaults in me no one else should see.

For the first time in years I felt a little less pressure; waiting to go through, going through; check flights, demerits, washing out. We had finished, and now we could *fly*, not Corsairs, not fighters but home, dive bombers but home. Wings and dive-bombers. In any case home . . .

" . . . Safe sweet home to Lord, that shining star."

Chapter 4

We parked on quiet, stately Second Street in the heart of the Garden District, September 10th, hot and no relief in sight. Sweat rolled down me even sitting still. We could hear the noise from the Douglas's when we got out of the car. War fever, this too; goodbye, coming home, a party for Wednesday afternoon.

Above us standing guard 200 year old live oaks, those tolerant oaks; through any number of wars and never shed a leaf over any of them; lulling and ages-old those delicate, strong oak limbs criss-crossing above the street, interlocking branches over gardens and porches with a shade that protected this part of the city more even than in the parks, and under these giants' arms—these natural giants that never seem to grow, no beginning no end—were some of the oldest and most beautiful houses and gardens in a city of unusual homes and grounds. Esplanade the first site of the old extravagant homes, but the Garden District had inherited the mantle; European graciousness, the villas of Italy, France, and Spain. As for the people inside them, well, they understand oysters, crabs, shrimp, and the thousand ways and sauces to serve them with. They understand care and concern for their kind, love and the tender mercies, but it is with food and drink that they compare with the world's best. In food and their gardens and houses—those pastel-colored wedding cake houses with iron grill-work, Greek and Roman columns, Italianate porches and custom balconies—custom-fitted around oak trees—French windows onto secret upstairs porches, arches and graceful patios in an endless variety.

"Heeeyyyyyyyyyyy . . . whataya drinking?"

Hugs and kisses from shining-eyed Tatie who always greeted me with something extra, "I can't believe this is my little Napoleon, but don't you look splendid and OH MYYYYY your WINGS!!!!"

My cousin, Bill, was at her elbow, "Well, whatdoyousay, cousin? Congratulations . . . "

"Doesn't he look splendid, Bill?"

Ha haa, "He looks okay, it's just Will in a uniform, after all." But he was laughing in the wry Douglas manner, part his own part my Uncle Willie, the one I was named after, who elbowed his way to us, hugged my mother, yelled his greetings in his gruff and still tender manner, three sheets to the wind and working on four.

All the Barclays were there, and the Ogdens except for Pat. Uncle Wallace, Aunt Alice, little Alice, and Neville on crutches, back from the wars but in uniform, a tuck in his pants where his right leg had been. My good cousin, Wallace, in marine khaki dress uniform, new lieutenant's bars. We moved toward each other and greeted. Wallace, very tall, like a dream poster for the Marine Corps, introduced me to his sloe-eyed beauty of a fiancée, Martine Fletcher, from South Carolina.

"I repeat," she said, "you *do* have a good-looking family."

"Not shy, is she?"

"Nooo," Wallace chuckled, and turned to her with their own joke.

Sewanee was on a two-and-a-half-year program, he told me. He had just received his commission in the infantry.

"So, you got your wings?" spoken in the friendly rivalry of the cousins, all eleven of us, who learned of each others' movements mainly through our mothers; offspring of the four sisters, more than cousins less than siblings. "So, what will you be flying and how soon before you go overseas?"

"Two months, they tell us—"

Before I could finish I was pounded on the shoulders by 'Little' Aphra Douglas, Tatie's daughter. She was, maybe, the healthiest and most exuberant of the cousins; big, terribly strong, a dark, swarthy beauty, with shining brown eyes, dark gleaming hair, cut in a short bob. She practically spun me around to meet her fiancé, a first lieutenant in the air force, his silver wings prominently displayed.

"Willy Boy, I want you to meet Dan Campbell, my husband. Well, actually we'll be married on the 25th of September. Can you make the wedding? Sure, you'll be there. . . . Actually," she interrupted herself,

"Dan's from New Iberia, and he's a cousin of a good friend of yours, that fool, Jack. What do you guys call him? Cacksy Jack? Yeah, it was the only doubt I had about Dan."

We shook hands. Dan seemed calm and tough, as capable as anyone of handling Aphra.

"So? Welcome to the family. What do you fly?"

"Well, right now, I'm in B-26s."

"My God!" I got an immediate flash from identification classes: heavy medium bomber, short wings. The flying whore.

"Does Aphra know what they're called?"

"What? *What's that?*" she bellowed, in true Douglas style.

Wallace and his fiancee Martine shuddered and laughed at her shout. Wallace's shoulders were shaking.

"Watch it, Ogden," she yelled over to him.

"Yes, she's heard all about it," Dan told me.

"Heard all about what?" She turned back to us.

"About the B-26,'" he said.

"Oohh, the flying prostitute? With no visible means of support?" This was daring talk, war talk, and we all were aware of it.

"Actually I'm scared to death of them," she added. But even her 'fear' was torn to shreds in the way she faced it.

"Where are you stationed?"

"Well, we *were* stationed at Barksdale Field in Shreveport but we're taking some planes up to Connecticut, transferring them, actually. We're just overnight in New Orleans. Landed out at the lake-front—*just barely made it, too.*" He chuckled.

"I don't want to hear about it," said Aphra.

"That field was not made for B-26s."

"Yeah. It's an E-base. Did you say you're leaving tomorrow?"

"In the morning. For Connecticut."

"Connecticut?"

"Yes, you want to go? We've got room."

I started laughing. Madness. Leyla. Boston.

"Are you crazy?" Aphra hit me. "You just got home. Aphroo would kill you! Don't you dare take him, Dan!"

My mother was called "Aphroo" by the cousins.

There were 20 or 30 people there and every one of them I wanted to talk with. Neville, back from Africa where they had fought with Rommel, was holding forth to fascinated cousins and aunts.

My cousins, Corinna and Monk, were both with navy officers and both engaged. And Uncle Wallace! Slightly stooped but very regal and, I found out from my mother, a hint of trouble between him and my wonderful Aunt Alice. He gripped my shoulders and, smiled, "*Oh, don't you look fine!*"

I would have gone through pre-flight school again for those words from him.

"Uhh, Pat, you know, is, ahhhh, instructing, on the west coast. He *loves* it!" he told me in his deep, slow, wonderful tones. I was a little boy again, waiting on his next marvelous pronouncement.

Aunt Alice came over, upon hearing Pat's name, and immediately announced, "I don't worry about Pat. Pat can take care of himself. He always has. Now, Will! What. kind. of. plane. are. you. flying?"

Uncle Wallace excused himself and turned for a drink.

"Well, I wanted fighters but I got dive-bombers."

"Now! Are you worried about *that*?" she said fiercely.

"Worried?" I laughed, "I just wanted a faster plane."

"That's the *ticket*! I. just. knew. you. would. feel. like. that! I. tell. you. I. *knew*. it."

"Knew *what*, Alice?" Martha ("Maboo"), the youngest of the sisters, came into the little circle, congratulated me on my wings, and wanted to hear ALL about it.

"Oh, Martha! These. young. people. are. so. DAMNED. brave. that. it. just. makes. me. cry! Will, flying DIVE BOMBERS! But. Will . . . tell. me. something. Don't. those. planes. come. STRAIGHT. down. out. of. the. sky??"

Dan, the B-26 pilot, pushed in, smiling. I had heard about it so often I felt I had already done it. "Yes, we come straight down. But in order to make a 'track' straight down we have to . . . " I showed them, with my hand, "See? More than 'straight' to make a *track* straight down."

"Will! I. am. *so*. impressed! I. just. can't. tell. you!"

I felt guilty, even though it was only a matter of a week or so before I was doing it. I loved her fierceness . . . .her vehemence, of course, but something more, her pride and admiration for things she didn't really know about. And I have a feeling it bothered my good cousin Wallace, being so close to that vehemence. Perhaps it bothered my uncle as well.

Maboo wanted me to meet the two fiances. "Just family," my mother had said to me earlier, then discovered boyfriends, girlfriends and soon-to-be husbands and wives of cousins. My mother suggested I invite Faye, or someone. I called, and Faye was thrilled and would meet me there at the Douglas's.

Uncle Willie came over. He had volunteered his services to the army and been offered his "majority," and was leaving in ten days for New Mexico for some very secret project. "Yes, nephew," he said in his gruffest voice, "I wouldn't ask you to salute me, except for the fact that . . . " every other word was an interruption to shout at someone, take a passing drink or a breaded, fried oyster."You didn't shoot down any Germans up there in Arkansas . . . or Georgia or wherever it was. If you had done what I told you to do, shoot a few Germans, I would make an exception to a shavetail lieutenant, but not now." He laughed loudly, "Nosir-eeee. You better salute and make it snappy."

Maboo was back with Corinna's fiancé, Tad Nicholls, a great badminton player, who had gone to the nationals and placed very high, and Corinna at his elbow, cheeks full of mischief, and laughing eyes. In another minute up came Monk's fiancée, ambling over, stooping to meet everyone he was so tall, Guy Hammell, from Mississippi, studying medicine at Tulane, courtesy of the navy and a classmate of the Moonfixer's, whom he praised as being near the top of his class.

Bill's fiancee, Beth Sewall, from Virginia was, as far as I could see, a blond-image, in speech and mannerisms, of my aunt Tatie. She had a graceful manner, clear eyes, and a great kindness. They were going to be married in a few months. Bill, now an ensign, was instructing the ROTC in naval procedure at Tulane.

"What about Carl and Arthe?" Bill asked me.

"Well, you know they've had their second child, a little boy. And Carl's instructing in P-40's at a base near Mobile."

"The 'P-40'?" Bill walked me back to his room where he had his record collection. He wanted me to hear a particular piece of music and some of his new blues records.

"I'm not sure what the 'P-40' is," in his careful way.

"You know, the shark-teeth decorations on the cowl. The Flying Tigers are using them, in China."

"Ohh yeah, oh yeah, yeah, I know the plane."

I was stunned that he didn't know. If I had been born ten years earlier I would have been over there flying with them.

Bill was not as loud as his father, not as careful and gentle as his mother. When the war broke out Bill was making speeches against the war to students. He told me he felt a little ridiculous preaching about peace in a uniform and so, " . . . instead of taking off my uniform, I took off my views," he laughed, a mocking laugh at himself. I knew it was more complicated than that.

"I'll put on this old blues while I look for it," he said, picked up a record, chuckled, and fitted it to the turntable.

He played an old cobwebby version of "That's Yo' Red Wagon," a song we used to sing at the dances. As usual Bill prided himself on having the original. "The singer is Six Toes Johnson. I think he comes from Houma, Louisiana."

He touched the needle, and the tinny, country sound of "Six Toes" came to us:

> "My mama nevah like' me.
> My papa stay' away.
> Dat's de reason honey,
> De way I am today.
>
> Yeah, well, dat's yo' red wagon.
> Dat's yo red wagon.
> Dat's yo red wagonnnnn,
> Keep on roll'nit A-long."

"What's going on in here," Corinna Barclay, bringing with her an aura of the noise, the glad-talk, the roar of the other rooms. Corinna had a sort of wide-eyed adventurous innocence. I thought of Wallace and me being caught playing strip poker with Monk and Corinna.

"Well, WILL, I didn't get chance before this . . . your *wings!* Congratulations!"

How like Maboo she was, even holding the drink with the same careless grace, as if it weren't there.

> "Oh, you can squeeze my lemon, baby,
> Till the juice run down my laig."

"What did he *say?*" Corinna exclaimed in amazement.

The little needle scratched on:

"She de meanest woman I ever seen

Ask for a glass of water, she give me gasoline."

"HERE it is," Bill said. "Now, listen to this . . . I just got this. I believe it might be 'pirated,' illegally transcribed, but just listen. You know the piece, 'Flying Home'? This *may* be the original version."

It was more enthusiasm and wildness than music.

"Do you like it?" he asked. "Can't you just picture those guys at some base in Africa . . . and the news comes in, they're going home, they're *flying* home, the next day?"

It reminded me of pre-flight and that music when we fought up and down the aisles in the mess hall.

I listened again, flattered that my older cousin would explain it to me. He put the needle back to the beginning and played it again. Not music as much as yelling. Not the intoxication of war but the intoxication that went with it.

"Listen, now, after this scat-singing, 'baoobeeedoo doo bee dooobee' and so forth, they sing that line—'*We are flying home, we are flying home, we are flying home!*'—*eight* times. EIGHT times! I think it's unheard of."

He played it again and something was happening to me. "We are flying home!" Yelling more than singing. Joy. Relief. Madness. Impossible walls scaled.

Something was happening. The wildness in *me*. I was home now, making a decision and didn't even know what it was. Home. I was already home, but . . . flying . . . *home*.

Brucie came in, "Will, Faye's on the phone."

Uncle Willie charged in and through the gravel I could make out that some young damsel was uhhhh out there uhhh calling for me, and that after I uhhh dealt with her I should come into the kitchen because he had a most secret formula for mint juleps and he would show me how, " . . . for a small fee, of course. And, incidentally, I told her, *Lieutenant* Vairin was occupied but I'd see what I could do," he said with a devilish laugh.

Tatie came in and pleaded with us to join the party; everyone was having so much fun. Mamoo ducked in and immediately started dancing to the old blues. She didn't even hear the words. She held out her arms to me and tried to swing me around.

Bar, my short, red-faced, hunter uncle was happy and a little "tight" as they said. "Heeyyy, well, lieutenant, congratulations!" No trace of the angry uncle who had caught us at strip poker six years ago, which I found difficult to erase.

Faye just wanted to make sure where the place was. Her mother was actually going to trust her with the car.

In the kitchen Uncle Willie was crushing fresh mint from their garden downstairs. "Grows wild," he said, "right out under the spigot," in his fearless voice that made the walls buckle. Crushed it, added sugar, water, gave me a big wooden mallet and a large cloth with ice cubes bound up inside it.

"There, nephew, I mean lieutenant, turn that bag into crushed ice for me! Give it hell!"

I pounded for a minute or so, he took it from me, showed me how, flipped it over, pounded and then gave it back to me. I smashed it into powder. We took the crushed ice, extracted the tall iced tea glasses out of the freezer where they instantly were frosted, bound the napkins around them, put the ice in the glasses, added crushed mint/sugar mixture, stirred ice and mint, added bourbon, a sprig of mint on top, put the ten or so mint juleps on a tray and carried them out, leaving two for ourselves in the kitchen, went back, toasted each other, and started in on the next batch. All the time something was buzzing in me, home, home, wild words, abandon, crazy happiness surging and I couldn't explain it.

Lucille and Henry were helping the Douglases that day, Lucille not as fat as Sally—Sally, the standard—but blacker; Henry nodded and smiled, cleaned and kept busy. Uncle Willie was very gentle with them, joking but so gentle. Loud and gentle. They had to feel how gentle he was. Seven dollars a week and carfare, but gentle.

All of it was the war. Faye driving to meet me, wings, the party, speeded up talk, we cousins drinking together, the special world's-gone feeling . . . flying home! We are flying home! I couldn't quite explain it, the unthinkable, all the unthinkables, of Corinna hearing those words, and flying, flying home. The time was jazzed ahead. Could it be the world my parents and uncles and aunts had always inhabited? Or the war?

Lieutenant. Officer and gentleman. Wings of gold.

Aunts and uncles proud of me! All sins forgiven.

"We are flyin' home . . . We are flyin' home!"

Suddenly it grabbed me around the throat! I was . . . already on the way!

" . . . you hear the excitement?"

Hear it? I felt it.

Bootchie gone . . . walking to Sear's drug store with that stolen nickel to play the Iron Claw machine. Pages in Rex. Don Zimmerman, All-American, getting drunk. One hundred twenty four cucumber sandwiches.

Tatie served *Pompano En Papillotes*. Heart-shaped bags. Corinna came over and started singing, "We have it every day!" We laughed. Was she getting drunk? She was only a little happier than her normal happy state.

I wheeled around and caught Dan, not sure of anything, and had to yell in his ear, "You got room for one more?"

"To Hartford?"

"Yes!"

"You mean it?"

"Yes! Somebody. . . . I've got to see."

"You got yourself a ride." He clapped his hand to mine and gave me a number to call. They'd pick me up at seven tomorrow morning.

When Faye arrived, little tiny-teeth, beautiful dark hair around her head, a gauzy dark blue dress, I guess it seemed serious, introducing her to the family. In the middle of the continuous roar, Bill shouted, two feet from her, "Faye, do you know what virgins dream about?"

"No," she said, innocently.

He got that wry little grin on his face and above the roar, "YOU DON'T? *YOU DON'T KNOW WHAT VIRGINS DREAM ABOUT?*"

Faye was suddenly burning red.

Mamoo came up, merry-eyed. She had never met Faye but she knew Faye's mother.

"Be careful of this guy," Wallace told her, "He'll get you into a gutter and cut your feet on glass."

By the time we left I had had two of Uncle Willie's mint juleps and was trying to apologize for the family, but why? Why the hell?

She handed me the keys and we drove down to the French Quarter, had coffee and beignets at the Cafe Du Monde.

It was now a date. And I didn't know what to do with her. I was sick with anxiety about the flight tomorrow, wild with it, with my sudden power. I'd have to pack and tell Mamoo. Connecticut? In a B-26? The flying whore? I didn't know anything about the north. How far was Boston from Connecticut? Back to Florida by the 15th? With luck we'd be in Connecticut tomorrow evening, the 11th. Deland, Florida on the 15th? Five days.

Faye was sympathetic about the dive-bombers, too sympathetic. All of her friends were "hostesses" in organizations that entertained the officers, mostly naval officers in port for a week or so, and there were "tea dances" and "coffees" for them to meet and "entertain" the young officers. I had no idea what was happening. Not with Brucie, or Paige, or Little. World gone mad.

It was dark when we got back to my house. We parked in front, arms around each other and faces next to cheeks. I smelled her perfume, her hair, felt where her arm joined her body, put my thumb under her arm, wondering about sliding my whole hand around to her breast. What the hell would happen then? Should I tell her about Leyla? About going to Connecticut tomorrow? I put my hand on her breast very lightly, and just as hesitantly her arm released me, pushed my hand away. I let her push it away and dropped my hand to her waist and down, pulling her to me from her waist. Her arm was around me again and I was kissing her hard on the mouth.

I almost felt sorry for us. Would she open her mouth again? Should I push it open? Pry it open? I grabbed her roughly, pulled her to me, felt where I'd watched so often through those evening dresses, the swells moving so predictably, grabbed her lower and harder than I ever had.

"*Will*," she said.

She was sort of asking if I knew what I was doing.

"What?"

"Willlllll."

I didn't even want to go farther. It was all too painful.

She moved to me, I kissed her again, and she allowed her head to fall back against the seat.

Surrender or despair?

I was a mole, groping through the earth. No, a mole with questions. I didn't even *want* to go on with whatever it was I was blindly groping for. Just let me go off to the wars and when I come back I'll know what to do.

Did she *want* to break through the whole thing of "nice" and "niceness"? Could I talk to her about it? Could I talk to anyone about it?

Was anyone else in the whole god damned country worried about this at the age of 20? Her head against the seat, legs almost sprawled in the front seat. A piece of meat. Just like me. Two pieces of meat. With heads full, full to the brim, of the most ridiculous nonsense. Just one or two more little details and I might have cried my heart out, or laughed my head off.

"I've got to get the car back. Will I see you tomorrow?"

"I'm not sure. I might have to take a trip. . . ."

"Where? *Tomorrow?*"

"Connecticut!"

"Wi-illll!" Her head was off the seat, "You just got home!"

Then she *was* mad. Hurt. Crying. I couldn't explain to her. Not all at once, anyway. I didn't have much to say, but she had enough for both of us.

I wasn't "serious" and maybe I never had been. She had waited so long for this leave, had written letters and letters to me, told everyone I was coming home, accepted invitations for us, to parties, to supper.

I couldn't answer any of it. But I was . . . well, not as wrong as she seemed to think. Then again, maybe, Christ. Maybe I was totally wrong.

"I'll call you tomorrow," I offered, knowing, in the same instant, that I probably wouldn't.

"You call if you want to, Will Vairin, but I'm not answering."

Off she went. I watched her car to the corner as 'the body' drove away, out of my life.

Chapter 5

Pearse and Mamoo were still up. He was sober and they were being very gentle with each other. They were smoking, my mother with a cigarette holder and Pearse like a tough newspaper reporter, speaking through a cloud of smoke; "Well, Squirt, you wowed 'em tonight!"

"What? You weren't even there!"

He grinned at me and let my mother explain, he'd arrived at the Douglas's after I left. "Which reminds me, Will darling, before I forget. Someone called you, someone who calls himself 'RM' He, umm, is getting married! And he wants you to be in the wedding—"

"What??"

"Yes, in Birmingham . . . at any rate he wants you to call him right away. He said that another friend of his is there, and—just a minute now—I told him that you'd just arrived home and, and, so, my darling . . . well, that's that, but anyhow, I left his number on the console and—"

"Alright, Mamoo, no I don't guess I can make it—"

"I should hope not my darling—"

"Mamoo, I've got to tell you—"

And so I did, just blurted it out, about wanting to see Leyla. How long since I'd seen her. How there was this chance and I had just found out to-night, the flight to Connecticut.

Pearse was smiling; foolishly it seemed to me, but doing the Man thing, explaining and asking particulars. When did I have to report to my next base? How long would I have to see her? All the details I hadn't even thought about. In fact he was helping it all to happen while she closed her face in her hands then left the room and I was there with Pearse talking through his clouds of smoke and his man-to-man talk. And suddenly I realized he was doing all this for me. And, a few minutes after SHE left, he leaned forward and told me it would be okay. She would understand but not to expect it . . . in the next minute.

"Squirt," he said, "I'm going to say this once only," and there was a kind of chill about his lips and lower jaw, at the lips and around the mouth a little pale, as if all the talk before this had been only a delay while he, or they, digested it and would react in time, "Now, this leave . . . well, she's been waiting for you a long time, Squirt. Your mother. For her to just let you go . . . well, I don't know if you can understand it, quite. You're determined to go, aren't you?" Then he nodded as if he'd answered his own question. "I mean you feel it's the right thing for you to do?"   At the last fraction he changed it from a question to a statement. Then he was just looking at me, smiling; a smile that I had seen before, when I found out it was also a smile of anger.

"You really love her? Leyla?"

"Yeah . . . and this is a perfect chance, a free ride."

"Alright," he said, dramatically, "go to it! Squirt. I'll make it okay with her . . . your mother."

How could I not admire him? Arthe and Brucie would never have this kind of a scene with him. They might even have pointed out, well, it isn't *his* sacrifice, so he can be brave about it. To me, he was acting out the philosophy from *The Prophet*, their book, their bible, which they were always quoting and urging me to read.

Pearse told me I should go in and see her, and that he would stay in the living room till I talked to her.

I walked in and realized I had not been in her bedroom for an awfully long time. In fact, I had not been there since she and Pearse were married, except for that one night, the last leave. She was in the beautiful four-poster from the mansion on Audubon Place, lying there very small and frail. I couldn't help wonder about them in bed. And then about myself and why I couldn't just feel bad about leaving so soon.

She sat up and held out her arms to me. The tears had left paths down her face. Something broke in me. I was holding her and crying. The long desert the long gulf desert of not having seen her, not so much the time between leaves but the time between admitting I loved her and, instead, how I made fun of her, laughed at her ways. Why did I make fun of her? Why did I want to see her exasperated ("Sometimes I wonder why I had you children!"). We stayed hugging, maybe the longest hug since early childhood. Something was loosening, pouring out of me, a kind of anger. Even for the news when I got home, first about Wonderful, then about Bootchie. After all, someone had to tell me. I didn't understand my anger at all. Hugging and crying. I had come in to explain something. Instead I was holding her, starved just to hold her; not cursing, not trying to escape home. It was connected with my father. Tears for her, for him, for the way it had been, and, I guess, for me too, although that was the hardest of all to figure out. It was also, strangely, that I loved New Orleans. Loved being home. Loved it that Sally was back again.

"Will . . . " She tried three or four times to tell me something. I knew by her tone that she accepted the trip. It was okay. What else had it ever been? It's okay, okay, my boy, go on, do it. I love you.

She blew her nose, grabbed another tissue, sniffed, wiped and squeezed her nose ("Would you please stop sniffing and use *something*?" she'd tell me).

I was within an inch of cancelling the trip.

Suddenly she was steady and serious, holding me by the shoulders, "Will, there's something I've been meaning to tell you—"

"Well, I haven't seen Leyla—"

"My darling, if you'll just let me . . . I wasn't going to say anything about that. You're hell-bent on it so go. I was, and . . . my darling boy, have I EVER stood in the way of what you wanted to do? EVER?"

Outside it started to rain and was now coming down with a roar, with a kind of hell-fury, a typical New Orleans tropical downpour that might last for an hour or stop in five minutes. The smell of green, of earth came through the window. It was locking me in, holding me.

"—I wanted to talk to you about something else entirely. Something I've thought about for some time. You know, my darling . . . reach the matches and that ash-tray for me, will you?"

I did it and propped my head up with my arm. The rain, the very earth through the window, the green of it, coming through the window, even in the dark.

"I was going to say to you that you have a . . . a tremendous gift. A gift that draws people to you, that makes people love you. I've seen it all of your life. But that is not it, what I wanted to say to you. What I really want to say to you, my darling, is that that gift brings, or carries a responsibility with it, a responsibility . . . .do you know what I'm talking about?"

"Go on."

"Just that, my darling," she puffed on the long stem of her holder, the motion like FDR's, her chin up, and seemed completely recovered from the tears.

"These people who love you: me, Sally, your sisters, little Faye, Leyla, all of your friends, your uncles and aunts who love you . . . Pearse—"

I felt like scoffing about that one but I let her go.

"Just that, Will . . . people love you. You don't do very much, maybe to, um, deserve it," she laughed gently, coughed her smoker's cough. "Not that you aren't kind and noble . . . to your friends especially, but the thing is that they *do* love you—little Ned, for another—and you have a responsibility. Do you see?"

"No, I don't."

"You really don't, my boy?" She was looking at me shrewdly, rocking the cigarette holder between her teeth, ready to ask it again.

"Yeah, sort of."

"Well, I'll tell you, in case there's any doubt. You have to be a little gentle. A little more gentle. And a little more considerate . . . maybe even a lot more considerate, well, about your time. About your plans. Now, I don't want to go into it any more than that. Now . . . do you understand me?"

"Yes, but, you know . . . "

"What?"

"It's not my fault . . . I mean, if someone loves you. You can't help it."

She nodded, nodded, "And neither can they," she said. "And one of them is your mother."

"Do you want me not to go tomorrow?"

"No . . . you go. Your heart's set on it. You can just think about what I've said. That's what you can do for me. Alright? My darling? I don't want your arguments, your case, because you're quite good at making a case for yourself, I only want you to think about it." She was running her hands through my hair, slowly, deliberately—short as it was—with a sweet happy smile on her face, her confident smile.

I think I loved her purely. As purely as I ever loved her in my life. After her silence I told her I was going to call RM.

She called me back, and added, "I'm worried that I didn't get it over to you, Will darling—"

"I understand, Maw—"

But she was explaining anyhow, "That it's a blessing . . . a blessing, my dear, that can turn into a kind of curse . . . do you understand me now?"

"Yeah, I guess."

"I mean, by the word, a curse if the gift is not handled properly . . . I mean, I look at little Faye and I know she loves you very much—"

"Ha! Well, that's over!"

"What?"

"As of tonight."

"Will, I can't believe that."

"Well, it's true."

"Did you tell her you were going to Connecticut?"

I nodded.

She looked at me but said nothing. She drew in smoke and watched me, shrewdly.

"Well, I better call RM and . . . pack some stuff."

She took another drag on her cigarette holder and gazed at me over it, then said something else, quietly.

"What?"

"I just say, my darling, that I have thought a long time about what I just told you."

"Okay, Mamoo."

"You think about it, do you hear? My darling?"

"Yes, I will."

I kissed her once more and hugged her but it was the way I had hugged her for years.

Chapter 6

The B-26 looks dangerous and menacing even on the ground. The stubby chocolate-green wings and cigar-shaped fuselage didn't seem to belong to the same vehicle—"vehicle" because it looked more like a ground-hugging tank than anything designed to fly. As a plane what was it? A torpedo, released from a mother plane sent straight ahead to plunge into the target and explode. But, on the ground, with its tricycle landing gear holding that cigar-fuselage parallel to the ground, it not only looked menacing but—in part because of the rain and the lakes of water all over the parking areas—like a poisonous heavy-bodied water bug. The water was also in sheets on the big mat where the "Yellow Perils" of Naval Air Station New Orleans took off and landed. Today there was no movement and the big medium bomber was the only plane on the field not tied down.

The clouds were low and sullen, soggy, heavy, slow-moving.

"You ever ride in a 'twenty-six'?" Dan asked me.

Chuck Ritter, Dan's copilot an old country-boy from Arkansas, was jeering about Dan's question.

They talked about where I'd sit. I didn't much care, although I was hoping to lie down somewhere. I didn't tell them I had a tendency to get sick when someone else was flying.

"Chuck, get him settled, I'll fill out the papers in the flight office. We'll take off in about 10 minutes." He walked away and we climbed the little ladder behind the pilot's compartment into the Martin "Marauder," the flying whore.

My first impression was one of darkness, and equipment jammed into every conceivable corner, and of no escape. A dark trap. Chuck squeezed through the skinny walkway to the pilot's and the co-pilot's compartment, stepped up to the seat and motioned to the left seat for me. "Too bad," he said with his quick smile, "these are the best seats in the house but, don't worry, we'll trade off after we get up to altitude."

He took me back through the center of the plane, showed me how to get up in the turret gunner's chair, "This is probably the next best seat," he said. Up there it was a real fishbowl, with a 360 degree view of the world.

"I'll take this," I said, "If I have a choice."

"You got it! The other two are not crew, they're only passengers," he laughed, "Well, that's it, then." He showed me how to strap in. I heard Dan come back, chuckling, "Will? You okay?" I could hardly see him down below me.

"Yeah!"

"I had to tell a few lies to get cleared in this weather but we're set to go. You might as well stay strapped in till after take-off; I'll see you in half an hour . . . let you fly this buggy . . . "

Then he was back again, "Incidentally, Aphra's not too happy with me for letting you go," he shrugged.

I climbed down again, I'd forgotten about RM; I reached the pilot's compartment just as he fired up the left engine. A crack-pow explosion that filled the area with smoke, and then the right, but he looked around. I had caught the real flyer about his tasks; he was wearing the big donuts over his squashed pisscutter cap but tilted it off to talk.

"Are we going anywhere near Birmingham?" I asked him.

"Practically right over it. Well, between Birmingham and Atlanta," he yelled. The roar of the two engines was deafening.

"And we're gonna stop somewhere to refuel, maybe in Richmond . . . well, we're scheduled to stop there. Why? You have another girl in Birmingham?" He was laughing and alive, so different from the proper young guy I had met at the party.

Something had changed his blood; the plane, flying, the risk, something I couldn't explain.

I told him about RM's marriage. He considered it a second, then shook it off.

"Yeahh," he laughed, "I'd like to—"

"Well, anyhow, let me know when we're over Birmingham."

"Will do. . . . You gonna bail out?"

"Ha!"

"You better strap in, we're heading out."

I went back to my spot in the turret and we were moving before I climbed up. The thin rain was grizzling up the turret as we rushed into it. The brakes were groaning and rocking the plane on its big squashy tires.

This field isn't made for a B-26 Dan had said yesterday. If it was true for landing it was even more true for take-offs. The field, made primarily for the little Yellow Perils, was a big tar mat circle, identical to the one at Memphis. Alongside it were two fair-sized runways crossing before the circle and continuing after it, like a pair of scissors holding a big ball. The wind was five knots, shifting. We'd take off into it over the lake.

They were testing the engines. The whole plane was shaking like a horse gouged and held back at the same time. Getting ready, ready, ready. At the other end, if we made it, was "the north," Boston, Leyla. And I had the usual thought. No guarantees for even five more minutes.

From the taxi-strip we wheeled onto the runway for a running start, engines thundering. At the far end was a patch of grass, cyclone fence bounding the field, grass, the road, the sea-wall and the lake, all moving toward us. The whole plane was vibrating and shaking violently. Half the runway used up and nowhere near flying speed.

Three-quarters.

We were dragging and then lifting into the air, nose high and hanging on the props.

Grass-fence-grass-road-sea-wall-lake. Flying . . . northeast by the skin of our teeth.

They had dropped the flaps to clear the fence and were just now closing them, adjusting RPMs for climbing and cruising.

Then we were into the clouds while still in a turn. A dirty towel had been wrapped around my lookout post. This was like nothing I'd experienced; heavy, plunging through the air, not flying as I knew it.

I had no instruments in the turret so I had no idea of speed or directions. The turret was my castle, or my prison. In either case I was locked here till we gassed up or crashed.

I was thinking about RM's marriage, my mother's talk, Leyla, Faye, Little, Paige Burney, and all the other people I loved and had loved so far and exactly what my mother was trying to tell me. I wasn't ready for all of that. I was still testing my wings and she was trying to ground me.

It was a little cooler but my clothes were still wet from sweat and rain. Funny, I only noticed as it got cooler.

They estimated a flight of some nine hours, with a stop for gas, to arrive in Hartford around five in the afternoon. The base was a hundred miles from Boston.

They had let him take off because it was clear in a line from Montgomery to Tuscaloosa all the way to Canada. From take-off to Montgomery we could only presume that we were flying over the planet earth.

I alternated between not caring about the risk and wonder at finding myself here. Of Mamoo waiting for this leave; anger at the guilt, happy for the madness, if it was mad. Grateful for the feeling of who cares. Leyla was not involved. She was the end of a rainbow I hardly believed in any more. We called and called each other, maybe relieved, sometimes, when we couldn't connect. Holding something, holding on. Calling, calling back later. Even when we did talk it was the same. Her schedule and me going through. As for her father, nothing had changed. They monitored her trips back and forth to school; telephone calls and telegrams about when she'd arrive in Boston at the northern or Shreveport at the southwestern end.

The noise, the buffeting, was gone. Dan gave me cotton for my ears but it was my thoughts that took me out of the noise.

Suddenly we were in light. It yanked my head back and up. We were rising off of a level white carpet as far as I could see. Above me was a war of clouds, high above, twenty or thirty thousand feet, but this beast had chugged up and out of the mush of the Gulf of Mexico, Louisiana and Mississippi.

I watched those huge engines plowing us, dragging us through the air. If one of them stopped, with only these short wings to hold us up, the plane would go down like a brick.

Something was pulling at my pants leg. Dan was signaling to climb down. He was directly below me with a big sunny smile.

"Yeah," he said, with his husky chuckle, "We cleared that fence by a *mile!*"

"Yeah," I agreed, "a *country* mile!"

"Well . . . two feet."

"Hey, we missed it, right?"

"I've been trying to convince myself, ever since, but I don't quite believe it."

Up to the front cockpit, past the two other hitchhikers, both army PFCs sacked out on top of equipment.

"We're flying the Birmingham beam, right now. Another hour, forty minutes. Get up in my seat."

I hiked myself up.

"Ever fly twin-engines?"

"No."

"There's the yoke."

Chuck was flying with earphones cocked, listening to us and the radio. Suddenly he started yelling, "When I was first in flying—before the war—navigation was real simple: 'follow the highway out of town, turn left at the cross-roads with the Esso station, pick up the railroad tracks, and so on."

"What happened if there was fog?"

"You taxied along the side of the road."

I liked him. And felt sorry for them both. Well, someone had to fly medium bombers. . . . *And* dive-bombers.

"Alright if we let this gyrene fly the Betsy?"

"You've got it, lieutenant!"

I had fitted my feet to the huge rudder bars and took the black-handled yoke.

Chuck showed me the trim tabs, throttles, the double engine gauges. I was flying a B-26, "Betsy," the Flying Prostitute.

"We fly by the trim tabs," Dan explained to me. The aileron trim tab was over our heads. There was twice as much radio gear, radar, toggles, buttons, and about six gas tank switches. That and the tiny little windows. To look out to the rear was impossible. To my left that huge engine was chewing the air, to my right was Chuck and a piece of the sky.

Dan popped his big donut earphones over my head and I was in the orderly, calm world of radio and the Birmingham beam. Voices in the distance and a humming slow dit-daaaaa, distinct, clear, neat.

Chuck's voice over the radio although he was only two feet away: "We're flying a heading of about . . . well, holding a heading of zero three two degrees, if you want to fly the beam . . . ahhhh, don't worry about the beam. Just fly it."

"Can I roll it?" I asked him.

"Haaahaaa, whooo!"

"What? What did he say?" Dan yelled.

"HE WANTS TO ROLL IT!" Chuck screamed at him.

"Gimme that yoke! Aphra warned me about you!"

I tried some turns, climbs, glides. Oh, but it was slow to respond, like a sleepy soldier. And even in a slight turn it dropped like a brick unless the yoke went back hard as the wing dropped. We were plowing through the air at 210 miles an hour. The speed alone held us up.

Chuck had some music on the coffee grinder:

Dit-daaaaaaaaaaaaaaaa

"Whether near to me or farrrr . . . "

Daaaaaaaaaaaaaaaaaaaaaaaaaaaa

I was on the beam and put the beast into a slight turn to stay on it.

On one side of a beam is the continuous sound of the Morse code for "A"—dit daaaa. On the other side of the beam is the continuous sound of the Morse code for "N"—daaaaaa dit.

Directly on the beam the two sounds merge to send a continuous hum of daaaaaaaaaaa. Once a minute, the particular radio beam sends out its identifying call number or letters to let the navigator know what beam he's flying. As one approaches the beam station the signal becomes stronger, as one leaves the station it becomes weaker. At the very center of the beam, where the four legs meet, there is a pocket of silence about three seconds duration. Between the four legs (or beams) the clear letter sounds of "A" or "N" are broadcast continually.

We sailed over Birmingham. Three seconds of silence. No sirens, no fire-works. I wished RM the best and wished I could do it all, everything in the world, everything all at once.

"There's an oh such a hungry yearning,/burning inside of me."

I could hear Arthe singing the words in the house at 6031, when the world was not so new but much simpler.

Half an hour of flying that beast and I gladly gave it over. I slept. Dan woke me up to strap in, we were circling the Richmond base, getting ready for landing and more gas.

Chapter 7

We landed in Richmond and I ran to a little canteen: coffee, sandwiches, candy bars, drinks, and back to the plane.

Dan made out the new flight plan, signed for the gas, we stretched, ate, and were off again.

Chuck flew, Dan and I talked, he in his cockpit turned to me, me standing in the skinny aisle between them, yelling over the huge engines on either side of us. I told him about the cousins, the aunts and uncles. He told me about growing up in New Iberia, fishing and hunting, and all the time with an eye on New Orleans, Louisiana's big bad city. The two army PFCs were still asleep and hadn't stirred since New Orleans. Dan took over and I went up to my turret, my sky watch. A high overcast had moved in. The frozen north.

Below us was the U.S. at war. Troops on maneuver, trucks, buses, troop trains crisscrossing the country; goodbyes, hellos, letters, cries for help, telegrams, "Regret to inform you. . . . " Rosie the Riveter, factories around the clock.

Leyla had no idea I was on the way to see her. That was the best thing about it. The chances, the chances and this beast of an airplane. I had called Leyla after getting our wings. Not even sure she was there. Not sure of anything. Bertram Hall.

"Leyla Herndon?"

In a bubble turret watching the country, my country. Over New Jersey, the northeast with its tremendous cities, the industrial north, Atlantic coast, Nazi subs out there, the cold.

"Who shall I say?"

After losing 20 battles are we about to win one? If this beast holds up another half hour. Circling the field.

"Lieutenant Will Vairin."

Coming in fast, wheels and flaps down. Dancing with Paige Burney at the Southern Yacht Club. Standing at ease with new wings, the admiral and Dubya D., "Yeah, that's him! 'Three days with wheels!'"

"I've flown around the world in a plane.

I've settled revolutions in Spain . . . "

"*Lieutenant Will Vairin—to see you.*"

The flight was like our time, the whole thing between us, the world on a string. "So long, Will. Good luck in Boston. Call this number—Flight Operations—for a ride, to Florida or points south."

A screech over the phone, from where I was standing.

Outside of Hartford, hitching, big green issue bag with uniforms and flight gear, gabardines and new wings, all new. And new luck.

Two hours from Hartford to Boston, and a taxi.

Well, Cambridge is across the bridge. Radcliffe and Harvard.

No, that's Harvard. Radcliffe is—

"*Wiiiiiiiiiillllllll! I can't beleeeve it!*"

Elegant, quieter; is she actually in one of these buildings?

I could never quite miss someone, not till . . . I mean, allow myself . . . allow I *missed* them, until I was only seconds away . . . maybe closer.

"*Let me look at you!*"

A blink of the eyes, in her arms blink, in a plane, taking off, missing the fence, blink.

I closed my eyes, allowed my arms to register. Her body against me . . . flying, flying home, I couldn't stand to open my eyes. Home, oh home! Her arms, hair, different. Different enough to really be? Slimmer? Wirey? Same container?

"God! Will! Is it really *you!* I'm gonna faint. I don't be*lieve*—"

"Leyla. It was like—" I snapped my fingers.

Each hug was collecting bits and pieces from the accident that had blown us apart. Gathering ourselves against the shock. The flight and those engines riveting my brain. Lost in her hair, "Ohhhh Leyla . . . Ohhhh, Leyla!" Breathing her. I couldn't help the tears that made her cry too.

"Will, Willlll, ohhh Will . . . " listening too, the story on her voice those months away.

If we could hug all others out, hug out the time away. The girl at the desk looking, but she knew the war. Leavings. Killed, love, missing. For alll we knowww.

We went to a little bistro coffee shop, filled to bursting—Harvard students, M.I.T. students, Radcliffe—most of the male students wore their dinky ROTC whites (Cadet whites, "I'll take vanilla!" we yelled to each other). Yeah, dinky, but these guys were *here*.

Over the tiny table we could touch foreheads and as long as we were in contact nothing, nothing, nothing. Not even . . .

The world was all pink, pink balloon buildings, we pushed them along with our smiles, a flick of one finger, only we could hardly talk, hardly think.

"You love me?"

"Oh God, Will!"

"Leyla . . . "

"God, Will . . . don't you see? Don't you know?"

"Leyla . . . I *had* to do this. *Had* to—"

" . . . and your *wings! Lieutenant!*"

She blushed, saying it. Her beauty floored me. I had no idea why she was blushing, but all of her innocence, her soul peeled away. The planes of her face more definite, freckles paler, perfect teeth and gums, lips agonizing in their curves and changes when she spoke, then smiled. Even her red-gold hair, held back and off to one side. I hated and loved it.

Leyla had leaped up and shouted some name, dragging the person over.

"Lil," she practically screamed, "WILL!" Threw back her head, as if she had produced me out of a hat.

The dark-haired "Lil" gave me such a look, studying, "Sooo, the famous Will! I was beginning to believe you didn't exist."

While Leyla positively gushed, spouted information about Lil, her "enemy," two hundred laughs over that, Columbus, Ohio, lived next door, fell in love with my picture, explained about this visit.

"How long will you be here?"

Leyla and I looked at each other.

"And where are you staying?" Lil asked, in a teasing way.

We started laughing and couldn't stop.

"You're both crazy, that's easy enough to see."

Lil, in the first minute, had been more practical than either of us in our hour . . . hour? Twenty minutes?

"I don't know . . . either one," I told her.

"Listen, I'll leave you two love-birds, I have a test in twenty minutes, but I have an idea, if you want to try it. For a place to stay. Call me, Leyla." Only she pronounced it "Lilla." And disappeared in the crowd. We sat down again. Head to head. The waitress came back for the fifth time, couldn't decide.

"You want some soup? They make great soup."

"SOUP???"

We were laughing so hard the waitress left again.

Her hair was full of glints. Gold. Red. Green-gold-red-sun-colored. When she paused to say something, just to draw in her breath, I knew reams about her. I knew books about her. I knew her history, her family, all the thoughts in her head, in front of her, the thousand things just at her lips, where her lips, the agonizing curved heart-breaking lips made me see, feel it all, instead settle for crushing those lips as close as the madness, not love madness, just mad madness.

In my heart of hearts did it matter what had happened? So life-full? While I was away? In my heart of hearts? But just as I decided it didn't matter, just then; as I was saying how I knew one person in all the north and had come up north, was with the one person, and what did it matter what happened while we were . . . up HE comes, bronzed, in his dinky whites.

"Ohh, hi, Derek!" Blushing? Embarrassed?

He was looking at her, not at me.

Then he looked, at the moment of introduction, "Derek, this is Will Vairin."

"Oh, uh, good evening . . . Lieutenant," and shook hands but it was more like a salute.

The bastard was in awe. Handsome, young smoothie, lean-jawed, dark eyes, and at ease, usually.

"Derek was in an art class with me," Leyla explained.

"Nice to meet you, Lieutenant." Then he was leaving.

"That's so funny," Leyla almost clapped her hands, "he was actually afraid!"

"Yeah, he was ready to salute . . . But, Leyla, the question is, are we in love?"

She put her head in her hands, then looked up at me and held up all the fingers of one hand and two from the other.

"What? . . . Ohhhh!"

She was mad. Hurt.

"Leyla, my . . . darling."

I'd never called a girl 'darling' and I was stunned at myself. "Seven? *Seven children*! That's what you meant . . . I *knew* that! Leyla!"

I was happy, touched, only she was hurt that I didn't know immediately. Her eyes were as suddenly full of tears. I pulled my chair around the tiny table and she hugged me fiercely, cried into my ear, "It's been so long, so lonnnng, Will, and you're here. So long away from you, waiting, writing, never getting . . . touch with you . . . I mean like . . . .so, even over the phone, like we've been together. Only in Memphis that talk, but at least I felt like we, like well, that we—"

"Yes, I know. You were so great . . . And so, since then, I mean . . . you saw guys . . . Derek and so forth?"

"I'll tell you . . . every detail…Ohh, I don't know. Derek . . . He's . . . "

"Yeah?"

I was introduced to more people. They stopped, and took up time.

"Will, I've got to ask you and I'm afraid to . . . .how long? How long . . . can you stay?"

"About two . . . two and a half days."

"Two? Two whole days? That's terrible, and . . . wonderful."

"I have to be back *on* the 15th."

"I've got it!" Leyla's eyes lit up, "Norrie's roommate. She told me she'd lend me her car. She owes me lots of favors. I'll be right back. Oooooooh, give me a kiss."

The waitress was back.

"What kind of soup do you have?"

"Split pea, minestrone, and clam chowder."

"Aright, I'll have split pea . . . and some coffee. You want to order? Or you're going?"

"Nothing."

She started to leave. Once she got two tables away and I pulled her back. We'll go get the car together. No. Alright. Back. *Don't move one inch.* How can you leave? I just got here. You want me to stay? No, go.

"A cup or bowl?"

"A bowl."

"I love the way you order stuff."

"I love you."

"No, I mean—"

"It only took half an hour."

"Don't move. Be right back."

"Just a second. *Is this really us, here? Boston?*"

"Cambridge."

One more kiss; lips, teeth, tongues.

Leyla got to the door, came back, I saw her move, threading through tables. Only it was me moving, back to me. I was getting up. Each greeting was like the first, after months. She walked into me, kissing till every thought was driven from my brain.

"Ooooh, ouch—" people at the next table were laughing.

"I can't leave you," she said.

"Let's go."

Out past tables.

"*Heyy, your soup!*"

"We're coming right back."

The poor waitress. Off into the fresh dark evening and back to Bertram Hall, where I had left my bags behind the desk. No Men Above First Floor.

Girls signed out, signed in, had curfews and passes. But there are ways and ways, Leyla told me. I wondered. Well, I waited and wondered.

Fifteen minutes she was back down. Pouting, "No car . . . BUT," the sadness was an act. "We have a place! A PLACE! FOR US!"

Lil would have to take us there, but she'd already called. Lil would be down in a minute. Her test was cancelled.

"I'm 'na have to watch you," Leyla said, ominously, "Lil would jump you in a minute. I *know* her. And Bess, my roomie, and four others want to meet you. They're dying to meet you. They've all seen the picture I have on my desk. Here comes Lil."

Dancing down the broad staircase leading to the mysterious upper floors came Lil. She had on a black scarf partly wrapped around her head, red-red lipstick, assured air. She was good-looking and would someday be a beauty, just a little baby fat.

"Alright, now, here's the deal. These boys have the top floor of a house not far from here. And there's an extra room in the attic. Well?"

"Great!"

It was already nine o'clock. Boston was jammed. The whole east coast was jammed, they said. The Merchant Marine, navy, army bases, wives, and families coming and going, transport planes flying in and out, troop ships leaving for England, liberty ships leaving and returning; tankers, battleships, aircraft carriers.

People made reservations three and four weeks in advance and still got bumped, reservations were lost. It's the war. Yeah. The war, the war. And now these guys were extending themselves for Leyla and her flyer, her "fiance." What did we really want? Just our privacy. Only the most difficult thing to find in the whole country. Now we had Lil, as well. We huddled together and followed. "I think Lil's in love with Derek," Leyla whispered to me. "He's one of the guys who lives there."

"Derek again . . . so, you've been there before?"

"Yes, to parties and stuff."

"..and 'stuff'?"

"Will?"

"WILL?" Leyla shook my arm. "Lieutenant?" She shook me again, dug her chin into my neck, her mouth in my ear.

She shook me and stopped. Lil had wandered on before she realized.

"Will, don't! Just don't. I *love* you! And that's *all*. Isn't it? YES," she decided.

"Yeaaaup."

"Ohhh, you're mad . . . "

"Come on, you guys, it's in the next block."

"Will! We haven't even been alone yet!"

Off we went.

A salt-box, she called the house. White with gray shutters. Rang a bell. We were buzzed in and up a narrow staircase.

"Hi, Randy! Is Derek here?"

"Shoo-wa waaa's," the one called Randy announced. "They should be back . . . " he looked at his watch, "They're bringing back some grub." Ho ho, 'grub,' they were all in the Navy.

"Well," by this time we were at the top of the stairs.

"Randy, this is 'Lilla' and her fiancee—"

"Sure, I know Leyla," said Randy.

"Well, they have no place and Will is about to go overseas—"

"Hey, I *know*! I heard! It's alright. I'll show 'em the place. Right this way, uh, lieutenant."

We shook hands. All of this group, so far, seemed to be, well, quite eligible, as my sister, Arthe, would have said.

"Rich and good-for-nothing,' most of 'em," Leyla told me.

Randy walked us into a narrow kitchen, reached up to a handle and pulled down a long sliding ladder, flicked on a switch, "Here it is," and walked up the ladder.

Leyla looked around with a dazzling smile, "Ain't we got fun," she whispered, squeezing the words out. Then she walked up after Liz.

I dropped my doubts and knew, if I never knew it before, that I was blessed. I could hardly breathe. Our hideaway from the world? Our place? Two hours ago I wasn't sure of anything.

The attic had old sea chests, steamer trunks, drapes hung on unusable lamps, racks of dresses. The roof slanted down except for the dormer, on that side was a low bed with a mattress on it next to some porthole windows, well, squarish portholes. Next to the bed was a little night table and a lamp.

The bed was kind of dusty, with only a spread on it. We stood, all four of us, and surveyed it.

Inside I was screaming leave, just leave. But no. Randy had suddenly become a mother. He'd go down and find a bulb for the little night-table lamp, and get us an extra sheet from somewhere.

No, Leyla said, she'd get *her* sheets and blankets.

"Stop! Just stop! Lilla, will you let me do that? I know the girl on duty, Kate . . . Kate something. Well, I know her real well, let ME get the sheets and tell me which blankets and I'll bring 'em right back. Okay?"

But Leyla had to go back and get some stuff anyhow, and I did too.

"Well, I'll sign you out and sign you back in again. With Kate . . . Kate what's-her-name.

She's on till two or sometime."

"Lil, you're a friend. An enemy-friend."

We had no key, but Randy would be there and probably the others as well. Oh, Jesus. And while it seemed it would never never end, it finally, by eleven o'clock, was done. My bags would stay behind the reception desk for the night, get 'em in the morning. I fished around for toothbrush and razor. Back at the house the whole gang, plus 10 or 15 more guys and girls, had come back from "Shoo-wa-waaa's" with beer and fixings and we met everybody, and I was the flyer and what kind of planes, and is that training really the world's toughest? Well, we're proud to have you, sir. Hell, yeah, the least we can do for a Marine flyer. Damn! And *what* kind of planes? Been overseas yet? And so on, most of which was okay and very admiring but at last we were up the stairs, the ladder was pulled up after us, and locked, and there we were. Safe and smiling in the dark attic. September, Boston, the great gut-busting war out there somewhere, and us in our hideaway.

Our little lamp light worked. Leyla made our bed. I watched and watched her magic.

"You want me to—"

"Look, Lieutenant, I'll *tell* you when I want you to move."

She made me chuckle. I sat on an old elephant footrest and watched her smooth and pat everything into place, around and around the bed she went, around, making it perfect and beyond that, then I grabbed part under her frilly, gauzy skirt, part legs, part skirt and tackled her onto the bed.

"Ohh, Will." She said in her tiniest voice. She was crying and huddled. "Will, I'm scared. I really mean it. I'm so happy I'm scared to death."

Moments . . . apart, travel and miles, time together. And our feeble words. Not even touching what had happened.

"Push that shade out, please? I mean the light?"

I pushed it and the light on our bed was pale yellow, evening yellow on the blue spread. If only this far, I thought. Only this far is enough. If just this, for disappointed mother, angry Faye.

Leyla was lying part on her back, twisted so her back was flat, her hair, red-gold, spread out, her hips turned, her skirt yellow, orange, pale green in swirls, above her knees. My hands behind her knees and I loosened the hold.

"You're scared? Leyla? With me?"

She turned as if she'd been shot. "No, no, Will. Not scared of *you*."

I pulled her so she had her head on my chest, a pillow under my head, our bodies not touching.

"See?" she said, "We never had this . . . before. Time to be together and . . . talk. Just us two. This will be the first time. Right? No one's car to get back. No one's waiting for me—"

"I know . . . "

"But scary, too, right? But GOD! WILL! Two days? Does this count? Is this *one*? How long? Exactly?"

"The 15th. I have to report *on* the 15th—"

"The 15th of September? Florida?"

"Yes, you nut. September 15th, of this year."

"What's today? Oh, God. It's almost the twelfth!"

"Well, that's it. Tonight, tomorrow, and the next day."

"Three days . . . well, two days?"

"You were scared a few minutes ago."

"No, it's . . . Will, you're here, and I'm still getting used to you being here."

I thought of us in that little dive, kissing when she came back. All of the compartments of my brain melting.

"Will . . . this is kind of silly, but I've got to go . . . "

At the other end of the attic was the little stall. The door closed behind her.

Something had changed. Flying? The war? Seven? There's no after-the-war-for-us?

So simple what we had back in Marshall. Off to the lake and we went at it. Now I didn't know. I mean, how she was feeling. Would we even do it?

The "sea" below us roared on. College high jinks: beer, booze, broads. The war way out there and who-knows-what's next.

"Gotcha!" Leyla pounced on me.

Mouths, tongues, lips, off came the clothes—t-shirt, pants, shorts and before I could finish she was on the bed, nothing on, gleaming yellow golden in the lamp-light.

"Leyla . . . ."

"Don't talk . . . just . . . come here," she laughed. I wanted to fall on my knees and thank someone, myself for listening, for grabbing Dan and that chance to get here, Bill for *Flying Home*, for telling Faye, Mamoo and the leave, flying home instead. Leaving anger and hurt to come here.

I moved down in bed and she lay like a queen, gently moved her legs for me, and I passed myself through her wetness, back and forth, so good I had to wait, just so good I had to wait.

"Ohhh, Will, phhhhhhewww."

Crazy, crazy with her.

"Ohhh, God, Willll, phhhhhhewww, what are you *doing*? . . . I can't *stand* it."

So tight and sweet pushing in, my mind pinked off to the sweetness.

"Ohh, my darling, my darling," our mouths were locked, her fingernails gripping my cheek, one hand on my back pushing, squeezing. Squeezing, squeezing, holding on.

It lasted an hour, or five more seconds. She was erupting, groaning, straining me to her, and there was no stopping, we sailed through a sound barrier, on and on, Leyla gurgling, "Good, ohh good, good, my darling, so good, ohh, ohh, yes, I want all of it in me, ohh yes, Will, you're in me, I love it, I love you love you, ohh you *let* me, you *let* me this time, ohh, heaven, heaven's what it was, Will, you don't know, you're just, oh," she was thrashing about, laughing, "you're just a *man*," she started giggling, "I didn't mean that, you . . . bastard . . . " squealing, squeezing me, gripping my back, tearing the skin off me, "Ohh, go' . . . I'm sorry," laughing, "Ohhh, WILLLLL," she said, in a sudden discovery, her voice brand new, sparkling.

She squealed, laughed, and then coughed me out. "Ohh, no! I didn't mean for, ohh, damn, Will. . . . Will?"

I didn't want to talk. I didn't know what to think. I hadn't hesitated for a second about coming in her. Not for a second. At the crucial moment everything said keep on.

My chest and shoulders were off to the left side and I could see her face, her eyes in the dim little lamplight open, her lids closing like a cat breathes, cloooossing, opening slowly, staying open, clo-o-o-o s-sing. Breathing so deeply, so softly.

"Are you purring?"

"*Yes!*" She said, delighted that I knew.

"Ohh, Will, I love you, love you. I'm so glad, I'm so glad we did it . . . like that. You don't knowwwww."

"Yeah, but Leyla . . . I mean—"

"Shhhhhh, don't worry. I think it'll be fine. I just finished my period."

"Just finished? *Isn't that the worst time of all?*"

She started laughing. I was in her hands, the entire being of her held me in a way that was frightening. At the same time I felt miles apart.

"Ohh, Will, oooh I love you . . . give me that face."

"God damnit, answer! Isn't it?"

"Will . . . " but she wasn't fazed, "you're so funny, so scared. No, it's not the greatest time but it's not the worst. I just finished, *just* finished. I, um, well, I have a very heavy period for three days, and this is the sixth day. The worst is between the tenth and—"

"Leyla . . . we really have to talk."

"Will. . . !" Suddenly she was gentled, all concern. She reached her hand for my face and I turned and kissed it on the palm. Kissed her palm, licked it with the tip of my tongue.

She moaned and gave her hand to my mouth. I could feel a stirring in me. I licked it and bit the fat side of it.

"Ohh, Will," she moved her legs against mine, "You make me so weak . . . I could die . . . right now and die happy. I can't explain how it makes me feel. How it makes me . . . now, you better stop kissing my hand or ohh, stop, I'll be all *over* you."

She jumped up, straddled me, her hair hung down, tickling my chest, her big beautiful breasts that I'd never actually studied up close, her hands holding my wrists, pinning me, her wet lips, clear eyes full of mischief.

"You wanta fight?"

"Noooooooooooooooooooooooo," she leered.

"Well, what the hell *do* you want to do?"

She got down close to my mouth, "You figure it out."

She was talking in my mouth, talking, actually saying something.

"What? What did you say?"

"I told you what I wanted but I'll only say it into your mouth: mmfmlslkmmfmlslksshsltickliemmm?"

"WHAT???"

"I won't say it again, even to your mouth, ohhh, God."

"Ohh Jesus, oh, yes, Leyla."

She slid back, reached her hand down and put it in her. She stayed on top, with her hair hanging down, moving, moving, her eyes closing like a cat breathing again, enjoying it in some way, in some way deeper than her body.

"Oooooh, Will, ooohh Will, do it again like that, will you? Please? Please? *Ooooohhh Goddd, Will, it's happening . . . right now . . . , ohhh Will, oh yes, I love you love you, ooohhh yes, Will, love you, Will, hold me, hold me, hold me . . . tiiiight.*"

Her talk drove me, her body furious against mine, grinding so fast she was rocking against me, holding, humming, out of control, thrashing, until she couldn't move and I had to heave her over and finish again without any more of a thought about what was happening, holding it deep and deep in her and out and deep again, as if I were trying to peel away my very prick then finally still but throbbing, throbbing, throbbing.

We stayed and stayed that way, clinging to moments, afraid of the slightest change, the least change, jealous of every second's passing; having and wishing for it at the same time.

I was dying, no, dead, never to open my eyes, never come back. We were still moving, notions of how to move, where, which way, all of that going on without us.

When I ventured to peep out, her eyes were gone, her mouth was open, and her head slowly flailing back and forth.

So peeled back for me to see, so open, so brazen and straight.

I woke up once, Leyla was sound asleep, her hair a very poem of soft curls, loops, eyes closed, nice lashes closed down on cheeks, then I slept, woke up with her watching me, waiting, recovered. I think she had just come back from the stall.

"One knocked-out lieutenant, if you ask me."

"I didn't think I was coming back . . . from that trip."

"Will, what do you call it when you . . . you know—"

"What?"

"When you are at the end? *The glorious finish?*"

"Umm—"

"You don't say 'orgasm' do you?"

"Um . . . 'coming'."

"Yes, well, when you uhh 'come', oooohh, I'm still feeling it, still feeling it so much, do I call it 'coming', too? When a girl, a woman does, gets that, that feeling, orgasm, it's called coming too, right?"

"God, Leyla . . . I never talked like this with anyone."

"Is that bad? Do you think it's wrong?"

"God. Just . . . I just never did. Never dreamed I would with a person I . . ."

"With someone you love?"

"Yes, that's it . . . with a person I love—"

"But that's the person . . . the very person you should, the very person, the person you really should talk it ALL over with, right? Do you think that's wrong?"

"No. Right. I mean, yes, Jesus . . . yes, Leyla. Yes."

"Do you know a really lot about it, Will?"

"No . . . a lot of talk. You're really the first. The first *real* one, the first real times."

"And since I *told* you to go ahead. You *DIDN'T?* During this whole time you were going through you didn't?"

"Leyla . . . okay, it happened a couple of times. I mean a couple of girls. Well, three times, three girls."

"You rascal, I knew it. I sort of well, I can't explain exactly. I wanted you not to feel, *not* to . . . feel tied down, *not* to . . . you know. I explained it on the phone. Well, I really meant it. Oh, Will, there's so much to talk about. If we talked from now for the whole time—"

"Alright, then. You said you'd give me a blow-by-blow description, the guys . . . and what happened . . . that Derek . . . and so?"

The talk might have sounded brave but I started shaking.

Leyla hugged me, hugged me, rocked me, hugged me. "I love you Will. I honest to God love you so much. Love you, Will, all the way."

I was shaking all over. I don't know why. And her beginning made it worse. Like a preamble to what I dreaded. And why? I know it, I knew she loved me.

"Tell me, Will . . . tell me!"

"About those *three?*"

"Noooooo. *Tell* me, Will."

"I love youuuuuu . . . ."

"It sounds more like a growl."

"Go on, tell."

"Hold me."

"This is going to be complicated . . . I can see that."

"There's not much to tell, really."

"Go on."

"Well . . . just . . . "

"Just go on."

"Well, there were lots of parties, especially at the beginning of last year and, alright, don't interrupt me, just hold me . . . like this . . . yeah . . . and all of this getting to know each other, mixers and stuff. Between Harvard and Radcliffe. And, just these parties. Most of us away from home for the first time in our lives. Lil and I got to know each other, a whole bunch of people on my hall, that end of the hall. And, well, after one of them, I had met this boy, a junior, and the four of us, Lil, some boy she had met, and, umm, we went over to their place, drinking something.

"Before I knew it, Lil and this boy were in bed. Real late. And she was going to stay over. The one I was with asked if I'd stay over. Around, I don't know, two or three or so. I didn't want anything to happen and I told him that. He agreed. Just sleep. Okay, he said. We hadn't even kissed or anything. And . . . " Leyla heaved a big sigh.

I was trembling all over, watching her hands clenching together.

"My baby," she said. She held me tight, fiercely. "My baby, I love you, love you."

"Sure, I'm *here*, now." It seemed so weak, so easy, I love you.

"Will. . . . You're asking me. I could lie to you. It would be so much easier ."

Okay, okay."

"You're shaking all over, you're just *shaking*—"

"Just go on. Tell . . . "

Leyla kissed me and, maybe to find our way back again, it turned into drinking-each-other, covers kicked off and I was on top of her again and almost like rape plunged into her, but she was wet and coming back at me, hard and fast, it lasted and lasted a long time before the final seconds of loving-hating, grunting surging plunges into the sweet maw of her, and the whole time holding me tight, to soften the hard back and forth, holding me, almost trying to stop me. I don't know, maybe she was thinking of this guy, maybe *I* was, to plunge him out, wash him away, to ruin the memory before I even knew it. When we finished there was no talk for a long while.

"Did you do that . . . Will? Out of love? Or—?"

"I don't know . . . I don't know . . . so, go on, and . . . I'll know . . . later. I guess."

"Ahhh, Will. We've got to just stop for a while. We just have to talk. All of this 'telling.'

Whatever I tell you, whatever you tell me. What is it for? If not to understand each other better . . . . . . then what's it for? To hurt? "

"No, Leyla, the thing that hurts, I guess, is even in Memphis, when you were being so . . . generous . . . . . . you had already done it. Am I right?"

"Will, I said what I said on the phone for the reasons I gave you. You weren't promised to me. I wasn't promised to you. You're going through training—"

"The god damned war. It's all the *war*. Do whatever . . . and call it '*the war*'."

"That's not what I'm saying—"

"No, I'm saying it."

"But that's not what *I'm* saying. I loved you . . . I've never stopped loving you. I love you now more than I ever thought possible."

"Ohhhh, shit."

"Will . . . maybe it's not exactly like you wanted it. Maybe I'm not exactly like you wanted me to be."

"No, you *are* . . . " I had to admit it and that's what hurt; "More than anyone. But you talk about children and I see the war, flying. And—"

"So? Now, *you're* using the war. You know, in one of my philosophy classes we talked about the philosophy of 'as if.' Vaihinger, I think it was. Sometimes to discover something we have to act 'as if.' And for the war, we have to act 'as if' it will be over one day. Just 'as if.' And we know it will be. One day."

"Very pretty," I wanted to belch but I couldn't work one up. She turned away.

"Alright, Leyla, Alright. I. . . . . Alright. I'm wrong to get mad. I guess . . . I hate the idea. Losing you, even for five minutes. Let's go on. And . . . it's hard to say it right now, but sometime, back then, not this last time, before then, I didn't even want to go back to being two people . . . "

Leyla turned back, her face wet, smiling.

In our silence I noticed that the party was over downstairs, or the noise. Time still changing things. A little after three, her watch said.

"Shall I go on?"

"Yes."

"Hold me."

" . . . So, I stayed over. And, he had his arm around me, then we were hugging, he kissed me, and one thing led to another, and we did it."

"Once?"

"Will? Do you want . . . alright . . . once that night and once early in the morning."

"And did you see him again?"

"No. I didn't really like him. In fact I detested him."

"I don't know which is worse. You do it because you like him or do it even if you don't."

"I'm just telling you, Will," she said, with a kind of warning. "I don't say I understand it . . . "

There was a pause. And I was dreading it, "So, that was in September?"

"So . . . ?"

"So, go on."

"Will, is this any fun? For you or me?"

"I just want to know . . . Jesus, I don't know what I want to know. I feel like my body has been off to Radcliffe. And I don't know what it's been doing."

"Will . . . that's the sweetest thing you ever said. You're breaking my heart." She took my face in her hands, "I want to marry you. Whatever I did, whatever you did. I want to marry you. And have your children. Our children. That's what I want. I've said it over a thousand times."

"Down on your knees . . . "

"No, Will! This is no joke. You can't embarrass me. You can say no, but you can't embarrass me."

I had been looking at her for so long I wasn't seeing her. It was our voice, our body, our red-gold hair, pale skin, with the dark red hair between our legs I still peeped at, no matter how close we had been.

"Leyla . . . you're way ahead of me."

"I know that."

"You . . . *know* it?" I was knocked back, laughing. "Well, not very modest, are you?"

"I knew the first time I saw you." Leyla spoke with angry confidence. "That first time. You came up and started talking to me about New Orleans, and I was thinking, 'I already love him.' But that was only part of it. Everything that happened was like an answer to questions I always had about HIM. THE guy. It took you 20 minutes to ask me out, and it would be safe because we'd double-date with someone I knew. That's so funny. If you had said run away with me, I'd have said, sure, let me get a couple of things. But it took you 20 minutes to ask me for a date—"

"That's— Leyla, I just can't believe . . . "

"Swear to God!"

"The first time I talked to you?"

"Swear, I swear, I'll swear it on my deathbed."

"That's the—"

"Ask Annie. I told her. I called her that night. I wasn't going to say 'no' to you. *Never* to say 'no' to you."

I was exhausted; the trip, that takeoff, talk with Mamoo, anxiety of getting here; I was speaking from an exhausted bewilderment, "So, then. *You've* found the one *you* want. Now what about him? Does he figure? Does he get chance to say 'yes' or 'no'?"

"Yesss,"she said slowly, and thoughtfully.

"Darling. . . ." I felt a strange kind of surrender.

"Do you want to sleep? And Will, just one more thing. What I said to you in Memphis, on the phone. That's no more than I'm saying now. I'm spoken for. And . . . please, please . . . *so damned serious.*" Her face one inch away, it was making me cross-eyed.

"'Serious'? I'm not 'serious' I'm dead . . . one knocked-out lieutenant."

Chapter 8

" . . . the town of Brindisi, at the boot of Italy, fell yesterday to British troops. Sardinia was evacuated by the Germans, and the Italian fleet has escaped to Malta and surrendered to the British . . . "

Through the porthole windows came the first light of day, and the news from a radio that must have been in the window downstairs. As in every city across the country, the news poured out to America on the half hour, with interruptions for an invasion or surrender. Then it was Louis Armstrong growling, "When It's Sleepy Time Down South."

"Some guy . . . alarm clock radio," said Leyla, eyes closed, and opening; "*Will*! Ohhh, my happiness. What time is it? How did we let the night get away?"

"We didn't. Well, a little of it."

"I brought a washrag but no towel. I've got to wash up," Leyla kissed and was off to the other end, holding her skirt around the lower half of her body, still swaying under it—hair more red than gold in the light halfway down her back. God, just look at her. The door closed on her and for the first time since getting here I was alone and thinking.

RM's married! Phewwwwww. And dive-bombers. Maybe I can't get a ride back.

"Here . . . " she was holding out the washrag but we were looking at each other . . . "God! You're *here*!"

It was 9:30 before we were down our ladder, made sure we could get back in, sat down and ordered at a bakery-coffee shop one block away. We got sweet rolls to take back with us, promises in a bag. After the breakfast rush there were only two other tables occupied. The newspapers were full of the Italian surrender. MacArthur had captured some base in New Guinea. And the new navy F6F fighters had done well in their first test against the Japanese. Then we were sitting there.

" . . . so beautiful!"

I thought of the White Corpuscles, if they could hear me now. But there it was: ropes of hair, clear greenish blue eyes, skin so white, straight nose, dazzling mouth and lips. Other people stared. I felt like walking over and agreeing, "Yeahhh, just look at her!"

Leyla's head was down, staring at nothing.

"What's wrong? Is something wrong?"

"Well, yes . . . there *is* something."

"Do you have classes? I mean do we have the whole day?"

"*Will*!! You think I'd go to classes? When *you're* here? When we're *together*?"

"Well, I thought—"

"Will . . . and . . . I want to talk. And this is it. Will, something is not . . . I don't know but something is bothering you. I mean, I was so astound-ed you *got* here . . . I still *am* . . . I didn't even want to leave our little hide-away for breakfast. And I'm dying to get back there, get our clothes off and be together, totally. And I'm worried you don't feel the same—"

"I *do*."

"No, with you it's different!"

"No, it's not."

"Yes, Will, it *is*."

"Well, it's bound to be a *little* different."

"Is it? Why?"

"Well . . . we're different people."

"*Are* we?"

Actually I was feeling a little lost. And challenged, at the core. Up-rooted. Between bases . . . between everything. I wasn't a flyer on the way to the final base before 'the big show,' I felt like I was stopped and now, yes, something was strange, was . . . wrong? She was not only beautiful, amaz-ing, baffling, a mystery ancient but no, not ancient or new, she was . . . out of time, not in time. And, what seemed to me, a whole town full of people ready to worship at her feet.

Yes, and more even than that. I was . . . admit it . . . out of my league.

"Leyla, I tell you there's nothing wrong," even as a little worm worried my brain.

"And I say there is. There is, there is! Now please think about it, please really examine it and tell me. I love you and I want to know."

"I love *you*, Leyla."

"See? There's something there. Some little . . . tit for tat."

We ate in silence. Was there something? This was the longest time we'd been together not speaking, not touching. I thought about hearts breaking. My own heart. And the trouble is there *was* something that was almost drowning me. Could she have seen that? What if that's not what she means?

"Well, maybe . . . a little thing. I don't know. Do you want to talk here or go back?"

"Listen! Here it *is*! We'll go to my dorm. I'll get some stuff and then, THEN, you lucky devil, I'm going to give you an alcohol rub, at *our* place."

Leyla had worked in a hospital one summer as a nurse's aide and she'd show me what she learned. Off we went to old Bertram Hall. She'd get towels, a pan, everything. But it wasn't forgotten, what she was worried about. It hung there. And I was sick with worry about it.

"Alright? Would you like that?"

"Sure."

"Would you *love* it?"

"Of course!"

"Will? We don't have much time . . . and this little something . . . I don't know, but it worries me."

She grabbed my hand, forced my eyes to meet hers. "I said that, Will. Cause I felt, just a little, last night, late, and this morning, that you weren't quite with me for part of the time. Something, something's getting to you."

" . . . . "

From absolute bliss I was plunging.

In 40 minutes we were back in our lair. Leyla had taken a quick shower, gathered her stuff, brought Bess, her roommate down to meet me, and we were off again.

Leyla thought Bess looked like Brucie. She was one of those tiny, perfect-featured dangerous women, a little ball of fire, full of purpose. When I said that to Leyla she was shocked, agreed that Bess was a very determined young woman and had one of the highest grade point averages in the entire school. "Her father is an admiral . . . in the *navy!*"

I was laughing at her, "Leyla, there *are* no admirals in the army!"

"Well, you know what I mean. . . . Alright, Mister, get those clothes off. I'll allow a sheet over certain parts of your body. Till I get to them, that is. Now, start talking."

She put hot, hot water into the pan and soaked the washrag, rinsed it, beginning with my hand, wrist, arm. It was a chance to watch her, do-ing me. "Just lie there . . . and talk," she said, busy with my limbs.

"You make it tough, nurse." But then it wasn't funny because I was going to have to say, to risk all of this. "I don't know how to say it. But I think it's . . . New Orleans." From that point it took me five minutes to get any farther. Doubts, fears, deep deep fears; aunts, uncles, family, and, finally, "The . . . the whole 'nice' girl thing. I guess . . . " I said it, leaning to her, not defending it, simply stating what it might be.

Leyla was working on my left foot. Watching her made me feel guilty. Everything she did was nice, direct, all-the-way, straight ahead.

"I don't understand what the 'nice' has to do with us."

"In a way it doesn't."

"Well? . . . Okay, bend your leg and put it on the towel, lift up."

"I can't tell you. Leyla, I can't say. It's not a problem with you. It's me, and the damned New Orleans thing."

"Well, exactly what is the 'New Orleans' thing?"

"Well, we've moved so fast. Me and you. To my mother a kiss meant engagement . . . the whole 'nice' thing. I can't put it any better than that."

"What!?"

She stopped rubbing my knee, totally stopped.

"Look. Leyla, you're . . . "

She had put down the washrag, looked at me, steadily, waiting. But waiting as if she already knew.

"You're . . . too much, for what I've known."

"What the hell does that mean?"

"I've never met anyone . . . never gone with anyone like you. Never thought about marriage, really . . . but when I *have*—"

"You mean, Will. THIS is not 'nice.' Is that it?" Leyla said it very slowly. Menacingly.

"No . . . that's the problem, Leyla. Not *this*."

"Will, you better explain. I'm getting some strange feelings—"

"It *is* nice—"

"You mean the sex is nice? But it's not 'nice 'to have sex?'"

"Leyla, I'm trying to say what I think might be making you . . . feel something's wrong."

"Do you love me, Will?"

"Don't ask ridiculous . . . I can't even tell you. . . . Of course I love you. Yes, yes . . . yes."

"Don't be 'nice,' Will. I don't think of *us* with rules, but you do. This is important. I want you to tell me if you love me or if you'll fly off and say 'that was nice . . . but not *nice.*'"

"Leyla, oh, we're in it now, and I hate it. At breakfast, at that place, I thought of losing you. I couldn't stand it. And I don't know why . . . why I don't completely 'allow' it. Wait! Just try and listen . . . the three girls, the three I did it with—"

"Not 'nice' . . . definitely not 'nice.'"

"Leyla, you make fun of it. Okay. But that doesn't help. And you're right. But I'm up against something. All of my life it was this way. You've made me see something. But, Jesus, there's a whole life of that. . . . My mother, when I was real young . . . please listen, and don't laugh. Leyla. And don't stop what you were doing. When you stop I begin to feel that *we* are about to . . . stop."

"Go on . . . "

"You love me?"

"Umm," she made a noise in her throat, but began with my right foot.

""No, Leyla . . . no good!"

"Will, of course, of course, of course, of *course* I love you."

"Okay . . . " We kissed, but it was a little chilly.

"Go on."

"My mother, I don't know what got into her, told me that 'No real man does it till he's married.' Now wait. Even at that age, I think I was eleven, I knew it was stupid. See, 'men' she said, the women, well, that was, of *course* the women. I grew up and thought about it. See, I made fun of it. *In my head.* But I was the last of my gang . . . to do it. Now why? There's something . . . something that stuck . . . when she said that. Okay? Okayy? Leyla? Tell me, you know what I'm saying?"

I was miserable and her looks didn't help any. I lay back on the bed wanting to hide from her looks. To hide my miserly, chicken-shit thoughts.

"I'm not nice. Right? I'm definitely not 'nice,' Will. I'm not the girl for you because I'm not 'nice.'"

"Ohhh, Jesus Christ . . . "

Leyla brought her head close to mine. She had on a pale blue cotton dress with nothing on underneath.

"So that's it, Will?"

"I guess so."

"So, this whole thing was a real kick in the teeth . . . to everything you believed in? From the beginning? Even in Texas?"

"Jesus, Jesus, I don't even know. You're the one who said something was wrong. That's all I can think of. That way back there . . . way back there, this is . . . " I couldn't help being ridiculous. "Way back there, this is not allowed."

Yesterday, we'd have been in a total embrace. Now, only her hand on my arm, and a puzzled look.

"Leyla?"

"I feel like a town . . . that's been . . . that Spanish town."

"Don't! Don't! *You're* right!"

"Is seeing the body of the person wrong? Especially the person you love? To love that? To love it, to . . . fuck? See? All of that is *wrong*? That's what you're saying."

"Leyla, God, can't we forget all of this? Let it be? Why did I even try and talk about it?"

"Because, Will, something was happening. We made love last night, I don't know how many times, and this morning. Was it wrong? I say, of course not. But something was happening with you. Then you were so worried about what 'happened' to me while you were going through training. I did it with that guy I told you about. Then Derek. I'll break your heart for you, if you want the truth. Derek and I did it right here, on this same bed. I think Lil knows that. Something perverse about her. But you know what? I don't give a god damn. And I learned something from it. It was no fluke back in Texas. I love you, that's what happened. With Derek it lasted a week, ten days. That was enough. But I love you. I loved you the whole time. Can you take that? Can you understand it? Well, that's my history while you were going through training. And god damn you, Will. Can you take that? That's the truth. I feel like . . . like *smashing* something!"

She was furious, heaving breaths. Crying. "And I'm sorry I did it. Not for any stupid reasons either. And you know something else? I liked it. I loved it. Even with that first guy. Is that a curse or a blessing? That I like sex? No, it ain't 'nice'! No! It's LIFE, Will. And to the Junior League, LIFE is not NICE! Can your New Orleans 'niceness' take that? And can you take it that I love you? Even *though*? Can you take that? And answer that?"

She practically flung herself at me when I opened my arms to her.

"Take your dress off."

"No! I want some answers. Was it wrong? What we did last night? What we did this morning? What I want to do with you all afternoon, and to-night, and all day tomorrow? Can you think of a better way to spend our short little time together than being in bed? Being as close as we can get? Can you? Do you want to go sight-seeing? Be a tourist? See Boston? I want *this*. . . ! And I want it in me. Where it belongs. I want *us*. Together. You hear me? THAT'S *NICE*! *Really* nice! I'm going screaming crazy at the very idea of what's stopping you, what's stopping me. How can you let it? How can *I*? Because of some stupid schmaltzy pretend-aristocracy?"

She went on and on. Slowly, slowly, she cooled down but not before I was roasting. I watched and listened, oh yes, I listened, arms back of my head, and sweated, even though mild outside through one of the open portholes. She sat up, stood up, marched back and forth, hardly watching me, talking to herself more than me, burning. I had never seen her passion in earnest. This quiet, full-of-life Texan, eighteen years old with my life in her hands. Where had it come from? Stevens High School? Her one full year of the big college experience?

She stopped. Deliberately unbuttoned her dress, took it off. I had always thought her breasts how full, how fierce, but suddenly they were proud, unashamed. No one put them down, and no one would. 'Here we are,' those pointers said, 'Ain't we nice? Dainty? Full of questions? Full of life?' Her nipples looked out dumb with life, turned dumbly and still intelligent with life to gaze out on a world they demanded/insisted a taste of.

"Will, I want . . . something special. That's what I want for us. Something not ordinary. And I see it in your eyes. I want you to be a great flyer. That's something. Not the real greatness, maybe, but it's a beginning. I wanted you to fling yourself at it and not worry. Sure, I'll go about my own life, but I'm caring for you. Trying to make it right. I saw something in your eyes. Not ordinary. I saw it at the very beginning. I saw it. I couldn't help it. I want you I wanted you, I want you but I didn't want to stop you. I don't want to ever stop you. I believe *everything* I said. Okay? Now. I want to go over your body. I want you to go over my body. I want us to do it slowly and examine this whole thing of *wrong* and *nice* and *right*. I was doing that while I was bathing you. I could go on, or . . . no, I've started, let me finish. I'll tell you about it. You do me and tell me. How is my body? How is yours? Then they'll say hello to each other. In the real way. In the nicest way possible. And, *by God Will, you've got to understand!*"

I watched and listened. She put her head down next to me. I rolled over close to her not touching. Her face was burrowed into the mattress. I could only see her hair spread out, but even spread and still it lived and breathed.

"I talk too much. Her voice was muffled.

"No . . . no! Ohhh no."

"Alright," she looked up. "I'm continuing with your bath."

More hot water and she was back in a minute.

She had done both feet and up to my knees on both legs. She took the cloth and washed my right leg, knee to thigh.

"Good, strong legs. Tough. Good skin. Is this 'bad'? To touch? For you? For me? Right up to the top of your thigh. And now the other one. Oh, you do have nice swimmers' legs."

After she 'washed' each one she put the washrag away and dried it with her big fluffy towel, leaving the washrag in the pan of hot water. Then she rinsed it out, squeezed it and rubbed each part vigorously.

"This is called a yogi bath," she said. "A little part at a time, wet down and then rubbed."

"My skin feels great where you rubbed it."

"It's great for the skin and circulation."

Then she began on my hands, up to elbows, upper arms, shoulders and back, then down the chest to my stomach. Crooning; " . . . tough arms that I love, good skin, hands and fingers that hold me so delightfully, squeeze me, tickle me . . . nice broad great strong flyer's chest and neck I love and have to kiss at the same time," she did, nuzzled my neck, bit one ear, "— a little extra, the patient will have to pay that back. Oh, but this is a love patient, my love patient in love's hospital and the doctor insisted on special care for this one because he's gonna be a dive-bomber real soon and won't get such special care where he's going so this has to last him for, ohhh, as long as he can stand being away from his nurse, nurse Leyla . . . "

She dropped the cloth again, dried off my neck, chest and ears. "And now for the stomach and those special parts, so important and personal, so NICE—*you hear that?*—well, this stomach, now how good and hard it is, how like a washboard across the middle, those bands of muscle, relax now and let it be loose so I can massage it. Oh and now into the hairs that grow so thick and this young soldier standing up in the forest, so cruel and straight. He needs such tender caring, such sweet and tender care, the little man, warm and wet first, and again, oh yes, and again, and then dried off very gently, ohh, so stiff it is. Ah it needs a little kiss because it stands so straight at attention." And she actually kissed a kiss on the very head of it.

"Umm, Leyla . . . for God's sake . . . "

"What's the matter, aren't I caring for it nicely? Is it crying a little bit? I'll take care of that. The maid to her warrior, that's me to you. I'm not sending you off to battle. I'd keep you here forever. Now, roll over. Your back, your neck, your butt."

And she did them all. I couldn't grasp it. I didn't know, I didn't know what to do with this close, slow attention. Crooning over me, over my body. Moving from one part to another.

"I accept all of this, Will. Just let me."

At some point I felt a great restfulness. My life in her hands. She had felt me, and touched me everywhere.

I fell asleep without even knowing how it happened, and woke up, no idea how much later, face down on the mattress.

"How the hell did that happen?"

"I love you."

"Ohhh, God, God, God, Leyla."

"Alright, are you ready to bathe me?"

We hugged. Hugged. Then I thought of Leyla and Derek on this same mattress. I pushed it out of my mind, but it gave me a sudden sadness. What did *he* think? What did he say? About us up here? 'Now it's *his* turn?'

"You're stiffening up. I can feel your back."

"I was thinking of you and Derek. Why did you tell me that?"

"Damnit, Will! *That's* not it! It's not the PLACE, or *him* that's sacred it's us."

"That doesn't help me."

"Look at me. Do you love me?"

"I never loved *anyone* before. I don't know what to do about it. I could drown looking at you, but I'm afraid if I see old Derek again I'll kill him."

"That's all idiot talk. Come on, give me a bath."

Off I went for hot water. What's dirty? What's clean? Our washrag is clean. Contains *us*. Thoughts were going through me very slowly. Something was actually turning over inside of me.

"I'll do your hands and arms, then your toes and legs."

Her hands and fingers were just parts of her. But I got the feeling suddenly of—

"Talk! Tell me what's happening while you're doing this!"

"— Well . . . your fingers belong to your hands, your hands to your wrists and arms . . . see . . . all of it connected—"

"Yeah, the knee bone's connected to the thigh bone—" she sang it.

"Stop it, Leyla, stop it. Something's happening, just don't say anything . . . quiet. Fingers . . . fingers . . . fingers are part of you, no less than breasts, and everything is *you* as much as everything else. Soooooo, everything is *you*, equally *you*."

"Yesss."

"Delicate fingers, each one to your hand, so fingers and breasts even your, what do you call it? Your puss?"

"What??? I call it my . . . my . . . *What did you say?*"

"Well, let's just say 'puss.' So, if your fingers are nice, so's your puss. And if your puss is nice so are your fingers, and if your fingers and puss then your ass, too, all nice."

She sat up suddenly, almost knocked the pan of water over, "That's *it!* Will—"

"I know it . . . I *know* it!"

"See? Either it's *all* nasty, dirty—"

"Yes . . . *all* bad, or *all* fine."

I was stunned at my own discovery.

She hugged one arm around my neck. One fine arm around my good neck.

"So lie back. Other arm. Yes, so smooth the skin, so firm . . . and all the little freckles—"

"Ugh, I hate 'em."

"Oh ho! You mean freckles aren't nice?"

"Don't pull that jazz on *me*, New Orleeeens."

"No, don't *you*! Freckles are 'bad'?"

"Well, I'll need a couple of days for that one."

"I love 'em."

"Yesss?? Really??" Leyla was genuinely surprised.

I washed under her arm, her shoulders, looking down the nice slope of the breasts, and a little finger walk down to blind nipples whose eyes suddenly poked out again.

To her feet and toes. She was jerking, tickled. I slowed down and held her feet, held them still.

"Nice calves, not too much flesh."

"Not enough."

"Wrong. Nice curve not big. No excess. I love that too."

"Ohhh, Will. I don't accept things about myself very well."

"Tonight's the night. I mean, the day."

"Isn't that a line from a dirty joke?"

"What kind of education have you been getting up here?"

"Well, to tell you the truth—" she giggled.

I did her legs, allowed the sheet to come down just over her little puss. This was the very stuff of some of my wilder dreams when I was young. And here I was acting 'clinical,' the warm washrag in my hand, kneeling between her legs, watching the color mount in her cheeks as she leaned up on her elbows to watch me. I had her left leg bent at the knee, washing the smooth pinky, white, orangey skin, bent further so I could see the left cheek and some red hairs peeping out from under the sheet. Rubbing, sensing, working to keep my mind—

"What are you thinking . . . you've become very quiet; doctor . . . nurse . . . impostor."

"Phewww, lady, I'm just the gardener. They slapped a rag in my hand and said go in there . . . "

Only not so funny. Sure, all parts of the body are . . . parts of the body, but some are so hidden.

Right up to the end of that leg I carefully rubbed.

"I love your long beautiful legs, and I'm nuts to just love your whole body."

"You're doing it."

Yes.

I soaked the washrag, rinsed it carefully. Adjusted the sheet, gave a little pat to the mound, the first time ever in my life I had not tried to get a touch. Then did her right leg. The same pale orangey pinky skin, not splotchy but changing colors, thousands of shades between pink and pale orange and, when I went over it, of spots almost red. Again I came up to the juncture of leg and body. Raised the leg up, saw the cheek, little hairs, the indentation where leg changed to buttocks, wiped so carefully—

"Hey, you're not talking."

"Too much going on. I'm being hit . . . from . . . Dreams I used to have as a little kid . . . these beautiful women, holding me captive. Ohh, God. What did they *want* of me!?!"

"Poor little boy."

"Yeahhh. Once I read a magazine called *Racy Detective* and in *Racy Detective*, Racy Defective, this guy did 'unspeakable things' to this girl. 'Unspeakable things'? The phrase stayed with me for weeks. It became, in my mind, things so wild there were no words for them. I wondered about that. I wanted those dream girls to do 'unspeakable' things to me. I mean, things so outrageous they couldn't be imagined. WILD things. Things that would rip books apart if they tried to put 'em in."

"What a battle inside of you! The WILD and the NICE."

"That's it, and now, I'm calmly, sort of calmly, washing this beautiful leg, with just a peep at the holy forbidden, just the tiniest few hairs before the entrance . . . Leyla, my mind is a junk pile . . . and I don't know if it will ever be fit for use again. I don't think about flying or the war . . . I have this vague worry about getting back. Getting back where? I'm not sure anymore."

"Alright, Will, now my stomach. And the 'holy forbidden.'"

"I don't know if I'm ready for this."

"No? Then back to the garden with you!"

"Wait! I'll try."

I got between her legs, wrung out the washrag and started on her upper stomach, watching the glaze in her cat's eyes. I wiped and massaged just below her ribs. "So delicate, and strong at the same time. Strong and vulnerable."

"*Very* vulnerable."

I washed her belly button. I'd never even seen it closely before. Flat stomach, tiny volcano. She liked me to touch it, wipe it, give it attention. For some reason I bent down and kissed it, and her whole body curled up around me, arms and legs clasping me to her, as if I had put my nose in an open flower and the petals had closed around my head. She let go after gasping and singing for ten wriggling seconds, flopped back, arms outstretched.

"Now, why is that? Why so sensitive?"

"I don't know."

"Okay, Leyla, here goes."

I put the warm cloth on her mound and held it there for a while. She was not so calm about it either. She closed her eyes and kept them closed.

"It's all the same," I couldn't help saying, "All the same but there's a mystery here."

"Center of pleasure."

"Yes."

"Well, physical pleasure anyhow."

I spread her legs wider.

"*Look!* I *want* you to look," said Leyla, in a faraway voice.

I scooted down and looked at the mesh of red hair and shiny little lips. Calmed myself, just look. Just look. How neatly made. God, the hours I'd spent just thinking of this.

Very carefully I put the warm washrag up to it. Leyla moaned, her body was shaking.

"Relax sweet, sweet Leyla."

"That's easy for you to say."

"No, it isn't easy for me to say *or* do, just try."

"I'm trying."

I looked. Pushed her legs wider. Then the whole idea of what we were doing knocked me over. How could I do without this . . . my adventurer?

"Leyla, I love you. I love you, love you. I love your puss, I love your legs, your head, I love every finger, every toe-nail and every hair on you. And—

"Shhhh. . . . You've *got* to! *Will*—"

I had been slowly moving the warm washrag back and forth and she was out of control. Bucking against the little washrag, reaching for me with her hands, scratching my shoulders, arching her back. "But, please, Will. Slowly. Put it in real slowly. And let's do it . . . do it, ohhh yes, so slowly, or I'll explode."

When it was all the way in, I was holding her around the waist, she was holding my face, looking, looking, looking beyond my eyes, "Will . . . I'm *coming* right now . . . I've been coming since you first put . . . the first instant. . . . Uuuhhh, I can't stand it any more, fuck me. Fuck me, Will!"

We were jammed together going at an unbelievable pace. She was driving me back even though she was under me, with a kind of shivering motion. The frenzy had struck us down. Death couldn't have stopped us.

"EXTRA! EXTRA! MUSSOLINI RESCUED
BY NAZI GLIDER TROOPS!"

"Hey, boy! Paper!" an upstairs window opened and a man shouted.

Our eyes were locked, we were lying side by side.

"I've got to call, today. I've got to find out. How many planes go out? Where? Will they tell me over the phone?"

"Just hold me."

Our bower, our fortress against the world and people selling "news" about it and trying to make us join up, and me about to. Mussolini "captured" and "freed" while we bathed, wrestled, hugged, kissed.

"God, I'm starving."

"So am I."

I was laying between her legs, feeling the heat from her sweet puss, the same stirring, the same yawning drive to be filled, to fill, to climb that hill again. Instead we dressed; my gabardines, her blue dress.

"Will you wear your whites? Come on, wear your whites!"

"My bag's still over there, but later, okay?"

We checked with Randy. Yes, he thought he'd be here when we came back. Two hours, we told him. Then, on an impulse, he gave us his key. Told us where to put it on our return if he wasn't there.

Chapter 9

We walked along Massachusetts Avenue, "Mass Av" they called it, and I was saluting back to the ROTC boys, saluting back to navy seamen with ribbons, guys I should have been saluting by all rights. Stealing glances at each other, trying to see, to take pictures, Leyla alternately laughing and blushing as I let go of her hand to salute.

In the Greek restaurant the swarthy, black-haired waiters were very busy, and between the kitchen and dining room a seaman—brother, cousin, with new battle ribbons on—talked to the hustling waiters and cooks as if he had all the time in the world. Maybe he did. A ship shot out from under him, days in oily cold water? I felt the newness of my wings, my bars. Well, my time was coming.

Leyla felt none of that. I was a hero already.

I used their pay phone and called Base Operations at Hartford Air Force base. Two calls and I got through. Dan's name meant nothing to them. They could not give out information over the phone. Get there in the morning, wait in line. Yes, they had flights going all over. How often? Exactly where? "I told you, lieutenant, we don't give out that information over the phone. 'Z'a war on, you know."

"Can you take my name down? For a flight south?"

"South?"

"Yes."

"Can you be a little more specific?"

"East coast. Florida."

"I'll put it down, I'll post it but. . . . If you're here and there's *room!* Okay? That's how it works."

We were clicked off. I fed quarters into the machine and walked back to our table. I was leaving Leyla and could no longer help it.

Walking back from Hartford to Leyla. Oh, how she sat.

I explained about the base and getting a ride and I could tell she was feeling it. I was withdrawing. No, worse, I was being withdrawn.

I knew it was hopeless when I watched her eat and envied her food, watched the fork enter her mouth, saw the lips, the teeth, her hair down on one side, so rich, so full of glints.

"God, let's go . . . back."

"I know, Will. Only we're supposed to meet my two other roommates at the Algiers, the coffee place at three. Remember?" Her right hand came across the table and joined mine. Even the squeeze of her hand, so healthy, direct.

"Look, Leyla. I feel like . . . I never thought I'd be saying this. . . ."

I don't know if I got the words out. But her face told me. Flushed, full. Her hands went to her face.

"I don't think I can stand being without you," I explained.

"Will. Will. Will. I know I can't stand it. Not after this time."

"I said it, right? Did you understand me?"

"Yes. That's what you said. Are you backing out?"

"Hell no. But you're not answering."

She got up, came around to my side of the booth, pushed in and kissed a kiss so frank and full that it went into my mind and smoked my brains out of my ears, until there was nothing but the two of us, then only kissing.

When we came back the waiter was standing off a few paces.

"*We're getting married!*" Leyla announced to him.

In an instant there was the old Greek father and the seaman who had been standing around, waiters, diners were coming over. It was the war, yes. The crazy bastards opened up wine, everyone toasted and cheered. It's the warrrr!! Long live warrrr!!!

The old father was telling us about Greece, how something is done in Greece but his accent was so thick I couldn't get it. No matter, he put a big hand on my shoulder and wished us well. And when I went to pay the check. "No!! No pay!!! Tomorrow yes! Today? No! Todayyy, free ride!! Ha haaaaaa! *Yes, no payyy!*"

He got so much pleasure out of it that his son started laughing at him. He shook his head, fiercely. No matter his son. What's right . . . in the world? What's wrong? No matter. We live, we die, pay, pay, pay, tax', the war, ev'ryt'ing. Well, here was one thing he could control.

"Remember!!! You remember!!! Hokayyy?"

We rode out of there on a wave and down the street toward the Algiers just a little after three o'clock. "Ohh, I can't stand it, Will. The whole street is dancing in front of me."

Another block and she asked, "What happened? What prompted you, just then?"

"It came over me. Calling the base, talking about flying back, time, watching you eat. It breaks my heart, I know I've said that about you. You break my heart. To watch you do things breaks my heart. I can't stand it to think . . . and no plans? Like a prison sentence—"

"You *are* funny. Am I going to hogtie you? Pin you down?"

"I never thought I might . . . want you to try."

"I WILL. Then I'll do '*unspeakable*' things to you."

"—done for." Only I couldn't stop smiling.

"Did you actually ask me to marry you? Without choking on the words?"

"I think so."

"Would you say it again, please?"

"Sure. Marry me. Will you? *Will you marry me?*"

"Sure, lieutenant." We stopped again, her body against mine, body I'd bathed and studied.

"Will you?"

"Yes."

"Marry me?"

"Yes."

"Will you marry me? I'll marry you if you will."

"Yes, yes, yes, yes, yes, yes, yes."

Chapter 10

We were headed out of Boston in Allie's car. My bag was in the back seat along with Leyla's overnight bag. The perfect-featured little Bess had come up with a bunch of 'A' stamps and we had three-quarters of a tank of gas.

I had to smile at Leyla, the way she managed things; now she was poring over a map and navigating for us.

"What did you ever do for Allie to deserve this?"

"Don't worry, I did lots for Allie, and she knows it.

"Such as?"

"To begin with I lend her clothes, then there's Danny, sooo, this Danny had a crush on me and I turned him on to a date with Allie and they're going together now, then there's Chemistry. Allie couldn't understand the equations and I helped her. *She* claims she passed Chemistry because of me. Then—"

"Okay, okay—"

"No, Will, you act like I don't do things for people."

"I was just laughing at your—"

"Will! Don't you think—" She interrupted herself to screech about us. I pulled over to the side, cursed out by the truck driver behind us, hugged and kissed. Happiness had nothing to do with it. It was pure madness. Happiness, mappiness.

The trip to Hartford was full of stops like that all the way to the big base where the medium bombers plowed their way through the skies; B-25's and B-26's on the base, along with the whole Military Air Transport System:

C-46's, C-47's, C-54's, twin-engine Beechcraft, converted Flying Fortresses and Liberators. We were given visitors' passes and drove on out to the flight line.

I left her in the car, studying Art History, looked back once and saw only her head of hair. I was truly walking the fence between here and there, between Leyla and the next step. Leyla had to get the car back tomorrow afternoon at the latest and I had to: " . . . report Naval Air Station, Deland, Florida, fifteen September, 0900 hours."

Pilots and crewmen slogged back and forth in loose-fitting flight suits, mechanics worked over the big medium bombers and transports. There was so much going on that a Nazi general in full uniform would not have been noticed. I found the flight office and ran into even more of a rat-race. Just outside of the large ready-room adjoining the flight office, service-men from navy and coast guard to paratroopers to Marine and army enlisted men ("doggies") all waited for rides "out." Some were home on leave from England others just in from the Pacific, or fresh out of boot camp, or on leave before going overseas.

I grabbed a short wiry looking pilot, and asked about a ride: "We're goin' to Kansas City . . . " a glance at his watch, "in fifteen minutes—"

"Ohh, I'm headed south."

"See that red-headed pilot over there? No, there! Check with him. I think they're goin' to Dallas, from 'Big D' you can get a ride all over the south."

I did, but Leyla and I were counting on tonight.

"What? Yeahhh. The marines!? Headed south? Are you on orders or just on leave?"

"I have to be in Florida, the east coast of Florida, the morning of the fifteenth."

"Heyy, Josh," he yelled, then whistled, pursing his lips and, to me, "I think I have just the guy for you."

He ran out, was back in a minute. "Hell, he's going down to D.C. lotsa rides out of D.C. He leaves in an hour."

"One hour?"

"Yeahh, check the flight board. Josh Pittsfield, if you want on."

Pittsfield was not only from Texas but had gone to A & M at the same time as me. A jock-swabber (cavalry). Did he know Dan Campbell? Nope, never heard of him. But they's a shit-pot fulla pilots on this base.

I was frantic to get out, but more frantic for one more night.

I asked at the desk if there were any flights for the south in the morning.

"I b'leeeve we have a Biloxi flight, leaving . . . scheduled to leave . . . around zero nine-fifty."

"How about Jacksonville, or thereabouts?"

"Don't know, don't know, dooon't . . . well, maybe Miami. Maybe. Leaving at eighteen thirty this evening."

"ANYBODY FOR L.A.? ROOM FOR ONE," a big goony looking tackle of a pilot bellowed out above everything else.

There was a pause of a full second before a young army private who had probably choked on his bubble gum jumped up screaming, "West Coast? That's me!"

The sergeant continued to me, "Be here half an hour before flight-time, with your orders, sir."

"Thank you, sergeant."

"Yes sir."

"Did he say L.A.?" Someone else, asleep at the wheel.

Planes were carrying orders and men to all parts of the country, dispatches, materiel, planes being ferried everywhere. Stuff coming out of Washington, Boston, New York, California, Chicago. The whole country in motion.

There was a lot to do. Get hold of Dan, call Mamoo, tell her the big news. Leyla's friend Lil had been the first one to know, practical Lil. 'You're getting married? When? What about school? Isn't Will going overseas? Do you have time?'

Suddenly I was running to Leyla as if my next breath was inside of the car, the black '42 Ford. She was in back lying down reading her Art History.

"God, Will! What happened?"

I explained it all to her. The madness.

"I know so little about what's going on, the war and all," Leyla said. "I feel stuck away."

"Leyla . . . I've been stuck in Arkansas, Memphis, Georgia, and Pensacola. Outside of Pensacola this is the first big base I've been to. And I didn't even see it when we got here. I ran off to find you."

I called Dan's BOQ (Bachelor Officers' Quarters) to see if he might know of a place, although he might object to the idea of us staying together.

They told me I might catch him at the Officers' club. I called there, he was paged and, suddenly, was on the phone.

He was amazed. And that I had Leyla with me. He directed us to the officers' club. In no time we were there.

Dan sort of rolled over to us, shook my hand hard and looked at Leyla as if she had appeared out of the ground, "Damn! Lieutenant! You don't waste time. I bring you up to see this girl and suddenly you're getting married."

"I don't waste time," Leyla told him.

We laughed and hugged for him.

"Does the family know about this?"

"Nope, you're the first."

"This certainly calls for a drink."

So we did. And did it again. Leyla and I had not had a drink together since, well, since the tequila in Texas.

"So, what now? Where are you . . . Leyla, do you, I mean, are you going back tonight?"

"No, we, uh, want to stay together tonight. Would you know of a place?"

"Oooohhh . . . ho—" He caught himself in the middle of some pronouncement and straightened up. "Let me think about that."

Off he went to check. We giggled and felt lucky, lucky, lucky. The place was crammed with people. Most of them were pilots and wore their silver wings, and their famous squashed caps, mark of the air force pilot.

In five minutes Dan was back, shrugging his shoulders, "No dice," he said. "I know the guy in charge of the Married Officers' Quarters but they're jammed. I told him you're newlyweds and just need a place for one night, but—"

The world was turning dark. Even now RM, Hebert, Dubya D. and the others were driving, flying, to our new base in Florida.

Dan had gone for another round when we heard his name over the loudspeaker.

Leyla was drinking scotch and water.

"Ohh, you little . . . you little yankee!"

"What's wrong with you? I drank scotch at home."

"Your father allowed that?"

"On special occasions," she told me. "Actually I don't like it. It tastes like smoke."

"Never tried any."

"You know, I'm going to be . . . "

"Um hummm . . . "

"Your wife . . . will that take all the fun out of it?"

"RM, I told you about him. He's now married."

"He didn't waste much time, did he? I thought you couldn't marry until after—"

"Till after we graduated. You can get married but you can't have your wife with you till after we finish dive-bombers, so—"

Dan came up, all smiles. "A couple just vacated a room, but you'll have to be out of there by ten tomorrow morning."

I jumped up, "Ga-reat! Dan! You're . . . you know, you're responsible for this whole mess-"

"What? What did you say, Lieutenant? Take that back!"

But it was a happy scene. And Dan *was* the cause of most of it; from my ride up, to getting us a room.

"That's really sweet of you," Leyla said.

There, her openness. Open, straight. Beautiful, straight, and dangerous.

"Thanks, Dan, for bringing this big lug up here."

"Hey, we're family now!"

Long-jawed Dan smiled, a tough and great woolly-bear friendliness.

"Maybe we can have breakfast together," he said. "Anyhow, I've got to meet some of the guys, we play pool Wednesday nights. Big stakes. And I'm sure you two don't need me along. But call my number early in the morning, okay? I'm not flying till eleven. And Will, you better call home and tell 'em because when Aphra calls I'm liable to spill the whole thing. You know, of course, I...*we* are getting married on the twenty-fifth of September. You're both invited."

Leyla gave him a hug and he was off.

"Oh, Will, what a great family! Brucie, your mother, they're great. And your step-father, what's his name?" She made a stab at it. "And Dan's marrying your—"

"My cousin. See, there were these four sisters—"

Dan came rushing back. "How the hell could I forget? Now, look. Married Officers' Quarters are right next to this building," he showed us how to get out to it, "See Captain Magruder, he'll show you the room." More shouted directions and he was gone.

We walked over and I think Magruder, a huge, and fat but affable captain, distrusted us, maybe too young, "Dan tells me you two are just married."

Leyla blushed, "Well, yesss," flashed him her ring finger."

I had no idea what she showed.

"Well, congratulations. Dan's a good friend. And, actually this is a little unusual . . . the couple staying here; *he's* going overseas in a week. Their stuff is locked away and . . . you'll only need it for the night, am I correct?"

"Yes, my flight leaves in the morning."

"Okay, this way," he stepped from behind the counter, waddled down the hall, up one flight of stairs, two doors in and unlocked it. "Can't give you a key, but."

"That's alright. Leyla, I'll get the stuff from the car. And, thanks a lot, Captain. This is really a great favor."

"Just a sec—" Leyla grabbed my arm.

"The charge is $3.50, towel and linen fee—"

Magruder waddled off down the steps.

"Ohh, my darling, we *are* lucky."

"What did you show him?"

She had a little green stone on a gold band, the stone she had turned to the inside.

I went to get the stuff from the car and she, she would be all freshened up and in bed.

I was in a state of wonder the whole time walking back to the car, driving it around closer to where we were staying, grabbing our bags and up the stairs. What were we doing? What had we done? In some part of my mind I heard 'the war . . . the war' then dismissed it with a shrug. We were being rewarded, this luck, for something we hadn't done. And now? Call home? This is the longest we've been separated for three days.

Leyla was still fully dressed, and worried; "Will, now just stop. Just stop and look at me."

I didn't often see her like this. And we did talk. I studied the planes of her face. I've chosen her, I kept thinking. But I was having these giddy notions. Playing house tonight. And there was something about her that was like Arthe. Not like her, exactly, but the LIFE of her. Something alike. They said "GOD" all the time. "God, Will!" It sent a pang through me whenever I heard it. But Leyla said it with an explosion of breath. A kind of pure energy, and it came from an inexhaustible supply.

She had grabbed me at the door of the squarish, brightly lit room, and made us both stop.

"Will, there's so much to do and say and we have about twelve hours. I don't think we should go to sleep. And we should really try and talk. Her eyes were blue and green. The blue of skies, blue brought to earth. The green was talking.

"Do you worry about what we've gotten ourselves into?"

Was it a plea or a real question?

Sure, we were over our heads. I also felt I couldn't tell her that.

"I feel like it just happened."

"Happened?"

"Yes. I didn't think I would say anything like that, and I did—"

"Will . . ."

"I mean—"

"I'm not going to hold you to this . . ."

Maybe it was the room; a MARRIED officer's room. We were 'married' according to that captain downstairs, and were taking a married couple's place.

"Tell me, Will."

She was agonized, and I had not often seen that. I had convinced myself that Leyla could not feel agony. She was gazing right at me with that direct stare, the green stare. And I didn't want to just hold her, hug her, in answer to this. I couldn't comfort her. I was in doubt as well.

And it was, suddenly, all in doubt. I was on the very edge of the next phase of training. I would become a dive-bomber and go out to the Pacific in answer to some yearning that had gripped me the first time I looked at those magazines. And seen that Corsair.

Suddenly we were stuck. We stood there, lightly holding each other, wondering whether to let go or tighten our hold.

"Well, I want to call home . . . and tell her . . . my mother."

"You're jumping ahead, Will. Let's talk first."

Only whenever she doubted, even the first sign of a doubt, my heart froze. I wanted not to move so fast. But something had happened to 'waiting.' I wanted her to wait but that meant I'd probably have to wait as well.

"Will? You're not answering."

"Leyla . . . I don't know what the question is. Let's drop it for the time being, okay? Let's drop it. I mean let's go back to easier questions . . ."

"Like . . ?"

"Like, give me a kiss."

Leyla didn't balk, or get stiff and unyielding. But she came to me with a preoccupied air.

We kissed, maybe the first kiss that was only a kiss. So unlike the kiss when we decided to be together, forever maybe. Her lips, ready to change, ready to be so much more. Magic lips, and now just a kiss.

She turned away and sat on the bed. Her shoulders drooped. I didn't know what she was thinking but I was afraid of her thoughts. I thought of Derek . . . and the other guy. Then others she hadn't talked about. Hadn't done it with but that she had looked at, watched, wondered about. I felt a little sick.

Leyla rolled onto her side on the bed, elbow at her chin. She looked like a child of seven.

I felt that same tug at my heart when I watched her reacting to something by herself, that tug at my heart only I didn't know if it was an ache for her or myself.

"Alright, what were you going to tell me?"

Watching her and thinking she's MINE! Then, in the next instant wondering if she was.

"Will, come here."

I lay down in bed beside her. She arranged herself so I was holding her, curved, pulling my arms around her. Then, in a tiny voice, "I think I'm ovulating, right now. I can feel it."

"What do you mean?"

"This is the time when I could get pregnant . . . so—"

"So . . . I'll do what we used to do in Marshall."

Her body seemed satisfied.

"Will, I just need you to say . . . "

"What?"

"Just no doubts, that's all! If you have no doubts I *want* to talk to your mother!"

"What about your father?"

"I'm going to have to do that—"

"I know—"

"I mean, I'm going to have to wait—"

"See, that sounds like a doubt to me."

"Will, that's different. I've got to have a little more time for that—"

"I call my mother, but you—"

"Will, it's not the same. Dad really objects to you. You know that. And my father thinks we've stopped seeing each other . . . "

"Leyla are we gonna do this or not?"

"Will, of course we are. Just try and understand. I can call him tonight, if you want. I just don't want to drop a bombshell and have you there for it."

"I give up. Let's go, I'm gonna call."

"And tell them?" .

"Sure, and you can talk, in fact, you'll have to talk with her."

"What do you call her? 'Mammou'?"

"Mamoo."

"Ma-moo. I like that."

"She'll love you."

"Well, Will, my folks will love *you*. As soon as. . . . Look, don't be mad about this. I'll do it as soon as I get back to school."

We walked down to the lobby and I knew; whatever I decided, whatever I wanted, all of my life it was go do it. We're going to Africa! Wonderful, my darling! China! Oh, won't that be exciting! I'm going to fly! Marvelous!

There was a group of three telephone booths just outside of the big lobby. The Married Officers' Quarters had the same buzz that permeated the whole base, only here in the lobby it was quieter. People were leaving, arriving, bags were piled everywhere, last minute instructions over the phone, hurried confabs, meetings at the field. Nothing stopped, day or night. Officers lined up before the booths to wait their turn. We were behind one nervous skinny officer in line for a booth. I glanced at him, wondering what he had done as a civilian and what had pushed him into the air force. He seemed a little older than most of the pilots around us.

The booth door opened, a burly guy left and *he* went in.

In another minute he was talking to his wife. His group was going overseas in 48 hours, he was on "forty-eight hour alert" and he didn't quite know what it meant either, but he wanted to know how to word the insurance. They talked about insurance as if insurance was a child they had sired.

I listened and watched Leyla. Her hair sprang out of her head. That alone told me so much about her. Would she take a dare? Only turn her in that direction. I was proud and, at the same time, a little, a tiny bit, afraid of her. Suddenly, she came over, slipped her arm around my waist. "Lieutenant-I-love-you, that's your *name*." She squeezed me. "Alright, then," the guy in the booth was saying, with no idea we could hear every word, "you first and then my mother, okay, yeahh, I miss you too, alright dear . . . say hello to everybody . . . " "I'll miss you too, dear," Leyla whispered loudly into my ear, "just make sure the insurance is in my name." She looked straight into my eyes with a laugh ready, a laugh waiting.

I rolled my eyes at her. The guy was halfway out of the booth.

We crammed ourselves into the booth and right in the middle of giving the operator the number Leyla grabbed me and we kissed a kiss as nice as any. I guess we were trying to say the same things. Her tongue reaching into my mind—so quick to dart in and come back, her mouth so wet.

"Yes, operator, New Orle . . . for Christ's sake, Leyla, New Orleans, yes." Pearse answered the phone. Husky voiced . . . drinking?

"Hey, Pearse! Will! Yeah, calling from Hartford, the air force base . . . "

Almost his first words were that he'd get Mamoo. The booth was so tiny and there were still the smells of someone who had been smoking a cigar, but Leyla . . . I could taste the smell of her. Then Mamoo's voice; "Heyyyyyyyy, my darling, you're in Connecticut? Did you get to see Leyla?"

"Guess what, maw?—"

"I couldn't guess in a million years!" She yelled cheerily.

"Leyla's right here with me . . . in this booth!"

"I don't believe it LEYLA'S RIGHT THERE???"

"Here she is!"

Our heads were so close together I could still hear Mamoo.

"Hello, Mamoo!" Leyla said, in a voice that was at once in awe, flip and happy. "Guess what???"

Leyla stuck the mouthpiece up to both of us, "We're getting married!" We both told her, practically shouting the words.

Then there was no doubt of the reception. Mamoo was shouting, "OHH-HHHHHBOOOYYYYOHHHHBOOYYYY"

Leyla's face was flushed red as a beet, and I could feel it. Being shouted over.

When she had calmed down she began asking us questions, not knowing at any one time which one of us she was talking to.

"OHHHMYDARLING BOY, WHAT A DAYYY AND WHAT NEW-WWSSS!!! I JUST WISH YOUR SISTERS WERE HERE FOR THIS, I JUST CAN'T WAIT TO TELL THE FAMILY. BUT NOW WHEN, WHEN, WHEN, ARE YOU THINKING OF THIS GREAT GRAND EVENT???? AND WHERE???? IN NEW ORLEANS??? PERHAPS??? OR LEYLA'S PARENTS' HOME IN MARSHALL???"

I took the phone, still with Leyla right there, breathing each others' breaths, breathing each others' thoughts. I told her we had just decided today, at about three o'clock.

Leyla looked at me and shouted, "No, Mamoo, *I decided a year ago, but it took Will a little longer!"*

She paused, about to break into a laugh and answered, "We don't have a time yet, but we will. We called you *first!"*

"Well, you get right on the phone and call them, call your family and do so right this instant. Both of you! And Will, please, please call me as soon as you arrive in Florida!"

I agreed, wondering if I'd ever get there.

She asked to speak to Leyla and I moved away and just watched Leyla's face. She looked like a child, listening and blushing. Her face actually speaking in its changes. Blushing, registering well, well, "Well, Mamoo, yes, I understand. And I love you too." Then she thrust the phone at me.

"Yeahh, Maw!"

And her final words about love and the family, accepting her and treating her so well, about love and responsibility that she had talked to me about before I left. "REAL responsibility," she told me. I was a little exasperated with her but it was okay, and I realized I might even have missed it if she hadn't said all of that. Leyla sat next to me/on me but was quiet.

"She *couldn't* have been nicer," Leyla was saying on the way back to our room. "She actually *welcomed* me into the family."

She sat on the bed, worry lines across her forehead.

"Will, I feel bad, now. About my family. Not calling them, but I just know they're not going to react like that."

We looked at each other.

"Will you trust me to tell them? I'm going to *tell* them we're getting married."

"Were you in doubt until you talked to my mother?"

"*Will!* Not for a second. I ought to hit you for saying that. Come here."

She held my hands and lay back on the bed pulling me on top of her. When my body touched her mound through her dress and her slip, I almost lost consciousness. I started undressing her but that wasn't fast enough. She was whipping her dress off over her head, her slip followed it, bra flew, panties slipped off, leaped on the bed, "Come here! Come here Lieutenant-I-love-you!"

The slip of arms around nakedness, texture of skin and hands, "God I love your skin."

"Will, I feel like your mother married us. Do you know?"

"Yes, now leave my mother out of this."

"Will, just stop a second."

She held my arms above the elbows, "Just remember *this* is a dangerous time, right now. I told you—"

"Yes, I know."

"Well?"

"Would it kill you if you were pregnant?"

"No, but it would kill you."

"You don't know me."

I eased into her and her eyes glazed over her hands squeezed my arms, her eyes closed. She raised her legs up higher, then put her feet on the bed and was pushing against me.

"I'd *love* it," she said. "And I don't *care*," she was acting the part, emphasizing the words against me.

"Yes, I'd *love* it," she said, "in fact I can hardly ever even *stand* it" pushing up against me, easing us in and out, and started a motion, twisting slowly around me, driving herself crazy as I went in and out of her, knowing it wouldn't be long, getting on track the train coming into the station.

"Ohh, Leyla, oh God; so great I want to go on . . . go onnnnn—"

"Will, *remember*—"

"Yessss . . . I want to, Leyla—"

"Will! You want to . . . ?"

"Yes . . . yesss, I love you, I want youuu."

"Then do it. *Do* you?"

"Yes!! Yes!! Do *you*?"

"Want to have a child?"

"Yes . . . do you?"

"Yes, Will, yes, yessss—"

"I do, I do! I want to . . . *whatever* happens."

"Will, oh do it! Do it. I'm coming, I'm COMING, COMMING, WILL, OHH, DO IT, don't stop!"

The tremendous spasm, the clutch of holding holding squeeze-holding, biting throats, cheeks, mouths seeking, finding, breaking apart to laugh, cry, gasp, looks and eyes changing places, eyes actually changing mine hers, hers ours ours mine.

Leyla's mouth curling around the words, "Ohhhh yesss, Will!" In a permanent yesss, "That was the greatest, greatest. . . ." Then burst into tears that tore her heart out and mine with it, great wracking sobs such as I'd never heard before, squeezing me so I could feel the very fountain of tears coming from her.

I was still inside her, realizing we had torn the book in half and then torn all the pieces. We had done it before without worrying, without counting the cost but this time we knew be*fore*.

"Crying because . . . " she said, wiping her nose on her arm, and laughing, "that poor man, going overseas, talking to his wife about insurance and *we'd* never, Will, do . . . that! And *my* mother . . . *my* father . . . and their little girl, maybe about to have a baby and they don't even know about us . . . and that fat man who brought us here, maybe's missing someone. And . . . *you're leaving!* And I hate myself for cry-cry-crying . . . because . . . I'm *crying*—" She started laughing about it and not wanting to.

Within an hour she *knew* she was pregnant. She knew it; "I feel it Will. Something's actually happening in me!"

Chapter 11

Dubya D was engaged to RM's sister! Mulligan was pounding me on the back. Evan (Coon-ass) was there, Scott Lee, all of us in the same boat. Wings! Lieutenants! Officers! Imposters! Madness!

"And you're *married!*"

"Yeah, Yeah," RM admitted, again, "I told you to get your ass down there. Now look what's happened!"

Dubya D's tongue came out and wrapped around his chin, "I'm not marrying you, it's your sister— "

"Hey! Hey! Bruh-in-law, I'm joking . . . Hey . . . Dubya D!?"

Happiness had sneaked up behind me. The whole gang together again, minus Tony, that bastard.

First meal at the Officers' Mess. Table cloths and napkins, heavy navy shipboard silver, mess boys waiting on us, serving us individually, marine guards saluting us at the gate-island entrance to the base, and overhead the very blood of us, formations of SBD's sang their ongoing reminder—we were closer by a huge step to the big show.

"Why didn't you tell me you were goin' up there to get married! I was calling your house in New Orleans!" Evan yelled across our table, and four other heads turned to me.

"Listen, Coon-ass, I'm not married!"

Hoots and screams and I know my face turned red.

For the first time since leaving Leyla I was feeling marked, and regretted it, not shame, exactly, it was a mix of something that wasn't going down well. Dive-bombers and marriage. War and marriage. I wasn't regretting

Leyla but, maybe, a kind of weakness about her. I couldn't explain it. It was like a wound with no location. There was the war and then Leyla . . . Leyla and pregnant. But is she?

Hebert was the only other one who felt we should be in fighters. Not much difference to the others. Well, here we were, hauled along into dive-bombers where I didn't belong, so, to say I didn't expect much was an understatement.

After lunch I went to RM's room. I had to talk to him. Our program would begin tomorrow; movies and talks on the SBD, checkouts tomorrow afternoon or next day.

Duke Ellington's "I Got it Bad and That Ain't Good" was playing on RM's little record player, and he was bent over, nodding to the music.

I needed RM. Hebert would just look at me with a blank stare. Dubya D, who was rooming with RM, walked out to the head and we were alone.

"Okay, Willy, I hope your problem's about Leyla and not dive-bombers. Cause we' done that one, awreddy, at Pensacola. Tony's in fighters. Big deal. We got our wings. Our bars. Here we are—"

"No . . . it's not fighters or dive-bombers." I could hear Sally, in the kitchen, singing the words to the song. "Is that the Duke? The Duke of Ellington_e_, Sally, my cook calls him . . . .well, RM, it makes me feel . . . shit, I'm in it up to my ears."

"Tell _me_, I'm an old married man. I been married eight days."

"RM . . . man, I think she's pregnant!"

"Leyla?? Jesus, Willy . . . you work fast. Did she just find out?"

Dubya D walked back in and I signaled RM to shut up.

Hebert walked in; he was going in to town. He was the only one of us with a car, so the four of us, along with Scott Lee Hunter, Texas's gift to Dive-Bombing Squadron 12-C, our new designation, piled into Hebert's speedy Ford for the trip.

Deland was a town happily forgotten by time, not unlike other central Florida towns of 5 to 10 thousand. It had a bank building, a neat little college, a town hall, market, movie, a cozy little bar, dry cleaners and a stoplight where two wide avenues came together, the stoplight hanging from some wires swung in the light breezes. Even here in the middle of "downtown" were large moss-covered oak trees.

We were on our way back to the base after cruising a few streets, buying toothpaste and such. No one suggested a drink at the one little bar in town to celebrate our first day, our reunion, partly because, well, we were a little in awe of the new base and the program, but just out of sight was a powerful guts-urge to stamp our "coin" on the world's surface. Dangerous, vulgar, wise, snap-cracking dance to some whip in the clouds.

Scott Lee, with a crafty smile on his rugged pan told Hebert, "Hey, stop and ask those girls the way to the base—"

They had to be from Stetson, the small college set way back from the road, surrounded by the graceful oaks and pine trees.

Hebert was outraged. "*I know how to get there!*"

"Well, ask 'em . . . *ask* 'em . . . ask 'em what time it is!"

"Down, boy! You're engaged to my sister!"

"Stop the car!!"

Hebert pulled over and Scott Lee asked—we were in our gabardines, shiny wings prominent. "Excuse me," not an often used expression with him, "Um, excuse me, but do you ladies (!) know where the Naval Air Station is?" Scott Lee was a serious, earnest and dedicated officer, I mean, where the big FLYING base is? You know, there's a war on and we're here to protect you ladies and, umm, we're looking for that base, you know, where those glamorous dive-bombers practice? That's our plane, incidentally, and we have to get out there so's we can better protect you? *And* the country, of course. Hmmm? Do you know where it is? Ohh, these? These, here? These are my wings. Yes, fliers, yes, very dangerous stuff.

She seemed to have missed the overtones but, when Scott Lee finished asking, the cute blond nearest the car opened her mouth and out came sugar and caramel, cake and honey.

Hebert was terribly embarrassed, embarrassed for us all.

The instant she finished talking Hebert thanked her and tore off, disgusted, "Why didn't you ask her when she got off from class? Fer gosh sakes."

"Wallll, you took off too quick!" Scott Lee answered with a sleazy grin.

"Man we got to get out there! There's a war on, remember?"

"Yeah, loose lips sink ships."

"Buy Bonds," said Dubya D.

We shook our heads over Evan Hebert; he was a wild man in a different dimension.

Deland, Florida, deep in the Florida orange-belt, home of one of the beehives along the east coast; fighters in Daytona, Jacksonville and Sanford, dive-bombers at Deland, torpedo-bombers at Fort Lauderdale. Further south was a P-base, 'P' for patrol bombers, at Miami and another at Key West for submarine patrol. The east coast was navy and marines, the west coast and the middle of the state was "Army," air force fighter and bomber bases. The state was cordoned off in this loose manner to keep the two services apart.

The bases were, truly, like bee-hives; and like bees the planes were constantly coming and going, and no matter how far they roamed they always returned to the same hive.

Groups arrived every two weeks and every two weeks another squadron finished up and off to the west coast and the Pacific. There were faces familiar from as far back as pre-flight school and 'E' base. But we were still not sure whether the six of us who had gone through at Pensacola would be together; most were navy pilots but at least eight of us were marines.

In the afternoon we watched formations of four and eight come in to the field and then one formation of twelve in their elaborate carrier break-up; the first four down to the five hundred foot circle and into echelon, the other eight around for another circle, the first four breaking off, each one of the four coming in singly to land. Then the next four and the next. They were slow but there was something majestic about them, the famous Douglas Dauntless—the SBD.

Hebert had signed the two of us to a two-man room, and it was by far the best quarters we had since the beginning. The uniform of the day was khaki or gabardine shirts and pants with the little piss-cutter caps tucked into our belts when under a roof. No hats inside.

At evening meal one of the instructors, a lieutenant junior-grade (j.g.), told us about the program. It was much like what the fighters were going through, he said, only *they* got more gunnery and dog-fighting.

"What about wives?" RM asked him.

"No wives allowed when you're going through dive-bombers . . . "

"I know that, but what about visiting?"

"You're on your own," said the 'veteran', and everyone laughed except for RM. "You're paid every two weeks," he told us. "And, Daytona's only twenty-one miles away. There's a fighter base there," he said. "F4F's and F6's." Then he looked at RM, "Lots of women in Daytona!"

"Shiiit . . . " RM said under his breath, spitting it out, staring him down.

"Just joking," the guy said. Half a foot taller than RM.

"Well, that's a rather dumb god damn *joke*, for my money."

There'd have been a fight just abeam of the table if we hadn't stopped it.

RM had told the navy bastard off and we were ready to back him to the hilt. Only problem was the 'bastard' turned out to be an assistant instructor. After supper I cornered RM again.

"RM, I really need to talk with you tonight."

"Awreet, my man, we'll do it."

When I walked into his room he was madder than at the meal. "Makes me so PISSED off." He even punched the wall; "I shoulda popped that bastard."

"Listen, RM, that jerk would have as much chance with you as tryin'-to-sandpaper-a-lion's-asshole-in-a-telephone-booth!"

"Well, I've got a big mouth."

"Hey that smug bastard deserved it. Only he'll probably be our instructor."

"Awright, Willy B, what's your problem. She's pregnant, right?"

We were alone and the door was closed. The others were gone to the Officers' Club or unpacking and knew we were going to talk. We nursed two beers.

Maybe the displaced feeling was because WE were not quite in it yet. As for Leyla and myself, now that I had the 'old married man's ear,' I didn't know what to say.

"Ah, well, shit . . . RM, it's not . . . Christ, I really love her. And at the time . . . "

"I know . . . I get away from her, from Clare, and it all seems unreal. Anyhow, she's coming down in two weeks and I really can't wait. That sonofabitch at the table. That cocksucker!"

"Yeah, now RM! Don't get started again."

"Okay, 'dad.' . . . OH, sorry, bad joke. So, now, tell me . . . alllll about it."

At the thought of our time together, so private, so much our own, the very thought overwhelmed me. Impossible to describe. I drank some beer, "Well, you catch me up first. The wedding and all. I thought about you. I even asked the pilot about stopping there. We flew right over Birmingham—"

"Yeah, you told me . . . well, it was a real small wedding. Dubya D. was there, he stayed at the house the whole time. My father came down. Hadn't seen the old . . . codger for three or four years. He and my mother parted ways about eight, no, ten years ago. Little church wedding . . . Anyhow, Clare and I, you know, we been going together since high school. You knew that, right? Hell, even before that. I never even thought about . . .

well, any long range plans without her. Anyhow, the bride wore white . . .
" RM snickered, then turned away. "Awright, Willy! You didn't come in
here to talk about that—"

Tremendous banging at the door and Evan burst in with Scott Lee and
Mulligan right behind him, "Heyy, come on down you guys. These . . . jok-
ers are tryin' to get me drunk, come on!"

I had never seen Hebert even take a beer before.

We got them out of the room; yeah, right, sure, we'll be down there.

"These guyzzzz!" RM said.

"Well, I guess . . . this is all so new to me. Even taking the trip; I didn't
know if she'd even be there. Wild ride, in a B-26. Then we were together,
just the two of us, for the whole time."

"Yeah, I understand, but, Jesus, you were just there for three days, Willy,
are you sure she's pregnant? And, now don't get mad at this, but . . . if she
says she's pregnant . . . I mean you see what I'm saying? Willy, this is just a
thought, but, has there been anyone else? I mean, you don't need to answer
this but . . . you were there for three days and she says she's pregnant? I
mean, how does she *know*? Well, I mean, could she be *saying* . . . ? See...?"

RM was sweating over it, trying to explain something about this and I
didn't, at first, understand what he was talking about. He went on because
I didn't get it. "I mean, if she's so sure about it, and you were just up there
for three days . . . you see?? What I'm saying? I just mean . . . "

Suddenly my whole body had turned warm, then hot. What had I done,
talking about this, like it was some very ordinary—

"Willy, don't, misunderstand, I'm just throwing stuff out, you know? I
don't know her at all, so, I'm just wondering about it, just asking, see? You're
a great *friend*! So . . . ?"

I was afraid to understand what he was saying. "No, you don't understand . . . at all. See, we *decided* . . . I mean, during the . . . TIME." I
stopped. He didn't understand.

"I can't explain her, RM. She's so honest, she's like a saint. An angel . . . "

"Okay, my man, but angels don't get pregnant . . . at least—"

I felt terrible. RM was not making fun he was only saying the usual
things. Maybe I would have said the same to him. "Okay . . . I know what
you're saying. Alright? I hear you."

"I hear you knockin but you can't come in?"

Again he made me think of Sally. Sally said that, from some old song.
"RM, you got to listen. This whole time was like nothing that's ever happened to me. You see, this is not just . . . a piece of ass, okay?"

"Great, Willy. I'm glad you said that. So many guys"—RM said 'guyzzzz'—"marry the first halfway decent gal they can get in bed, you know?" RM spoke as if WE understood.

"You don't know Leyla . . . RM, she's different." At the same time I was being crushed. What did I know about it? Not only was Leyla the first 'nice' girl I had done it with, she was almost the first of any kind. And why was I defending her? She didn't need defending, *I* did.

"Well, that's part of what I wanted to talk with you about. I mean, I mean it was a crazy time, RM, we were . . . I mean, we were talking about it. She was ovulating. She felt it. We were doing it . . . and less than an hour later she *knew* she was pregnant . . . Christ, I maybe shouldn't be talking about all this."

"Willy, relax, you don't need to say any more."

"Well, I've got to, now. See, she knew, before we did it that night. She *knew it was the time* . . . and she told ME, do you see?"

"Hey, buddy!" RM came over, bent down to me.

"Well, she still might not be . . . pregnant . . . might *not* be. I told you that because she told me she was. Shit, I can't explain. Don't tell anybody! You're the only person who knows."

"Hey! I'd cut out my tongue first, okay? *We've* sweated it out, Clare and me, waiting for her little friend, she calls it. I was just saying . . . ahhh, I don't know. Forget it, Willy."

"Pheww, no, *I* don't know. But, do you think that's possible? To know? So soon after?"

"I don't know . . . women can get these feelings . . . I don't know. Well, what are your plans now? You gonna call her? To make sure?"

The dive-bombers were coming down then recovering, coming down singly, over and over doing their night glide-bombing, not far from the base, only a mile or two. Rocket trains on rails. Nice, but I was getting numb.

"You gonna make an honest woman of her?" RM was joshing now.

"Honest!?" I couldn't get the rest out.

"Get her down here, Willy! Get her down here, some way . . . I mean if you're sure about what you're doing."

Sure about . . . what I'm doing? "I've known her for two years, since Texas days . . . "

"So I take it back, Willy. I didn't mean anything. See, man, it's just talking, you know. If she's pregnant, and when."

"I never knew anyone like her. But, man, when I left, in that buggy from New Orleans, and we almost didn't make it on take-off, l never thought—"

"That's got to be love, my good man, to fly across the country in a B-26! I hope she appreciates that."

"I told you about that long talk from Memphis?"

"Told me? I was *there*, waiting for you. We even listened to some of it."

"You sonofabitch."

"Willy, marry her. Is she beautiful?"

"Beautiful?! Jesus Christ, yes."

"Marry her. Get her down here. Call her tonight."

"I know, I know, but . . . "

"'But' what?"

"Flying. Overseas. Dive-bombers—"

"Yeah, there's a war on. Buy bonds! You know . . . other things go on, too! Willy . . . right?"

They were back, pounding on the door. Hebert's eyes were red, Mulligan was screaming about how drunk he, Hebert, was. Pointing out, practically sticking his fingers in Hebert's eyes to show us. Hebert was blushing, knocking Mulligan's hand away, protesting, then laughing, and, in all, quite proud of himself.

It was eleven o'clock before I could get away and then I couldn't call. There was a guy in the booth and that decided it. Call her tomorrow. But something was happening, the longer I waited.

First lectures in the morning, checkouts tomorrow afternoon maybe. No more dual controls, no more training planes. From now on checking out in a new plane would mean a talk, cockpit familiarization and off, by yourself. We were flyers, as the admiral said. 'Za-war-on' as we said, and I had been oblivious to all of it for the last five days.

Chapter 12

It was after midnight; sleep was a wish, far away.

Big day coming up. New squadron together for the first lecture; film on the SBD, cockpit-checkout and maybe first flight in the Speedy D, if planes available.

I couldn't sleep because I kept saying I can't sleep, and I couldn't stop saying it.

At three in the morning I walked down to the phone. Picked it up, heard the buzz and "Operator," put the receiver back and looked at it, waiting for help, as if the phone itself should call Leyla, as if the operator should know, should get her up and make it okay. The longer I went without speaking to her, the more I began to wonder about RM's words.

I went back to the room, watched Hebert sleeping. Did he envy me ever? Did he envy anything? Evan was a simple machine. Hungry he ate. Tired he slept. And flew with more native talent than 99.9% of the people going through.

Sometimes we talked about his childhood. Adopted. Catholic parents puzzled by this man-child they'd legally called down upon themselves. The kid wants a pony? Get the kid a pony. The kid does wrong? Spank him.

"Shucks, I'll be a cowboy! I'll go out west. Well, [snicker] they caught me ten miles out of town. Stuck my little . . . butt in the station wagon, tied the horse to the bumper and . . . back we went. But, I tell you . . . after *that* . . . well, they didn't cross me. I mean, I didn't get away with a whole heck of a lot but it seems like things were easier after that."

I couldn't sleep but suddenly Hebert's alarm woke us up. We dressed and down to breakfast at the BOQ; 'reassembled eggs' (powdered), orange juice, toast, two pieces of bacon, coffee and milk, as much as we wanted. Down to the Flight Line and up the hangar stairs to lecture room B-2.

"We have two months," said the lieutenant commander, "to prepare you men for combat in a plane you may only have seen in aircraft recognition or read about in the papers until you came here. Two and a half, three months and you'll be flying this plane in combat."

The very thing I'd been waiting for half my life, only I was hearing her voice over his.

He told us how lucky we were to have Major Gaines (marines), and full Lt. Crow (navy) for instructors. The major nodded to us, Crow stared ahead. Both had flown the "D" in combat. Lt. Crow at Midway, off carriers, and the major at Midway and Tassafaronga Point. The commander left us in their "very good hands" and out the door.

"One day we'll tell war stories," said the unsmiling Lt. Crow, lean and bent and leather-skinned, in answer to a question by one of our unknown squadron mates, a black-haired handsome devil of a new lieutenant—new as the rest of us—who wanted to know about their experiences in the Pacific.

Lt. Crow's tone squashed any "talk" and if it was to come up it would be under very different circumstances. Lt. Crow was as dark—full-blooded Iroquois—as the Major was ruddy and fair as a baby. But when it came to "war" these two understood each other: Why talk to these young hotshots? They've got it all fixed in their heads and nothing we say will change it.

In any case the look between them was not for us, us fledglings. Their eyes had seen and their bodies had been there while we were asleep in school, riding bikes, growing up: Kolombangara, Papua, the Coral Sea, Bougainville, The Solomons, Borneo. The names still melted my bones, and I was torn down the middle about Leyla. Somehow, in some way, I had already fought with the marines in those stubby little Grumman Wildcats over Guadalcanal. In a real way I was a little acorn.

We were each given a stapled handbook on the SBD-2 (Scout Bomber, Douglas, 2nd version) which we would take a test on tomorrow.

We looked at each other guardedly, but with more care than usual. We twelve would go through the program together, fly formations in the speedy D, and become dive-bombers.

Tall, pale John Mulligan I had known at pre-flight—long-distance runner, Mr. Cool from New York. RM, Dubya D and Evan, of course, were known. Scott Lee at E-base in Memphis and Muncrief at Memphis, another Indian, slow and stolid, married to his childhood sweetheart, now pregnant and back home in South Carolina. How different he seemed to me. How different our situations. Leyla's parents still knew nothing. I felt like I didn't know much more than they did.

The only other one who struck me was the guy who had spoken up in the class, asking what action they had seen. The list said Segura, Jorge.

We got back around lunch time. I called Leyla and waited.

"Not here," the voice said.

I called again right after lunch and was standing there with the phone in my hand when Hebert rushed up, "Come on, gee, leave the poor girl alone! I fixed it for you. Four of us can check out right now, I told 'em we'd go. Scott Lee and RM are already down there."

We were running to the car. I was feeling the first wave of relief.

"Man, I haven't read the god damned handbook! I haven't even opened it!"

"Shucks . . . " Evan started giggling in his child's way.

"Is that your answer? You crazy bastard? You fuckin' coon-ass. I don't know where anything is."

"Heyyy, watch your tongue. I can . . . WE can fly that bugger. And I read enough of that . . . that 'manual,' to know we don't need to read it. I found out where the throttle is—" he started with his insane giggle, his 'bad kid' laugh. "The throttle . . . that's all we need."

It was infectious. What did it matter what happened, what I did with my body? I was coming back to the world: flying, us, the war.

Hebert was laughing so hard at himself he couldn't go on. Flying was a joke, and all the manuals in the world weren't worth the paper they were printed on. I shared that with him, in a way, but there was a wildness, a screwy difference. Meantime he was whipping around corners, passing jeeps with high-ranking officers in the back.

"Well, you bastard, I told you, I haven't opened the book."

"Listen. All those manuals . . . you c'n just take em—" the giggle again, "—and besides," he interrupted himself, "books don't fly planes, pilots fly planes. . . . Throttle, mixture, flaps, wheels. We can figure it out—"

"Yeah? Well, where are they?"

"They're all right there . . . in the cockpit." Mad laughter.

"*Finger* it out, you mean! Man, you're crazier than I am."

"Listen, I know you. If I'da gone down there and checked out in that plane before you, you'd have been mad as heck."

He was right and . . . it would be fine with Leyla. Meantime, we'd fly. Oh yeah! Waves of joy, of don't give a shit.

Evan caught me smiling. Whipped the car into some questionable parking area and we were running across to the hangar.

The major was there, standing around like a slightly fat little boy in flight suit, helmet dangling from his right hand.

"Are these the other two?" he said to no one because there were only three of us there.

"Yes sir," Evan told him, ready to salute, only the major had no hat on, and neither did he.

"Now, you boys know the handbook, is that correct?"

"Yes sir."

"And the field regulations?"

"Yes sir, in the back of the handbook, right, sir?"

"That's right. Alright, then, go into the line shack, they'll have the planes ready. The other two have already gone out."

"Yes sir."

Evan hadn't said "sir" so often since he'd left home. I knew nothing about the field, the regulations, or the plane, and Evan knew next to nothing. I followed him.

At the lockers in the dressing room we were all laughing, hurrying on with our summer flight suits, one piece suits that zipped up the front with wings in leather sewn on the left side and, under them, "2nd Lieut." our names and "USMCR" Marine Corps Reserves after them.

RM said he'd walk me to my plane and explain where everything was. He had studied the handbook for an hour.

He stood on the wing next to my cockpit and explained the starting procedure while the plane chief held the fire extinguisher and gave me a 'thumbs up'. I stuck the handbook in the map-case down by my right leg.

It started with a loud explosion. I jerked the throttle back and it was idling. RM pushed the mixture control forward just as it was beginning to cough, " . . . your prop setting's here, on the throttle quadrant, just like the 'J'. Wheels, here." RM had his head inside the cockpit yelling, the prop wash buffeting his body outside, "Landing flaps. Prop . . . I said that. Dive flaps over here. Ummm, brakes as usual, top of the rudders. Here are your trim tabs. Just drop your left hand and you'll hit 'em. I'll set them for take-off." He did. "okay . . . gas! . . . gas . . . that's okay, leave it on main. Awreeet? You got it?"

He was out, then in again, "See this little catch? That locks your cock-pit hood open. Flip that inside and then wheel the mother closed. Yeah, this regulates your cowl flaps. Leave 'em full open on take-off, close 'em down after . . . according to your cylinder head temperature. Okay? See you up there, *loo*-tenant."

Down off the wing and running to his plane.

We were supposed to take them up, singly, find an area in the sky clear of other planes and feel it out. Somewhere between eight and ten thousand.

We were using cloth "issue" helmets with the built-in earphones and attachment to plug in to. The goggles were large and curved to give ample space for visibility, and the microphone was on a hook to my left.

Our squadron was Hawkeye and I was Hawkeye Four. We had to report in and request takeoff and landing by that identification. We waddled out to the end of the runway and, no matter what we wanted, these planes were tough and the engine made a good powerful noise, a tough clatter, and when I goosed it, a detonating clatter-roar.

I didn't know how to check magneto drop-off so I ran it up and it sounded clear.

"Hawkeye Four for take-off!"

"Hawkeye Four, cleared." The tower flashed a green light.

The huge roar was new blood in my veins, courage flooding me. And with the various settings still new in my head we—me, the handbook and the plane—went down the runway and flew off the ground. Wheels! Wheels! Where did he say? Okay. I pushed the handle up and felt them tucking away, gingerly eased the prop control back, left full power on and climbed away in a gradual left turn. When I realized "we" were off the ground I was coated with pleasure and smiling absolutely unconsciously. Suddenly, the altimeter was passing five thousand and I was sitting at 5000 feet talking out loud, "Yes, this is Lt. Will Vairin, dive-bomber pilot, U.S. Marine Corps. Flying the SBD-2. Diving? Nawww, it's easy."

At 8000 I cleared to the left and to the right. No one close. Took out the hand-book, turned to the cockpit blow-up and checked over dive flaps, okay . . . cowl flaps . . . yep, landing flaps. Okay. I closed the cowl flaps to halfway.

I started checking the trim tabs and fooling around with them, adjusted the rudder trim, took the torque pressure off the aileron trim tab and started yelling. I must have yelled for a solid minute before I could calm myself down.

I thought of Wonderful and the Corpuscles. It was like swimming the river. I was at eight thousand feet looking over the handbook to learn something about the plane I'm flying.

The flight was scheduled for one hour. Half the time in familiarization; stalls, climbs, glides, turns, and half the time shooting landings at a field ten miles to the west of the base.

At a little over 8000 feet I cleared the area and tried some stalls. Holding the nose up to test its flying characteristics, not knowing from experience just what speed a plane will stop flying and stall out. I had power on but not much and the controls were getting mushy and unresponsive at 70 knots, but I held it and kept the nose high, down to 66 and holding, slowing still, and then, last look at 62 or 61 it seemed to give a flutter, almost a sigh, and then the nose just slid down past the horizon and we were in a slight dive. I let it have its head, as if I were jumping a horse, let the stick come forward, gave it power, pulled it up and tried it again. Yes, it was a very "honest" stall. Lots of signals, lots of advance notice before it let go and slid down through the horizon and toward the ground, wings level. Over and over I tried, till I knew just exactly how far I could take it, and knew by the feel of the stick, without looking, what the speed was, how close it was to stalling. With full flaps and a lot of power I could hold the nose up and get it down to 58 knots.

The only other dive-bomber I had ever heard about was the German Stuka, the famous JU-87 with the fearsome, hideous shrieking dive siren.

Landing flaps drop down from the trailing edge of the wings but dive flaps, of perforated metal, open both above and below the wings. I hit the dive flaps lever and the plane slowed down in a very ungainly way. I flew around like that for a time, making some gentle left and right turns, and then peeled over and let it drop down. Even in the cockpit I could hear the whine build up as the wind went through those perforations. I dove through 3000 feet and suddenly I *felt* like a dive-bomber and well, maybe, this dive-bombing . . . well, it'll have its peculiar thrills.

I was screaming and kept on screaming, roaring, screaming.

I screamed till I thought I'd burst a blood vessel. I *wanted* to burst a god damned blood vessel! Hell, that's what they're for. You wanta live forever? Hell no.

At last I was not only closing on the war but flying a first line plane being used even today. The Australians had them, the British had SBD's on carriers and they were being shipped to the Russians.

I think I graduated in those minutes—unable to realize what was happening till now.

I located the landing practice field and from 7000 I could see it easily although it was a nice cloudy day, with big cotton puffballs over 40 percent of the sky.

I rolled over, hit the dive-flaps lever and was heading down, almost straight down. The dive flaps gave a feeling of hanging in the air at 190, 200 knots. At 5000 and still at a good angle I closed the flaps and felt it jump ahead and a smoothed out feeling, the needle said we were slipping through the air at 280 knots, still going down, king of all I surveyed, I dove on and circled the field and picked out three other SBD's, two on the ground, one coming in. Then I saw another two in the landing pattern.

I took my interval at the upwind end of the field. I still had to lose a lot of speed so as not to overtake the plane in front of me. I pushed the wheel lever down and felt them fall into place.

I popped the landing flaps abeam of the spot we were to land on and began turning in, the plane in front of me hit and I could see little puffs of smoke come out from the wheels. It veered a little, then he was straight and picking up speed and was off again, no idea who it was down there; RM, Scott Lee, mad Evan, or some stranger.

Down around, watching, head out of the cockpit, only occasionally allowing my eyes to touch the instruments, speed and height over the ground. Already I felt at home, that it couldn't betray me. It was like riding a bike, making a turn, head out watching the street and making the adjustment from seeing the street and what was needed. It came to me again that we'd be going overseas in these, or a newer version.

We shot landings, me and my four unknown fellow pilots, at that lonely little field in Florida set among the scrub pines, landings witnessed only by two navy enlisted men on the 'Bloody Mary'—white crash truck with red crosses on the sides—at the end of the runway and off to the side, waiting, a little ghoulishly perhaps, for an accident.

We got back to the field, landed, hauled our chutes and jungle-packs (inflatable life raft, emergency rations, paddles, whistles, dye-marker, pills, rum, inside of a neat square pack between the parachute and the seat cushion), sweaty and free, and something had changed in me. Leyla had moved to the side a little. I needed . . . I needed her, yes, but this was a drive I was more familiar with. Squadrons were going through. Down and into meals the sweaty pilots rushed out to fly again, the buzz, the talk was of flights and bombing runs, strafing sleeves, formation flying and forever the noise, like a cloud covering the whole base, squadrons coming in, taking off, engines roaring, the strong smell of aviation gasoline.

The entire base was caught up in its own life. No one was worried about torpedo bombers or fighters. Here, the "Speedy D" was everything. The instructors and everyone who had a chance to fly or work on it loved the plane, even knowing it was slow. It was stable and dependable. When the lift in the wings was gone the nose fell through the horizon, wings level. Unlike the beautiful and treacherous Corsair which, with no warning, went into a vicious spin. "The Widow-maker" it was called and even that I loved about it. But the real thing about the Wings-of-Gold-Corsair-Widow-maker—415 miles an hour straight and level—it was the fastest plane in the world. Beautiful and dangerous: *La Belle Dame Sans Merci.*

In some strange way it was bound up with Leyla, with loving and losing, with the most romantic death; bloody, flaming, heroic, sad, beautiful and fast. I couldn't begin to explain it. It was a voice saying all the right things but I wasn't getting a picture.

The second night after getting to Deland I got the phone and caught her.

"Will . . . Is it, oh, God, I didn't mean to start with all of this, but—"

"Leyla . . . I love you . . . I love you so much . . . " Only . . .

"Will. . . ." She was crying. Actually, almost bawling over the phone, and not caring that I heard it all.

"Will . . . it's been so awful . . . " she started laughing, " . . . so wonderful-awful. I had to. . . . HAD to hear you say that. Had to hear your voice. Give me a number where I can reach you."

"Leyla, are you . . . ? Well, you know. Are you—"

"I told you, Will!"

"But you haven't had any tests or anything."

"No! Do you think I should?"

"Have you told your folks, yet? About us?"

"Noooo, and, Will, I feel terrible about that. If you were only here . . . "

"I *was*." And felt worse than terrible. She had told me she'd call them. Was she lying? That she'd do it? And now what?

"That sounds very cold, Will."

"Yeah?"

"You're mad."

"Sure. You should've called . . . you said you would."

"Will. I don't know if I can stand it."

"Me neither." I was going to tell her. Even if it wrecked us. Divorced from Leyla. Divorced even from myself. All the dirty jokes I'd ever heard. What-women-are-really-like.

She was calling my name and I wasn't answering.

"Leyla . . . " I almost choked saying her name, "Are you sure?"

"Sure of what?"

"Sure you're pregnant?" Only that was not it.

"Do you think I should go see a doctor?"

"I love you . . . " Only it was goodbye, goodbye.

"Will . . . it's been so awful, not having you . . . " she was crying again, and, "I had to hear you say that . . . "

"What? 'I love you'?" Goodbye, ohh my throat hurt.

"Yes . . . that you love me . . . I need it."

"Leyla. . . ?"

"What, Will? Something's up. Something's bothering you."

"Yes."

"I feel that coldness again . . . Will?"

"I . . . don't know how to say it."

"Just tell me. Haven't we been honest with each other?"

I couldn't speak.

"Will? Tell me. I love you, no matter what. Tell me!"

"Leyla . . . are you sure?"

"About what?"

"That you weren't pregnant. . . ?"

"*What?*"

"Before?"

"WILL!!! What are you *saying?*"

"Just that!"

"What are you saying? What are you SAYING? Ohhh, Will! Did it mean . . . nothing? Just nothing?" But her voice was fading.

Then she was gone and I was left with my awful doubts. Not even doubts. My awful . . . my evil thoughts . . . and the phone in my hand.

Sorry. So sorry, sorry. I had just said it. Just said it. Knowing . . . knowing all the time. I called back, called back six times. No answer, or else someone told me she wasn't in.

I went back to RM's room. A whole pile of people were in there. I signaled to him and watched Evan laugh that mindless little kid's laugh and envied his uncluttered life of action. RM walked over and we stepped out of the room.

"Man I have done it now."

"What happened?"

I told him.

"Willy, how? How you did it, how you said it is so important."

"RM, I love her so much. What the fuck do I do now?"

"Get her down here."

"RM, man, she won't even answer the phone."

Chapter 13

The program was roaring off the ground. We had intelligence briefings, more navigation, ship and plane identification, movies, instruction, briefings before and after every flight. In between flights, lectures and movies, I was calling Leyla and couldn't get hold of her. Something had happened and they all seemed to be in on it.

"Bess?"

"No, this is Allie."

"Allie, this is Will. I've GOT to talk to her. I'll walk out of here. I'll go AWOL and go on back up there if I can't talk to her. I've got to! Please. Tell her I love her. She's got to forgive me. I want to . . . tell her . . . "

"Just a sec . . . " the receiver hit something and she was gone.

"Hello, Will. This is Bess. Allie is going to talk to her."

"Please, tell her how sorry I am. She's got to forgive me. I've got to get hold of her!"

"She's missed all of her classes, since—"

A new voice now, "Listen, Will, you almost killed her. She's still recovering. We had to . . . well, anyhow, she's okay . . . she's okay now, she's fine—"

"What happened? What do you mean? *Now* she's fine?"

"Well . . . I'll let her tell you about it. If she'll come to the phone. *I'd* rather not. Allie is talking to her. This is Lil. I think you're a *fool!* I don't know what got into you but I think the world of Leyla. She's the most honest person I've ever met in my life . . . and maybe the best!"

"You're right. I was crazy, Lil. But I *love* her. I was crazy—" I couldn't go on.

"Well, here's Allie."

Again the phone was given over and I got the terse message, "Give me a number where she can call you tonight . . . around eight o'clock. She'll definitely call you, around eight—"

"Is she okay?? Tell her I feel terrible . . . and I can't wait to hear from her. Please tell her I love her . . . " then with a rush of blood that almost spoke for me, "Tell her I love her to death. Please tell her that. Okay? Please, Allie?"

I repeated the number, made her repeat it and we hung up.

Then eight o'clock had come and gone, nine, and ten o'clock and still I sat there in the big lobby watching others get their calls. Screw it, fuck it. I had been sitting there reading magazines as if I wanted to do nothing else. I even brought the handbook with me, figuring I'd at last get chance to look at it but I couldn't bear to open the thing. Hebert was right. Besides, hadn't we mastered it already? I didn't want to read about settings and proper procedure.

I left the room, closest spot to the phone, and felt like I was leaving her. The pull on me to stay and wait was almost physical. In a way I was closing the book on her. I went to RM's and Dubya D's room. They were talking, listening to Benny Goodman, the trio or the quartet. "Ly-o-Nell" RM called Lionel Hampton, "On the viiiiiiibes."

I listened, not adding much. Cursing myself. Why worry about it? I had lost. So, there's flying and the war. I'll be like Hebert, I'll fly, and go to Daytona with the guys. So simple before Leyla. Only my dreams and waiting for the war.

"Charlie Christian on the geeeetar," RM told us all, strumming some air notes. Then the music turned moody, "So Rare."

RM looked over. "Did she call?" He mouthed the words.

I shook my head.

"Formations tomorrow," he said. I nodded and left.

Down the hall, across the lobby. And a note on the door. "Leyla called, 2230. Call her."

I didn't even go in. With one side of me I understood completely and forgave her for not calling. On the other hand all of my earlier numbness had turned to anger. I was walking down to the phone when the seaman on duty almost passed me.

"Lt. Vairin?"

"Yes."

"Telephone call, sir."

I walked faster; delighted, angry, mad with love for her, ready to kill her, unspeakably happy, cautious not to show it . . . well not too soon.

"Hello?"

"Will?"

"Yes, Leyla?"

"Will . . . "

"Leyla, are you alright? I'm so sorry, so really sorry."

"Will . . . Will. I don't know. Is it all over?"

"I love you. I love you. Are you really there? If I could just be there, you wouldn't say that."

"Yes, Will. My darling. Oh, I don't know how I can say that . . . now . . . I don't know how you said . . . what you said."

"Will you listen?"

" . . . . "

"I don't know *why* . . . I was hurt . . . and talking to RM—"

"The one who's married?"

"Yes, I was talking to him . . . I mean it's not his fault, but—"

"I just don't know, Will . . .when I heard you say that, I couldn't believe I was hearing it. It was no longer you. My mind blanked out. I think I fainted. I couldn't believe it. Couldn't believe you would ever, that YOU, I just kept saying you KNEWWW. Other people could talk like that but not you, not *you*."

"If I could only be there . . . we could *be*."

"Go on. I want you to . . . make it . . . okay. Will?"

"Leyla you say that . . . and . . . "

"Yes, like I'm not sure I know you . . . you said that and I felt lost. The ground opened up. Nothing anyone ever said made me feel like that."

"Leyla . . . if you can just forgive me. It's got to be the same. It's got to be . . . You didn't tell your father, your mother, about us. That hurt me so much. You told me you would. I thought you didn't really take it seriously. I mean, I felt like you'd *never* do it. And that hurt. You didn't tell them. You were too afraid. It made me feel, well, I was serious but you weren't. Also, that you gave me your word . . . your word that you'd call and tell them and, since, you didn't keep your word about that . . . that maybe . . . maybe I couldn't believe you. "I was just angry. I couldn't believe you hadn't told them. But I know that's no excuse—"

"That was wrong of me—"

"No, Leyla . . . it's no reason for me to say what I said. I don't know how I said that. No matter what—"

"Will, I've never felt so empty."

"Come down, Leyla. We'll get married down here. That's IT!! Come down. Please! I don't care if you don't tell 'em. Come down! I don't care if you don't *ever* tell 'em, just come down and we'll get married. Sometimes I feel like I'm suffocating without you. I was ready to leave and go up there . . . "

"I don't know what you would have found."

"Leyla, you have to tell me, what happened?"

"I've never been so sick. . . . The hospital . . . and . . . well, bleeding."

"Leyla!!"

"Yes, the whole hall got involved. I passed out. I never fainted before—"

"Leyla, I feel terrible . . . " I also felt as if I had aged ten years. I was deep into something I couldn't stop, couldn't handle, couldn't get out of. No turning back. She was everywhere I looked.

"Well, and Will . . . " Her voice sounded ominous, strange, broken.

"What?"

"I don't know how to say this. . . ."

"God, Leyla, *tell* me."

"Will . . . help me . . . get over this."

She was sobbing, heart-broken, heart-breaking. I was crying without ever having heard what it was.

"Will?"

"Yes?" I could barely speak.

"Ohhh, Will . . . "

"Leyla . . . should I come up there?"

"Will! You CAN'T!"

"Tell me . . . tell me, Leyla."

"Will . . . I don't know why it should be so hard, but—"

"Leyla, I'm going crazy . . . just tell me."

"Well . . . I *was* . . . I *was* pregnant, Will—"

For a minute or so I had no idea what she meant.

"I *was* pregnant, Will. The doctor said it looked like I had a miscarriage—"

Just when it seemed she had recovered and was gaining strength Leyla was sobbing huge heaving sobs, wracking sobs that came right over the phone to me.

"You're *not* pregnant!?" I was still trying to digest the fact that she had been.

"No," she whispered in such an empty, desolate voice that I could feel her very soul laid out on the voice coming over to me, dead, or dying.

"Ohh, Leyla . . ." I was stripped of wings, commission, name, background. We were two souls yearning, pulsing a hurt forth and back. I didn't know where I was, who was hearing this, what time it was. I felt like a lighthouse whose light has gone out on a stormy night watching ships crash on the rocks. Calling, calling on myself for help, lights out, no one home.

"Will . . . listen, I'm okay. I'm okay. That was, well, the last of it. I really am. I'm okay. I may cry a few more times about it, but I'm really over it."

"Leyla . . . I love you so much. I love you more than ever. That was . . . our child." I couldn't even believe the word. "Did *I* kill it? Ohh, Leyla."

"Will . . . no, no, Will. I can't really talk about that right now. It's too much. I didn't know if I'd be able to call you but I did because . . . Well, but, now, all I can say is I'm over it."

"I called so many times. I can't believe I left you up there. But even if we got married we couldn't be together for two months, while . . . I mean now, right now. I mean—"

"Will, we—"

"I mean we could get married, on a weekend, but we can't live together, till after—"

"Will, I know . . . I know . . . and when you were calling, part of me wanted to speak to you and another part couldn't do it."

"Leyla, *will* you marry me? Will you come down?"

" . . . Let me think, alright? I've got to think about it."

"Oh, if I was only up there."

"I couldn't stand it right now, Will. I don't know how I let you go, but I couldn't do it again."

"I flew today. This afternoon."

"You DID? Oh, Will!" We were back again, her voice told me! "How was the dive-bomber? The SDQ?" She was laughing but it was still so close to her tears I could hear both in her voice. "Did you put that plane through its paces?"

"Yeaaahhh, I'll tell you all about it."

It sounded like, 'I love you.'

"WHAT?"

" . . . I love you."

"Heyyy, does flying do that to you?

"*You* flying . . . ."

Chapter 14

"What are you messing with that *girl* for? You better forget all that stuff. Besides," Hebert's evil chuckle slipped out, "time for that stuff after this thing is over . . . if we live that long." The censored chuckle was Hebert the child, forbidden to laugh about death, sex and the bathroom. "You can't fly with a wife! Look At RM! As the man said, 'Fly now, wives later.'"

We studiously avoided saying 'after the war,' as if the whole thing was a poker game. Don't count your chips; don't even talk about your 'chips' during the game.

For whole blocks of time I knew Evan was right. Time enough for "all that" when . . . well, if we're still standing. And she's still waiting. Then, again, is it 'fair' to marry? And leave a young widow? Dubya D was talking about getting married before we went overseas. Sarah and he were *both* talking about it, so why should the guy be blamed? Mulligan, Scott Lee, Jorge Segura, Dubya D., RM and I often argued about it . . . about "the right thing."

RM would scream at Mulligan, the cool New Yorker, who talked about responsibility, and how *he* wouldn't marry, "Nooo way, not with a war on."

As if he'd tried it during the Spanish-American War and the Civil War before that—and it had not worked out, no sir. "Get married just before going overseas? No good! It's not right."

"Not right? In whose mind?" RM would turn away in disgust, "Don't give me that shit!"

I admired RM., loved him in a way, and Mulligan; well, I enjoyed Mulligan. The only thing wrong was that RM had been in love with Claire since grade school and Mulligan might never settle down. He was in love with running around. With Leyla and me it was totally different. And with Dubya D and RM's sister? That was different too. It was all different. Still, we argued about it as if only one position was right.

"Brffsk, ahem," said Mulligan, assuming a stance, "I just believe in being *responsible*."

"You're responsible for your hot nuts," Jorge told him, "now shut up, and let's go, we have a briefing in ten minutes."

FORMATIONS AND CARRIER BREAKUP

"The idea . . . ," the major drew some little stick airplanes on the board, "is for the leader to make it easy for his wingmen. Set your throttle and leave it alone. We'll cruise at 1850 r.p.m.'s. If you're a section leader set your throttle a fraction faster than the leader and, in a turn, sliiiide to the outside if you're overtaking the lead. If you're falling back sliiiiide to the inside . . . " He showed with his fat hands, turning his slightly chubby body to follow his hands. RM jutted his jaw out 'seriously,' and caught my eye.

"If you must add throttle, bend your head forward *first* . . . " He did it, in a jerky motion, tucking his chin in, "in order to let your wingman know about it, *then* add throttle. To take off throttle . . . head *back* . . . then ease off throttle." He showed us that too.

"We will be in three groups of four each . . . staggered UP. Three leaders. Each leader smart . . . *smart*! Change throttle settings only when you have to. For the Carrier Breakup back at the field, the first four break off, go down to the 500 foot circle—" all of these with swirls and circles in chalk on the board—"the other eight go around again, the second four then break off, the last four go around again . . . okay? Make it nice!"

The ungainly twelve of us headed out to sea at 7000 feet past the up-staggering cloud formations; stately, graceful and slowly changing shapes.

Above the twelve planes, one bee of an instructor stung us with his commands.

"Hawkeye eight, 90 degree turn to the left."

"Roger, Hawkeye eight."

The rest of us, cueing on the lead four, wide or shallow turns to stay in our relative positions without changing throttle. Within each four the wingmen make their adjustments, sliding to the inside or outside of the turn, crossing over if we're slow or fast.

"Hawkeye four, take the second section . . . "

"Hawkeye four, Roger."

Hawkeye six pats his head, points to me. I've got it. He slides out, drops back onto my left wing, the four of us cut inside the turn of the lead four.

Work, learning, dancing to the short commands. Watching, judging, sailing out, sliding in. Changing leads, sweaty and thrilled with the exacting routine—hard, greasy blue and white-winged bodies passing over, passing under, fifteen feet away, these tough birds in comradely formation, heading down and in to the field, down to lunch after the morning's practice for war, last schooling before the big show, the great grand Pacific islands and glory, the all of it, even the clouds above our south Florida base put there by a god who knew we needed them like that; immense, girded and bound, spiraling way up there. Above me the last four swing in, drift to the outside to stay behind our lead while the mighty clouds holding their own formation sail past.

Down we go, controlled dive for twelve planes, into position around the field, big turn heading upwind over the runway, the lead four break off 'step down' from 8 to the 500 foot circle, our eight hold straight ahead, into a turn, an 800 foot oval around to the same position again, my four the kiss off and down to 500, pass the lead and I'm free to land my lone-at-last dive-bomber, taking interval on the last of the first four.

The clouds above us spiraling up to 40,000, still the morning pictures jostle for a place, the whole so delicate, so strong; our platform of twelve against the immense white towering cumulonimbus and a memory from Pensacola; instructor screaming to his chickens, "Jesus Christ, get out of those clouds!" And the sing-song flip answer from some cadet, forever unidentified: *"This is Jesus Christ! Coming out of clouds!"*

Ah, well, we were like Jesus, or at the very least like angels, coming down and in, coming home, hot and sweaty out of clouds both flying *and* sitting down to fried chicken iced tea with lemon wedges ice daggers and a ton of sugar, between ground and sky, flying eyes, hands and talk in glory speaking, reaching, laughing, cleansed and ready for the up of our down-up existence, sitting there in the down of our up-down lives.

The eyes of America were on the American and British campaign for Italy, the "soft underbelly" of Europe, as Churchill described it. Only our troops were going nowhere. "Heavy fighting around Naples." Every day it was "Heavy fighting." Mud and rain, rain and mud and no air support for the tenth straight day in and around the mountains above Naples. American dead coming down the mountains on mule-back.

News from home: Dan and Aphra married. Dan on his way overseas. The wedding had been beautiful but "Oh so rushed . . . the date moved up because of his orders. Oh, and little Aphra looked so beautiful. Everybody asked about you. And, my darling, Jack, you know, they believe, is now in Italy. Little Wallace is on guard duty somewhere in the Pacific . . . "

I had to smile at her words, 'Somewhere in the Pacific.' People wrote letters to an APO address in the U.S. From there they had no idea where their letters went.

As for 'Come down now, we'll get married,' there were things about myself I didn't understand. And I couldn't talk to anyone about them.

Well, right now, this instant, I didn't want to. Not because I didn't love her but because I didn't know how we'd do. Would it be like Cambridge? We'd never get out of bed. And something else; I hardly knew how to word it. It was right *now* what to do? Could I really handle it? Husband? To that dynamo? How would she be? Would it all change?

Other times I felt, sure, come down! Get married now!

Then again, I wanted not only freedom but Leyla too. To fly and have a wife? I might as well sign up for Patrol Bombers. Fly at ninety, live to be ninety.

"Be careful now!"

"Alright, honey."

As for the miscarriage I hardly understood it. Add it to so much else I didn't understand.

Fly now. Wives later.

Every flight I disappeared into the world of the twelve of us: the 'us' of us, the way I felt about the Corpuscles, Robin Hood, freedom. Even signing for a plane, lugging chutes out, hands to the chilly metal, looking at that tough bird I'd fly; rude, brash, loud, cutting into the air and the hell with everything quiet. Throttle fire-walled. And it didn't stop on the ground; up or down, eating lunch, even waiting for the weather to lift.

Wings, sky, space, speed, landing, take-off, formations of us together in risk, death only wing-tips away, the flight marriage till-death-parts-us loyalty that doesn't stop on landing, hasn't stopped since our wings, only that detour in Cambridge, and like Cambridge come down in love. Deeper and more mysterious with every flight.

Chapter 15

DIVE-BOMBING, said the big letters on the blackboard in the briefing room.

The base itself breathed the words.

Lt. Crow, 'Chief Duck Honking,' RM's name for him, would lead six of us the major would take the other six.

RM, Dubya D, Evan, Jorge, Mulligan and I went with the Chief—we did call him Chief to his face, and he liked it. For the Chief's briefing, in front of the ready-room, parachutes over our shoulders, held by leg straps, we strained to hear the few words he gave us: "I'm in 49 . . . Rendezvous over field . . . angels five to target . . . echelon 10,000 . . . I'll drop twice . . . observe . . . then begin . . . Keep interval . . . call in each dive . . . carrier breakup . . . meet here . . . questions?"

He picked at his ear, looked down, no one spoke, he turned away and walked to his plane.

We followed, chutes on shoulders and laughed at RM's imitation: "Chief . . . Honking . . . up . . . Dive . . . carrier . . . questions?"

Out we went and maybe just as well. Movies, lectures, diagrams: whatever, we were ready for the step beyond it. Too bad we didn't have smoke bombs to mark our hits, rocks even.

I took off after the Chief and bent the throttle to catch him, pulled in close off his left wing and *felt* Evan slide under me onto his other wing, RM. sailing into us from the side and out to Evan's right wing. Joined at 3500 and continued climbing to 8000 then to 10,000. The Chief held up three fingers, then *told* us "three," and we picked up the voice of the observer at the air force bombing range to the west, calling in the "hits'" of the B-17s. The Flying Forts were using the famous Norden bombsights. Top Secret. With the new bombsights the B-17s and the B-24s could, we were told, put an apple in a barrel from 20,000 feet. Yep, we heard all about it as we climbed for our bombing runs.

"Six-two, your last drop-six-o'clock, 300 yards . . . " Silence for ten seconds: "Seven-five-your-drop eight-o'clock, 1000 yards . . . Five-seven-your-drop—"

"Heyyy," it sounded like Scott Lee, "How 'bout them APPLES?"

"Yeah," another voice sang out, "Where's the barrel?"

"That barrel better be 600 yards wide," and wild laughter from another voice.

"Hawkeye one, *knock it off!*" was the Chief's comment and longest speech of the day.

At 10,000 we leveled off. "The lake," said the Chief. He swished his tail for echelon and we swung out in line off his right wing, like a flight of six ducks. Another twenty seconds and he kissed off, rolled over so pretty and maybe every kid's dream; his body rolled over and fell from the sky, an Indian 'bird' to the god of great risk. I counted then gave RM our Indian "How" sign and rolled over after him, popping the dive flaps on my back, elevator trim forward, found the lake, electric sights imposing that dim yellow target over the whole area, centering on the very center of the lake, straight down, hanging on the straps, feeling the very pull of 6000 feet, winding down, 4800—" . . . not below 3000 feet"—feeling, waiting, one last glimpse at 3300, made the imaginary drop, flaps closed, jammed it wide open, saw the Chief climbing to my left up ahead, screamed on after him, thrilled to my bones at the game; for what else was it? A game the government (all governments?) had devised for us to play, the greatest game of all, the life-death game and they picked up the tab for the whole thing, even the funeral. Yeahhhh, caught him going up with speed to spare at 5000 and the others catching up, a flying accordion coming together sucking up air for the next great note—we were high, high, diving through space separately and together climbing for our next effort.

They had warned us don't become hypnotized; concentrating on wind drift, position, centering on the target and run out of altitude. Just one more second to get it, just another sec—

I was walking to the room after a workout with Ziegler, feeling the sun on my life, my very life a shell projected into space, a long arc going up, way up there and still more to go. It seemed to connect with a kind of release to the world. Ever since I had been on the track of flying, the war, and training, my view had been raised, not in a vague way, but now closing in on the Far East, all of those names that touched my heart: Borneo, Sumatra, Java, Empress Augusta Bay. I stopped on the sidewalk between the BOQ and gym, forced myself to admit it, bursting out of my skin with it. Happy, satisfied, happy.

Ziegler was a college wrestling champion from Oklahoma and was showing me some basic holds. He had a bull neck and long ape-like arms. "You have good balance, good reactions. You oughta take it up . . . after the war," he told me, not once but twice.

'After the war'? It made me uneasy. None of us said those words. The very words were a jinx. Not during it, no, no!

I was on the way to my room after the workout. Last flight Saturday, and none tomorrow.

Then like burglars looking for a bank to rob: Scott Lee, Jorge 'The Black Beauty,' Dubya D, Mulligan, and RM with a bag full of bottles.

"Lookin all over for ya, Willy Babe! We're *goin!*"

"TO THE BEACH!!"

"Daytona!!! Babe! The beach is callin'!"

"Where in the hell you been?"

"THE BEEEEEACH!!"

Off we went in Jorge's long wreck of a convertible, a Buick circa 1934, newly bought so new, in a way. Off to kill the time between now and the next flight.

It didn't matter about the trip, miles, speed, or daylight. Nothing mattered to and from the base, or while there, or here, or in between, only here, now. 'There'? There is after! After what? After now? Time pulling us to the great action, the show, so any *time's* good on the way to closer, closer to the mighty Pacific. The world's ours till then and after. Drunk before drinking, only explain it get drunk, yes, 'n order explain it, no, clear it up, *catch* it? No, prove absolutely *prove* . . . or be able to . . . to what? What the fuck difference . . . hollow walnut shells with toothpick arms and legs and a mad fly trapped in the nutshell moving arms and legs to get out. We'd jig on till the fly died. Well, weren't we flyers? With a strength that screamed out for use? Didn't we have it in our eyes? Our hands? Our legs and reflexes? Our kingdom the very skies? And didn't the world depend on us to turn back the menace?

Did we want to tell the world? No need; they *know.*

We got one room, registered in the name of the straightest looking one at the time and went right up, ordered ice and chasers and drank.

Alright, no one leaves till he's drunk. Well, there's only six so it shouldn't take long. Especially if everybody tries. You aren't trying, you sonofabitch? Come on, TRY!

You have to stagger. No one leaves till he passes the stagger test.

"Shit! Man, you're not staggering. Here, drink this . . . No, *I'll* fix it . . . Lieutenant, it's already *fixed*!! . . . Don't spill that, you ass, that's the last bottle of banana mint brandy they had! Yeah, and a little gin . . . *Fixed?* . . . Caaaaaugh, that's not a drink, that's *straight! straight*!! . . . Just drink it and shut up so we can get out of here! . . . I'll fix him one, I'll settle this . . . Alright, then, YOU drink THAT shit . . . Gotta draw the line . . . I tell you that stuff tastes like hydraulic fluid . . . Officers and gentlemen, I have a speech. . . . Let's stagger out to the boardwalk, give us your speech later . . . LET'S FOR CHRIST'S SAKE, GET OUT OF HERE! ! . . Nobody leaves till I give my speech . . . AHEM . . . Wait a second, WHO'S NOT STAGGERING??? JORGE, YOU FUCKER, WALK THAT UN-STRAIGHT LINE FOR US. . . . That's it! No, for Christ's sake, no more, I can't stagger any better . . . Shit, you call that a stagger? . . . Listen, my aunt staggers better than . . . Yeah, your face staggers me! . . . Nobody leaves till I give my speech, AHEM!"

RM clapped a hand over Mulligan's mouth. "Al*right* . . . "

Mulligan's feelings were hurt. He grabbed the telephone, "Hello, desk? This is 401. There are some rowdies up here and I want them thrown out!"

"Good," Scott Lee said, "now you'll have to pay for the room!"

"What? It's not paid for?" Mulligan croaked. "Desk? Cancel that last call! I'm giving them one more chance!"

Mulligan, who also thought he could sing, loved speeches and never got past his introduction.

RM was our goad. He lost patience more quickly than anyone, particularly with Mulligan, who wanted to be the wise old man, the Advisor, and because he came from New York (Brooklyn) took on the air, and rarely referred to Brooklyn, unless it involved the Dodgers or meant he was unique.

The six of us staggered out of the room an hour or so later to the big casino at the end of a pier, wide enough to drive a big truck over. The pier ran out into the ocean for a quarter of a mile.

The bar was a block long and there was a huge dance floor.

I was at the bar but couldn't talk. Some girl. Pretty hair. Nice forehead. I tried to tell her about Leyla but I couldn't, not a word. The bartender cocked his head at me. No words. He cocked his head again. I pointed at a bottle of bourbon. I could think and remember and hear but no words.

"This one?"

I shook him off and pointed. I was also clutching the bar. Think okay but no talk.

"This one over here?"

Up and down.

He took the bottle down and asked, "Now what do you want with it?"

I couldn't say, but he finally found it and added ginger and ice to the bourbon and gave it to me.

I put money on the counter, took the glass, she put change in pocket.

What did he think? Why serve? Going over to fight the war? Dead in another month, let 'em go?

The girl? So natural. Smiling, took my arm. We walked away, big barn on the water to pier. Like dances, New Orleans and Paige Burney. I tried and tried. No good. Paige! Where are you? Leyla? No, Leyla like a cloak. Like night-waves-stars that I was trying to reach, pointing, reaching. Did the night ever have such an eloquent spokesman?

"auggh . . . ele . . . grawwkk"

"I think you've had enough to drink," she said, but she stayed. She did everything but say it: flyers, overseas, giving their lives. What can we do for them?

We took advantage, every offer, asked for more and took those. What no one seemed to realize—we were happy risking our necks. If we hadn't been flying we would have found another way. Drunk? They're blotting it out, trying to forget. How can you blame 'em? It's the war. God love 'em. We owe them everything. If they could only hear Evan how he'd fly for the Nazis if they gave him too much trouble, or kicked us out. To fly, to fly . . . I understood him, but I'd have to keep the cap on old Evan. This was our chance, our only chance. I also believed, yes, the Nazis were a bad crew but it didn't figure high. As for the Japs we didn't pretend to understand them— to hate or admire.

I was throwing up into the ocean, long heaves like the waves rolling in to the beach, somebody holding me, talking Okay, 'It's okay, okay!' The shit it is! Couldn't talk, though, couldn't talk. 'It's okay, okay!' Like shit is. Ohhh Jesus, agaaain, oh shit, ohhh God—

'It's okay!!'

Finished. She? Somebody gave me a rag. Kleenex. I couldn't get rid of her. Throw up all over the place and she's still here. Back inside to the table. Scott Lee, half dead looks up: "Slap the Jap 'fore he wipes us off the map!" His head flopped down on the table.

"Someday," he said, talking with his head resting on the table and no effort to pick it up, "I know, I know, the war and all, but someday we gotta take a leaky old boat across the Pacific, y'know? I mean a' old rusty boat, y'know? A real SCOW! Ya understand, Willy? Wanta go? Heh? Willy?"

The juke box was screaming out, "Try a little tendernessss!"

"You wanta dance?" My date, my female helper, my nurse.

" . . . " I couldn't speak. Could just barely walk and without her help probably couldn't do that, laughing so hard I almost broke a tooth on the table.

"Willy? Huh? Wanta go? 'N old scow?"

"Come on, you can try! I'll help . . . "

Scott Lee looked up, asking me about his rusty old scow, a cigarette butt pasted to the side of his face, "Cross Piss-if-ic . . . old scow?"

Jorge, 'The Black Beauty' came over with some tough-looking youngish girl, and they discussed it.

"What the hell is wrong with you, Scotto? What's with this old rusty scow that might sink?"

"Yeaahhhh!" Scott Lee breathed a huge sigh, ". . . might sink, ya *get it?*"

"I get it alright. You're whacked out of your noodle. Let's get this straight, now."

Jorge knew Scott Lee was hanging on by a thin string, and happy to disengage the remaining fraction. "You don't want to take this trip in a nice safe liner, right? It's got to be old and rusty, is that it?"

The smile on Scott Lee's rocky face was pure gratitude.

"Yeahhh, got it! Willy understand' Not . . . be . . . *safe.*"

Scott Lee and I shook hands. We had agreed about safety a few days ago. But Scott Lee couldn't get enough.

"Come on, let's go dance, you can try—"

"What'sasense? What's'sense, 'm ah right? 'Fno risk . . . no fun, right, Willy Babe?"

I was almost speaking. We shook hands again.

"Let's go dance," she said.

Dubya D came over, maybe a little less drunk than earlier, "Take a crap on the Jap—"

"No," said Jorge, "slap a loose liver-lickin Jap 'fore he sinks a ship fulla crap—"

"Nooo, I got it, loose lips sink chinks—"

"Loose bonds buy lips."

"Wait! Chapped-Jap lips lick laps fulla crap!"

"Buy crap—"

"Sink bonds—"

I was trying to explain to her, what's her name? I kept thinking I could speak but no. She stayed and stayed, I don't know why. I couldn't kiss her, throw-up she saw it all, fact she helped wipe me up. What did she want?

Then it was Sunday afternoon, the shades lifting on beach, swimming. Beer made it better, half out of uniform, through the gate, saluting the enlisted marines. And back. Great to be back. Great on the beach. Great how we'd jounced along on the back of Time, oiling its wheels, stoking its engine from beer to banana mint brandy—flying the whole time without planes.

Fly in the morning. Today? And three notes: Call. Call Leyla. Call.

Chapter 16

Leyla had called from her grandmother's on Sunday and it was Monday night before I caught her—2 flights, 2 lectures, films on the Pacific, airplane recognition, intelligence briefings.

I told her I couldn't talk, people all over.

"Well, *I* can talk. And Will. Two things. One, and most important, You, ohhh, you don't deserve this, youuu bastard."

"Hey—"

"Shut up. Now, listen. Oh Will, Will, this is so exciting! Now, what do you think of *this* . . . "

What did it matter what she said?

"—so Allie and I, Lil and Bess are ALL going to come down there! Alright?"

"*What?*"

"We're all four coming down!"

They were collecting coupons, buying, stealing, begging gas for the trip.

"Leyla! Leyla! Evan, my roommate, Evan?"

"Yes, the wild one—"

"Yeah—"

"—who rooms with the other wild one."

"Well . . . Evan, Evan siphoned some high octane gas, some aviation gas, from a wreck. He has a twenty gallon drum in our closet right now. Full to the top!"

"Twenty gallons? That'd take us . . . God, that'd take us . . . I don't know how far! Oh! Will, I can't believe all this! And, wait, you know what we're doing? Every gallon of gas we're plotting on our map. Allie's little car gets about 19 miles on a gallon and right now we're almost to South Carolina!"

"Yeah, but *when*, Leyla? When?"

"Well, I have to wait and so, my dearest flyer . . . you do too. Ohh, isn't it exciting? I can't believe we're doing it. We have promises of gas and when we get it we're going to hop in and OFF to Florida where the dive-bombers play."

"Hey, with that aviation gas you'll be flyin' low!"

"—hoping for Thanksgiving break . . . but, God, that might be too late, right?"

"Yes, ohh well, yeah, well we finish up around November fifteenth, depending on weather—"

"So *soon?*"

"I thought I told you, but, well, *weather* is a big—"

"Listen, we're coming down! And you can bank on it . . . even if . . . we have to sell our bodies!"

"Leyla! . . . don't talk like that!"

"Just joking . . . Will? I was joking. But now I've made myself cry. I love you so much. Will, Will, Will."

"Hey, look," even as the dream was receding, "Leyla, if you *can't* make it—"

"I said we 're gonna get down there!. I'm doing this, for *you*. Some . . . great," her voice got dreamy, "grand . . . adventure, like . . . you're gonna laugh . . . a *CRUSADE!*"

———

The fever, the disease hit us shortly after that talk. She was coming down, I could count on it and forget it. As for the twelve of us going through, we looked in each other's eyes and saw a glaze-mixture—happiness, a rocklike conviction that we were being called on at last, that we were needed, then a cover of joy which increased daily as we became more and more familiar with the SBD, knowing we were one month away from overseas. We flew two and three flights a day, with briefings before and after each flight so close to flying because it was the future, the now and the past; what we were about to do, were doing, had just done, bringing it all back. 'Intelligence Briefings' on the war and films from all the major areas of action: the new Italian government declared war on Germany; mine-laying German subs still off the east coast of the U.S. The Russians had launched a major drive against the Germans from the bridgeheads on the Dnieper River. A huge raid by American B-17's on the ball-bearing center in Schweinfurt: "very successful," we were told, only we lost so many B-17's that day raids were stopped. The secret report said nearly 70 out of 291 shot down, and 55 damaged, so, almost half were gone or out of commission. We heard these reports not as outsiders, but for the first time it was ourselves we were hearing about.

In blacked-out rooms at one-hundredth of a second slides of freighters, battleships, fighters, bombers—the Zeke, the Jack (newest Zero), the Betty. We had critiques and briefings after every flight and, slowly, some ideas were changing. What, after all, did we know about it? One lecture with movies showed us how anti-aircraft no longer shot at individual planes but covered an area. *Not firing at planes?* That did stop me. An area? Not firing at planes? Nobody else was surprised, they took it in with all of the other material, just now beginning to convert young starry-eyed flyers into combatants. RM looked at me as if I were from another planet. "It was found," he told me slowly, "that they can shoot down a higher percentage."

"'Percentage'!? What kind of damned *war*—!"

They not only thought it was funny but quoted me, the 'war romantic' Was I crazy?

When we didn't have night formations or evening glide-bombing— sweet roar-singing down, clean of flaps—we went to Deland to our own bar, Ceci's-See-Through, where we slugged a few 'caps' of brandy in octagonal snifters—the new Lafayette escadrille.

At first Daytona was only for weekends. Back late Sunday night, then it was dawn on Monday, then maybe back on Monday night.

Four days after her call Ziegler dove into the target. The tough college wrestler with long ape-like arms, the one who had given me a wrestling lesson and talked about 'After the war.'

If his plane had been a bomb he'd have scored a bull's-eye.

Then Zimmer's engine cut out on take-off.

Death was looking for 'Z's that week. But Zimmer walked away, speaking his Yale-y drawl, " . . . thought I could get it under control before those high tension wires . . . "

Stood it on its nose, stepped out, down the wing and away from the smoking animal, talking calmly to the startled meat-wagon occupants.

Two more cut-outs-on-takeoff. Water in the gas tanks. All flights grounded. Off to the beach.

Dubya D. and RM were worried about us and said so.

"I only said flying's risky enough without taking chances."

I was irked; "What did we *choose* this for? To worry? To live forever?"

"*I'm* just saying . . . besides, Clare'll be here in two days, and I want to live till then."

And if Leyla comes? I mean, *when*?

Dubya D took it up, speaking to Hebert and myself, "Look, I've seen you guys since Pensacola . . . even Memphis, Will. And the trouble you got yourself into, dog-fighting with an instructor!"

"I didn't know it was a damn' instructor!"

"You've missed the point—" Dubya D said, with acid.

RM explained for him, "Willy, he's just saying that, with all the warnings at Memphis, Elimination Base, about being kicked out, why take a chance and dog-fight—"

"With *anyone*," Dubya D burst in, unable to stop himself.

And more of the same. Sad, sad we didn't feel the same about this world-saving skill.

Then Dubya D did put something between us, at least the two of us. "You know, Willy, even for the twelve of us, there are the Sanes and the Crazies, *and you two*," he said, as if the conviction had, at last, burned its way out of him, "are definitely not among the 'Sanes'."

Hebert was laughing his high-pitched giggle. Instead, I felt ashamed and hated it that some of us were trying to fly safe. No, we *had* to fly close, we *had* to zoom in to formations and skid into place 'hot,' we *had* to go down and kiss the earth. And until he spoke up I had looked on Hebert and myself as only "a little wilder." I thought we'd weeded out all of those who "give a shit" when they left for multi-engines.

At Pensacola we had won our wings. But here at Deland it had dawned on us—from thinking we were good to the realization. No, we were better than that.

They went on about it, "I mean, shit, Willy, you and Evan (and *that* bastard . . .), well, I mean, like this morning, your propeller was chewing my wing."

Then, on the ground, after a few remarks it was okay again. The happy fever. Nothing could stop it. Not the nights when we weren't flying, not the mornings before going up, not the weekends which we crushed. Every hour closer, another day, another week. Days ripped off that calendar in our heads and the going music. Beer in the afternoons on the beach was like cotton candy before the circus. How did we feel about Ziegler? His new wings and dreams of glory? Bull-neck and strong arms into the target? There wasn't one of us who believed it could happen . . . .to us. Well, maybe a few of the 'Sanes.'

So, the weekends got longer, back to base in Jorge's beat-up, long Buick convertible early Monday in time for the flight, hung over or still drunk. The "chief" glowered at us but the major actually talked to us about moderation. We decided the poor man was stoopid. You don't hear de duck honkin, do ye? "Lissen, you guys better straighten out," Mulligan told us, "Now, there's a little place in town . . . Ceci's, I believe it's called. I want you gentlemen to be there in one hour, I'm going to give you a talk about moderation. Yes, ahem."

These were important times. At "Ceci's-See-Through," named after Cecilia's blouses, we de-briefed ourselves. Besides, there were hardly any guys at the college and these girls, well, who else did they have? As part of the war effort we had to see to them.

No need to worry about getting drunk because you can't fly drunk, can you? Of course not. Scott Lee Hunter, our lone star representative from old San Antone, was not the greatest flyer ever to hit the Marine Corps, flew no better or worse on Mondays than any other day, so he felt it was okay to drink during the week as well. "In fact," Mulligan kept telling him, "you do *better*! I was watching you this morning."

"Yeah," Jorge told Mulligan, "well, I was watching you make love to that palm tree outside of the Baptist church in Daytona, Sunday morning. Did you get her name?"

"Look here, you've made an awful mistake—" Mulligan told him.

"Right! I forgot, it was the *Methodist* church."

Mulligan was so tired of hearing about how we had found him, in full uniform, wrapped around a small palm tree across the street from the church at ten o'clock Sunday morning.

"At least it was a *young* palm tree," said Mulligan, with a look at Scott Lee who had picked up a mother, and not a young one, and taken her out to the casino.

"That woman was forty-five if she was a day," RM reminded him.

"I was drunk," Scott Lee said, 'and besides . . . "

"'Besides', what?"

"I *liked* her," Scott Lee giggled shamelessly. He said the words in such a sneaky way, in such an underhanded way, that it became part of our lore. In the middle of a dive an oily voice might call out; "I *liked* her."

There was a fighter base just a few miles out of Daytona. They flew the tough-bodied pale sky-blue Grumman F4F, the Wildcat. When the wind was from a southeasterly direction they passed directly over the beach, and held the planes down a little longer than necessary to pass over us. We could watch their wings and tell how maneuverable they were—just a touch and a wing dropped or lifted as they hurtled out to sea. My heart went with them, fighters and the South China Seas.

The army and marines had landed on Vella Lavella. In the big air wars over Europe, which went on night and day, the damage inflicted was almost unbelievable but, too, the losses of bombers and fighters. 60 out of 300. These were truly air battles. Thousands of people were killed 20,000 feet over the earth every night, not to mention the bombed out towns. I was thinking of Wonderful, and his mother calling and calling.

German fighters hit them on the way in to the targets; American, British and French fighters opposed them. Then the allied fighters had to return to base for gas, and the anti-aircraft of the cities took over. That lasted until they left the targets. Then the German fighters came in again. With no escort and battered by anti-aircraft the bombers were an easier prey.

I was torn, wanting those air battles and worried about the slaughter. Americans in P-51's, P-38's, and Thunderbolts. And Wonderful Bob lost over there, Bob, whose father had wanted to marry Mamoo. Lost at night, 20,000 feet over Europe.

In India more than a million people died of hunger.

U.S. Navy planes had attacked Marcus Island and the F6Fs had done well again.

And here we couldn't go any faster than we were going so we managed a town girl in Deland, a college girl at Stetson. Daytona was for beach-combing. Secretaries and college girls found their way down for fun and sun on the big flat beaches of Daytona.

"I'm just thinking of those poor bastards over Europe."

"Yeah. I'm drinking to them."

"I believe we better have another round."

"It's the only honorable course."

Scott Lee, Mulligan and I had Deland girls and they were always for going out, if only to drive around Deland and park somewhere. We were back in Arkansas, smooching away.

It gave me fits thinking about Leyla. Was I any better than those bird-dogs, as RM put it. He, RM, talked to me like a father. Leyla's coming down so straighten up. After two hours of mooning and spooning I got tired of it. Scott Lee could go for an endless amount of time. Mulligan would start declaiming after a while—he really could not shut up for long. Scotto could lie there with his mouth against Nancy Ann's mouth forever. Once I asked him if he was in love with her and the look on his face said, 'Why didja bring that up?'

One night I decided to watch. The streetlight was shining on them, eyes closed, even mouths closed, pushed together. Nothing was moving, not their jaws, their mouths or their lips.

All four of us were in back; me and Jimma, Nancy Ann and Scott Lee. And we were all over each other. Jimma was a sweet, fiery girl with a conscience about the war and us flyers. Jimma had taken care of me the night I was throwing up, got my name from Jorge, called me, got dates for Mulligan and Scott Lee, and it really irritated her when we dropped a hint about our other girls or going out beach-combing. In fact it drove her wild. She kept guessing we were out for a good time but she wanted to believe different. "Are you guys out to get all you can? From anybody who comes along? Is that it? Well, and if it *is*! Well, you fly boys can just go straight to hell." Shades of Maryanne way back in Arkansas.

Now why was it I had to get the one with a conscience? Old sleepy Nancy Ann was there for the taking, she just lay back, put up her mouth and relaxed. As for Hilda, Mulligan's Hilda, she was crazier than any of us. She also had the car. And let Mulligan drive it till he began making speeches. Then she would make me drive and Hilda and Mulligan would get in back—Nancy Ann and Scott Lee hardly noticed the change.

Sometimes Jimma and I would get out of the car and walk and talk and I began to realize she was uniquely her own person. She loved a song called "Racing with the Moon," and she would grab my hand whenever it played. It was after one of her fits about trying to get every girl who came our way and I hadn't seen her for three or four days. We were on the beach when up came Jimma with Ralph, her rich, older friend and friend of the family, a person who loved flying and loved to hear about it—he had a heart condition, I believe. Ralph hung around with her and us. He was always available to drive us anywhere and usually had a couple of rooms on the beach for changing. Muncrief thought he was a spy.

Jimma told me he did it for *us*, out of the goodness of his heart, because he wanted to do something for the war effort, she explained, to do something for us "young flyers going off to war."and she was hurt because we took advantage of him. This was one of the things about Jimma that made me laugh. Of course we took advantage of him. He wanted us to.

So, Mulligan and I were walking the beach full of the going fever, in love with Leyla, half in love with my Stetson girl, her long beautiful hair and limpid "lake-eyes"—I thought about Cacksy Jack and falling in love every few minutes—and here comes Jimma. When we weren't flying or partying I put in some time worrying about myself and what, after all, was I doing and how many people could I be in love with and what about Leyla? Was she seeing Derek again? Someone else? Was I worth her little finger? And, more to the point, was I ready to get married?

Well, Jimma was very cool at first and then she asked me into one of the dressing rooms Ralph had rented so we could talk and I thought, alright, this is it. And I was thinking about Leyla and if I would or not, because even if I felt guilty about kissing these others I wasn't screwing them, just going a ways and that couldn't be helped. And so we closed the door and were on the bed talking, and she wanted to know if I was really serious about her and so forth and I was getting more serious by the minute because we were all over that bed and in between her lectures she was kissing me back and I'd think this is it, then she'd stop me again and talk and stop me for a while then give in again until it dawned on me that she was really in love and was trying to say something, and I didn't want to hear it, because to try and figure it out, what we, the twelve of us, were going through and how, for some reason, we weren't worried about being killed but there was something about it, what she was saying and about IT, too, that made me wild. The very something I couldn't even think about because it made my brain ache. I honestly didn't know what I or we were up to, unless it was exactly what she said, so, I mean, we knew but we couldn't stop it. Even Dubya D and RM keeping an eye on each other— RM married and Dubya D engaged to RM's sister, due to be married in a month—would get drunk and end up with someone and feel bad for a while and, ohhh shit, it didn't bear examining. We couldn't wait and we couldn't go faster, so it wasn't exactly getting everything while there was time but there it was, now come over here you little fox, no, now stop, just *stop* and let me catch my breath.

Outside the waves pounded the beach and those little tough-bodied F4F's were hurtling out to sea preparing for war and all hell breaking loose around us, in us, and Jimma trying to make sense of it all ohhh, Jimma.

One day I fell in love again. Four or five of us on the beach with three girls from Kentucky toward the end of our time when our heads were turning even faster. Well, RM was out of it and, as a matter of fact, he and Dubya D thought I should be out of it also and I was getting some heavy looks from them. And lectures about Leyla and exactly when she was coming down. Clare had just left. Sarah had come down with Clare for Dubya D, Evan was there but he was so shy he wasn't in it. When I joined them Scott Lee was talking to the most beautiful girl. There, that was it, sometimes I couldn't even remember what Leyla looked like. And, then, Leyla was wayyy up there. Well, this Pinky from Kentucky—the whole state was suddenly a cornucopia of wonderful things—and she was right next to me.

"Do you realize the second letter of your nickname and the second letter of my name is exactly the same?"

"Yeah, and 'Kentucky' and 'Louisiana' both have a 'u' in them?"

"Right! Maybe we should get married."

Her skin was so fair, her body and face so perfect and every word that fell from her mouth was a miracle.

Poor old Scott Lee had a flight and had to get back to the field. RM, Hebert and I had checked out in field carriers but Scott Lee needed extra time. Off he went.

"Hate to see you go, old man."

"Yeah, I'll bet."

"We'll protect Pinky, don't worry."

"Hell with you guys. Pinky don't speak to them while I'm gone."

"Not a word," she yelled after him.

We took the three girls, Pinky and her two friends to the fair, up in the Ferris wheel. "Ooooh," she gasped.

"'Ooooh!'?" I was in love.

Then I was diving straight down thinking about her. Hanging on the straps watching the earth come up at me. We had learned so much since those first flights. If we were coming down and the wind was blowing us off target we took a "step" over, corkscrewed around and straight down again. Aim, hit the toggle switch to drop, clean the plane of flaps still in the dive, feel the speed build up as the plane friction lessened, like an arrow in a dive faster than fighters. A power-speed climb to the roof of the world, sailing up gravity-free like our own strength unstoppable, up and up climbing with throttle fire-walled, sailing into formation again with that free wild blood-rush-blood-cleansing dive still in us.

The next squadron had begun training, and the next, and the next. We were ten days from finishing, depending on the weather. That drunken feeling was constant. It was a party from one activity to the next and on the way.

Leyla? I hadn't heard from her in two weeks, nearly three.

RM was telling us about the mess boys and how they were a sacrifice to the war. RM the great jazz-lover and fan of negro music wanted us to take the mess boys up in the gunners' seats of our dive-bombers and so it happened.

They were a little suspicious but there we were, five anyway, all ready to go. It wrenched my heart to see them, so primitive, so untrained. We had to do everything for them, explain how to put the helmet on—some of them had not even seen movies of planes—how to adjust the parachute, and explain what it was for, insisting nothing would happen.

Off we went; Mulligan, RM, Scott Lee, Evan and I and I knew that Evan and I would not have them use their parachutes no matter what happened. We'd land the plane somehow. Shit, they'd probably kill themselves jumping out.

We went up, flew formation for a while, turns and a little tail-chase. I asked my new rear seat gunner how he liked it and all I could understand was bubbles and noise from back there. I had explained to him how to use the microphone, to "key" the button at the top of the mike and speak into it, but once he "keyed" it he forgot to let go and the "shhhh" of his transmission was with us the rest of the flight.

When we got back I felt we were comrades, this grinning young colored man so foolishly proud and happy about his flight.

What courage it had taken for them to go up with us. What did they know about us? Maybe we would try and make them sick or scare the hell out of them.

"Mah'n we went UP deah. . . . How high we wuz??"

"About 8000 feet."

"Eight THOUSAND!!!" He staggered back.

We were lacking any further excuse to stay with them but something held us together, something absolutely new in my life. Somehow Sally was involved. Her primitive ways, her wisdom. For all of us, even Evan, there was a bond between us. They had trusted us and, well, we straightened up and flew right. They were thanking us and instead of saying 'welcome' I felt like thanking them. There were stars in young Murchison's dark eyes and a shine in his dark face.

After our staid squadron party, playing bingo and eating watermelon with the major, his wife, and Crow, Chief Duck Honking and the Duck's wife—both wives watched us with a little more suspicion than friendliness because the chief looked on us as a "wild crew"—we went back and had a private party in RM's room and invited the mess boys, the ones who had flown with us, and got to know a different kind of wildness.

These mess boys were out to get drunk and "right now!"

They hoisted and put down whatever we had. We were laughing with them and at them; RM was giving us his faces, his lightning glance meant, 'ja see that?' 'Look!' 'Watch this!'

No doubt of it he was on their side and, again, his idea was *do* something for them. It impressed me and yet, what's he up to? Why is he doing this?

Then I saw the way they acted and it touched me, maybe more than anything in my training so far. Here was a whole population that I had, all my life, taken for granted. And their lives were being interrupted too. They also had families and wives. They served us young sprouts, us officers, and we didn't want to hear from them. We wanted more of this or that and no backtalk. Only recently we were hearing, with increasing frequency, "Ain' got no mo'." It was now something of a rebellion.

Only RM was different. He let them play his records when he wasn't there, he arranged our flight with them, he had them in for drinks. And they had responded like kids. Happy kids. Then the party. There was Dean, and Murch (my crewman), Biker, Bill-bob and Tiny.

Dean and Murch were the leaders, the talkers, and by the looks of it those two, at least, would be drunk inside of ten minutes. They drank explosively, as if the whole thing might be stopped in the next instant, no idea or care what they were drinking. Here's to ya, "Shoooo, man!"

First we were drinking with glasses and ice but soon enough were toasting each other, all sorts of toasts, and drinking straight out of the bottles. Glenvale Castle, a scotch no one had ever heard of. "Aged" it said but whether for a half hour or a month was anyone's guess, only these guys, these new . . . friends might as well say, didn't question it. Hadn't we taken them flying? And gotten them back to the ground safely?

"Listen, a good landing is when you walk away from it in one piece!"

"Or just walk away from it."

Why, shure, I'll have some of that . . . and some of that too. Shooo, *whatchew laughin at Tiny?*

"An' here's to you . . . offsahs, you pilots!"

They drank. We drank. Passed bottles around, each one saying a few words.

Mulligan: "Yeah, we're pilots, we pile it here and we pile it there."

"Wait! Now, one thing . . . one thing. . . . How long [giggle], how long it take to learn . . . dat?"

"To fly?"

"Yeeeeeaaaahhhh. How long?"

"To fly like Scott Lee??? Shit, no time at all!"

They laughed. We laughed. Pass the bottle.

"To the messhall men!"

"Yeaaaahhhhh," we all drank to that.

"To the pilots . . . wait . . . to de bes' pilots on DIS base!"

Ohhh, we drank to that. Yes. And just as I was wondering, because we had been drinking an awful lot in a short time and they, those guys, twice as much as we had, when suddenly Murch was doubled over laughing. "Heah, gimme heah—" Did a little flippy sign with his fingers for the bottle, grabbed at it and almost fell but the intensity, or determination, held him up. He was composing a speech, "We boys in de mess service don't know whaaaayaahh . . . " a wild swing of his bottle arm, "WHAH we goin' in dis navy but ahmna tell yew boys, yew offsahs, scuse me, ha haaaa, Lawwwd . . . " Dean and the others were doubled over laughing at Murch, but he shushed them and, still laughing, "no mattah whaahh ah is . . . nomatta*whah*, ah'll serve you ginna-mins with de greatest pleasure," he drank a long drink and passed the bottle.

Dean was touched too and with a glint and confident smile, "Lissen . . . ef ah be's on de USS. . . . Whatevah be de USS dey put me on, ahmna treat yew flyboys right!" He drank and passed it and around it went. Each person adding something. Toasts to each pilot, to each messboy.

Over to Tiny, who had been quiet till now, "Hey!!" he shouted. "'Ah don' care ef ah be's on de USS *CAWLIFLOWER*" he shouted the word to the skies, "Ahmna treat yew boys RIGHT!"

"Heah, gimme dat. Ef ah be's on de USS *STRINGBEEEEEEEEEEN*, ah sees any you ginnamins, ah do enny*thing for yew*!!"

Pilots from other squadrons were trying to get in to see what the commotion was, they were pushed out. Zimmer came in and warned us, there were complaints about the shouting and noise from this room.

The bottles were empty, the mess boys were falling over chairs, laughing uncontrollably. Tiny was halfway to the floor, his knees locked together, feet splayed out laughing. We had to get them to their quarters without the mess officer seeing them.

" . . . DE SS COLLARD GREENS!!!"

"Shut up Murch . . . Shoooo."

We took them out of a side door and walked them all the way to their barracks and the whole time it was more of the same.

"Ah don' care WHAT it is . . . "

" . . . de SS *ANGELFOOD CAKE*, AH HELP YEW BOYS, CAUSE YEW DE BEST . . . "

Endless handshakes all around and again, slaps on the back, so long, take care of yourself and good luck, good luck, good luck, yeahhh.

We came back, drunk and talking just as sentimentally and really drunk, maybe dangerously so but we all understood what had happened. It was with us forever, maybe more for Scott Lee and RM and me and Evan, all being from the south. That's when I realized that Evan had disappeared . . . maybe an hour before, 'cause that good Catholic boy might steal aviation gas and even an airplane or two but he was no drinker. Well, neither was I, and when he came up to me with a worried, mischievous, cracked-grin, he not only knew I was drunk but had to tell me twice:

"Man, you better straighten up. That gurrl is here to see you!!"

"Whaaat?? Girl?"

"Yeah, from Massachusetts, you know, *your wife-to-be!*"

Chapter 17

Hebert, all spiffed up and ready for supper, cap in belt, hair still wet from a shower, caught me outside of our room. He was laughing, no, snickering.

"Great friend!" I stared at him, wondering, really wondering about his clean life; mass in the morning, gas scavenger at night. A boy scout gone berserk.

"Heyy, don't blame *me*! Ha, I didn't make you drink all that stuff. I cleared outa there when you guys started all that toasting. Nooo, don't blame it on *me*."

"Well, Christ! You're *laughing*. I'm drunk! And this is important! Where is she?"

"'She'? There's four of 'em. Down there in the lobby, I guess. That's where I last saw 'em. With a bunch of bird-dogs hangin' around."

Through that crowd and suddenly, with a screech, she was in my arms.

But everything else was unreal so that fact took its place alongside the party in RM's room. Hugging. Looking at her. She had to know I was drunk. Holding that body, looking at all the faces suddenly dear to me. All the faces in hers.

"Will! God, you . . . smell . . . you're a little drunk? Will!!!"

She hugged me hard, trying to get past the drunk.

"You're here! Here in Deland!" I was trying to get my two sides together, the drunk talking to the other because the drunk had no problem with miracles it was the other one that didn't believe.

"Now you know how I felt? You see?? Do you know?? Do you see??"

"I see. I see, yes I see!" As a matter of fact I wasn't seeing too well. And focusing was an effort.

"I told you we were coming down! I *told* you!!"

I was beginning to notice things. RM, Hebert (grinning, then laughing outright), Scott Lee, Mulligan, Zimmer, Jorge and at the edges of this half circle were the big three; Allie, Lil and tiny Bess.

Lil had it all planned.

The whole base had been transported to Cambridge.

They, the three—somewhere between sisters, deadly enemies, chaperones—greeted me with a guarded excitement. I remember that. And whatever Lil felt she had a plan and was itching to lay it out.

Hebert signaled that he was going in to eat. Jorge, the dark one, came up and I introduced all of them—mainly with an idea for Jorge, Scotto and Mulligan to take them out.

We moved over to a corner of the big lobby, Lil announced: "Will, we made this trip for Leyla, and . . . for you . . . and . . . for the hell of it," everyone laughed, "But we certainly hope, ha haa, that your roommate can part with some of his airplane gas for—"

"For Christ's sake," Jorge shushed her up, "You want us to be strung up by our thumbs?"

"—sorry about that. Well, anyhow, you got the idea . . . "

"It was a fantastic trip," Bess said to me in a whisper of friendship. I was playing it over and over in my mind. That picture was very clear. Also that Hebert had not gone in to eat, had been looking . . . yes, at Bess. Evan the pure. He was still here, not in the mess-hall.

Leyla squeezed my hand hard, "You smell like a brewery!"

I shook my head, "I'm sorry, sorry, oh Leyla."

"It's okay . . . Lieutenant-I-love-you," squeezing my hand with all her strength.

"Yeahh, it's really drunk out," said RM, red-faced and laughing, then walking away.

Lil was telling us all they were going to take Leyla and me to town or wherever and leave us to our own devices. They were going to get a place out on the beach or in town, and we'd meet for breakfast, or sometime later in the day.

I thought, RM knows places, Clare and he, and started in to the mess hall to get RM, but Leyla pulled me back, "Ohh, no!" she said. "You're not getting away, youuu drunk!"

"Scotto . . . RM, get . . . RM . . . RM knows . . . I'm sorry . . . "

"Don't say that any more, Will. You didn't know . . . only. I just wish . . . ohh, it doesn't matter, it'll be okay."

She *was* disappointed. And it kept coming back to me.

Scotto brought RM back and I introduced the whole group, and they laughed because I guess they had already done that, or maybe I did.

Meanwhile Mulligan and Jorge were making moves; all very polite: How long did it take to drive down? Oh, really? And from the girls: You're all pilots? What kind of planes?

RM told Lil, who stood almost eye to eye with the flashy RM about a place in town, a little hotel where Clare stayed when she came down.

"Do I look terrible?" Leyla was saying, and more than anything it made me look at her. My head was spinning and I kept catching her on the go-round.

"God . . . you're so *drunk!*"

"'*Terrible*'?"

"Can you even see? Well, we didn't get any sleep. We drove straight down and just switched around driving."

"'*Terrible*'?"

"Yes, damn you, can you answer?" She was pulling on my arm, looking so fantastic, even spinning around.

She yanked my arm again, waiting. "You're drunk, youuu drunk!"

My nose in her hair when, from far away, I heard Lil telling everyone, " . . . so those two can not be counted on for anything."

I looked up, the Black Beauty, Jorge, had moved over, grabbed my arm, "Look, son, my boy, ahem, yess, ahem" imitating Mulligan, "if you'd like to borrow the car for tonight??"

"Oh, yes. Great . . . *Dad!*"

"'*Dad*'? What is this? He . . . *he* can't drive!"

Meanwhile, Mulligan, the perfect gentleman, was talking to Allie, then looking at his watch, 'Let's see, the invasion begins in abouuuut,' then looking up, a few more words to her.

Jorge jogged my elbow to watch Mulligan.

"Yeahhhhhhhh!"

"The oooollld smoothie," said Jorge.

So, when I looked up again, or when I got the next installment of what was happening, the girls would go to the little Crown Hotel in Deland to freshen up. I was to take a shower, then Leyla and I would follow in Jorge's car, The Boat, with Leyla driving. Jorge, the gentleman, gave me the key, told her he trusted me, " . . . even drunk. Besides, The Boat is indestructible."

Mulligan, Jorge and Scott Lee "The Old Scow," who had started talking to Bess, would get Evan to drop them off in town and, and . . . was Evan going?

"The gas!" Lil said to me, before they left, "I'm holding *you* responsible for that! Will? Lieutenant? Do you hear me?"

A shower and clean clothes, brushed my teeth about three times so I was now clean and drunk, and kept thinking oh, two hours, just two hours to recover.

We found Jorge's Boat, the long Buick convertible.

"No wonder," Leyla said.

"What?"

"Nothing."

I started it for Leyla and was happy to let her drive to the hotel. She slid over, I walked around got in and Leyla was arms around; "Ohh, Will, Ohh, Will, I'm here and I love you and you're so *drunk*, and when will you be alright again?"

"I'm okay."

She was explaining about Lil . . . I was dreaming of an hour, one hour to collect myself . . . that Lil was a great friend, only a little bossy but she did things that had to be done. She had the feeling, Leyla told me, that if *she* didn't do it, it wouldn't get done.

"Jorge's . . . he's Spanish."

Leyla laughed hysterically, "Will, you're so drunk."

"Stop, Leyla. Stop the car, drive over there. *Stop!*."

"Why? Are you going to get sick?"

"No!"

"Are you feeling sick?"

"No! No! No! Just stop!"

She pulled off the road into the campus drive and stopped under the oaks, turned off the engine.

"Leyla, I'm . . . drunk, but you have to listen. I have to tell about the party, why . . . the party."

Every time I said her name I was coming closer to realizing . . . she *was* here. All I had to do was be here too.

"Yes. I think it was real . . . sweet . . . thoughtful that you flew the mess boys. The one, 'RM,' told me, while you were taking a shower he was, kind of, chaperoning me and told me about it . . . You took them flying? The colored mess boys?"

"See, it was a party for *them*, after the flight. I couldn't leave. You should have seen. We *couldn't* leave. And Leyla . . . Leyla, I can't say it right because . . . I won't say it again, the stuff we drank, but something happened, and, see, it wasn't just drinking. Okay?"

"Will, I came down for us to be together and . . . I don't know, to find out how you feel. And I want you to know I'm not *mad* . . . I just wish—"

"Wait! Got to explain . . . so glad . . . you're here and so, well . . . what I'm trying to say it wasn't just getting drunk . . . See, after the flight RM had them into the room for drinks. The mess boys. So important . . . I feel like I can't. Say it—" I felt like crying. Huge lump in my throat.

"Go on, Will, tell . . . just tell it."

"That's the problem. I don't know if I can—"

"Alright. Alright, I'm listening."

"Well, I've told you about Sally. New Orleans. My cook. I grew up with her. You have to meet her. It's about that . . . these colored boys, these mess boys. Something I didn't see, till RM. Well, RM used to talk to them. They'd come in and listen to his jazz; Duke Ellington, Count Basie, so he got to know them. And that's how he arranged it. Take 'em up? Sure, okay. RM's a good friend, I'd do it for RM. Then we saw them out there ready to fly, pushing and shoving each other, laughing, but ready. You know that takes some courage—"

"Wait. You mean these mess boys don't fly, ordinarily?"

"No, Leyla, the mess hall, the 'Officers' Mess' is all they know. Never flown. Don't know up from down. And that's what got me, at first. Then, this young . . . Murch was gonna be with me. Leyla, they're like *us*, young, crazy. But, no college, no education. That's not it. I guess I've always taken for granted that coloreds don't go to college . . . no, not *that*. They don't *know* anything. *Anything* . . . 'bout . . . the world. No, that's not it. . . . But it struck me. How we're different. . . . And, you know, Leyla, I'm getting less . . . drunk—"

"Well, yes, ahem, ummm," she said, imitating Jorge imitating Mulligan. 'Course you are.'"

"God, can't believe . . . you're here. Alright, maybe that's when it started. Because, see, he was flying my rear-seat, the rear-gunner's seat. No controls back there, so the guy in the rear's helpless. I mean, it's up to me. That's why most of us wanted fighters. Just one person. Responsible, you know . . . one . . . so—you see? This is something . . . *southerners*, and all the time, without *seeing*. These guys . . . forgotten. No one cares . . . what happens . . . worries about them, and so, the war, *see*? Leyla . . . I love you . . . so glad you're here! . . . but nobody pays attention, and what is war for them? Washing dishes, serving *us* . . . younger than they are. I mean, no chance of getting out. Serving meals . . . Officers' Mess . . . Florida. See? The glorious war for freedom!"

Was I getting it? My head was gone, but I was getting a piece of it.

"So, we fit them . . . parachute, Mae West, helmet and they . . . so eager and excited, they were 'going up!' and maybe it started then. This feeling. . . . See? Doing for *them*. Not *them* . . . for us . . . understand? But all my life I've seen coloreds serving . . . sweeping . . . sweeping, washing so it wasn't that. It was now, *now*, two of us going to do something together. *I* had to help *him*. His life in *my* hands. ME serving *him*, see? Same plane . . . his life in my hands. I was explaining about parachute and how to use it, how to jump out and get free. And I was looking in his eyes and . . . Leyla, I can't *tell* you." I could feel tears coming out of my eyes, drunk or not, "Leyla . . . " She put her arms around me and hugged and hugged.

"I know," she was saying, "I know! It's okay. And, Will . . . something else . . . Will, I'm *here* and you're right next to me . . . and the trip so crazy but so exciting . . . okay, go on, tell me—"

I was afraid she meant okay for being drunk. Was that it? "Ohh, no!" she laughed.

"So, I looked at him, in his eyes. Innocent. I tell you I can't explain it. I saw myself . . . is that crazy?

"I saw him, or me, innocent. Okay? Waiting for me to tell him. I had his life in my hands. And I was so . . . happy. To do something *for* this colored boy. Leyla, they're not dumb. Not ignorant. Well, I mean, he's ignorant but intelligent, you know, *bright*. I could see it. But he knew nothing. I told him wait there and I went over to Evan and told Evan if something happens these guys won't get out. And we agreed, no matter what happens to the plane we'll stay with it, bring it in. And, see, Leyla. Not a hero . . . I'm not saying that, I didn't save his life, okay? Nothing went wrong. An ordinary flight but, you see, I *would* have. So, the parachute, for them, just something to sit on. I told him we wouldn't use it, no matter what happened. To forget it. Okay, so we went up . . . a tail chase, just kind of follow-the-leader, nothing scary. We flew and it made me feel—"

I was getting choked up again.

"I felt good. He loved . . . he *loved* it. He keyed the mike and started talking. Never took his finger off so I couldn't hear anything but him—not the other planes, the tower or anything else, just Murch screaming from the rear seat. He had the key held down the whole flight.

"When we got down he was . . . Just a little kid someone gave a treat. You understand, Leyla, he treasured it. I *know* that. I did something for him. For Sally. All these years, I was . . . aching to do something like that. I *must* have been. And I did. Now, the funny part . . . I was grateful. He's thanking *me*? *I'm* grateful. Leyla, now listen, because I'm a little crazy, and I don't know if this is right, but something *moved* . . . in me."

Leyla was crying, I don't know why. I was, she was.

"So, we had this party, for them, you know, in RM's room. They were toasting *us*. So happy they were wild. Being accepted by us, young, I don't know what, us fly-boys, they call us. And, well, we know they shouldn't be calling us that, they know it, we know it, but it was all fine. They drank to us, we drank to them, and, Leyla . . . you just got here, and I'm drunk, and I haven't even welcomed you, and I love you, but I had to tell you. They—"

We kissed for about five minutes and suddenly I knew she was there and she had been listening. She had been there all the time I babbled on. "And, just one last thing . . . they toasted us. They called us the BEST! We couldn't leave. Understand . . . couldn't . . . And . . . so, we drank, I don't know how much or what we drank, but those boys were drunk. I mean . . . *drunker*. They drank more than we did . . . drinking with the 'offsahs,' huge gulps of the stuff . . . terrible Scotch. God, my head's throbbing . . . well, anyhow, we got them back to quarters, and shook hands . . . Jesus, about a dozen times we shook hands, wished each other . . . oh Christ, slapped each other on the back, shook hands. So, I was crawling back to my room and Hebert, who ducked out, he ducked out, then Hebert tells me you're here."

I couldn't shut up, " . . . what is the war for them? You understand me, Leyla? See, this is about *us*, about the south. And what is the war for them? Serving meals at the Officers' mess?" I couldn't stop but I was un-drunking myself, to focus on one thing but the strange part was it was happening

now. I hadn't realized till I was trying to tell her, till it came out, not really
till now.

" . . . He held down the key and all I heard was bubbles and laughing
. . . no matter. He didn't know. You understand, Leyla? He treasured it. I
know that. Understand? See? My treasure?"

"Yes, yes, Will. I'm so glad you did that."

Drunk, with my feelings right at the top, ready to let go anyway, "I am
too, Leyla. So glad." Tears were rolling down my face. "I always cry with
you . . . so we *couldn't* leave. Toasting us. It changed my life, Leyla—"

"I hear you . . . lootenant-I-love-you now shut up for a minute. It's great,
now *us!* Me and you together, alright? US! I think it's great and now we're
gonna move right along and—"

"They called us the BEST—"

Leyla was crying too. Flung her arms around me. "It's okay, okay . . .
Will! That's beautiful. I really forgive it. There's nothing to forgive . . . I
think it's great you did it. Oh, my darling. So much we have to talk about.
Let's go to the hotel. I'll clean up and—"

"Okay, but one last thing—"

"No, just shut up, we're going to our own party—"

"Okay, one last last thing. I got a glimpse of something. And the glimpse
tells me these guys, these mess boys, they're *good.* Good as anyone."

"Hug me!"

"Do you see?"

"Hug me!"

Leyla had on an old sweatshirt and under it a thin cotton blouse and a
bra. I thought I'd touch those sweet titties, and didn't even know if oh, they
were mine to touch, or if everything was still on. I decided not to. It wasn't
right, mixing things, then my hands, on their own, and they were like
some tender squirming animals under my hands.

Then we got stuck there, frozen, afraid to move, while a strange sadness
came down on us. And I had the notion. So drunk and so clear. That we
wouldn't . . . that our 'seven' and that we wouldn't . . . because. Then it
closed down. But the sadness, I know it was the same. One sadness. What
time had done. What it would do. And I could almost *see.*

I was *seeing* and even drunk, or because of it, something opened, strange
gift. I was seeing ahead, the wonderful, the awful, the awe-full . . .
moments so good, so terrible, we missed them before they were fashioned.
All of my dreams coming true. *All* of them. And I was not so drunk, only
wiped out, and I lost that vision ahead.

Chapter 18

We backed up Jorge's old touring Buick, with the top up for a change—he usually left the top down and used bailing cans for water—and off to the hotel.

"Do I look terrible?"

"Leyla, come on."

"Well, do I?"

"You asked me that. You're . . . fishing."

"Yes, and what if I am? I need you to tell me, if I don't."

"Welllll . . . "

"Damn!"

"Listen, Leyla. You drove down here without a stop? Well, you look like you just took a ten-hour nap."

"I guess I should have called . . . but I wanted to surprise you."

"Yeah, I know."

"Like you surprised me up at school."

"Well, you did, you surprised the shit out of . . . Ohhh wait. Did I say 'shit'? Ohhh, sh- , oh, I'm sorry."

"You're not sorry . . . you're drunk."

By the time we got to the hotel the others had come and gone, how or with whom we had no idea.

The hotel was really a large apartment house with a haphazard numbering system, no chance of sneaking into their rooms. In fact Leyla had a hard time convincing the woman she was with the girls from Massachusetts who had just left.

"She's my fiancée," I told the woman.

"Well, that's very nice, but you'll have to wait right out here till she returns."

"Leyla, hurry."

I collapsed into an uncomfortable wicker chair and in almost the next instant Leyla was waking me up.

I opened my eyes and there she was, hair still wet.

"I hurried!"

"Okay," I said, in what I hoped was a brave tone. I had no idea what we would do. My mind was not working.

"Listen, Leyla—"

"Hey," she held me by the shoulders and forced me to look at her. "It's alright!"

Her smile sought out my secret eyes.

"You made it down here!"

"Lieutenant-I-Love-You . . . yes, now, we'll find a place, somewhere, anywhere and just be together. That's all. Okay? That's all. Maybe we'll have to sleep in whozit's car, Jorge's car. I don't care."

The woman at her little study table, her "desk," was watching us.

"Let's go."

"I don't allow men and women in the same room," she told us.

"You don't? How come?"

"Come on, Will."

"Because I don't allow that sort of thing."

"*What* sort of thing?"

"WILL! It's okay, we're leaving, Miss."

"No, I don't allow it. Leastwise not here."

"Will, for God's sake—"

Off we went, half a tank and Daytona only 24 miles away.

"Wanta see the ocean?"

"Sure!"

We put the top down and we could hear the cans in back, when we made a sudden turn. "Those are Jorge's bailing cans, to keep this thing afloat," I told her. Leyla was driving, then she pulled over, just for a few minutes she said.

I was cudgeling my brains to ask the right questions, to at least begin them; "So, how long can you stay? I can't stop while you're here. I wish I could. Flying, classes, movies and talks. Well, tomorrow morning I don't have to fly, but I've only seen part of the schedule. A flight in the afternoon, and whatever else they put up there."

That was the closest to getting mad I'd seen so far, "Will, I know . . . I'm not stupid, I *know* that nothing stops just for our visit! I know that!!!"

She turned away, anger and sadness.

"Well, Leyla . . . " I was thinking Leyla, sweetheart, lovely Leyla, but instead I asked her, "How long can you stay?"

"Forever!" she said, still with her back to me and rigid. Rigid with anger I discovered.

I grabbed her shoulders, almost aware of everything between my hands, and pulled her to me. "I even love the way you argue. I hated to say that about the schedule . . . but we're going through this machine, and it's not to the end of the cycle. Ten flights and we're done."

"We can't stay . . . I *have* to be back by next . . . I don't know. I don't want to talk about it. We just got here. In a way I feel like we're still driving down."

"I hate to say something that . . . what makes you sad, makes me sad."

At the same time strange about the program, happy nothing could stop it, how it had its hooks in us.

"I know . . . " She twisted around to me.

"Your guy was lucky," she sighed. "the mess boy . . . I'm lucky. . . . You're lucky. . . . *We're* lucky . . . lucky, lucky."

We started out to the beach again. Nice air, not too cool for November, driving east into the night, into the moon, first quarter moon going down. Or as if I were flying and Leyla next to me in the cockpit on a night flight crossing the ocean; the stars, the night, endless fuel and no interruptions. We could talk, or not, no pressure.

"Will, I'm *dying* for you!"

"You make me feeeeel . . . so lucky."

Daytona's light and, soon enough, the ocean. Up on a rise of the cement road and there it was, vast and roaring. The moon coming down over part of the ocean, light enough to see the big breakers roaring in.

"I think I'm over being drunk, mainly."

"Yes, you're coming back . . . a little."

We drove onto the hard beach until the Coast Guard flagged us down with a big flashlight. He saluted and told us that after sundown there's a sub watch, and no one's allowed on the beach.

The casino, okay, but not the beach. Oh, yes, the war, the Atlantic. France and England straight ahead of us.

"Okay. Thanks."

"Yes sir."

"I love to see you salute, how you salute."

"Oh, you love it, eh?"

"Yeah, wanna make somethin out of it?" She had a jouncy, braggy, little kid's way of saying things.

"Soon as we get a place."

"And," she said proudly. "I have some money. Compliments of my grand-mother. And she knows all about you. Well, something about you."

"Does she have to keep it secret?"

"Yes, for a time. And she thinks it's fine. I showed her your picture. And when she saw it, you know what she did? She hugged me. And gave me money to come down. Now, how's that for a reaction?"

"Yes, ahem, very fine woman! Yes. Now, do you have that little ring? The one that proves you're married?"

"Right here!"

The Florida east coast was dotted up and down with bases: the fighter base at Sanford, dive-bombers at Deland, an amphibious base north of Daytona, right on the ocean, torpedo- bombers at Fort Lauderdale, and a night fighter base down the coast, with radar training and Coast Guard stations every forty or fifty miles. Three or more amphibious training bases and others. Wives and relatives came to see sons and husbands, and places to stay were in constant demand, but Uncle Willie once told me that hotel managers always have a room somewhere which they keep for emergencies.

We drove south along the beach for a place. The moon, a little sliver, like a crib, or like a gondola, was practically sitting in the water, although it was still early, around ten.

OCEAN VIEW HOTEL—ROOMS BY DAY OR WEEK

I swung in and got out. Before I could even reach the desk the big paunchy desk clerk with the gray face said, "No rooms! Sorry!"

"Look, my wife is down just for a—"

"Now, it don't matter about your story, I still got no rooms."

"Well, I like this place and if you could find a room for us, just for two nights."

"I told you, we don't have any rooms."

"Okay," I started away, but stopped, "Listen, my name's *Joseph*, and my pregnant wife, *Mary*, is out in the car. Are you sure you don't have a room? Back in the manger or somewhere?"

The man was shaking his head, half-listening, then, "Your name's *what?*" His mask fell away and he actually looked frightened. Then he continued shaking his head.

I went back to the desk. "You don't have any place at all? Even a single?"

"Nope!"

"How about a closet or something? A room up in the attic?"

"I toldja . . . Lieutenant, but I can give you the name of a place where you might could get a room."

"Okay."

I took it down and left. It was north of the beach and I was feeling downed. I wanted this place, here.

"What did he say?"

Leyla spoke with such an eagerness, 'Well, and what's next for us?' It was okay, not something I had failed to pull off.

We kissed and held and her mouth, so soft and ready, so eager and adaptable, was enough of a miracle. I knew what she meant; any place even the car, with us in it.

"So, we might have to stay in Whozit's Hotel!"

"You mean? The car? I don't *care*."

"Really?"

"My darling. Nooo."

"Well, this guy gave me the name of a place but let's go to the Officer's Club first, it's just a few blocks away, and I have a hunch they've taken Allie and the girls there."

And, sure enough.

None other than Evan came charging over, flushed and happy, "Heyyy! Get your uhh, *self* over here. Excuse me," he said to Leyla, as if he'd been cursing, "we got a bunch of Indians to deal with."

"Coon, have you been drinking?"

"Not so's you'd notice it!" But his face was flushed and he'd been laughing too hard.

There at a big table a duplicate of what might have been the scene on any weekend night except for Evan and the threesome; Lil, Allie and Bess, and, I couldn't believe my eyes, there was old Nancy Ann, Scott Lee's "towny" with that group.

They cheered and yelled. Jorge and Mulligan had not stopped drinking from the party in RM's room. I don't know how they weren't laid out flat.

They all had Indian names, from talking about Chief Duck-Honking. Scott Lee was "Old-Scow-Crossing-Great-Waters." Mulligan was "Big-Wind" or "Wind-over-a-thousand-leaves." Evan was "Coon-of-Swamps," or "Mouth-Free-of-Garbage." Jorge was "Dark-one-of-Many-Names," since he was naming everyone. "No," Mulligan decided, "Driver-of-Long-Boat." He also had named me; "Chosen-of-Fire-Hair."

"No," said Jorge, "Will is, 'Clean-Spoon-Waiting-for-Soup.'"

"Wha-at?" said Leyla.

"You're the soup," said Scott, "but 'clean'? Well . . . "

"Quiet, Old-Scow, Face-of-Mountain, you speak from belly."

Scott had also acquired other names from having had so many extra flights for Field Carrier Landings which he didn't seem to get. "Eagle-of-a-Thousand-Landings," and others about wearing out tires.

They were charged up and rolling, they had named the major, "He-Who-Rolls down-Mountains," and "belly-of-good-things," and Dubya D. "Lemon-no-sugar." Mulligan's Hilda was, "Tall-Willow-No-Apples."

Scott Lee had a wasted silly look on his face but he seemed no drunker than earlier.

"Scotto! Old-Scow, you have field carriers at eight tomorrow morning! You gonna be okay?"

"San Antoooooonn!" he yelled back.

"Face-of-Rock-Mountain," Jorge spoke to Scott Lee sitting there in an alcoholic haze, "Great-White-Father, teacher of young eagles, Stomach-Full-of-Good-Things, say Face-of-Mountain, Hawk-of-thousand-landings be in Thunderbird soon after sun show face."

Mulligan chipped in, "Oh Eagle-destroyer-of-many-tires, no more fire-water this moon, cost Navy much wampum for new tires and hard earth-hit make thunderbird wings sag."

Nancy Ann waved, Jorge caught my eye. Jorge, Evan, RM and I were the only ones who had checked out in Field Carrier Landings so far and Scott Lee was not doing well.

"Scotto, 'Landings-Without-Number . . . '"

"Quiet, 'Father-of-Long-Boat' and you too, 'Used-Spoon,' at end of new moon Face-of-Mountain will check out in field-pretend-boat."

Nancy Ann was there by default only she didn't know it. Bess had chosen Evan. Scotto wasn't even disappointed, he had called Nancy Ann and told her to meet him in Daytona, after supper. When I told them we still didn't have a room Nancy Ann jumped to the rescue.

"I'll call Ralph, he'll get you a place."

"Ralph?"

"Yeah," Nancy Ann turned to Lil, whom she'd been talking to—Lil the beautiful brunette (with baby-fat) whom Jorge, the Black Beauty, had chosen—and explained: "This guy, Ralph, loves flyers and he, well, he sort of adopted these guys. He's got lots of money. I'll call him," and dragged Scott Lee along with her to find a phone.

"*Gentlemen!*" said Mulligan.

"Sit down, Big-Wind!" Jorge ordered, and Mulligan did as he was told.

Evan thought it was very funny and Bess, the over-achiever, the admiral's beautiful daughter, laughed along with Hebert.

"I've never seen her like this," Leyla whispered to me. "She must really like, umm, Evan."

Leyla talked with the girls a few minutes.

I heard only the last of it, Lil asking, "So you're not coming back?" And Leyla, to the whole table, "No, I'm staying with this fly-boy tonight!"

Evan almost choked on that one. Jorge raised his glass.

Lil looking directly at me, announced, "Lieutenant Evan 'Mouth-Free-of-Garbage' Hebert! *For conduct above and beyond the call of duty—*"

"That's 'Coon-in-Swamps'—"

"I told you no more talk about it to the whole world, or you can just *push* that danged car back up to Massachusetts," Evan warned her, but he was laughing.

Lil was bending toward him, apologizing.

"I agreed—" Evan said to me, "aw, I'll tell you later."

It had to be about the gas.

Scott and Nancy Ann came back and she was beaming.

"Go to the Ocean View Hotel and give them this name."

Within an hour we were back at, miracle of miracles, the old Ocean-View Hotel, Rooms by Day or Week.

The desk clerk was embarrassed but coughed up his room, "Yeah, Ralph rents those rooms four/five days at a time. You do realize that it's a single?"

"That's okay."

"That'll be no charge, it's on Ralph. No luggage? You're 'sposed ta have luggage and a wedding license."

Leyla showed him her ring and told him her stuff was at the other place. Tomorrow she'd get it.

"Well . . . bein' as it's Ralph's room," he started off with the key in his hand, up the stairs.

"Well, that's nice of him . . . Ralph," I said, trying to change the subject.

He led us up one short flight of stairs, unlocked our room and left us. The door was closed and we were together.

Slightly larger than a single bed, a wash-stand, a rickety table and bathroom down the hall. It seemed as if we had been waiting a week or more.

"Are we really alone? Are you really okay?"

We sat on the bed, side-by-side, hardly touching.

"You were drunk, and I'm so tired, but we're *alone*, Will."

Now I could feel it, in both of us, not only weary but so self-conscious; we'd been together four hours, our first four hours together, and only now turning to each other.

Hugging impossible position, bodies turned to each other, feet off the bed, trying to talk, to fight off eyes-closing, only know you're back, we're together, mouth of mine, eyes I trade hearts with, bodies we went over so carefully, learned so much and now clothes still on, eyes closing, Leyla you're crying; okay, it's okay, I was, *I* was earlier; yes, yes, you were, such good tears, oh, you are are *are* my darling lieutenant-I-Love . . . can't say, talk in my mouth again, talk in our mouths doesn't matter what we say. . . . Only together, the only only only thing, oh yes, my soul and my heart, I don't care, I don't care if we never make sense . . . say anything I want if I talk in your mouth then it's heart to heart down your throat into heart and back from heart to mine. Ohh, fly-boy, this fly-boy's red-headed lover, you love lover loves you . . . you . . . no, you . . . no, you . . .

And so sleepy, helping each to our selves unguarded, first miles then other distances, travels through clothes of first conversations off, off, off with that, off with first hugs, first smiles, and words, off conventions, off piercing bad scotch and buttons, driving, and talk, off belts, shoes kicked, shirts, her pretty cottons, bra so lucky, down to hair, skin, bare arms, hands to cup, mouths and breath, sighs on breath, and strength from that inexhaustible supply:

"Oooh God, *dying* for this, Will, I don't care what that makes me."

"So awful to forget. Never again forget . . . like this . . . us."

"Talk tomorrow, just . . . you know . . . "

"That's like, haaaa, ask me keep breathing."

Within even a minute Leyla was arching up straining like a cat stretching, straining to the utmost possible; "I'm ohh, Will, I'm . . . ohhhhh, what's better in the, what's love you sooo better, could I love you so soo soooooo in the world, sooo love you, could be in the whole world betterrr, God, oh God!!! Happening, Will! Ohh . . . ohhhhh."

Then undecipherable for minutes after, laughing hugged up, hugged up forever, last memories on earth.

Sometime in the night a spread over us not even then that it was me covering both parts of me, and gone again till bright day.

Chapter 19

"Telephone for Leyla Herndon," said the woman's voice.

Leyla had no muscles. I held her limp body before she began to come around.

"Lil and them . . . " she breathed, as if it were her last.

Her eyes found mine and without another thought she blessed me with a hug and juicy kiss on the cheek.

She put on her plaid skirt and a sweater over nothing, ran a hand through her hair, slipped on her shoes and started out the door.

"Goodbye!" she said, tragicomically. "Don't go anywhere."

She was back in five minutes, slowing herself down to talk. "Will," she said, catching my eyes and both arms.

"Yes? What's happening?"

"RM called the hotel in town to get you out to the field as soon as possible. There's a crash; he said, 'someone's down.'"

"What? They didn't say who? Jesus! It has to be Scott Lee, Dubya D., or Muncrief . . . "

We were in the car racing to the base before she confessed that it was Hebert, her eyes filled with tears.

"I couldn't tell you before—"

"But . . . Evan has already checked out of Field Carriers! We were the first ones! He wasn't even *flying* this morning!"

"Will, that's just what . . . I'm just telling you—"

"Crazy god damned coon-ass—"

Her agonized eyes followed mine then she looked down and came over close to me. She needed something too.

"Just hope to hell it's not him," I said, trying to be calm, although I was feeling sick, somewhere behind my stomach.

We decided to drop her off at the Crown Hotel—in fact I wasn't sure how they had talked their way onto the base yesterday. Movies and flight this afternoon another lecture . . . oh shit, Evan you fucker you better not—

"I swore I wouldn't say goodbye till we have to leave, so . . . take care . . . I'm hoping and, um, praying . . . "

Out at the field I ran into Dubya D., poker-faced, but I guess he might as well have been thinking out loud.

145

"Nobody knows much," he told me, and looked down.

"But he wasn't *scheduled* to fly!"

"Well, he took the flight anyhow . . . they think his engine cut out and he went into the trees."

"So, they're sure it's Evan?"

"Everyone else is accounted for."

"Shit! Shit!"

"Scott is up in the tower or the flight office, and RM's over there, they're trying to pinpoint where he went in. They've sent a crew out there, but it's swamp and jungle, so. . . . "

In the flight office they were asking me if I had known of his plans to take the flight. No, he just liked field carriers. No, he loved it all. No, it wasn't out of character to take an extra flight.

The morning was shot. At ten we reported for the lecture. Recognition: Identification Ships and Planes. The Intelligence Officer told us: "I know you're missing a pilot. I've told the Flight Office. As soon as there's news they'll announce it here."

The class began and ended, no news. Good news? He might be alive in the swamps, he might have been dead for two or three hours.

Scott Lee filled me in about Hebert's aviation gas. When Lil asked Hebert if she could buy some he first wondered how she knew about it, and then, after 'blessing' me out, he told her, "'Shucks, I can't sell it! I stole the danged gas from the navy, how can I sell it? You can have it. You'll need more'n that to get up there to Massachusetts.' Can't you hear him?"

"Scotto, you were on the flight—"

"Well . . . he was behind me in the pattern, cruisin' out, flying wide then coming in to pick up his interval, and the only time I saw him was once I looked back and he was really low to the trees, but you know how he's always. . . . Then Jeff was calling. The LSO in the jeep asked us to check in and Evan was the only one who didn't call. The flight was cancelled; we flew around . . . real swampy area, and came on back."

At twelve forty-five we got the report, they had recovered the pilot; no word whether he was in pieces, dead or critical.

We waited for half an hour near the field where the ambulance would have to pass. Then, way down the road to the field came the meat wagon with something hanging out of the window. Alive! And screaming!

We didn't know whether he was in pain or just nuts.

There they went on to the hospital, with "Moka" (Bird-brain, compliments of Jorge), half his body out of the window on the passenger side, yelling into a microphone, wires dangling from it, "Sorry, Major, I couldn't save your plane but I got the mike! And I'm safe! Yes, old Moka is safe and sound . . . "

By the time we caught up with the meat-wagon we realized he was drunk and raving.

One of the crew on the meat-wagon told us they'd found him paddling around in the swamps in his life raft, yelling and screaming, the emergency rum was gone.

Not content to have been hauled out of the swamp in one piece, Evan got away, walked out to an SBD on the line, pulled the chocks himself, jumped in and took off, without permission, without a fire bottle, without a flight plan, without signing. He took off in the face of a red light from the tower, buzzed the tower on take-off, buzzed us, buzzed the line, broke off over the runway (not in use) and landed in an incredibly short space. He had broken about twelve flight regulations in ten minutes.

It was not until that night that we had chance to question him about any of it. For now he was grounded and in big trouble. For a pilot to be grounded after an accident was the procedure but because of his "Unauthorized Flight Conduct" Hebert would undergo a hell of a lot more.

I called Leyla just before the flight and gave her the good news. She went immediately to tell Bess and the others. Useless. Bess had not remembered anything about his accident, even though Lil later said Bess seemed to be awake when told of the crash.

"Typical," said Lil. "Bess sleeps and nothing gets in the way."

How about tonight? The same lineup? Wonderful, said Leyla. Allie thought Mulligan was a perfect gentleman, well, until later in the evening. Bess was fascinated by Hebert and had never been with anyone quite like him.

"There *is* no one like him," I told her.

"—and Lil . . . well, it's hard to get anything from her. She has a secretive side, but I think Jorge's manner interests her."

"How about Leyla's date?"

"Ohh, I was hoping you wouldn't ask that. Wellll, I better try him again, he's . . . a real 'bronco' as we say," then she laughed, and I could hear one of the others in the background yell out a shocked, "LEYLA!"

"Now, one more thing, Lieutenant . . . " she whispered the rest, "WE are going to be by ourselves and talk. Tonight!"

They were going out for brunch, since it was already after one, and would go back to the hotel and then get ready for us.

When we returned from our navigation flight, sixty miles out to sea, a dog leg, and then back to the field, they questioned me, his roommate, about Hebert's habits and "character"; the Chief about his flight conduct and ability; the Landing Signal Officer; other pilots on the flight. We, his fellow pilots, convinced them that he never drank anything, that he was a clean-living (madman) and that he had just been drunk on the rum from his emergency rations. He had also been hit in the head (three stitches) and, so, he had not been responsible for his conduct. As for the excellent control exhibited during the flight itself, the perfect landing, the distance between the tip of the propeller and the ground objects he passed over, no one brought that up. And so, like a traffic cop who realizes a certain case would be more trouble than it was worth, they decided to drop it. With a warning.

Hebert was temporarily grounded, had to report to the medical doctor and to a psychiatrist for questioning.

"That poor bastard is in for a shock," said Dubya D. who was disgusted, "I mean the doctor," he added. "Commandeering a plane! Jesus who else would even *think* of doing that? That's what distinguishes the 'Sanes' from the 'Crazies.' At least you, Willy, had enough sense to take the time off."

Yes, for Leyla. Oh, well, I took the credit and shut up. And tonight, both Dubya D. and RM wanted to join us for supper.

"Just to give my blessing!" RM said to me, although he had already hit himself in the head a few times at the first sight of her, rolled his eyes, whistled and shook his hand (phew!) in his special way instead of talking about her.

The docs had talked to Hebert and found him okay, or crazy within bounds.

"I'd question the judgment of our resident psychiatrist," was Dubya D.'s opinion.

Hebert was also scheduled to fly our air-to-air gunnery flight tomorrow and, as a matter of fact, was going to pull the gunnery sleeve, our target, on the first flight.

Our next lecture was canceled. We showered and got to the Crown Hotel at 6:00 in two cars; me driving Jorge, RM, Dubya D; Hebert with Mulligan and Scott. The girls looked great.

"I'm totally recovered, so look out!" Leyla hugged me and whispered; only RM heard it, I think, and shook his head.

Lil wore a simple black dress that hit her at the knees, and walked over to Jorge with a small evening bag held at her waist, smiling a self-assured smile. Bess was studying Hebert's cut forehead and it totally confused that young warrior. "Shucks, it's just a cut!"

"Yeah, and he saved the plane . . . no, wait a second, he wrecked the plane but saved the life raft . . . " Dubya D said.

"*And* the microphone," Scott Lee added with a laugh.

"Yeah," Jorge added, "they send you out with a dive-bomber and you come back with a microphone. Does that sound like a fair exchange? Your new name is 'Moka-in-Swamp.'"

"Now, tell us about your flight after you got back," Dubya D. asked, "Did you break ten flight regulations or was it eleven?"

Hebert chuckled modestly, to Dubya D's annoyance.

"Old-Scow-Across-Great-Waters, you gonna call Nancy Ann?"

"Maybe," he grinned, "After supper. I'm broke."

"Do we have the room?" I asked Leyla.

"Yes," she said, with a quick little look, "but I think there's a question about whether it's on Ralph or not."

"Heyy, you guyssss," RM called to us all, "we could stay here in town and go to 'Ceci's' or whatever you guys call the place. They have good food there."

"Yeah, Ceci's-See-Through. I'm game."

That was the plan, with some griping, of course. No more nor less than if six White Corpuscles and dates were trying to agree on anything. There was also a question whether Mulligan would be allowed in.

"Mulligan, you Lounge Lizard, just behave yourself tonight."

Jorge enjoyed ordering Mulligan around, overseeing his behavior. Mulligan usually obeyed him. Leyla worried about it.

"Why does Jorge always pick on poor old Mulligan."

"'Poor old Mulligan'? Leyla, Mulligan is a raucous, loud-mouthed drunk. Last to leave a party, first to begin another one. Mulligan hasn't missed a party since he was fourteen."

"You'd never know it to look at him."

"Yes, he does have that respectable air, for a time."

Before we walked in Mulligan decided it would be best for him to personally apologize to Ceci.

"Mulligan . . . Pita Leenya," Jorge's obscene name for Mulligan, "No! No apologies, no speeches, just come in with us and sit down, and *eat.*"

Ceci, herself, met us and seated us. Aside from a long look at Mulligan she said nothing.

"I think it's funny," Leyla said to me, quietly.

"You're so beautiful!"

"Just . . . for you."

Evan and Bess, like two good children, moved in together.

I made sure that Leyla noticed.

"Would you think there goes one of the maddest pilots in the Marine Corps?"

"He seems very correct, almost frightened," Leyla observed.

"He *is*, right now."

RM sat on the other side of Leyla and, later, told me of her great eyes. "She's one of the most beautiful, naturally beautiful, uh, women, I've ever seen . . . next to Clare, of course."

He was telling us about Clare and how he wanted Leyla to meet her. They'd get along, said old 'Head-in-Music-Box.'

Leyla turned and looked at me eyes speaking, pleading. I felt the same way, much as I liked all this, the whole thing, the group of us—Leyla's family and mine. And Hebert back from the dead. We gave our order and I think it was Jorge who finally told him, "Alright, 'Thunder-bird-in-Swamp, let's hear it from the beginning."

And after some fencing and joking Hebert began.

He had been "skinning" over the trees, in between landings, holding his position in the pattern, Scott Lee in front of him, and suddenly his engine cut out. Dead. Nothing. "With only two hundred feet of altitude there ain't much choice . . .

"The area, except for the landing strip is nothing but swamps and jungle. I hit the landing flaps, they came down part way. 'Float it in,' they say! Ha! 'Float' a dive bomber? and set it down on top of the trees . . . "

Then Evan had, in what might have been a stroke of genius, or a madman—with him it was hard to tell—plunged the stick forward in the last instants of flight, when he was just above the trees.

The huge limb of an oak tree fell across the rear-gunner's seat, which would have crushed anyone in it.

Hebert was hit on the forehead. The cockpit was locked open for Field Carrier Landings, and he had climbed down to the swamps because the plane was still ten feet above the water. He climbed back into the cockpit, undid the jungle pack, carried it down, inflated the life raft, found the emergency chocolate and ate it.

"And the fire-water," Scott Lee reminded him.

Hebert just laughed, "Yeah, well . . . yeah I found the rum."

Bess was watching him with a look of envy, admiration, almost hero-worship.

"Why were you so low?" . . . "Why didn't you hold it off?" . . . "Why didn't you call?" Mostly the questions were from Dubya D., Rah-Rah's-Chosen-One.

Leyla and I were finished. No, no dessert, no coffee.

"Ohhh, so soon? What's the rush, Clean-Spoon-?"

Mulligan stood up, "Indian Brave no leave—"

"Big-Wind-Over-Dry-Leaves, sit down before Squaw-of-Thin-Blouses throw Big Wind *out*."

Mulligan gulped, and sat quietly.

That went on but short of force we were leaving. I had Jorge's car for as long as Leyla was here. Good guy, Jorge.

The girls made plans for brunch again. Our gunnery flight was scheduled for 0800, the second flight would be right after lunch if the weather held; rain was predicted.

Funny how we felt about it. Hoping for rain and hoping to fly; fighter runs on the sleeve; the ever-anxious go go go.

Leyla and I were off.

"Don't crash and burn," Hebert yelled after us.

"Did you notice that Bess and Evan were holding hands?"

Evan and love? I felt just a little betrayed.

We were heading out of town toward Daytona. Leyla put her head in my lap, turned, talking to my stomach, I clutched her head to me hard, hard.

"I want you. I just want you," she kept crooning.

Why was it, I love her so much but she tells *me*.

"I've never been so happy in my whole life. I want to keep driving like this forever, then I want you in a room, not even to share the night with us. A tiny room. Will?"

"Yes, my sweet . . . "

"Sweet what?"

"Angel . . . pheww! Never called anyone *that* before."

"Will . . . I don't know how much time we have but they know, they know I'm crazy. And so Lil is the one who has to think about getting back. And, meantime, I just don't want to see anyone else. I know you love the flying but I wish you didn't have to fly tomorrow morning. Just tomorrow. I don't want to take flying away, just tomorrow."

"Yeah . . . "

"Tell me. Will . . . we have to *talk*. About everything."

"It's like a crazy fever, but even if I wanted to I couldn't get out of this. We're going. Going, going, going. Even now. Even with you here. Every minute we're closer."

"And every minute is a minute closer to school again. But I don't think about that and don't feel like that. And, still, I'm almost afraid to go to the room because I don't think we'll talk. And it's not that I care if *that's* all we do, that's so great, our bodies' loving, with us, dreaming out of our mouths direct to each other. Isn't it? Do you think so too, Will? *Will?*"

"You angel, youuuu angel, it's true. And a dream. A living dream . . . I can't even say it. Leyla, the thing is should we get married now? I mean, well, suppose, I mean, going overseas, people talk about, is it *fair* . . . to you—"

"But, Will, don't you see? Already it's too late."

"It's how *you*—What??? Too late?"

"Yes. Don't you see? It's already too late . . . You know how I feel. Don't put it on me! I already said it."

"To get married? Now? I *don't* know how you feel."

"Will, it's too late. Too late. It's already too late."

My heart like a battlefield after a bloody battle, "God, Leyla, what do you *mean?*" I pulled the car off the road and stopped.

"Don't you see? Don't you realize? Bess gave me a perfect quote."

"*'Too late'?*"

"Yes! As soon as I heard this quote, I knew it was too late for any decisions; it's from the Book of Ruth; 'Whither thou goest, I will go; where thou lodgest, I will lodge: Thy people shall be my people, and thy God my God.'"

"Leyla, bring it down to us, and what you just said."

"Will, ohh Will. I love you, don't you know that? Can't you see it? It's really too late to talk about marriage because, you nut, we're married. That is me about you; 'Whither thou goest, I will go; where thou lodgest, I will lodge'"

The battlefield was green grass. Too bad if the timing, our meeting, and developments didn't follow a schedule. I couldn't even talk. She was so far ahead of me.

"Will? You okay?"

"You . . . wonder."

"Now, who's crying?"

"You've been down here two days and I've cried twice. And I never cry. Never cry. How come you're so smart?"

"It's not smart, I just *know* . . . some things, and I know what I have, and what we are."

"I don't deserve you."

"Oh . . . bullshit!"

" . . . Did you . . . did I hear you right?"

"Yes, you heard me right, and Will I don't want to hear you talk like that. I told you we're lucky. Lucky, lucky, lucky. *We* are. Not just me, not just you. And our children are lucky to have us. The children we don't have yet."

"You have no idea, Leyla. I worried, I wondered. What if something happens, and all the time I didn't even believe it! All that crap!"

"It is crap, Will."

"Leyla, I know it. I used to wonder, I used to want to be lost in it, lost in the big middle of a ferocious air battle, just to throw myself in it, in the huge maw. And then just the other day Dubya D. was talking about the 'Sanes' and the 'Crazies' in our squadron. About taking chances, like Hebert—me and Hebert he considers to be the worst—and I told him, I told him, 'I *know* I'm not going to be killed. No matter what I do.' I said it to irritate him, but it surprised me when it came out. I said it. I knew it. I know it. Isn't that strange? You see, I told him a secret, a secret I kept even from myself, and I wouldn't have said it to him except he was being so, so god damned safe, you know? And that's something we have to talk about, as long as we're . . . married."

"Talk away, only tell me like *this* . . . tell my right ear."

She was around me, her head to the right of my face, my hand on her leg, rubbing, holding, squeezing, oh such good flesh, "So, well, I don't know how long this can last, but, I mean, God, Leyla, you feel so good I want to scream. I want to get out and scream and tell all the stars how great you feel. Yeahhh, great, great you feel. Anyhow, I'll talk, as long as I can. Well, it is only the worry, about, what happens now, what happens? You go back to school? I finish up here, two weeks leave, I'm going up there for that time, just after Thanksgiving, and then to the great, Jesus, Pacific—"

"When do you finish up, exactly? Do you know? I mean do you know the day? Heyyy, my folks are coming up to Boston for Thanksgiving, with my grandmother, who likes you so much . . . she saw your picture, and . . . she'll love you."

"And meet your family?"

"You've already met them."

"Yeahh, well, how would they go for that?"

"I'll get my grandmother to invite you!"

"So, we'll blame granny!"

"Don't be sarcastic, Will. I'm just working on it."

"Well, how about telling them we're married?"

"Well, how about getting married first?"

"Jesus . . . when?"

"Listen, I just proposed to you and you—"

"You're proposing to a married man."

"Hey, Will. Are you fighting me? We're on the same side!"

"No . . . let's just slow down. If we're married then maybe we should really, in public . . . out in public. Now, wait, just a second. That's one thing. You took the fear out of it. Okay, yes, we're . . . my problem was what to do about it, how it'd work out. But RM and Clare worked it out. Maybe it's not the greatest way but . . . Stop! What are you doing?"

"Just licking your ear a little bit."

"Christ, I can't concentrate. You wanta go on to the room and . . . talk . . . Or . . . Hey! In the morning . . . before I—"

"Before you what?"

"Before I . . . "

"What?"

"Before I . . . fuck you right here!"

"You wouldn't dare!"

"Ohhh . . . hooooo!"

My hand was already on her bare leg under her skirt. The front seat of Jorge's big boat was more like a pullman couch. I hitched the seat all the way back. The main obstacle was her full and long skirt. Leyla had worn a white blouse that tucked into her skirt with a dark blue light sweater over it.

I rushed both hands up the skirt and hooked her hips and pulled them toward me.

"You mean it, don't you, you brute?"

"Yessss!"

Her left leg was against the seat, her right leg on the hump of the transmission box. She was not helping me, not stopping me, sort of watching.

"Are we parked in the middle of the highway?"

"You . . . you *would* ask that, wouldn't you?"

She giggled, but didn't help me.

"Ooh, Will . . . wasn't that the sweetest, craziest, funniest?"

"Don't change the subject."

"Where's our tequila? I could cry. The bottle—"

She was almost stretched out, her legs slightly separated, and I had my hand on her sweet puss, the heel of my hand exactly between her legs, my fingers on her and between my fingers and her very self the little puff of her mound and cotton pants with a tiny ruffle. So sweet I put my head down on that soft mound, with my hand still there. It felt so warm. Almost hot.

Leyla was cooing and moving, an action so slight that only if I held my hand still could I feel her body's slight movement.

"Ohh, my baby, you want me to, don't you?"

"You brute, youuuuuuu brute . . . yes."

"What did you say? I could hardly hear you?"

"I won't say it again. You're a brute."

"Are we married?"

"I married a brute."

She was on her elbows, her head was flung all the way back, her body offered. Her skirt up above her hips and my head inches from her little puss. I was delirious, daring myself, touching my head, my nose to that mound, taking the first tentative sniff and the sweet, strange, smell of her, just the faintest sniff of the sea.

Leyla moaned and had one hand on my head pushing, pushing me away? Pushing? Asking if that's what I wanted? Making sure, making me make the decision, giving me the chance to refuse this exotic dish. Cambridge was very clear in my mind.

"Oh, come here, come, come to me, Will, come up, ohh, ohh do it now, no more teasing, youuuuu—"

I left her for a second, two, three . . . buttons, zipper. No time to take off her pants, just pulled aside and her legs open. Ohh, how it went in, so welcoming, so warm, so close and wet and the pants sawing against me only made it sweeter where they stopped and she began.

No thought of stopping halfway; everything was blanked out except the fierceness of driving, driving blindly.

"Sweet, ohhh, sweet, sweetness, sweeet, sweeeet Will, my darling brute, you brute darling, ohh, yes do it, do it, sweet sweet Will, do it right inside of me."

"Oohhhh, ohhh ohhhh, my angel, OHH!"

Dreams turning real, coming true, white flowers shooting into her, shooting out, blossoming.

Then kissing, kissing, kissing, her very lips a welcome, her tongue, her mouth, laughing and talking down our throats and I could almost decipher Leyla's secret talks to my throat to my heart, " . . . inside me safe warm and wet where it belongs, stay forever, forever and forever." Only half heard, half understood.

"Leyla, do you think we're crazy?"

"What? Oh God, don't stop me now, I can't talk. You're still in me and I'm buzzing and humming with bee-love and honey."

Five minutes later I was moving away.

"Oh, don't, don't, ohh . . . you *did*."

"Leyla, we're going to the room where I'm going to do this properly, totally, completely."

"Heyy, this was proper and, fine, and everything."

I drove us to the hotel and the desk man; "This is your last night, isn't it? Are you gonna want it another night? Ralph just had it for the two nights. It's open, and—"

Leyla wasn't talking so I told him, I nodded, yeah. . . . He was destroying the mood. Leyla was carrying a little bag of stuff but he didn't say anything about license or luggage.

"Maybe I'll take a shower," she decided, took a towel and went down the hall.

I lay down on our bed, stunned at the last 24 hours. Hebert's crash, his flight, dinner, gunnery tomorrow, our own train, going, readying and, already Hebert having missed the navigation flight, was a stranger to the very latest of the squadron's doings. Then us. The dinner, leaving, leaving part of our very selves in that spot on the road and here, now . . . married?

What had changed? How was I different?

My sister, Arthe, had two children but, she said, she still missed New Orleans and couldn't wait to get back. Meanwhile at a base near Montgomery, with Carl, and their two, children, Arthe and little Carl. And Brucie engaged to some navy J.G. The one she had the blind date with, the night I got home.

Well, in ten days we finish and then? No matter what we did with ourselves. No time.

Leyla was back, 'chilly,' she said. Wearing only a little kimono that could fold up into a ball smaller than a pillow case, and wearing a towel around her head. Her soap-smelling freshness, her wet neck, damp smooth skin, legs squeezing us together. What was the good of talking?

There was only one subject, how to get closer. We were sitting in bed, facing each other, her kimono tucked into the crotch, leaning against me, me against the wall near the night window, looking out on the slightly fatter moon sliver, about to sit down in the ocean. My hand was at the juncture, pushing the kimono against her body, and she curled up to me as close as she could and what we'd been like the first time it ever happened, after Longview, about that time, and now this, on the highway.

"Youuu brute! You ravished me!"

Within a minute we were coiling around each other, exhausted and at it.

She hissed through her teeth in the grip of a passion so strong I could only go deeper, deeper, plowing, plumbing, sore, hurting, loving it, going over the top of the hurt to laughter, screaming, crying. A hurt ecstasy until I felt my brains were melting, into my arms, my chest.

"Ahhh, you make me . . . come and come. I can't get enough of you. I can't. I don't know what to do Will! How will I leave? Alright, let's stop and talk . . . just talk. You've *got* to tell me how you feel. About going overseas, and what you want me to do. I swear to God I won't touch you. You *have* to talk to me about it. No, I mean *we* have to talk. We, we, we, but you first."

As usual, as always, fascinated by this beauty, appalled and fearful. And that was one of the things I wanted to talk about . . . I couldn't stand to admit . . . the sex thing, released in her, for sure, could she . . . could she slow down while I was not there?

Old-fashioned as it might seem, the notion that once we were actually married, to everyone else in the world that we were married, it would hurt more . . . to meet other Dereks in the world and, just out of, well, I could understand it . . . too much life was her problem. I understood it and wouldn't, couldn't say it. If she had others . . . only the terrifying thing was, even so, I was helpless not to love her. At the same time ashamed of any feeling that blocked love. Just love, not jealousy, not doubts, just just and only love. I felt it and couldn't say. And the war . . . and guilty for the feeling I couldn't admit, *wanting* the war. And, maybe, the *whole* thing. The *all* of it: "Alright, Leyla, my darling, my life, or that's the way it's coming to be. My angel, now listen, there's no way we aren't going. It's now November the eighth, and between seven to ten days, depending on the weather— and, incidentally that's why I can't tell you exactly when we'll finish. No one knows; we have five more flights. And right now we're done with lectures and movies, just flying time, now. For the squadron, too, because some of them haven't finished field carriers—so how do I feel about it? When you're gone it takes over. And I don't mean just the flights, but a kind of well, don't-give-a-shit fever. So, we go into town, to the beach, get drunk—"

"And there are other girls? Women?"

"Not really . . . well, yeah!"

"I hate myself and being jealous, Will, but I am, too."

"Yes, and so, you . . . and guys buzzing around you—"

"You can't worry about that—"

"Of course I can't . . . I mean I can't help it. Damnit it's so sweet with you and then when you're lying there, so open, so giving, like a wide open flower and in the last moments, it could be, well, I mean, at times, I feel, for both of us, that whatever person, man for you, woman for me, that it doesn't make a lot of difference—I mean lost to everything."

"My darling, my darling . . . don't you realize and know it's *you*, it's you, and I only open to you. I can't explain it. I truly open, because I know it's you. What are you saying?"

"So, no men are tempting? No men look good? You haven't done it with anyone—"

"Well, Derek's been buzzing around me, yes."

"'Yes'? Have you gone out with him?"

"Just once."

"And—?"

"Nothing . . . well, he kissed me."

"Ohhh."

"Will, Will, darling. It doesn't mean anything. You're the man in my life. Do you realize all four of us are practically throwing this semester down the drain just to come down here? That they're doing this for me? And I love the madness of it and—"

"I don't know, I mean, about us. I know we love each other. I don't doubt that. And—I almost did it with one of the 'townies' last week. She's—"

"Is she in love with you? She is, isn't she?"

"Well, we would probably have done it if I'd said it. But I didn't."

"And so she wouldn't?"

"That's about the way it went, I guess . . . so, who am I to talk about what you're doing?"

"Oh, Will, Will . . . this is not it. With our time, our little time. . . ? "

"No, just say it again, that you didn't do it with him."

"No . . . I didn't do it with him. It was very disturbing though, but I didn't want to. This time has been more difficult than any time in my life. On the phone with you, fainting, the miscarriage. I swear I could cry my heart out . . . even now. It would all be so much easier if we were *having* it . . . the—" suddenly it was there, between us again, "It's not anything," she said, crying, sobbing, "It's just . . . just . . . *everything!*"

She started laughing at herself, wiped her tears, stopped, laughed, tried to speak again. "The time . . . and flying, and I love you . . . and . . . something *great* is coming . . . to *us*. A *great* time. Not ordinary, and not *any* lives but some kind of greatness . . . I want you to sleep and be ready to fly tomorrow, be ready for your flight, and I kept you up all last night . . . and I can't help it. I *want* to seduce you . . . I knew I was seducing you on the road and I want to just sleep with you and be with you and make it great for you and, just a second. I loved you so much, when you were drunk and talking about the mess boys, just telling that, I want us to discover those things together, so many great courses I've been taking, oh, Comparative Religion . . . religions of the world, places in the world I want us to go to, great works of art . . . India—"

"Stop . . . Stop a second, Leyla. *You* seducing me? I love it, but . . . but, let's just suppose, well . . . I can't really talk seriously about plans . . . no, no, Leyla, *that's it*. I CAN'T talk about it. It makes me *furious* to talk about it. I feel like—"

"Like it's jinxing us?"

"Worse than that. Like a guy counting his chips. It's not superstitious, it's realer than that. The chips aren't his till the game's over . . . the chips, our lives . . . the game's not over."

"But you said you *know* nothing's going to happen! You're not going to be killed—"

"Leyla, there's a little thing you don't understand and I don't know if I can explain it . . . "

"Go on—"

"Well, this guy Ziegler, talking about 'after the war' and dove into the target—"

"*He* dove? Ahh, the flyer becomes his plane."

"Look, I don't need to tell you this kind of stuff and I wouldn't but there's a connection. It's not exactly a superstition, but they point us, they point us at the war, the Pacific for us, and to think about anything else . . . it's maybe, in the whole history of civilization and all the wars ever fought, just another war, but it's hard to think about anything else. The next flight. Bombing. Strafing. Then somebody . . . Leyla . . . comes along and I'm thinking . . . children, the whole thing and, incidentally, if we go on like this it won't be easy to travel the world with a bunch of—"

"But I want that, *too*," she said, with a look of absolutely unearthly beauty. Her delicate and full lips and face poised to laugh, to plead, with a light, unearthly light . . . understanding, humor, grace, as if she knew, she couldn't have it ALL, and still hellbent for it. Maybe that's what she had seen in us, wanting it all, all, all.

"*There*," I told her, "there *is* a greatness in you."

"In us," she said. "Us, you big lug."

"Ohhh, God . . . Leyla . . . what is the best thing to do about now, and us? And how much time do we have?"

"Finish what you were saying."

"Well, I let the secret out, to Dubya D., to you. Maybe that's it. True, true, that deep secret, as long as . . . To let it out, no secret, no promise of safety, the promise, just a little kid—"

"Wait. Say that again?"

"True . . . the secret, the promise . . . a promise on the condition it's never revealed."

"And you let it out, so it's something that *was* true? Strange, Will. It gives me the chills, as if I had a hand . . . d'you see? You're telling *me*—then I'm to blame? I didn't *ask* you . . . but because I hear the secret?? That's ghoulish!"

"I let it out . . . but the game's going on, that's all, as long as I'm aware the game's going on. And too much talk about it—"

"Alright, but Will, right now, everything depends on you and the orders. Where you go, how long your leave is. I'll marry you, right now, tonight, if we can find some place open. Tomorrow, if you want . . . I have my bridesmaids with me." Leyla giggled, "I'm trying to talk only about now . . . I'll stay down here if you want, or go back and finish the semester, and wait for— *God damnit, Will, I can't talk without including the next few weeks . . .* "

"Leyla, for once you're wrong. Right *now* depends on me talking to you, looking at you, having you, not plans, now, here, us, in this little room, not tomorrow, not ever again not another hour later."

"But you said the word 'promise' as if . . . that's part of it, right?"

"Yes, and . . . Leyla, I've never told anyone . . . about this . . . and I don't know when it started but I think I was born with it. A promise that 'it' would happen. Then 'it' became flying . . . great deeds . . . war . . . then fighters . . . then it became the Corsair, the plane I've dreamed of . . . so I don't know . . . then you came along, and it's as if another train became joined to the dream, but it became incorporated and the promise was 'you'll have it all . . . ALL . . . all you've dreamed of and the *dream* and the *promise*—"

I couldn't go on, overflowing with knowledge an overwhelming knowledge of wishes-promises and couldn't distinguish if I had created it, whether it had come from me or was really 'out there.' "So, I'll tell you what. I want to marry now. In another way I want to wait till we finish dive-bombers then come up there—"

"Sounds like plans . . . but, okay."

"Maybe I can get RM and Clare to come up for the wedding. Or Evan, the first day or two of my leave. Yeah? And now I want you to tell your parents."

"Boy, you *do* pick the hard ones."

"You're mine?"

"No, you're *mine!*"

"Hey, I like that too."

"Will . . . I love you, forever. And I want seven . . . And I don't care about PLANS! Seven little hellions. I don't give a damn if we never get married."

"Ohhhhhh, that's what you'll get! Throw in India, and Africa."

Better than sleep and, still, we slept from five till seven, waked up by Leyla's little alarm clock. Up and out, me to the field, Leyla to the hotel in Deland. How long would they stay? Over lunch they'd talk.

Chapter 20

We waited in the ready room. Clouds were almost rumbling over the field, some as low as three hundred feet. RM was telling me he 'approved' of Leyla, "Yeah, and then some!"

Dubya D. chimed in, "Uhhh, yes, uhhh, Lieutenant, a worthy specimen of northern pulchritude!"

"Ha haa, yeah, only she's from Texas."

"Um humm," Scott Lee added, "great knockers, too."

"Shut up, Face-of-Mountain, I'll tell Nancy Ann you were too cheap to take her to supper last night."

RM pointed out a Lieutenant J.G. "the hero" whose picture had been on the cover of *Life* magazine a few weeks before. He was now an instructor. Lean, pale, unimposing. What had he done that Hebert or I couldn't have done? I was surprised at my own vehemence: he wasn't my idea of a hero. Not a Jimmy Doolittle, not a don't-give-a-shit Mike O'Brien, no hell-for-leather, gut-busting Spitfire pilot, just a guy.

We pumped Hebert about his interview with the head-doctor.

The "doc" had asked him a lot of "bull hockey," according to Evan. Then he got a stern note in his voice and recounted some of it, "I don't know what all he didn't ask me. Do you play with yerself, do you have any weird dreams and a lot of bull like that. An' just when I was wonderin' if he'd ever get aroun' to askin' me why I took the plane up, he finally did."

"So? Why did you?"

"I told him, shucks, I don't *know* why I did it. And he kept askin' me in different ways. So, finally I told him," Hebert was blushing, "I guess, to show them . . . jerks I could fly the danged plane. Case they had any doubts . . . in case they were blamin' me for that engine cutting out. The first danged accident of any kind I ever had."

"And he let you get away with that?" Dubya D. asked.

"Well, I'm here . . . " Evan chuckled, self-righteously.

"Did he suggest that you were knocked in the head, or anything?"

"Yeah, well, he asked me if I was drunk . . . although he didn't use that word, but he said, was I affected by all the emergency rum I drank. So," Evan laughed, "well, I figured I'd be smart and tell him, yeah—"

"But you weren't, right?" Dubya D. insisted. Oh, it burned him up about Hebert.

"No . . . well, let's put it this way, I was in my right mind when I took that second plane up, only a little . . . well, *excited*, shall we say," he began laughing, his little kid's high-pitched laugh, which made it as much of a mystery to us as it must have been to the doc.

"Yeah, it looked like it!" Dubya kept after him.

"Hey, what the heck's eatin' you, anyway? You angry because I'm not in more trouble?" Hebert rarely noticed sarcasm and how Dubya D was, usually, exasperated around him.

Dubya D. sized him up, "Nooo, I just think you're nuts, drunk or sober. And if you had been at five hundred feet instead of two hundred you might have made it to a clear area."

Next time I thought about it we were passing over the beach headed southeast out to sea and I was looking at Scott Lee's face twenty feet away, half-hidden by helmet and goggles.

The gunnery range was south of Daytona about ten miles out to sea and boats were prohibited in the area. The cloud cover had risen to a high overcast by the time we got near the firing range.

"Charge your guns!" We did; our shells dropped into the ocean.

Our tow target, Evan, was circling at eight thousand in the western quadrant of the target area. Evan's SBD was pulling a long, round sleeve, like a long straight sock on a cable two hundred feet behind his plane which we'd be firing at.

I was seeing Leyla's pale and beautiful legs over the whole formation. A week of this life and I'd be a shadow. Well, maybe a month. RM saw Clare every couple of weeks, and I know he missed her between times.

It was still so new for me, to "report in" every single day.

We were going into echelon, the six of us. The Chief and six of THE BIG SEVEN, as we called ourselves; RM, Dubya D, Scott Lee, Mulligan, Jorge, Evan and I.

Evan was now one thousand feet below us.

"Hawkeye Six, take a heading of zero three zero degrees, we will begin our runs in two minutes, this is Hawkeye one, over?"

Evan's twang came back at us, "Hawkeye Six, zero three zero, Wilco, out."

We paralleled his course, went into echelon and peeled off individually, turning back and down toward the tow, electric sights on, then as it was about to go past us turned back into it, leading the target less and less as we got closer to it, and as the deflection angle lessened, firing all the way from a 90 degree deflection to no less than 20 degrees, then breaking off, full throttle, down and to the other side of the tow plane and up to join the others collecting on the opposite side of the tow plane's path.

Six runs on each side and we were heading back to the field.

We were supposed to have another gunnery flight and maybe a third flight in the afternoon. Our squadron was on "priority flight status" and the squadrons behind us could be bumped from flights if there weren't enough planes for us. Scott Lee, Davis and Loomis *still* needed more time before they could be okayed for carrier landings.

On our door I found a note, call operator 206 in Boston, "collect."

I called from the desk and "Operator 206" connected me to the caller: "Go ahead, please!"

A beautiful voice asked, "Is this Lt. Will Vairin?"

"Yes."

"Umm, Lieutenant, I got your name and number from Leyla before she left. She told me to call if anything really important came up and, well, something has, and it's very important for me to get in touch with her. It's about classes. Can I give you the message or should I have her call me? Well, no, let me tell you the message and maybe she should call me anyway."

After a few more decisions, she told me, "I hate to tell her this but she is going to be dropped from two classes if she misses any more. I just got back from class a few minutes ago, well, half an hour ago. She's got to be in her first class on Thursday morning. Day after tomorrow. So, you might tell her that and get her to call me. She knows the number. Just tell her Dorrie . . . Dorrie Webster, she'll know."

Christ; even if we wanted to get married there wasn't time. I called the Crown and woke her up.

"Hey . . . I was just *dreaming* about you." She brought her sleepiness to the phone and I could see her hair sleep-mussed and eyes half-open. I gave her the message.

"Well, I knew. . . . Oh, I knew it, only . . . we just *got* here."

"I'll be over as soon as I can. Maybe you can stay for tonight? If you can, get the room in Daytona. The strangest thing, I've been missing you, already."

We ate, and were back at the field and in our planes. Seven more flights: two more dive-bombing flights with five pound smoke bombs, a hundred pound bomb drop, dive-bombing a moving target, evening glide-bombing, and laying smoke screens for landing craft.

Dubya D. was pulling the target sleeve on the second flight and, after the flight, dropped it on the field, then landed and blew a tire. The plane ground-looped and he had to fill out some forms. Evan Thunderbird-in-Swamp was snickering.

Before the phone call from Boston I asked Jorge about Lil and his only response was: "Ooohhff!" Delivered with his customary passion.

Hebert about Bess? "We're gonna write."

Mulligan on Allie: " . . . a statuesque flower, umm, yes, but in the final analysis not very cooperative."

I got out of the briefing and raced into town. They were in the lobby, packed to go.

"How long can you stay?"

Lil turned and pointed at their luggage. They had been waiting for me to get there. Evidently there had been some long and angry arguments. Allie was also in trouble. Her folks had found out she had gone to Florida and practically sent out an all-points bulletin for her. Bess was the calmest of the four. She was caught up except for the classes she'd missed. Lil had to get back, but for no particular deadline.

"How did they find out where you were?"

"Well, the whole hall knew about the trip," Allie said.

"I think my mother knows, too," said Leyla.

An aunt had called Leyla and, thinking it was a friend, the girl who answered told all. From there to Leyla's mother.

Hebert pulled up in his car with the aviation gas, container and all, and gave Allie three "A" stamps worth three gallons apiece. "Some pilot just gave 'em to me . . . I was talking to him about your trip and he said, 'here'!"

"This is too much, it's all too much," said the willowy Allie, "We're up, we're down, we don't have enough gas, we're fixed."

Having delivered the gas, and also the news that I was in trouble for walking out of the debriefing, Hebert turned to Bess and in his direct boy-scout's manner started talking to her.

Leyla told me, "Lil and Allie both say, okay, half an hour. We'll leave from Ceci's, where we went for supper."

We drove off. Leyla moved closer, "You know, we'll be together real soon. In a week or two we'll be together."

Close as she was she was moving away, as good as gone.

"Will you be able to get a ride up there?"

"Yes. Easy."

"Be careful, Will . . . no, I didn't mean that. I really didn't. I won't ever talk like that, okay? You can count on it. I love it the way you are. Even if you are one of the crazies." She was searching my face, anxious, beautiful, heavy-lidded, her face looking so simple. What *is* beautiful; wide clear eyes, sloping nose, good cheek bones, clear skin, the look, the life in the face. Quick mouth, so full, so changeable.

"Can you stop somewhere?"

"I'm going to."

"Off the road?" She teased.

I pulled off on a dirt road, one-track, no idea where it led, stopped it and we were hugged up so tight, so fiercely, a hug that would have to last us. I wanted to convince Leyla we didn't have to do it, just holding her would be enough.

I told her, and she knew it. "I know. I know, I know, I know."

I felt it would be a way of proving something, not to do it again. "Just because you're leaving! You understand? I love *you*, Leyla, us together."

"Yes, I agree. It'd be too heart-breaking, I couldn't do it. Do it and just leave? Just run off? That's the way we were in Marshall. You don't know how I felt, for days afterwards . . . "

"Okay, good. So great just having you, just like this—"

"Was it a mad, crazy idea . . . to come down? Tell me, totally honestly?"

"Leyla, it was the greatest thing that ever happened. It was the same as Cambridge only better."

"Oh, you were so drunk. But, you know, I hugged you that first hug and, know what?"

"Yeah, go on . . . "

"I was tickled to death. It gave me a chance to love you just seeing you, almost knocked out. And then about the mess boys. If I'd never been in love before that time just that would have done it."

"Yeah, you just melt like cheese."

"No, like ice cream and hot fudge, you're the hot fudge."

"Sooo, now your folks know. Now what?"

"You know the way I feel? Now that they know? I feel happy. 'Do your damndest,' that's the way I feel. I feel so great and proud of you and what we're like."

"Alright! And you're not afraid of them?"

"Not the least little bit."

"Now that's great. Leyla, that was a big worry. I know, they're not . . . they're different, but I expected you to say, if you can't go along with me, well . . . "

We talked about the phone call and the miscarriage. It was all happening so fast in Cambridge. And I had almost no experience. What she didn't understand was that I hadn't believed her. There was no excuse for it. No matter what she said I knew there was no excuse for it. I told her about RM but that didn't help.

"I guess when I found out you didn't call your mother and father I decided maybe I couldn't trust . . . I couldn't believe you."

"Awwww . . . Will, Will, Will. You know, we have *nothing* if we can't believe each other. We have nothing. *Nothing!*"

My heart was a desert and she was pouring sand on it, "nothing" saying it, echoing, reverberating down the corridors of my brain endlessly, "nothing," although she may only have said it two or three times. I was dead and gone. No qualifications, no . . . nothing.

"I love you," I told her, "and I believe you, and I'll never, never not love you and I'll never not believe you. And, for God's sake, Leyla, if there's any love in your heart for me, don't say 'nothing' again. Please don't ever say it again, that we have nothing. Please, please don't ever say 'nothing' again."

"Ohh, Will. I've been down for this three days and this is the third time. Ohh, Will," she started giggling, "you can dry up; I've taken all the tears out of you. Oh, youuuu, *if there's any love in my heart for you?* But Will, that's all there is. There's no room for anything else."

The time was up and we almost did it anyhow and from that time on it didn't matter—we were lost, doing or not doing it. We were flat on the front seat, knocked nearly unconscious and lying there, when suddenly a tractor was trying to get past us. The guy hadn't even seen us yet, and alright, I was up yelling to the guy, "Okay, we'll back it up."

Silently, in the last of the daylight, he backed up; we backed up with him and headed back for town.

At Ceci's-See-Through, Hebert was still there, even relaxed and joking.

"We're all packed, all your stuff is in the car, Lilla," as Lil called Leyla. "We've got some miles to go, so . . . "

Scott Lee, Mulligan and Jorge drove up, Mulligan driving Hilda's car! Everyone was goodbye-ing. Lil actually told me she forgave me. I asked her how she liked Jorge, "Well, she said, I don't *know* about that boy. But he's great looking."

Earlier, Leyla told me what Allie said about Mulligan, "'John,' she said ('John' for God's sake!), 'well, John is a real gentleman till he's had about four beers. Then? Look out! Good dancer! We'll stay in touch.'"

Out of the corner of my eye I caught it and turned to see Bess with her arms around Evan, simultaneously kissing each other's cheeks, then turn for a real kiss.

Lil gave Jorge a more formal hug. Mulligan was holding Allie around the waist, his face a foot away from hers, talking to her so smoothly. Mr. Debonaire kissed her twice. She laughed at something and they broke apart.

"I want your voice in my ear as soon as you get up there."

"Will! It was great . . . this last little time. I mean the TIME," she laughed, "but the time to talk, and . . . to love each other and, just think, we'll be together in . . . ten days?"

"Yes. So, promise you'll call, soon as you get there."

The rest, all the saying, tentative hugs from the 'bridesmaids,' watching that blue Ford take off—Allie at the wheel, Leyla out of sight—a dream, only a dream they're going, that I couldn't believe I wouldn't wake up from.

Chapter 21

Laying smoke screens for landing craft for a simulated island invasion, our first flight coordinating sea and air power. We rendezvoused at seven thousand at point "X-ray," two miles north of the fleet, two miles out to sea. We were in radio contact with the "invasion" fleet and, at their signal, we'd begin our dives—"no lower than two hundred feet"—hit the smoke toggle switches and, if everything went right, lay a smoke screen between the landing craft and the beach. The smoke 'lines' were supposed to be five seconds apart and successively closer and closer to the beach in front of the advancing landing craft.

The idea was to protect the landing craft from the guns of the defenders on land, which meant that, in an actual invasion, we'd be drawing heavy gunfire during our smoke runs.

In order to shorten our exposure time we had to make our runs, parallel to the beach, wide open. I believe the major and the chief were a little afraid of the results if they simply told us to pour it on during those low-level runs, but we were aware of it.

There was a lot of waiting, and endless chatter between the coordinator of the landing craft and the major. Down below us, getting dizzy, were the landing craft which were turning round and round in tight circles, the circular wakes of fifteen landing craft, waiting the signal to head for the beaches. It was the same with us, above them, circling, circling, while the chatter went on and on. Finally, the signal was given, the circular wakes were left behind and the landing craft struck out in a line straight for the beaches all this about twenty miles south of Daytona.

Thunderbird-in-swamp and I were fourth and fifth in line.

We were to start laying our smoke-screens in front of the boats and half a mile out to sea, parallel to the beach, then closer and closer to the beach to protect the boats as long as possible. Down went the third plane. Evan was counting, kissed off and, as we said, "Bent that throttle over the end of the throttle quadrant."

At one-thousand-five he was gone, I nodded, started my count. Already leaving Zimmer before I kissed off, then off and down, the plane clean and *moving*, and it was like being let out of school. All of our training, all of the waiting, all of the cautions, directives, warnings, out the window and down we go. I was laughing all to myself, watching Hebert ahead and out to sea a ways from me, he too was down on the deck, kissing those waves, screaming along and laying that screen of smoke. I hit the toggle and had no idea if it was pouring out the back, just watching those waves GO by, lickety-split.

"Hawkeye Four, Hawkeye Six, *two hundred feet*, I said *no lower* than *two hundred feet!*" I laughed in the privacy of my own cockpit.

After the flight, Hebert and I had to wait till we got to our room before we could really laugh about it.

"'Some of you, as usual, were not following instructions.'"

The magic of doing something we knew so well, even with variations, was not quite enough. Faster, steeper, *in* just a little closer from plane to plane. That was the real difference between the 'Sanes' and the 'crazies.' If we needed speed we had no hesitation in jamming the throttle forward, up to the fire-wall, and never a thought whether the engine would *take* it. The 'Sanes' considered the engines.

Glide-bombing at dusk; we roared down on straight tracks of air. Listen you townies that's us rocketing down, down, down on straight tracks. Then up we soared to do it over, and over again, down like no roller coaster ever invented, with no dive flaps to slow us down our SBD's were faster than fighters in a dive, faster than shooting stars, faster and more wondrous than the stars themselves.

Then it was over.

Our very last flight: DIVE-BOMBING, MOVING WATER TARGET. Coordinating dive times with the Chief's six and the Major's six, eight dives apiece with the little five pound smoke bombs; rendezvous of the twelve and a carrier breakup back at the field.

We were high for the flight, high all through it. Nothing had happened to us the entire two months, one major accident, Hebert, and one minor accident, Zimmer's cut-out on take-off.

We joined up and the Duck Honker led us out to the lake, climbing. At nine thousand over the lake we established contact with the target boat. They were ready for us. The chief shook us out into echelon and we were diving; first dive a dummy run, then the Chief off at two thousand to mark our hits.

Down we came, three twisting dive-bombers in our dives all at the same time, one releasing, the next at five thousand, another at seven and one just entering his dive at nine.

Great fun—the little boat was speedy and elusive, and had no rules to follow, just keep from getting hit. So we were judging wind, "leading" the boat so bomb and boat would meet.

They were having a hell of a time down there too. Sometimes they went in circles, two, three circles, then would strike out in one direction, reverse, cut left, head straight.

"Hawkeye four, entering dive . . . "

Dive flaps and down on that little insect of a boat, first getting directly over it, corkscrewing, then down. The boat had just come out of a full circle, the wind across his bow at five knots, hardly rippling the lake. I led the boat ahead and to the left, anticipating a left turn. At four thousand, all lined up, I felt, no, he'll turn right, and sure enough he began a swing to the left, a feint, yeah, he'll turn right. I led him to the right, corrected for wind drift and dropped at three thousand, continued on down and yeah, turning to the right as I cleaned the flaps and gained a great burst of speed and headed up to rendezvous.

"Hawkeye Four . . . your drop . . . thirty feet, eleven o'clock."

That would have been a hit for a bigger ship.

So it went, the game. And our first live target.

On and on we dove, joined up, climbed and dove again.

Cocky, we joined up and headed back to the field, graduate dive-bombers. The record for eight drops was an average of 65 feet off the target. Maybe I had broken it.

Now, all we had to do was make it back to the field. Nothing more stood in the way of going overseas! Leave! Leyla! I wanted to lead that foursome and not even touch the throttle, just hold our position, in close, swinging back and forth and gauging turns.

We got tighter around the field, our finishing squadron, show 'em how it's done. I was close in to RM leading the first four, Jorge in excellent position leading the last four. The entire twelve of us a still platform of twelve planes, and beyond and below our glances the field passing by, our twelve a separate planet, twelve plane planet cruising past earth. Our four up and to the right side of the first foursome as they kissed off and slid down to five hundred.

Hit the end of the runway by the time the last of their four was in his final turn.

Up the runway, into echelon, kissed bye-bye gave the "How!" sign to Scotto and off. Last landing. Flaps, wheels, bending this big tough dive-bomber, around and over the end, waves, waves, of excitement over me. Straight and in to land. Touched, banged it in tail first, rolled to the end and off the runway.

Walked off, ready to erupt, ready to scream, call her, ready to get drunk! No one killed! Evan a few scratches and we had done it! He walked over, we screamed, pounded each other on the back but hardly said an intelligible word.

On to the Pacific! Out to the world! On-on-on to Burgundee!

Chapter 22

I called Leyla. She screeched and yelled down the hall to Allie, *"Will's finished up! They've finished up!"*

"Well, God, Will, so exciting! What about the leave? "

"Youuuu, sweet angel. I'll call you the first MINUTE I get the word."

"You had better!"

After Leyla I called New Orleans and told my mother. When I told her about the plans to go up and marry Leyla she was disappointed that it wouldn't be a proper marriage with invitations and so on.

"Well, my darling, you know best."

Why did she talk like that? It was out of her code. I didn't know what was best. I didn't know anything. I was just acting and reacting, like a puppet on a string.

Terrible, wonderful days. November 20th, 21st, 22nd. We cursed Washington. We had been pushed through with "Priority Flight Status" as if they had special plans for us.

Where are our orders? Our leaves? Don't they need us?

"The Nazis wouldn't treat us like this!" Evan confided to me on the third day. "Give us a couple of those Focke-Wulf 190's, I betcha we could show those P-51 jockeys a thing or two." It was Evan's idea of a joke but the scary part is he meant it.

Marcie, the girl with the limpid "lake" eyes, on the phone. The girls at Stetson were having a big house party in Daytona and already had a beach house. And they wanted *us*. They wanted to be wild and "go crazy."

RM was counseling me, "Man, I hear you; Marcie doesn't mean anything to you and you're just going out there to get drunk but . . . well, we can get drunk here on the base, or at Ceci's. I mean, it's your business, but you're practically married."

"No, I *am*!"

Then Jorge started with his, "*Evvvvvvvvreebody goessss!*"

RM tried to slow it down, "Yew guyzzzzz."

Then Scott Lee and Mulligan joined in: *EVVVREEEEEEEEEEEEEE-EEEE-BOD EEEEEEEEEEE GOESSSSSSSSS!*"

In the end all seven of us, even Hebert went.

Well, they had trained us as dive-bombers, shown us how to destroy bridges, forts, buildings, foxholes. We had had aerial gunnery, strafing, seen movies on explosives, invasions, war and destruction and here we were— destroyers without a mission. It was obvious that our notions of "going crazy" and theirs would hardly be the same. The girls were divided about us for a while: half of them thought we were "fun" and the other half wanted us arrested.

When the Coast Guard intervened, with attack dogs and searchlights, we were running naked up and down the beach liberating the sand-flies. They chased us right to the door of "our" house where the girls welcomed us not at all.

When the Coast Guard six had us naked warriors surrounded with searchlights, billy sticks, guns in holsters and attack dogs snarling and frothing at the mouth—"Call off your hush puppies, before they get hurt!" we told them. They were in a dark and snarling circle around us and began asking us questions. We told them: "Ah ah! Loose Lips Sink Ships." And "Loose chinks slip blips!" And "Crude Krauts Kill Coast Guard!" And "Loose Pups Lip Crap," all of which we thought was end-of-the-world-funny, having finished off, in the hours before they caught us, an ice-barrel full of domestic champagne, rum and watermelon juice mixed together with a walking stick—the house was furnished. The man who owned the house had hats and shirts and pants that fit some of us.

When we found our own clothes and the Coast Guardsmen discovered we were "officers and gentlemen" and were waiting for our orders overseas— we let that slip even though it might sink a few ships—they apologized and told us about Nazi subs off South Carolina and that the beaches were off limits after dark, even to admirals. We could have been shot, they said.

"Wow! Gee, we didn't know THAT!"

It was only the sixth or eighth time we'd been stopped during our two months' stay. Later we sat in front of a big wood-fire, although we had been swimming earlier, and talked a little. I was feeling foolish and sentimental. Hebert was all for going back, Scott Lee had gotten sick about four times on the beach, Jorge was glassy-eyed, RM was waiting to go but, meantime, was talking to Marcie about marching bands, because she was in the Stetson band. RM had been in Auburn's band and was having fun trading notes with the lovely Marcie. He whispered to me, "Yeah, I know. I'm married but I'm not dead."

I loved Leyla so much. But Marcie . . . did I love her too? No, I wasn't going to start that. And Pinky? And Jimma, and Faye? Of course I loved Leyla like no one else in the world, but what about the others? And if it was true for me, wasn't it true for her also? 'I'm married but I'm not dead' said RM. 'Everybody wants to do it with everybody else,' said Cacksy Jack. It was all a mess. But even to *think* about marriage was . . . no, just let us go overseas, slay the dragons then come home and sort it all out.

Cacksy Jack fell in love every five minutes, and was now missing 'somewhere in Italy.' Amoss the Mouse, Ostoyc, out in the Pacific in landing craft. We had laid smoke screens for the Mouse off the Florida coast a few days ago. And Jo-Jo? The Moon-fixer? Old Ned Needlebutt. In bed for life? Why hadn't I written to them and where were they now?

Next day, the 24th of November, it was raining; everything was "down." We were finished with flying but the weather affected us anyway. Aerology predicted rain all day, morning flights cancelled, afternoon flights were Standing By. RM was nodding to the music, Benny Goodman's Quartet was playing "Smiles."

Zimmer's face appeared at the door, "The orders are in," he said calmly. "Pick them up at the Administration Building."

I don't think RM even turned his record player off. We were running through the rain, got there within two minutes; burst into the quiet office where all of this work went on without our consent, concern or notice. We lined up and received the heavy khaki-colored packets with our names inked in on the front of each packet.

Each packet contained four sets of orders. We tore them open like kids with Christmas presents, let's see what Santa brought.

"Night Fighters!" I couldn't help but scream it out.

Hebert had it too. RM, Jorge, Mulligan and Muncrief the same, only RM had read the whole thing and had some questions about it.

They had split us in two. Dubya D., Loomis, Davis, Scott Lee and Nadell were going to San Francisco, for something described as "Extended Duty."

Zimmer was going to be an instructor, staying here!

Yeah, but when? When? When?

'Five days travel and twelve days proceed' for the west coast boys.

The wording of our orders must have been dictated by a team of lawyers after a drunken brawl. But the five and twelve days was for the West Coast group. The rest of us 'Night Fighters'?—already RM was arguing with my interpretation—well, we had to report "directly . . . in conjunction with the Night Fighter program." We had three days to report to Naval Air Station Red Beach, Florida, which was one hundred sixty miles down the coast from Daytona, November 27th. Thanksgiving be damned.

And no leave? Three? Two and a half days?

"What do you think?" I asked Evan.

"What do you think, RM?" RM had hardly spoken a word since we'd gotten the orders. We had run back for lunch but stood there just inside the entrance, stunned, trying to discuss the very indirect way our orders read.

"Well, Willy babe, I'm not so sure we got Night Fighters—"

"What???"

"If it's Night Fighters why doesn't it say so?"

"Well, it does!"

"'In conjunction with the night fighter program,' it says."

I couldn't argue any more. For sure whatever it was, it was not a welcome sign. Instead of saying 'you must be there on the morning of the twenty-eighth,' they said, 'your orders are effective as of the twenty-fourth of November, one day travel and three days' proceed time.'

But evidently we "Night Fighters" were not going overseas because we did not have leave. It would be more training of some kind, although it said nothing about further training. RM had also pointed this out. Apparently, whatever we would be doing required no further training.

I couldn't possibly talk to Leyla about it. Was there a chance we would *not* be night fighters? I told them I had filled out a form, at Memphis, and in answer to what kind of duty I had put down, as a second choice, Night Fighters.

RM, with a sarcasm that I wanted to kill him for, reminded me: "*You* have even talked about how little those forms mean. You think they're worried about some form you filled out? In Memphis, for Christ's sake? Willy? *Think?* Do you believe they looked through those forms—"

"*I'm just TELLING you I put it down on a form!*"

I was losing a friend, a close friend. From the first day I had known him at Pre-Flight. We were about to square off . . . but over what? Because I wanted Night Fighters so badly?

"Look," said Hebert, and he really did stop us, "you guys can beat each other's brains out for all I care but it's not gonna make a heck of a lot of difference. The place is about one hundred and sixty miles down the coast. Let's pack up our crap and get on down there. This guy, I don't know where he gets it, but he got some gas for me this morning. We can find out the deal down there and, if nothin's happenin' we can continue on down . . . I don't know, Miami er some place."

Strange about the "West Coast" boys. There was already a separation between us. Even Dubya D. was different. He gave us his frosty smile and wished us well, we shook hands and that was it. Contrary to what Hebert thought about me "and your mess!" I was ready as soon as he was. Scotto, Jorge and Mulligan caught us and couldn't believe we were leaving so soon.

It was no good trying to stop Hebert, even for an hour. We'd see them down there, and off we went. Leaving NAS Deland, the girls at Stetson, Jimma, Ceci's, the wide beaches of Daytona, the whole thing.

We, RM, Hebert and I, straightened it out. "Hey," RM said. "If we get night fighters, great. I just don't think they'd take a bunch of dive-bombers and stick 'em in night fighters!"

It made sense. What was wrong with me? But if *not* night fighters what did it mean?

"That's what we're goin' down there for," Hebert replied, undoubtedly the simplest and most direct comment of the day.

Chapter 23

Red Beach Naval Air Station, eighty miles south of Deland, was like the one we'd just left. Bachelor Officers' Quarters and Married Officers' Quarters farthest from the field. The Officers' Mess identical to Deland's. Red Beach was in the middle of the orange belt and the base and town were separated from the beach by the Indian River which, under one name or another, runs almost the entire length of the east coast of Florida. Then, in place of the dive-bombers there were the sleek-looking F6F Hellcats, midnight blue with white stars, and radar bulbs on their right wings. There were rows and rows of the little fighters.

They put us up in Visiting Officer Quarters. We had lunch at the BOQ, and a trip to the field to see those sleek F6F's. Right over our heads a section of two F6s shot over. One laid its wing almost straight down and broke off. The engines made a ringing sound as if the planes were harnessed to a million little bells. I wanted one of those night fighters like a dying man wants life.

But what were those old Helldivers doing over there? And, even older, from the British Navy, the Brewster Buccaneers?

Nobody could answer our questions. And no one could explain our orders either. We were told only that at our meeting, for our group, a group of fifty, it would all be straightened out.

I couldn't call Leyla. I didn't know anything. My heart was poised between a great hope and the most bruising defeat. And despite my hopes I had the feeling that the great train with all of my promises and dreams . . . the great train of my life had slipped the tracks. RM's question kept coming back. Why assign fifty dive-bombers to become night fighters?

We dumped our stuff in the temporary quarters, went down to Miami and crushed two days.

There were fifty pilots in the small assembly room. Mulligan, Jorge, RM, Evan and myself among them. All fifty had gone through dive-bombers, and all of our orders read: "*in conjunction* with the night fighter program."

An irritatingly skinny, navy full lieutenant came in, bobbed his Adam's apple at us a few times and broke the news.

"Your duty, here, is as Auxiliary Pilots . . . "

"'*is as*,'" RM leaned over and whispered in a disgusted stage whisper.

"That means," he explained, "your duties are to help train the night fighter pilots."

"And what does that mean?" a disgruntled voice asked, almost a whine.

"How long do we do that?"

"Yeah, when do we get overseas?"

A hundred more questions hung in the air, when he stopped us, "You are on temporary-permanent duty, here," he told us.

"Permanently-temporary, or Temporarily-Permanent?"

There was a roar of anger, questions to the wall, the ceiling, to each other. Now the lion tamer was also getting angry. He did everything but shake his twin bars at us: "These are your orders! I'm simply reading them to you—"

It was midnight of the last night of my life. All of it flashed by me from Leyla to pre-flight to Texas A & M to dances at the yacht club to football at White Corpuscle field and the day of my long bath of dreams, on back to Aunt Alice and *On on on to Burgundeee*.

We were outside. Hebert explained it all. Three hour night flights. Check-out tomorrow, the schedule to be posted, names and times to check out in the SB2C (Scout Bomber Modification 2, Manufacturer Curtiss).

But what does it mean? Temporary? Permanent? Those old dive-bombers? SB2Cs? Faster than the SBD but not as dependable.

Night flying . . . three hour flights? For the night fighters to practice their airborne radar? Cowboys and Indians? And we're the Indians?

"Hey, that's all I know," Hebert told me impatiently, "Look, I gotta go check on my car. I found a mechanic who can help me work on it. See you back at the room."

It was monumental. What to tell Leyla? What to tell myself?

The idea of marrying seemed out of place. The dream shattered: grow up, fly fighters, go to war and throw my life at it, then come home marry Leyla, New Orleans, kids and . . .

Who was that guy? With the Adam's apple. Navy Lieutenant Who? No one seemed to know. We turned to each other and I thought I could see death's ashes in the eyes I looked into. As for my own train of vows, wishes, dreams, my own dream of glory? I couldn't breathe. I had been promised. And betrayed. We would fly from three to five hours a night and were "off" the rest of the time. I didn't want "off," I wanted everything, *everything*. I wanted "on" twenty-seven hours a day. I wanted the big test, everything demanded of us. The meeting was coming back, whether I wanted it or not.

"You men are on temporary-permanent duty."

"What the hell does that mean?"

That was as close to a rebellion as we came.

"Well . . . temporarily, or until further notice, this is permanent duty for you pilots."

I could feel, if not hear, dreams crashing on rocks. Not even the promise of new planes—the Helldiver, faster than the SBD, a plane which was replacing the "D" as fast as they could be turned out.

Call Leyla? And tell her what? The promise had been dive-bombers and orders overseas, marry on the leave and go. Now? Marry and what?

Most of us hung around the general area but every time one of those speedy midnight-blue Hellcats went over, bells ringing—jaunty, joyous, fast—it was a spike in my heart. I asked RM what he thought about it.

"Well, my man," he drawled, "It ain't the end of the world. I'm gonna get in touch with my sweety and look for a place for us."

Jorge was not speaking. Mulligan was grinning about something. I turned away from them. Finally Jorge turned to me, "You know something? I tell you we're going. I feel it in my bones. I don't care what that guy says. You and I, we're *going*."

I didn't quite believe or disbelieve Jorge but it was the bright spot of the day.

I called Leyla at her grandmother's and was lucky enough to have her answer the phone. She was there for Thanksgiving.

"Leyla, I don't know, quite what's happening. But . . . my sweet, sweet angel, I can't get the leave . . . right now, and we're not going overseas, or not any time real soon."

"Oooh, Will . . . Willllllllll. . . ."

I could hardly talk.

"We're . . . training night fighters. Oooh, Leyla, no, it's actually . . . I can hardly describe it. And we're stuck here."

"*Where*, Will? And how long? And your leave?"

I told her where we were and gave her the numbers to call.

"Will . . . that's . . . that's a crusher . . . and you don't know when?"

I couldn't tell how much concern was about the leave and how much about overseas.

"There are fifty of us . . . stuck here. RM's looking for a place."

Silence.

"What did your folks say?"

"Ohhhh . . . they were very upset. They don't think we know what we're doing. They want me to stay in school. We're off till December 2nd, then papers and exams. That's not important and so Will, Will, Will, I love *you* in all the world. And I'll do what you say. Do you want me to come down there? If you want I'll leave school after Christmas . . . "

"I told you that RM is looking for a place for him and Clare didn't I? Well . . . "

"Do you want to . . . .find a place? . . . Will, are you teasing me?"

"Yes, I mean 'no,' but let me sort this out . . . I'm still in shock."

"Well, so am I . . . Bess got a letter from Evan!"

"Really? Does she really like him?"

"Yes, I think maybe she does. There's something about him, she says. 'He's not a talker, he's a doer,' she says. Isn't that funny? And, sort of, wonderful?"

"You're sort of wonderful—"

"Will? I want to tell you something, just a little thing. I really want to tell you, only . . . maybe I shouldn't."

"Tell! Come on."

"Well, it's only a little thing—"

"Leyla!" I was laughing despite all of my ridiculous and wrecked news.

"Well . . . You know, sometimes, you . . . call me . . . oh God, this is silly, well . . . you call me, sometimes, you call me . . . 'angel'? . . . Ohhh, I'm ready to hang up."

"Don't you dare."

"Well, I just want to tell you. . . . It makes me feel, I can't even describe it . . . I don't know, maybe it's the way you say it. And, well, that's all . . . is that ridiculous?"

"You angel, you *angel!*"

"You don't know what you're doing to me, but . . . it's good. It's marvelous. Ohh . . . And so what am I going to do about you . . . and, I'm sending you something. I won't tell you what it is . . . "

When we hung up, I felt the glow of whenever I talked to her, also that I was over my head. It was my move and I was stuck.

Chapter 24

We had a lecture and a movie on the SB2C, put out by the Curtiss-Wright company. Strange combination of selling it to us and giving us information about a plane we'd be flying.

Lt. Farrell, whom we called "Fowler," and "the Fowler," stepped forward and decided that was the moment to tell us that acrobatics in the SB2C were forbidden because the tail, as always, is secured by only three bolts.

"The plane is also *condemned*, right?" somebody yelled out to him.

"It is *not* condemned," the 'Fowler' yelled back, red in the face.

"I've got a friend on a carrier who said the tails come off. And it was condemned!"

"That's not true. They were—" suddenly 'Fowler' was having to shout against the frustrated screams, "THE SB2C-1A WAS CONDEMNED FOR CARRIER DUTY BUT NOT—" By now there was so much noise nothing could be heard. He kept screaming and suddenly was fearful. Yes, it was out of control. Once again it was like a tide rising to open rebellion. He signaled to the corpsman, the lights went off, the film began, people shut up. The movie opened with dramatic music and some flying shots of the SB2C-1, taking off, diving, landing on a grassy field. Very wide landing gear and, in all, a good looking plane, big but good-looking.

Then, the inevitable, earnest, conspiratorial voice: "Let's get up and take a closer look—"

"Let's not and say we did!" Jorge shouted from the back.

Hebert was pulling at my shirt, and in a loud whisper, "Just show us the throttle!"

In a few minutes he was at it again; "At ten thousand feet, what are we supposed to do, get out on the wing with a screw-driver and adjust the carburetor?"

I was too downed to join him.

We checked out in "the Beast" as it was known, and found it bigger, faster and more unwieldy than the friendly tough SBD. And after five to seven hours of familiarization were briefed on our main duties, as targets for the night fighters.

As if that was not enough we were told that the designation "Night Fighters" would soon become All-Weather, or All-Purpose fighters. The F6F would be replaced by Corsairs. The final humiliation.

For our flights we had to report by radio at a pre-assigned altitude to our scheduled ground-control radar operator—any time from sundown till dawn—the ground controller would direct both the target and the fighter in such a way as to simulate night-fighter interceptions. Once the ground controller had us on his radar screen we, the targets, the "bogeys", would switch off our running lights. The ground radar operator would direct the target across the path of the fighter and give him directions: "Cowboy six, target crossing from right to left, angels nine, speed one sixty, five miles, over?"

If Cowboy Six's airborne radar could pick us up he'd report in: "Roger, Star, one bogey, four miles, crossing from right to left, over?"

"Roger, from Star Base, proceed with problem, over."

Back and forth the constant patter went as the fighter closed in for the kill. In this game, and night after night, we were the robbers, the Indians, the bad guys. We flew straight and level, listening to the fighter "spotting" us, closing in then shooting us down.

"Splash! One Bogey!" That'd be me, down in flames. Ten or more times a night for each fighter, three fighters a night. One hour flights for them, three for us.

Occasionally, I would wait till the big hero was a quarter of a mile behind me, whip around, get on his tail, close, and while he was still whining that his target had disappeared, close in and report, "Splash! One Cowboy!"

The ground controller might laugh, but then I would have to bend over again and assume the position, target for a trainee I could fly rings around.

The war had moved almost beyond reach, and it was not striking me over the heart any longer. All fifty of us bogey pilots were faced with the distinct possibility that the war might end without our help.

RM and Clare found a place within a short walk of the beach, set up house and according to them were as happy as any love-birds. And, coming so soon after the disappointment, I both envied and hated them. How could they turn so quickly and easily to just *living*? They kept asking me to come out, and it cut two ways. I was pulled and, at the same time, detested the idea. I did not want to see them in their little hideaway.

Christmas came and went. We were into '44.

The war went on. Pilots were married, killed, divorced, had babies, went to "work." Life on the base continued; people worked in the tower, fixed airplanes, sorted mail, crashed, swabbed decks, typed, filed, and everything else people all over the world do.

It was like my time on the farm at A&M. The darkest of my life. I stopped calling Leyla.

In February came the definite news that night-fighters were being phased out. The new designation would be All-Weather Fighters and, oh Lordy, Corsairs would be replacing the F6F's. The last nail in my coffin. Bogey pilots in condemned dive-bombers, targets for Corsairs. Shot down over and over again by the only plane I wanted to fly.

For the others, "playing house" while a war was going on: buying groceries, playing bridge, sending the kids to school, while the English, French, Russians, Australians, Germans, Italians, Africans fought, died, froze, were shot down, bombed, and the Japanese and Americans in the Pacific were captured, killed, dove down funnels, spewed bombs and bullets, starved to death on by-passed islands, well, to be in Florida playing house seemed almost evil.

I couldn't even answer my own questions. Why not get married? Set up housekeeping like RM and Clare? I couldn't explain it but it made me sick. Playing house on the beach? With a war on? It was somehow so opposite every dream I'd ever had. Train, fly, overseas, come home a hero, and *after* all that. After . . .

Only, since "there's no after the war for a fighter pilot," you've got to enjoy married life *before*. I had no answer to my own logic.

RM kept it up, come on out, Clare's a great cook. Then one day Hebert and I agreed to come out for supper.

"Uncle five-eight, your new vector, two seven zero, over?"

Working for Uncle Sam.

We did what they told us to do. Came down from our flights, drank and talked, watched red flares go up from the field; a flat tire, wheels-up or a real accident. Drank more coffee; registered planes coming in, going out, the ringing of a million bells for the fighters, the heavy growl-hum of the Beasts, checked tomorrow's schedule in a life that had now adjusted to the war as NEWS.

Then one Bogey pilot was killed. Engine failure on take-off. Forty-nine to go. And then another. Vertigo, air-sick, they think. He dove into the ground. Both took place at night.

The marrieds lived their bridge-party lives, their little dinner party lives, and I was almost as disgusted with the others; partying, drunk every other night, trying to screw everything that walked. It's the war, it's all the war.

Mulligan and Jorge had joined the party circuit. I was between groups. Hebert and I had our own war, but I sometimes went with the partiers.

Two months passed. What was it all about? And what was I going to do? No possibility of getting out and I either had to get Leyla down or . . . or what?

What would it mean if I didn't get overseas? Did it mean I should start thinking about after the war? If there's no after-the-war for fighter pilots, is there a during-the-war for bogey pilots?

The one touch Red Base had with the war was the navy and marine pilots returning from carrier duty in the Pacific or from Guadalcanal. The marine pilots had truly borne the brunt of the first part of the war: Hotch Hotchkiss, Jack Mintz, Sam Lyttle, Smoky Thompson and four or five others were Guadalcanal pilots now going through the night-fighter program. They were tough, strong, don't-give-a-shit flyers, and now captains, who'd take a chance or bet on anything. They gambled, they caroused, they played poker for high stakes and the games went on for three days in a row. In some way they had been screwed to the wall, and no longer played by the books; they were angry at something unnamed and unnamable. So were we, the "bogeys." Especially after we found out that the planes we were flying, the SB2C-1A's, had been condemned. There was a natural affinity the one group for the other, but they had already passed the test— these veterans who had seen the toughest action—had faced the lion in his lair and come away with honor. F4F's against Zeros.

It wasn't that they wouldn't talk about it, they *would*, only it was not like the guy at Deland who had given his interview to *Life* magazine, telling the public about honor, glory, the flag and victory. With the Guadalcanal pilots it was different. A shrug of the shoulders, a laugh, a few words.

"How were the Jap pilots?"

"Great! . . . Tough! . . . Excellent!"

What else was there to say?

How was it, really, on Guadalcanal? The food, malaria, flying, fighting, returning to gas up and go out to fly again?

"It was like shit!"

Not good copy. No long articles. No heroics.

MARINE ACE SAYS IT WAS LIKE SHIT!

Nights, after flying all day, shelling attacks, jump out of cots into wet fox-holes, fire back at Japs breaking through the lines only a hundred yards away, and attacking them face to face.

The Japs sent their bloodthirsty message to the tough, exhausted marines—pilots and infantry: "Banzaaaaaiiieeee, the fucking Marines shall diiiieeeeeee!"

These Guadalcanal pilots, now all captains, the survivors, were our natural friends and allies—unhappy misfits that we were—and they enjoyed our reputation as "wild" and rebellious.

RM spoke to me about the whole thing and, of course, I was talking to Leyla for a while . . . hurting her, I knew, in some way I couldn't rectify.

I was waiting, waiting to see for sure if there was some distant chance to get out. RM and Clare already had a month and a half of being together. Leyla mentioned that.

I couldn't begin to explain it. It was as if I were an actor in a play and had suddenly forgotten my part. We could fly the SB2C's as often as we wanted, so we flew.

RM took it like work; flew his flights, saw us bird-dogs once in a while, invited us over for meals, went swimming. He and Clare shopped in town, listened to records, wrote letters and made friends with other couples.

People sent for home-town sweethearts, married them, lost them right there. Wives kissed husbands goodbye before every night flight as if it was the last time they'd ever see them again and only grunted when they got in bed hours later. Hubby works and the wife has a little part-time job or cooks and sews, gets pregnant or all four, and worries about her pilot-husband, about baby-sitters, play-schools.

I couldn't make the transition. Maybe for Leyla and me it was already over. I couldn't forget her, but I was stuck. The war was a dull ache in the back of my mind but it kept me from making any decisions. The 'war' had spit us out here; not over those lovely islands in the South Pacific, not Burma, the Empress Augusta Bay, or the South China Seas, or Europe where the G.I.s were being kissed and welcomed into neat little Italian towns. The war had been promised and now I felt betrayed. By whom?

Leyla was going into the last semester of her sophomore year.

Chapter 25

When they told us no acrobatics, they were simply refusing to acknowledge what we were bound to do. If we got killed, okay, but they had warned us.

They were like a doctor telling a poor man with five children to take a six-month vacation out west, and if not then HE, the doctor, was no longer responsible. The working stiff can't afford the vacation and we couldn't afford not to see what these clunkers would do. These "doctors" knew we would ignore their advice.

Three bolts? Either they didn't know what they were talking about or they were massive bolts. Hebert and I took two planes up to ten thousand and tried them out.

We used channel three, 'our' channel.

"Hey, your tail's still on!"

"Yeah, so's yours."

"Congratulations!"

We could see each other, plane to plane, grinning away but had to talk using our mikes.

We did rolls, we did Immelmans, four-point rolls, eventually we did everything but snap rolls. We flew on our backs for at least thirty seconds and nothing happened except for a lot of dust and debris from the floor of the plane.

We talked about coming in some night on our backs and going past the tower upside down. That'd fuck 'em up good, seeing the green light where the red light was supposed to be.

We flew for hours every day and began pushing these trucks to the outer edges of what they could do. To *snap* the wing of a dive-bomber over takes a strong arm, and we began to break up like the fighters; "No," Hebert said, "like those fighters *should* break up." And we did it right under their noses. We broke off, wings pointing straight down at the ground and hauled back on the stick harder and harder each day, dropped wheels and flaps, held it in very close to the field and did a steep continuous turn to a landing, all power off.

No one said anything so we kept it up, steeper and tighter, closer to the field, more and more of a spin to a landing.

185

Because a lot of the bogey pilots were bringing the planes back early, with complaints, a new directive came out: all utility planes (SB2C's) will be tested each day before night flying blah blah blah. 'It's not the planes, colonel, it's the pilots who are not air-worthy,' we told each other, laughing. So, there was a lot of 'testing' to be done. Hebert and I were down at the flight line every day and each day we tested three or four planes apiece.

The first official complaint about our flying came via a memo to the line shack where we signed for the planes. We came down one day, laughing about our break-up, and the line chief told us we were wanted in the flight office.

"Were you two," the flight officer said, "in those planes that landed just a few minutes ago?"

"You mean the 2C's, sir?"

"Yes, I mean the two SB2C's that just landed. I mean, lieutenant, numbers #326 and #334. Yes, that's what I mean."

"Umm, yes sir, I believe those were the numbers."

"Look, I'm not going to waste time with you guys. Five minutes ago two SB2C's came in, those were the numbers, and there haven't been any others in the last half hour, do you want me to send for the sheets on those planes to nail this down?"

"No, yes sir, we just came in, together, yes sir."

"Well, I want to know just what the *hell* . . . that was the god damndest breakup I've ever seen, and I've seen a lot. You're both on report, for dangerous flight conduct. Dismissed."

Once out of the office, Evan was highly indignant, "Why, heck, it's safer the way we fly, stickin' in close to the field."

Actually we were flattered and happy to have been noticed: ". . . the god damndest breakup he's ever seen." Well, how about that?

Yes, they'd like to clip our wings, and if there was ever a time when Hebert, the Mad, wanted to talk about flying for the Germans this was it. I didn't want to hear it about the Nazis and the Focke-Wulfe again. We were trapped, all fifty of us. It would do us no good to argue, not that we flew like that for safety's sake. Evan was a good, solid, totally unschooled madman and had to be protected from the world. I told him to swallow it and shut up. Would we continue flying that way? Of course.

The base was far from the action but people were also getting killed here. Four in the first month. Two Bogey pilots and two night fighters. Life went on.

We had another Bogey Pilots' meeting. And the first order of business that Lt. J.G. Farrell took up was a new directive just out: "Around the field, the following specifications will be observed: Speed will not be in excess of 165 knots in the traffic pattern—"

Boos and hisses.

"Hold it! Hold it! That's not all. The angle of bank when breaking off over the runway will be forty-five degrees. Got that? Forty-five degrees. Some of you think you're flying fighters, you're breaking off at a ninety degree angle. And it must be stopped."

There were screams and hoots.

"Forty-five degrees, the angle of the dangle!" Someone shouted.

We made his job as unpleasant as possible and, always, hit him in the vitals: "When the hell are we getting out of here?"

We went to him after the meeting and told him of our idea; having the new night-fighter recruits fly as "bogeys" for a few months, and *then* go through the program. That way they would be better night fighters and *we* could be fed into night fighters.

He laughed as if it were a ridiculous notion.

"I did hear this," he said, "if it's any consolation: someone said, I won't mention who, 'If they'd send those two overseas they'd be heroes in a week or else dead.'"

What did we have to lose? We continued landing and breaking off exactly as we had always done. We came screaming into the landing pattern a hundred miles over the "speed" limit and bent those wings straight down at the ground—forty-five degrees and another forty-five to make sure.

Then one day Captain Sam Lyttle informed Evan and me, after swearing us to absolute secrecy, that he had been asked by an "important person" in China to form a second flying tigers group of volunteer pilots. Would we be interested? The Soong dynasty banking house was behind it.

What?? When??

Before he would answer anything more he told us we might have to renounce our American citizenship and become, at least temporarily, Chinese.

I looked at Evan and we laughed.

"Sheeeucks," Evan said, "Gimme them papers, I'll sign right now."

"No question about it," I told him.

What kind of planes? What was the deal? When? How? For God's sake keep in touch with us. Definitely count us in.

He wouldn't show us the rest of the list but he told us they were all good pilots, the best ten he could gather together, and we would hear about it as soon as he did.

I was right to wait about Leyla. If this came through we'd be leaving for China any time.

For weeks we lived in high hopes, and the more we thought about it and discussed it the less we cared about our citizenship. Every few days we sought out Cap'n Sam.

"Well, most important, I hope you guys haven't said anything."

"We haven't said a word. We're just waiting."

"Because I think, I *think*, the colonel's gotten wind of it." The only additional detail was that one of the Soong sisters, Chiang Kai Chek's wife, was behind it.

The hope alone changed everything. He told us again that Evan and I would definitely be among the ten. This Guadalcanal hero had chosen *us*. He wanted wild pilots and *good* pilots and he had them. Meantime Leyla, so sweet and honest was finally losing patience.

January:

I'm packing my bags.

Leyla . . .

February:

What are we doing, Will?

Ahhh, Leyla.

Do you want me or not?

March:

We could have been together for three months. Three months! Do you realize? What *is it* Will? Is something wrong?

No, absolutely not.

Do you love me?

Yes.

Then what is it?

I don't know.

She hung up.

Chapter 26

It had been a strange day. Evan and I were going out to RM's for supper. He wanted to talk to me about something. Me not Evan. That day we took two "Beasts" across the state to play with the air force planes. There was a P-39 base in the middle of the state and P-51's and P-38s a little farther west.

We got into their formations, had dogfights, followed their landing patterns, whether they liked it or not. We flew along the beaches of the west coast of Florida, about five feet over the water, waaaaaaaaave to the girls; just passing through, doncha knowww.

We got separated and I caught a lone P-39 Airacobra, a good-looking bust of an airplane. I dove on the character and, unlike the area patrol at Memphis, this guy was ready to fight.

Why not? After all, any fighter could beat any dive-bomber and so we went at it. I don't know if the plane wasn't any good or if it was the pilot but I got on his tail and stayed there. I shot him down a dozen times. He couldn't shake me. Soon enough he was just flying along straight and level. I pulled up on him and saw a rather fat pilot just sitting there. He looked over at me and shrugged. I was looking at a dead man if he ever came up against a Zero, or a Focke Wulfe.

I found a formation of P-51's and had trouble keeping up with them but then they got into a strafing circle and I took my turn, came down in a dive, just as they did, no ammunition but I did everything else. I figured they'd take my number but what they would do with it I didn't know and didn't much care.

We got back separately, showered and went out to RM's and Clare's little cottage for supper, a mile or so south of the pirate-like 'shipwrecked' Driftwood Inn, twenty yards from the ocean.

We stayed till about midnight reminiscing and drinking. RM told us that Dubya D. and Sarah, "Rah-Rah," had been married on the west coast, and Scott Lee and he were now "out *there*." And flying *torpedo bombers*!

We were a little drunk on martinis and Clare's wonderful meal. Hebert and I were both scheduled to fly from two till five, RM from three till six, the dawn patrol.

RM's lecture to us was partly serious, partly for Clare's amusement and also so she could thank her lucky stars for safe, responsible RM rather than one of the 'crazies' for a husband.

"Now, from what I can gather," he started in on us, "Not that I'm around the base any more than I have to be, but from what I hear you two are creating your own war; acrobatics in the beast, which you've been warned about, dog-fighting with the air force, hot breakups around the field, day *and* night. Now the point izzz—

Hebert was laughing like a bad kid, and began to show RM and, incidentally, the blond beauty of a Clare, just how we came in; "All's we do is" his hands were coming over the runway, one-two, close together, "like this and then," one whipped away from the other violently, "and around, like *this*, in a . . . ha haaa. . . . in a well, a, well, ha haaa, yeah, in a—" and we both finished it together, "a one-turn spin to a landing."

"Well, I probably shouldn't encourage you but the other day the commanding officer of the base, Captain Wynton, saw the two of you come in to the field from 'testing' planes, and God knows what you were really doing but, anyhow, he saw it from the flight office. Now I heard this from none other than Cleary, that con artist . . . anyhow, according to him the captain almost fell out of his chair. 'Who the hell is THAT?' and so forth. And, according to Cleary, when they found out it was you two, Cleary defended you, 'Oh that's the way they come in, but captain, the two of them are always taking extra flights, they test planes almost every day and, sir, they never miss a flight.' The captain said something about, 'In *dive* bombers! . . . never saw—' and so forth. In fact, I'm sure that's the reason we're gonna have a meeting with the Fowler in the next few days."

Clare was a perfect California blue-eyed blond, from Alabama. For a minute or so I actually studied the face to find a flaw but apart from a small skin-colored mole on the lower left cheek, with a couple of hairs, oh maybe a quarter of an inch long, she was flawless. It was as if the mole held her to the earth. She wore a long peasant skirt of some flowered material gathered at the waist, which didn't hide the swell of her perfect, well, ass, as she walked back and forth to the table. Nice breasts, sweet manner, and a way of looking at the speaker which was enough to turn anyone's head.

"Well, *Ritch* tells me"—she called RM "Ritch"—"that you have a beautiful red-head, Will, just waiting for you to say the word and she'll be down here."

I nodded and Hebert whooped.

"Well, it's none of my business, but we'd love to have her down here . . . maybe we could even rent a big house together. I mean, if you wanted to."

"Yeah, I . . . " I couldn't say more without offending both of them, their life, *and* Hebert.

I watched RM and figured I couldn't explain to him. I guess I had joined Hebert. A life of flying, and waiting, still, for the war to take us away which had nothing to do with THIS: apple pie, baked with her own lovely hands, a meal for old friends—he makes the drinks, she handles the food—then bed together and having it whenever you wanted.

But given a world at war and the madness . . . well, the life here, the easy life was, God, almost evil.

And on the other hand, why wasn't it the perfect time, even *if* going overseas, to eke out all the pleasures, before the world came up and knocked you in the head?

Just before we were about to leave, Muncrief, the stolid Indian, who lived in the next house over with Imelda, his wife and their little baby, knocked at the door, came in, "Just for a second . . ." to tell us that Don Loomis was missing, "since, ohh, 'bout 10:30, I mean to say twenty-two thirty," he smiled a slow smile, "Last contact around twenty-two hundred." Muncrief, after a few more words was out the door again. "Loomis," he had told us, "never liked night flying."

"Well, I gotta be gettin' on back to the base, get ready for my flight," said Evan.

Then RM made his proposal, strange enough at the time, and I don't believe Clare knew about it till he opened his mouth, "Willy, I'd like to talk over something with you, if you don't mind staying a few more minutes . . . I can give you a ride out to the field in time for your flight . . . okay Evan? Old thunder-bird-in-swamp?"

"Shucks . . . I kin make it back okay, I reckon."

"Don't crash and burn," I called after him, our usual salutation.

He left and the three of us had coffee and it didn't begin right away but soon enough RM was at it.

"Look," he said, "and don't get hot at what I'm about to say . . . I'm speaking as your lawyer, and your counselor, and your father as well, so don't be disrespectful . . . okay?"

"Shoot, dad, I'm listening."

"No, make it as a friend . . . but Willy, what are you doing? Wait! Just a—let me say . . . before . . . I just don't understand your *program.* I'm not, I'm trying not to bring Leyla into this but, Jesus, I don't understand it at all. It looks like you're either trying to kill yourself or be court-martialed, or both. And, I can't help but bring it in. You're in love with Leyla, right? At least you talked to me like you were. Shit," Clare didn't wince a bit, "I care for you, Willy and I think something's wrong. I don't understand Hebert and can't say as I ever did. He's a different case-study entirely. Anyhow, *is* something wrong? You're angry because of the orders? But what is it you're embarked on? So . . . go ahead, tell me."

I was pleased and uncomfortable at the same time. If somebody hadn't brought it up I don't know how long I'd have gone on without saying anything. Was Leyla gone? Was it all over? I truly didn't know and was deeply saddened and couldn't get around to thinking about it, resolving anything about it. I was turning hot and cold while he was talking, while Clare looked soberly on.

"I don't know, RM, exactly, what you think I'm doing. Sure, it's a lot of . . . shit," I had hesitated then went ahead and said it, in front of her. "I hate it . . . being here and stuck."

"But what's that got to do with her, Leyla? Maybe I shouldn't tell you but Leyla called here and asked . . . "

"She *called?*"

"She called yesterday. She thinks something's wrong. She knows you and I are good friends . . . "

"She actually called."

"She loves you—"

"I don't think I understand it, either."

"The thing is, Willy, who are you taking this out on? Does she get the blame for it? And what are you gonna *do* about it? That's it. And don't tell me about fate and heroes and flying down the funnel of a Jap ship and ticker-tape parades—"

"For your *body*! When it's shipped back," said Clare.

We both laughed. He went on, "Remember the lecture you were upset about? The movie at Deland about antiaircraft and how they fire at an area, not even at planes? You came out, really shook up?"

"Yes, yes, sure."

"Well, *that*, Willy babe, is war, the way it's fought now. Each brace of antiaircraft guns covers an area, they don't shoot at individual planes any longer, they just send up a wall of antiaircraft. The day of heroes and individual combat is *over*, Willy. It's not war like it's s'posed to be. Right? Individual combat, knights on horseback—"

Clare interrupted, "Will, forgive me for just asking straight out, but why not get Leyla down here? Why not?"

"Okay," RM jumped in too, "Get her down here, marry her, we'll find you a place on the beach, and begin living again."

The implication was clear. The way Hebert and I were going at it was not "living."

"I tell you plain, lieutenant, she's really hurt. She knows you love her but she doesn't understand this—"

"Yeah, well, there *is* something I can't tell you—"

"You've got syphilis," said RM.

Clare burst out laughing.

"No . . . there's a crazy chance we might go overseas. And one more thing. You know, despite dive-bombers, I was happy at Deland. Happy, raging, wild to go. And mad about her at the same time—"

"Look, you wanted to go overseas. You wanted it a lot more than I did, but we landed here. Now the thing is you're here. And whose fault is it?

"Nobody's—"

"Then, Willy, it's not taking 'advantage' of anything; it's only admitting you're here. You're here and stuck. She's there. You love her, and told her you'd marry her—"

"Yes, and if we'd gotten the leave, and orders to the coast, I'd be married now."

"If the war ended tomorrow would you marry her?"

"Yes. But . . . I'd feel . . . cheated—"

"That's it," Clare spoke up again, "I want to hear about being 'cheated'."

"I can't explain it."

"I don't get it. Willy, what is it?"

"I've dreamed about it. Wanted it all my life. The great test, the challenge. Then *after that* . . . AFTER THAT, marriage and the rest—"

"Yeah, down the Jap's funnel, or ram the battleship with your 500 pound bomb, after shooting down 27 Zeros . . . Christ Willy, that's like a child's dream. Down the funnel and THEN come home to get married? . . . Pull the sword out of the rock, slay the dragon and get the damsel? There's no after-the-war-for-fighter-pilots. Do you know what that means?"

"Sure!"

"Willy, it means you're *dead*. Swallowed up in it! See?"

I let him go.

"You think you're gonna get it out of your system and *then* come back? Not the way you would go into it."

"Something like that." I was hanging on, embarrassed and grateful at the same time.

"Willy, it's a dream and a fairy tale. And what you're trying to find is not out there. Maybe it wasn't ever there, not even in the first world war, when they dropped a bouquet over the enemy's airdrome. It was only in those *Air Aces* magazines. Did you think of that?"

"Well, then I want to see that . . . for myself—"

"And you're gonna be mad and pout till you get overseas? And lose Leyla? And all for a dream you have about *war* and what war *really* is?"

"I can't explain it."

"Willy, that's ducking the issue."

Things were getting hot and I was reduced to firing my last salvo which, I knew, would be a slap in the face . . . to them, out here on the beach in their cozy quarters.

"Look . . . no, I give up."

"No, tell us."

I looked at them, both intent on the conversation, and I felt a kind attention, a loving attention.

"Will, I think this is very important," said Clare who only knew me through RM, blinking her acknowledgment that this concern might be only conversational. And added, "You know, when Ritch and I got married, I didn't feel that gave me any more of a hold over him. It only made me feel at rest. That he could go overseas but that we were, it sounds old-fashioned, 'promised' . . . do you understand? It might give him some strength when he got over. Alright? I know you guys and your superstition, not talking about 'this thing' till it's over, and I respect that and, right now, even more than you guys do, I'm worrying about Loomis. But these things happen whether Loomis is overseas, or here and married—"

"Loomis could be in bed right now—"

"Maybe forgot to sign in on his plane sheet, it's happened before."

I liked what Clare said. As for Loomis, it didn't look good.

"We better be on our way," RM said looking at his watch, "It's 1:15, and you gotta be on station at 2:00, my boy."

"Look," I told them, "it *is* the war . . . and while it's going on it just seems, almost, sacrilegious to—"

"What?" RM pounced on me. "To enjoy yourself? Have fun?"

"To be playing house," I told them. There, it was out of the bag.

"'PLAYING HOUSE'?" Clare was furious, RM was choking.

"Allllllright, I *thought* so," said RM

"Will . . . that makes me furious," said a red-faced beautiful Clare. "No matter what it looks like to you or how amateurish our beginning seems to you, we're beginning our *together* . . . hear that? Our *together* lives, because a WAR isn't life, alright? I think you have it backwards, the *war*'s not real, but our life together *is*. I don't mean that, because war's *real* enough, it's just *madness*. People who've never seen each other, never known each other, nothing against each other, going off to kill each other—"

She wanted to add more but was suddenly abashed and looked to RM.

Instead, that warrior decided we had to go in order for me to get to the flight line, take off and be on station at two.

It wasn't a great leave-taking. Although I should have been apologizing it was more Clare, and she took my two hands and told me she had a prose-poem she wanted to lend me, for as long as I wanted it. "Mark Twain's 'War Prayer,' have you read it?"

I had never heard of it.

RM told her to forget it, we had to go and were out the door before she came running up to the car and gave it to me. They had a second together. Their kiss was like a curse, and I felt it whether that was their intention or not.

I was feeling pretty low, about my comment and, now, seeing it through their eyes. Thinking about Leyla, hanging up. She's never done that before. Have I lost her?

"RM, I'm sorry I said that."

"Don't be sorry. Conversations begin when we start saying what we really think, although," he stretched the word out "it was something of a low blow, if that's what you really think."

"Well . . . Clare gave me a lot to chew on. I never looked at it like that—"

"Smart girl, Clare. Hides it behind those honey looks. I always told her she has a good head but never had to use it . . . she got by on other things."

I knew he was angry but was putting it off for the ride in to the base; through that lane of royal palms, and over Point X-ray, the wooden bridge across the Indian River, where every plane entering the traffic pattern passed over in order to check in. Now the traffic was the 12 to 2 flight returning—sixes, 2C's and twin-engine Beechcrafts, full of students from radar training flights. I liked it. I loved the flying, night or day, those planes lofting down and in from altitude, tired and wild with speed they came singing in and down. But, have I lost her?

We went right out to the field. RM had another hour and a half before going up.

"You haven't called Leyla since she hung up on you?"

"No. I guess, I thought that was it . . . I mean, I thought . . . till I find out about this plan."

"This secret?"

"Yeahh . . . and, please tell Clare I'm sorry."

"Hey, Willy," RM said, and I felt our friendship had been restored, at least partly.

"I wanted to hear some music tonight. Nat 'King' Cole, Slim Gaillard, Lion*ellll*."

"Next time, Willy. Meantime, *call* her, for Christ's sake."

Chapter 27

I checked with the tower as I taxied out for takeoff, "Any word on 47, over?"

"Negative, 58, from Citrus. We're taking names of pilots for a search at Oh-eight hundred."

"Put me down."

"You're *on*, 58, Citrus, out."

Hebert and I had each tested three planes today but, even without that, flying these beasts was more familiar than walking, than going to bed, than brushing my teeth.

I jammed it open, started down that dark alley lighted with flare pots on each side, eased the tail up slightly, waited for it to gather speed; off the ground, wheels up, cockpit closed, cowl flaps, prop back, stood it on its tail, and turned away from the field climbing, and wondering how I could not have called her back. Well, if the Flying Tigers came through we'd be in China before she could get down here. Was that why I hadn't called her? I could not answer my own question.

I was down at five. The sky was turning from black to grey. Hebert and four other bogeys were in the dressing room waiting for the search. On the makeshift blackboard was the news:

BIG MEETING: ALL BOGEY PILOTS!
1400 HOURS, TODAY, LECTURE ROOM 'C'

Obscene comments, drawings, curses all around the words. The fury of the comments and the discovery that everyone, outside of RM and one or two more, hated this duty was surprising. Hebert and I cursing the duty in private was one thing but to discover that everyone was furious, and fury was the word—that was news.

"What the . . . heck is *that* all about?" Hebert asked the room, pointing to the notice.

"I don't know," stocky Balt answered him, "but 'the word' is that he's gonna clip your wings . . . yours and Willy's."

"And what time is this gonna take place?"

"Two this afternoon . . . fourteen hundred to you."

Three hours' sleep and we were back to the flight line for the search at eight. Loomis I remembered vaguely from dive-bombers, tall and earnest, with a shock of hair cut like a country kid's, a sincere sort of goony bird, very proud of being in the marines."

" . . . he never liked night flying," Muncrief had told us at least three times.

Just before the search we were put on hold. We stood around waiting for news. Behind it all I was itching to call Leyla but there was no phone.

Ten search pilots were now ready to go, including RM who had been waiting since six. Then the flight was definitely put on hold. Ten minutes later it was canceled.

An SB2C had been spotted in a cow pasture six miles south of the base. It was off a little dirt road off of a paved road south of the station.

I don't know why, maybe because we were ready to fly and had been stopped, but everyone was piling into cars to go. There were six of us in Jorge's big Buick and the mood was giddy. Going out to see. What? Meanwhile the war stood off and above us all, like a huge thunderhead that was passing us by. Behind the thunderhead I could see Leyla's face.

We made the correct turns and spotted the big beast in the field, propeller blades wrapped around the fuselage, wheels up but apparently not very damaged. We parked behind three other cars of navy pilots, crossed over the barbed wire, and in a kind of frenzy, not quite running, walked up to it.

Why doesn't he get out?

We could see the pilot, cockpit closed, sitting as if posing for his portrait. Closer to the plane we slowed down. More cars were being parked, more pilots coming to see. We became very orderly and even formed a line without a word about lining up.

Each one of us stepped onto the wing, up to the cockpit, looked in, stood for a few seconds, even politely turned away and walked down, stepped off the wing, strolled off to stand and look from farther away.

There were about 20 of us, marines and navy, for once quiet, tamped down not by the sight but the fact of death in this pleasant field, this ungainly downed blue and white starred beast downed like a rhino in midcharge whose legs folded underneath and still skidded forward, mass and speed working out this final problem after death. But that's what we couldn't figure out.

I walked onto the wing, on the strip of sandpaper at the root of the wing, and saw Loomis for the last time and, really, one of the first. Loomis had been one of us in name only—an all but unnoticed part of squadron 12-C. I went up to the cockpit and looked one look at him, sitting, hand still on the stick, eyes open, a fly crawling confidently across his face.

The plane looked like it had been in a minor accident.

On the way back, Jorge asked, "What killed him?"

No one answered Jorge. No one knew.

When we got back to the base everything took on a miraculous hue and I was operating mechanically while I looked and watched people, as if I was watching life itself: people greeting, shaking hands, talking as if . . . as if we would always be able to depend on such things. Hands. Fingers. Voices. Laughter. I went to the mess office, got a bunch of change, fingered the quarters, thinking, feeling the hard coins, called Leyla, deposited coins. She was out. Gone. With no hope at all I left a message, "I love you, please call, Will." Hours went by in a strange procession. We ate lunch and then, in that same strange mood, Sam Lyttle, Cap'n Sam, caught me after lunch, walked me to a corner of the lobby. His first words were so shocking I knew I wasn't hearing right. "Look, I hate to tell you because I know how you and Hebert were counting on this but it's all off—"

"*It's* . . . all off? *What* is? Surely, not—" My mind was blinking off-on, but he was still talking, then his voice came back to me.

" . . . The colonel found out . . . got hold of the list . . . 'Resigning your citizenship'? He was ape-shit! He'd court-martial the lot of us . . . yours truly today . . . *this very afternoon—*"

Dreaming? Was it a dream? Surely, he couldn't be talking about . . . about "it" the Flying Tigers?

"Well," I asked Sam, amazed, "Aren't we free? Aren't we free to go somewhere else? Isn't China an ally?"

"'Not during war,'" he said. "'I'll court martial your ass . . . today,

Captain, I'll put you under house arrest if I hear one more squeak about it!'
I tell you, Vairin, he was *raving!* He ate me up one side and down the
other, 'You're a grown man, for God's sake, you think you can go fly for the
Dragon Lady? This is not a comic strip!' And a lot more. So that's it.
Finito! No ifs ands or buts. He was ready to court martial me for what I've
already done. I'm sorry, Vairin, and all I can say is I'd have been proud to
fly with you boys but as for that scheme, it's—"

He put out his hand. I took it. And that was all. He left. And like a
match touched to tissue paper the dream was ashes. This tough, swash-
buckling gambler, Guadalcanal flyer, a hero who had the financial backing
of the biggest banking house in China, derailed by a guy with silver chickens on his collar.

I lay down, crushed. I had been promised. *I'd* get over there. And, somehow, in Corsairs. And now? I took Leyla's last letter to bed with me, while
I secretly watched Hebert at the washstand wetting his hair then brushing
it. Brushing, brushing. I could see his face and the reflected face in the
mirror, and I could see Loomis's face behind the cockpit plexiglass.

I had that familiar feeling, failure and hurt at the back of my throat.
Last and best chance. A dream gone wrong. I tried again to read the letter.
Hebert was stacking his clothes—he had a mountain of T-shirts and skiv-
vies and washed them every two weeks.

The colonel was acting like we were a vital part of the "war effort." Well,
he hadn't seemed to think so until he found out he was about to lose some
of his boys to the Chinese.

I couldn't face telling Hebert what I'd just heard. Down the tubes, China,
the Far East, the South China Seas, all gone. Telling him, out loud, would
be like telling myself and I couldn't stand that. It wasn't gone till I told
someone else out loud.

I started reading the letter, stopped, jammed it in my pocket, went down
to the lobby and placed the call again. Bess answered this time, "Please
have her call me. It's very important, Bess." Left the number again in case
she'd lost it, picked up the letter as if I was picking up a piece of my lost life.
I flopped on the bed.

"What's eating you?" Hebert asked me.

"Nothing."

I held the letter in my hand. Now I've lost Leyla *and* the war.

> *I'm sorry about the situation, and not going overseas (and the leave). I hate*
> *your being . . . thwarted. Not that I understand it too well. This drive . . .*

We've been studying some American writers, Dorothy Thompson and this wonderful quote about Hitler, 'Nazism . . . is the enemy of whatever is sunny, reasonable, pragmatic, common-sense, freedom-loving, life-affirming . . . ' I like it, especially, that it's the enemy of whatever is 'sunny.' You know, Will, we are 'sunny.' Our lives are going to be 'sunny.' We're with the sun, the light people.

And when you call me an 'angel' that's how I feel. It makes me feel 'sunny.' Maybe it's irritating for me to talk like that when you're not feeling 'sunny' about things, but it won't be forever. That's as close as I'll come to those awful forbidden words. And one more thing, another quote, from Dostoevsky (sp?), but I can't find the book, it was about you, I thought, and this character, 19 or so, who wants to give his life to help solve the world's problems (I thought of you) and how, if only he could devote some years to study and ideas about it, how he could come back to the world's problems and, with so much more wisdom, throw himself at the world's problems, with his whole force, mental and physical . . . there, I hope I haven't ruined it, I'll send it when I find that book.

I look back on our trip and it seems miraculous. Planning and doing it by ourselves. Well, my darling Lieutenant-I-love-you, it was miraculous. And it helped us. Don't you agree? Please answer this last question. Sometimes it is so clear and vivid, but other times, I hate to say it . . . it's distant and like a dream . . .

I stopped reading and watched Evan folding his skivvy shorts and T-shirts. He was like a busy pack-rat about his clothes and had at least 20 sets of each, rolled up and stuck away in his closet, for the great flood or the end of the world.

The date on the letter was January 15th, '44. Would she still say the same things? In March? Have I lost her?

When I finally told Hebert he didn't say a word, just a certain grimness about his mouth. He went on stashing his clothes in his methodical way. Then, suddenly, "*It's all off?*"

"That's what he just told me."

"You know what I'd like to do? I'd like to steal some danged planes and go down to South America."

He got wilder and wilder, mapping out a life for us. We'd smuggle diamonds, we'd get an island and mount antiaircraft. We'd hold the bastards off. We'd have wives and children and start a danged NEW country. He went on till even he was laughing at his mad plans. And all the time rolled his T-shirts in tiny rolls and stashed them away, ready for the end of the world.

In early April Leyla would finish another semester. She was about to begin her junior year. According to RM, she couldn't understand my hesitation, and I couldn't explain it. And now the Flying Tigers, gone without a trace, a pipe dream we had fastened on. Only, like any plans one depends on, it was not letting go. For whole minutes I would catch myself waking up and wondering, which is the dream? We're going? We're not going?

In my own mind, in my own heart, I had made a compact with the powers that work these things out . . . Corsairs—and glory in the air.

"Come on, we got that meeting! I hear *we're* going to get it. No more hot breakups, no more one-turn-spins. That comes direct from 'Lover Boy' Cleary." The one who had conned his way into scheduling the rest of us.

There was a knock at the door."Phone call, Lieutenant Vairin."

The radio in the lounge announced the Russians had recaptured Berslov, and the RAF had dropped more than 3,000 tons of bombs on Frankfurt, the heaviest raid of the war. P51s with disposable gas tanks were now able to escort bombers all the way in and back from the targets so US daytime bombing was being resumed. The war was a living character in my life. Where was it now? What was it doing? I called as we were about to go out the door to the meeting.

"*Will!* I was just about to call *you!* This is amazing!"

"Leyla . . . I just got some news that's changed everything. Will you drop whatever you're doing and come down? Come down, please, my . . . angel. Come down and let's get married?"

"WILL!"

"Yes, now! Come down now. We can get a place, there's a place I can get out on the beach, near RM and Clare—"

"What's happened? What has changed? Why haven't you called? Or written?"

"I can't talk about it. And a few people were almost court-martialed over it."

"Very mysterious—"

"Leyla . . . you're not answering. For the first time it's clear to me. I'm not going overseas. We're not going anywhere."

"I'm sorry I hung up, Will . . . but there didn't seem to be anything else to say . . . Do you really want this?"

"Leyla I just didn't want you coming down if there was a chance . . . I mean if I was *going*."

"You almost said it again. Between me and going overseas . . . you see—"

"Leyla, save my life and come down."

"Will, do you see what I'm talking about?"

"Look. It's not competition. Don't think of it like that. You can't think of it like that."

"It's hard not to, Will . . . with you it's overseas *or* marriage D'you see? RM and Clare—"

"Will you, please? Come down?"

"Beg me."

"'Beg you? I'll come up and get you!"

"Now, that's more like it."

"I had supper with RM and Clare last night . . . RM told me you called."

"That was supposed to be secret."

"I'm *glad* he told me. Leyla, until he told me I thought you might . . . have ended it."

"Oh, Will . . . sometimes . . . you're such a fool."

"Anyhow, I accused them of 'playing house' when people were dying all over the world—"

"Are they still speaking to you?"

"Clare was outraged—"

"Good, good. Will, that was very cruel of you. I hope, *hope* she did tell you off."

"It wasn't just telling me off. She told me some things about, oh, the war—"

"I wish I'd been there."

"Yes, so do I. That would mean you're here now."

"Ah, Will, Will."

"I never thought of it that way, they see the war as an interruption, I'm seeing it as, Jesus, I don't know what, maybe tied up with why we don't allow ourselves to speak of it in the past . . . you understand? Leyla, my angel, for God's sake come down . . . Clare gave me a Mark Twain essay, 'The War Prayer.'"

"Oh, we read it in American Lit. What did you think of it?"

"Listen, Leyla . . . I haven't read it yet—"

"Will, I'm supposed to have a class now, can I call you later?"

"Leyla. . . . We need to talk *now*."

"Okay . . . okayyyy." The two words were as different as night and day. The first impatient, the second one giving over, giving over with a sweetness that was so like her.

"Will, then talk to me . . . "

"Leyla . . . you're a . . . blessing, and I've got to tell you something."

"Yes, darling—"

"Don't be sweet. I might never get it out."

She laughed, "Alright, youuu bastard, tell me."

"Leyla . . . I have trouble—"

"Yes."

"Trouble . . . admitting . . . Saying it. Feeling . . . Missing you. Do you see?"

"No, but you tried to tell me this before."

"Leyla . . . that's not what I'm trying to say. See . . . I just always felt that first comes the war and give everything to *that*, then *after* that, marriage and children—"

Will! *After???* Give everything to the war and . . . Don't you *see???* No, you don't get it!"

"Yes, after . . . doing that, giving myself to *it* . . . First! Then coming back and us and our children, our seven children. Anyhow, now it's all changed . . . We're going nowhere. The pact is broken . . . "

"*Pact?* You've lost me."

"It's a long story. Anyhow, we're not going and so please, please, come down, come down now . . . Leyla, you seem so far away—"

"No, Will, I'm right here. Waiting for you. But I want to know, for sure, that this time there are no reservations. And you've really given up this obsession with the, excuse me, the damned war."

"None, absolutely none, Leyla. Oh, my God, can you really, will you really come down and let's be together?"

"Yes. Yes and yes and yes, yes, yes . . . and yes."

"And listen, I have only this tiny one little request—"

"Will . . . you worry me."

"Will you marry me?"

"You heard me. Now, what is this tiny request?"

"It's not a big thing . . . but these *wives* . . . have premonitions and cry, give them numbers of planes they can't—"

"Will, I ought to hang up. Damn you! The only thing I worry about is . . . being up here while you're down there, flying. I want to be there . . . with you. Not to control you! God, Will. I *love* you!" There was a long pause, "saying 'I love you' Is so senseless—"

"What's that mean?"

"It means I want to either start raving or shut up."

"Leyla, I'm feeling it now . . . missing you, I'm aching for you. Come down, please, my . . . angel. Come down? Now!"

"WILL!"

"Yes, now. Come down now. There's a place out on the beach, near RM and Clare. I'll send you the money for a train."

"My grandmother will take care of that."

"Will you leave school, and just come down?"

Hebert was pulling at my sleeve.

"*Will* . . . you call . . . out of the blue—"

"I know . . . I know—"

"And you want me to just—"

Hebert, pulling at my sleeve, "Just a second . . . Moka, just a second—"

"We're late!"

"Who are you talking to?"

"Listen, Leyla . . . my angel, can you call me tomorrow? This time? With a definite date?"

"Will . . . don't 'angel' me now. You're exasperating . . . I'll call you tomorrow. Same time."

"With a definite date!"

"Yes. No. I'll tell you now. Can you wait till April . . . April the ninth? Definite!"

We hung up. Hebert was halfway out the door.

"Meeting now, wives later," he yelled. I caught up with him and we drove to the meeting.

Chapter 28

⌒

The room was jammed; every chair filled and pilots lining the rear wall. The Fowler, Full Lieutenant Farrell, and short fussy Captain Spatzler, marine, were still waiting when we walked in.

Forty-five of us, everyone minus Laurie Heath, non-conformist, Buddhist—pacifist some said—Loomis's room-mate, who'd go home with

Loomis (or his body) on emergency leave. The kind of leave no one wanted. Heath very quietly drunk, out at the beach house.

The crowd, the animals, wouldn't quiet down so Farrell began anyhow, waving a sheaf of papers at us, "When you first came to Red Beach," he shouted, and repeated it. "Alright, quiet down! When you first came to Red Beach, you didn't know what you were getting into, but . . . but, *quiet down* . . . from the beginning . . . " he looked us all over, "I have been working on orders for you. I know that most of you men have been waiting to get overseas, and waiting for this news for a long time . . . "

'Waiting'? Eighteen months, like lightning through my brain, then four more and it's just 'waiting'?

" . . . This time has not been wasted. You knew it could be used to perfect your flying—"

Deland and a tremendous war opening like a morning glory, through the last steps before flying off to make our fortunes, cast our bread on the great waters, knock heads with the world, as innocent as purely drunk on the vintage that great year, wine-air vintage 1943, at our otherwise quiet bar of dark mahogany tables . . .

"You pilots rank among the top flyers for night flying time, in the world . . ."

patio beyond French doors, huge green elephant ears nodding lightly in air come down from the sky off ocean touching bougainvillea brick wall and poinsettia powder-red, air of sea flowers through glass twining thoughts and heavy-bottomed octagonal snifters, cognac for new Lafayette Escadrille, Ahab in some Peruvian port, so spilling over so hopped up still coasting on the last flight, in class planes slanted into sight through glass out again, like that flying slanted in slanted out, rags of lecture-flying-drinking until nothing could stop the gaze so deep in laughing-wonder and late heavy sun . . .

"For the most part you men have done an excellent job, at very frustrating duty, I admit . . . for the *most part* I said, which brings me to some new directives—"

Pensacola and single engines, last outpost for old-line heroes, Little Johns, Jolly Robins, the very last Mohicans in an organized madhouse. And Marines, oh yes, golden wings from Montezuma's halls to the banana kingdoms, and single-engines? No choice except for those freaks with their 'learn a trade,' because there *is* no after the war for fighter pilots.

"So, the Beast, the SB2C, as it's presently being flown is *not* condemned. It's a good plane, rejected by the navy for *carriers* . . . *HOLD IT*, rejected only for—*carriers!*" His last words drowned out by screams, hisses, cackles, boos.

Graduation morning; wings, uniform, shoes, teeth, faces shined for knighthood and orders for the post-graduate eight weeks before war. A beautiful sight and all their parents should have seen it and died happy afterwards; seeing themselves in the still-too-good-to-be gull-winged Corsair, world's fastest, while marines on Guadalcanal fought for their lives.

"Well, they're in! Effective after you've completed five months of your current duty and after relief arrives," he waved a sheaf of papers, goading, infuriating the room, "but first these directives—" in the roar of questions Farrell calmly put the orders on the bottom of the pile.

May, 1943, night train for Memphis, news in half-light:

Bougainville gone, Singapore taken, Bataan—far eastern Alamo—new tradition, new history, and all the way to the Indian Ocean, Malaya, Sumatra, Borneo, Celebes, pearl divers, sarong wearers beautiful mixed race women and, fine, let the war be hard and long, let it wring us out, use us up. Destination Memphis, drunken sleep and thoughts so far away that train unrelated to the war took us nearer, through the night, heading east it drew us west.

"Okay, I'll read 'em," Farrell pulled out another sheet, "And you can listen or not, but once you've signed these you're responsible, so *wake up*: Flight conduct in the pattern —"

A big "JESUS!" greeted that; Fowler paused, noted where it came from, did nothing.

"—Some pilots have been breaking off much too steeply over the run-way . . . these so-called 'one-turn-spins-to-a-landing' are *out!*"

This was greeted with screams. Was he staring . . . .at me? At Hebert?

"On breaking off, your bank will not exceed FORTY-FIVE DEGREES!"

People were pushing us, laughing. Others were exasperated, laughing, yelling, BULL-SHIT! . . . JESUS CHRIST! . . . ."

Spatzler stepped forward, "*You know damned well when it's 45 degrees . . .* "

While Japanese rolled over thousands of square miles—Australia threatened, endless China toppling endlessly, Gilbert Island, the Marshalls, Wake—sinking battleships and theories, cruisers, destroy-ers, merchant ships, downing hundreds of British, American, Dutch planes.

"And another thing," Spatzler told us, "you men can play around but we're going to start cracking down! These orders . . . " he looked over to catch Farrell's eye, "are not effective immediately. It'll be another month, and meanwhile we continue as before . . . no, I mean, *not* as before! Lieuten-ant Farrell and I are damn' tired of the colonel and the captain blaming your conduct on us! Some of that flight conduct around the field is . . . is *crazy!* Is . . . *LAWLESS!* We're not nursemaids and you're not children," Spatzler was screaming at the entire room. "You're marines!" He said, even more flustered, "And just remember that!" Spatzler was convinced that to imply we were not marines, even for a day, was to roast us in hell. He moved back, nodded to Farrell who, surprised at Spatzler's vehemence, held up still another paper, "Pilots will not lower wheels in excess of 200 knots, since it puts a severe strain on the entire hydraulic . . . I think that's all . . . now!" Spatzler touched his arm, they conferred, Farrell turned, grinned.

Farrell, the good salesman, had slipped these directives to us under the gimmick of new orders but now, after the greens came dessert, meantime the low roar had grown for the last 20 minutes, the group would have their meal or the trainer.

And from that tight little isle: blood, sweat, and kidney stones: 'We shall fight on the landing grounds, we shall fight in the fields, and in the streets; we shall never surrender.' With that cockeyed British under-statement that put lumps in throats and tears in eyes thousands of miles away.

"I think that's . . . *alright*," he told the roar, which almost swallowed both of them, cracking out their, "Quiet down! . . . Hold on! . . . Damnit, quiet down!" Exchanging co-misery glances, missing each other in the near-panic.

"While I've been reading these directives . . . Captain Spatzler has checked the roll. There's one person missing—"

"Lucky bastard!"

"*Silence!* . . . You were told that one hundred percent attendance would be expected. Does anyone know where Lieutenant Heath is?"

Balt lifted his heavy arm, "It's his day off . . . besides, his roommate . . . was Loomis."

"You were told by the colonel that all such meetings would require your attendance, whether you broke a leg or—"

"I don't know if he broke his leg," Woodruff, the merry duke, told Fowler, with more poise than Fowler had shown all day, "but he couldn't walk so good when I saw him last."

Relief for the crowd and they took it laughing, almost yelling.

"Make a note of that, please," Fowler told Spatzler.

Then Farrell leaned back against the desk, holding them one instant longer with his dark thin significant smile, and suddenly, the man with fiend in his veins, held out the last sheaf of papers, the magician had at last produced a rabbit, "I have here your orders, authorizing gradual inception into the night fighter program—"

A wave of noise crashed, rolled forward. Cursing, loud outright contempt for the system and all orders, these included and anything else from Farrell and, finally, not *his* words, not *his* interpretation, the Bible itself: "Alright! Here it is: ' . . . In accordance with specifications . . . herein outlined . . . authority contained . . . order MCVFN134CGU55 of above date hereby modified to read, those pilots currently serving utility capacity, VFN Night Fighter program, Jacksonville Command, and desirous, to be incepted type Marine Night Fighter program 2BUVFMN for further training and duty involving combat aircraft overseas *upon proper relief* current duties or proper replacement . . . their current duties for release to aforesaid duty . . . '"

Hebert hit me on the arm, smiling and unaffected by the way the Fowler presented it. I understood only a mist around 'combat aircraft' and 'overseas.'

The ground-school classroom had erupted again as Farrell waved still another paper, not having answered anything.

What's it mean? When? When *what*? When do we start training *and* check out in fighters? The meeting had given birth to 20 meetings. Excited, skeptical, cynical, haranguing, yeah well WHEN? And Farrell screaming against them information they yelled back for and still no one SHUT UP! Three times, four times and somehow we got hold of the word April. Replacements? No! He didn't know, maybe a week. Replacements? NO! Checkouts. Fighters. Early when? No, No, No, QUIET!

Up on the table, "Sign up with 'Lover' Cleary in the flight office, those who are interested in night fighters . . . priority to those who have flown the most hours since arriving Red Beach. Pilots and flight hours, in order of those with the most flight time now being mimeographed and will be posted—"

"Everything is mimeographed," muttered Jorge, "the number of women you screwed is now being mimeographed and will be posted."

Farrell continued, yelling, "And when relief comes you will go through *five* at a time, by *fives*, in other words, groups of *five*—"

"*Eight?* . . . Did he say fifteen?"

The meeting had adjourned itself, first standing, then out into the hall, an excited, angry pushing mob of nearly fifty and a different meeting, the real meeting which once in the hall did not move, everyone in a rage swept up in this need to argue, to prove you were right all along and their god damned 'those desirous,' furious that no one cracked a whip saying *go* or *stay*, or get out there and save the world, no, only 'those desirous.'

"Hell yes," long tall Gondran was screeching, like the Moonfixer at the ref, "I don't care what, I'm signing for it! I'm sick of the Beast and sick of target-life."

Stocky Balt arguing with him while most of the others stood around like it was already too late to choose but just listening. Woodruff, the merry duke, up to Hebert and me with Balt after him, "What do you think?" Balt at Woodruff's cocky elbow smiling uncommitted, Mulligan over with Jorge, then Waylie against Simmons or whoever stood on that side, "I volunteer for nothing. Not even a pay increase." Very good, oh ho, sound sound advice, then Jorge grabbed me, "Okay? Did I tell you? Is this it? Shall we go? Shall we give 'em a break?" feeling more enthusiastic than that crazy prophet here it is waiting for us—Jorge at the first meeting four months ago, the 'temporary-permanent' meeting had felt it in his bones—Jorge through that herd of unhappy bulls had grabbed my neck, a secret, low, hissing, happy for it all, as if Farrell, back then, had given us orders, 'Listen, Willy, I told you, we're *going*. I *feel it, right here!*' Jorge grabbed himself by the balls,

Jorge the wild-eyed whose visions didn't bounce up and down over Fowlers. And at such a time, the strange light in his eyes, not at the milling group but at me, the two of us, and now again.

Then the group seemed to explode like a bomb, rose up, opened out, arguing, flattered, insulted, irritated, glad, even afraid—the slightest creaking movement of the big machine—excitement and a kind of center in the biggest knot where Waylie, the calm one, and other cynics stood off Gondran and three more, now vehement for signing while Waylie with his cohorts grinning fiercely; Waylie the cock-of-the-walk only none came forward to meet him. Now Sinkowska, full of hatred, "Look at this . . . just look! A bunch of kids," angry they needed reminding, angrier the longer it took, "Children, for Christ's sake," then to Waylie about them all, " . . . a little piece of paper and they think they're going overseas tomorrow . . . reference bullshit, authorized up my barracks bag, XPM17 thousand, combat aircraft, come on, boys, jump in your flyin' kiddie Kars, take a crap on the Jap before he wipes us off the map," turned to the advocates of signing, coolly, yes he thought they were wrong and hated Farrell hated them hated his own country-peasant-sucker background and wasn't falling for nuthin'. Yes, *hated* Fowler and wouldn't follow him for free beer. Waylie the scoffer laughed at them, he simply liked it here, but Sinkowska would have none of it and none for no one else: "Does the order say *when*? Do the orders say April? Or does Full Lieutenant *Fowler* say April? Did Fowler say where replacements are coming from?"

To Gondran now so raging he could hardly speak; any less and he would start swinging, "All I said was . . . all I said god damnit . . . I'm signing on the chance, just the—"

He could get no farther. Others began, as Muncrief, bursting out with it first not talking yes or no to aid Gondran, ready to hit out, cry, or start screaming and running in tiny circles.

I watched Gondran and too felt the pain of *choosing* war and Fowler's 'forty-five degree bank' and, way back there of Leyla and what all of it meant, then back to the indignity 'those desiring' war, the big parlor game and the one or THEM responsible for all of it falling out like it always did. No, let them beg first. Only in the next second ready to run for the chance, sure, let's go, and did, at Jorge's suggestion, that the five of us; Jorge, me, Hebert, Mulligan, and, hell, Woodruff, Balt and RM if he's not too deep into the married life, and, okay, Nevers too, little rat-faced Nevers who was into revolution, "Let's go, let's blow up the moon!" Hey! Here are seven suckers, eight, no questions asked, Woodruff talking where to find Cleary, back to the room, back out, alright? Yeah? The crowd moving down the stairs on the far side of the hangar, rain forgotten remembered again, the six and Nevers, seven, eight? Pushed past the crowd collecting at the huge hangar doors, pushed off from the building, the rain came down harder and Hebert for his car, No! To FLIGHT! Coming back, wha . . . ? There, like the pause of confused pedestrians under the wheels of a truck and in the middle of two crossroads, Hebert confronting Woodruff the merry duke who'd have killed himself in a Maserati if not in a plane, "Hey? Yes?" and Balt's big-shouldered shrug, "Suits me!" And me, Will, who had prayed, lamented for so long I was meant to go and not just any way, alongside little Nevers, "Come on, let's get off the earth, out of our skins!" Talking, cursing Jorge, laughing no matter what in the rain and to flight? On the second rainy decision, we took off straight running flat out hangar-bound to Cleary's list, breaking with the old life there in street-raining-decision, back into the hangar up the stairs to flight to Lover Cleary and the new life, even dry shirts now wet from rain, Hebert next to me, just ahead Jorge's shoulders moved under his shirt, Woodruff on the other side we flew in tight formation already a team to fight together die for each other no, no, all five six or eight up Fifth Avenue to ticker tape blizzard. The war so simple. Not for this or that stupid reason but for us to fight and win in.

Into the office in line and RM! You too?

"Yeah, I'm married but I'm not dead!"

We laughed. I looked behind and saw Peters in line. We were laughing, making ridiculous hand movements, blowing up battleships, flying *under* battleships, shooting down Zeros . . .

"Don't push! It'll be a long war, look alive you fighter pilots," 'Lover' Cleary, the one among us who had seen a need, someone to schedule the bogey pilots. And rarely flew anymore.

I took the indelible pencil from Jorge and signed the paper, twelfth on the list, but knew Hebert and I had more flight time than anyone else on the base.

All flights were on hold, rain was coming down in erratic sheets, although reports were it was going to clear.

Hebert and I took off in a race for the beach, breaking all records, hit the end of the bridge, Point X-ray, so hard we didn't smack down again on the wooden rattling construction for five feet, straight through the avenue of royal palms to Milton's Place, where ocean and highway met, for the big muster, the beer muster and meeting, the real meeting without Fowler: ten of us, same ten who went out to see Loomis, same day Cap'n Sam said no to China, Leyla yes to marriage, day of orders, day of beer, of who'd signed, who didn't, why, how, where, when, of what's it matter let's get drunk and will the weather hold?

It was already clearing so out to the fast-clearing sky and first planes of the day shot over us, out to sea.

We left them with their beer, and stripping our clothes ran for the Castle and our wet deserted beach, dove into an ocean as turgid green and beautiful as any picture of the Spanish Main, only here not boats down to the sea but planes winged out a hundred feet over our heads whirling clattering bursting engines winging planes into the east light blue against stark gray sky breaking up to tender blue and pink, yes, ohh, yes, we're going, waves spilling salt froth snapping bubbles washed and pulled dancing living thinking legs and feet. Then into the castle, showering, singing before a good supper no matter what we ate.

Gradually the others drifted in and over to Heath's room, quieter because death lived here, where Heath still so drunk he couldn't have walked let alone to a meeting, pointing at, pointing ridicule at Fowler, marine corps, navy and only sorry he'd not been there for his impression, "And don't tell me about Willy Vee, American eagle, I know he's all signed up."

And even talked to me, until he realized, "Not talkin' to you, dumb-bastard-up-the- runway-on-yer-back-at-night . . . "

Heath's head swung wildly at the dizzy thought, then mumbling something, stared around crazily at us and he, he at their mercy. His fingers got past a ridge of covers, the arm sprang backwards, head hit pillow neck twisted.

"He's crazy," said Hebert, and really meant it.

Chapter 29

For days following the big meeting there was jubilation and celebrating. Then the wind went out of it. There were flights to be met and nothing was changed. Some said there *were* no orders; the idea was to keep us in line. Others were convinced it *had* to be true. And when something *has* to be true the lack of conviction can be measured by the ferocity. Others had found a kind of groove here. The war was over there. There's death and risk enough here at Red Beach. The 'work' was reasonable, three to five hours of flying a night, one day a week off, the war be damned. Talk of orders and overseas was so long overdue that it was only a vague reminder of the heroic life, the harder, cleaner life of struggle and, perhaps, death overseas.

Others had settled down. Children were conceived and born here. Life went on. Flying at night was onerous and, for some, frightening, but all in all a life they could live with. In almost all of the groups there was some guilt. In Europe and the Pacific people were performing heroic deeds; killed, be-medaled and honored. The attitude for many was, let them have it.

And yet at the call to arms even some of those had signed up. Wives and husbands fought and some of them, brave cowards, had their names removed from the list. Others, on second and third thoughts, wanted their names added. For The Fowler and Spatzler "the list" had become a nightmare. Hebert withdrew and confessed to me. Farrell was furious that the 'orders' had come with the unfortunate phrasing, "those desiring." Since he had said, or the orders had said, "those desiring," it must then include room for those *not* desiring, or at least not right at the moment. It was no longer clear whether Farrell had used the words or they had been written in the directive from the Jacksonville Command. No, he would not allow copies of the orders to be seen.

What was RM's position? What did Clare have to say about it? RM smiled a wan smile and left his name on the list. The average life span of a fighter pilot in combat, the world over, was still 30 minutes. Yes, he knew that.

Of course people were killed here, too. In fact, there was a rumor of a congressional investigation about so many killed at Red Beach. Eight pilots—four bogey pilots, three students, and one instructor—in five and a half months.

For me and Evan, and those first days after "the orders" we conformed to the new restrictions— within 20 miles an hour and 15 or 20 degrees of bank—after a week we went back to our old ways with a vengeance, screaming into the flight pattern at just under 300 knots and breaking off, wings pointed straight down to the ground, holding in tight to the field in our one-turn-spins, coming out of our spin and hitting, tail first just at the very end of the runway in use. It had nothing to do with "perfecting our flight skills," as "The Fowler" put it, it was a matter of pushing the planes to their limits, as well as pushing the powers-that-be. It was also a matter of anger. We were flying and risking our necks here since we were not being called on to risk them anywhere else in the world. And as the days went by the orders seemed more and more a pipedream, a hit of opium to calm us down.

I bought a car, five days before Leyla was due, a once-green Ford, circa 1923, as Dubya D might have put it, for 165 dollars, from one of the newly graduated navy night fighters who was headed to the Far East. The car had been handed along from one night fighter pilot to the next. The upholstery was not in great shape and it sometimes jumped out of second gear, but it had "nuts" as we said. The green paint was fading in spots and Mulligan called it the chameleon. "Yeah, sometimes green, sometimes powder gray," said he.

I took over the house from the car owner, Ensign Alvin Newcomb, who had lived there for two months with his high school sweetheart and new bride, Shirley. What the hell, I bought their bed, too, and a bunch of other stuff from them, the refrigerator and stove. I disliked Ensign Newcomb from the beginning, and it grew. He was very breezy: "We're the Mustang squadron. I'm Mustang Seven, we probably worked together. We leave in four days. You can sell it to someone when *you* go overseas."

Just shut up and go.

Then one day I was standing in the house and it came to me what I was doing. The furniture he had left and I had bought. I was getting very tender. *Our* bed, our little house. I hardly believed any of it, I was just taking steps toward April tenth.

The house was a log-cabin box and cost 75 a month with a month's deposit. It was a quarter of a mile from RM's and Clare's. It was built on a slight rise near the end of one of the sandy roads to the beach off of Highway #1, the old north and south highway, and was close enough to the ocean for us to hear the waves pounding the beach on windy days.

On the sea side of the box was a living room facing the ocean, with a couch and small section windows the entire length of the room. Off of that a little dining room, half the size of the living room. Beyond the dining room was the kitchen. Opposite the dining room was the bedroom, the bathroom was next to it, between it and the kitchen. It was a perfect box. Well, if Leyla didn't like it we could find something else, but we'd start off here.

The base chapel and chaplain could be obtained free of charge for weddings but I didn't want to be married on the base. Leyla and I were talking almost every night and I'd promise things and then have to report the following night. I discovered I was a great promiser. When Hebert was around he would laugh and shake his head.

"Yeah, listen, I'll get that done tomorrow."

I also discovered that there wasn't a great deal we *had* to do in our flying lives. One 3 to 5 hour flight every night and, when we felt like it, testing 2 or 3 planes. That was our war effort.

Three days before she was due, I found myself standing in the empty kitchen looking at the bed, and then our "dining" room. It seemed a little, well, ugly. The walls were pea-green and faded. The kitchen was battered and had an air of hopelessness. Sometimes I really did feel that Leyla was an angel. And it wasn't that our place should be luxurious, but it should not be like this.

The outside of the house was the best thing about it. It looked like what it was, a cabin made of half logs. The other windows, the side windows, were chunky pioneer windows framed by logs, the kind from which you shot Indians with a long-gun.

I couldn't figure out what it was that bothered me. Maybe I was picking up thoughts from other transients who had used this passed-through cottage. It was not a house in which people lived, made plans, and raised children, it was a house in which a couple lived for weeks or a month then he goes off to war, the bride back home to wait. This brought up the orders again, and a moan of life-dreams. But Leyla was so full of joy it made me forget that. It was all going to be fine. I did not mention the orders, then I decided, just in case, I better tell her. I also told her it was all very indefinite. And I left out "those desiring." The most infuriating part of it. War is an option, folks, for "those desiring."

I went over to RM's and Clare's, and found Clare in shorts and sandals. She greeted me like a buddy, "Heyyy . . . how about some iced tea?"

"I want some help."

She laughed and told me to sit down. A hot breeze was blowing in from the sea. RM would be home any minute, she said.

I had left Evan out of the wedding plans; my two sides were not to be mixed.

I was about to join a fraternity, the married pilots. Evan and I risked our lives without a thought. We came down laughing about something we'd done, "Wow! That was close!" My very blood was cleansed every time we flew. And Leyla insisted she did not expect me to change.

I watched this blonde beauty, RM's wife, get ice and glasses, reach for the pitcher of tea in the fridge and realized what a southern custom that was.

"Clare . . . do you worry about RM? When he flies?"

"No," she sat down with the glasses, passed a plate of lemon slices, took out a cigarette and lit it. "Not really. Not like Imelda . . . Imelda Muncrief does. Now that girl sweats out every flight. Some other wives worry like that. Clinging to their husbands' necks before every night flight, calling the base if he's ten minutes late. Are you worried she'll be like that?"

I had to laugh. "I'm worried about all sorts of things, but I really couldn't take that," I told her, "We've already talked about it, though. Anyhow—"

"Did you read 'The War Prayer'? In the book I gave you?"

"Not yet, but I swear I will."

"It's very short, Will. Only three or four pages."

"I'll get to it. Anyhow, I can't stay long but I wish you two could help me a little with the wedding. I want to talk with you about it. And I'd also like for RM to be the best man."

"Ohh, WILL, he'll be tickled to death. Is Evan going to be in it?"

"I don't know. Evan is . . . you know, 'Fly Now Wives Later,' so, I don't mention it to him."

She laughed, "One of the flying madmen bites the dust."

"A mechanic called us the Trouble Brothers."

"Wait . . . I think that's Ritch, now. Anyhow, of course we'll help. When is it going to be?"

RM came in, gave Clare a big kiss and jived with her a little. They were going out to supper and she was supposed to be ready. He had flown the mail to the radar stations at Fort Pierce and Stuart, a five-day rotating job we all had to take.

"Tell him, Will," Clare said, beaming.

"Well, old man, old Head-in-Music-Box, I'm about to take the big step, you know, and I'd like your help. Sooo, will you be my best man?"

"Why, *hell* yeah, my boy." RM grabbed my hand, shook it, looked flushed and pleased. "That's an honor, lieutenant. I won't lose the ring—"

"Oh, Jesus! The *ring*!"

Clare thought it was all very funny.

RM asked, "Hebert is not going to be in it?"

"No, we'll let Hebert buzz the place."

"DON'T," he said, in mock terror, "don't and say he did."

"Alright, can you think of a place? And some guy, who's not too religious?"

Clare spoke up, "Well, you know, you'll probably have to have a talk with the person who does it. And you can more or less tell him what you want."

"Yeah," RM added, "and if he objects we'll have him burned at the stake."

Clare was still digesting it, "Sooo, you've decided to call her down and 'play house?'"

"No! We're going to begin our *together* lives, as someone once said to me."

"Allllllllright, lieutenant, that calls for a hug."

She got up and came around to me, we hugged and I felt all was forgiven.

"You planning on changing your . . . umm, your *ways*? I mean, you gonna break off at 45 degrees from now on? Stay out of trouble?" RM said carefully.

"No . . . I'm *not*. And, to change the subject, I've taken that little log cabin just south of here. The other guy, 'Mustang Seven,' just left. The one you told me about."

"You took it! That's wonderful," Clare said.

I moaned, and they laughed.

"I do not know what the hell I'm doing anymore."

"From what Ritch tells me, she's beautiful. I can't wait to meet her."

"She's a beauty alright, no question about it," RM added.

"—just a mountain of things before she comes down."

"We'll, help. Really. Call meeeee . . . tomorrow afternoon and we'll get someone to do the honors, and we'll think of a place. You want a church? Or—?"

"I'd like it to be outside. Maybe at the Driftwood?"

"Why not?"

We hoisted a beer together and I left feeling worse and better. The fucking little Ford jumped out of second gear. I'd forgotten to hold it in and for a minute the world seemed a dark place. Rings and houses, weddings, and all the things to be done. What about plates? Sheets? Kitchen stuff?

I called Leyla and she was gushing.

"Ohh, Will. It's going to be so great, no matter what. Do you hear me? No matter what! It's going to be great. And fun. I'm going nuts. I can't wait to get down there. I'm leaving in TWO DAYS! My grandmother is giving us some stuff. Sheets and silver and stuff. And Bess is definitely coming down. And maybe Lil."

I called Mamoo and told her it was out of my hands. She wished and she wished and she wished but I had given her absolutely no notice and they, she and Pearse, were so broke. Pearse was between jobs, or, rather had started a new job and things were tight. She insisted that I call—no, not now—that I call Brucie, at the house, a call for *her*, and Arthe; she gave me the number in Alabama where Carl was instructing in P-35s, or something.

"Mamoo, there *is* no 'P-35'."

"Well, my darling, as you know, I don't know a great deal about these things. Maybe it's a P-75! But the point *is* . . . maybe it's a Pee *Pee*, for all I know, but the point, the point . . . oh, you think that's funny, do you? . . . well, I honestly can't keep track of it all, at any rate, you and Leyla are going to *have* to get to New Orleans the first time you get leave. To meet the family . . . ohh, won't that be something, though. And Sally, too, you must phone and tell her. She's not working today. And you know, of course, that Brucie is engaged."

"Yes, Pete? The ensign? I met him, the Yaley she was going with? In fact, I believe she had her first date with him the night I tried to fix her up with Hebert."

"Well, he's exceptionally nice!"

"Well, he better be."

"And, now, I'm going to call Leyla's mother, in Marshall. The name is 'Herndon' right?"

"Yes. That'll be good to call her, I think she's, well, not exactly in favor of it."

"Well, my darling, I can understand why she might be concerned and a little worried. In any case, all of my love to you two, and you take good care, oh, my darling, good care of her *and* of yourself, and you inspect every plane before you take it up, do you hear me? And my heart will be with you and please please write and tell me all about it. And call me on *that* day, do you hear me? Oh, I just wish that everything weren't in such a rush, but that has been your whole life, I suppose. Let's see if there is any news. Oh, Shep is in India, I just heard. Pat is still instructing out on the west coast. Little Wallace is in Pearl Harbor. No news on Bob Cameron and I think they have given up on . . . on his being alive, I know how that must hurt you, as well. And your cousin Garth Deupree is safe. He was one of ten survivors. His ship was, umm, blown up, and, well, anyway he was one of ten who were saved. The rest were, I believe, well, tragic and terrible, burned in the explosion and fire and oh, how I hate the whole thing and wish it were over but, at any rate, *he's* safe and recovered and is now stationed in Washington . . . "

Full Lieutenant Farrell, the Fowler, gave me a three-day emergency leave and Cleary, our desk-pilot in the flight office—in return for all the planes Hebert and I had tested—was going to take me off the schedule for an additional three days.

Hebert wanted us to take a couple of planes down to Cuba and back, non-stop. He had it all figured out and was certain we could make it, if we leaned out the mixture. He was also pushing for another air show down at Star, the radar station and outlying field at Stuart. Nevers, another bogey pilot and wild man, little rat-faced Davey, wanted to fly with us and had been promising some friend of his he'd give him a ride. Bud Harrelson, the controller at Star, got a kick out of us and let us buzz the place when the commander was off the station, but all that would have to wait till after the wedding.

Hebert wasn't down about the wedding, "I just think yer puttin yer head in a noose is all I been sayin.' She's a danged pretty gal and all that but geeesh, hooo, marriage is so, ha haa, permanent."

"Well, I'da had you as best man, but I feel like you're sort of against the whole thing."

"No, you got me wrong, lieutenant, I'm not against it. I jus' hope you know what you're doing. An' I'm not sure you do."

"I've always known exactly what I was doing, right?"

"Right, yeah, sure, lieutenant. Now what about Jorge and Mulligan and Muncrief, the cigar store Indian, and his wife? They gonna be there?"

"All of you better be there."

"I'mna buzz the cotton-pickin' place. Out at the Driftwood, you say? Eleven hundred?"

"Yeah, and Bess'll be there too."

"Yeah, I talked to her. I'm gonna show her how to suck the roof off of the Driftwood Inn."

"Now, Moka. Don't do anything I wouldn't do."

"I won't, and that roof is coming off, I'll guaronnntee ya, as we say down in bayou country."

Everything was set. I picked out a ring from a piece of string she had sent me, knotted in two places. She'd have to come in and try it on when she got here. And no, the man wouldn't give me a charge account. "Yew boys'r in an outa here so fast I can't keep track of you. You gonna have a double ring ceremony?"

I got a flash picture of a corpse with a gold ring being cut off of the finger. "No!"

RM and Clare had reserved a reception room at the Driftwood Inn. The marriage was to take place there, in the breezeway that went straight through from sea to land and, on the land side, opened to linen-clad tables, covered by an awning. The Unitarian minister, Mr. Charles Preston, a nice enough lemony older man with a sparkle in his eye, said he'd make it simple and suggested a couple of passages, one about times of trouble and one about love. I think he wanted both of them. I picked the one about love. I knew Leyla would like it. It went on a little bit but it was good. I asked him, apologizing and asking him not to be insulted, but not to, well, add a lot of other things. He smiled and agreed, although he gave me a look which I couldn't decipher. RM told me that the fee was whatever I wanted to give him. Mr. Preston took down some information and said he'd get the rest from Leyla on Tuesday.

I borrowed 200 bucks from Jorge and gave some to Clare for sandwiches and punch. Flowers? She'd get some and let me know. Room at the Driftwood for Bess? And for changing? Yes. Will, you should take her somewhere, some little trip. Palm Beach! I know a great place and it's not too expensive. Shall I call them? Yes.

Full Lieutenant Farrell, the 'Fowler,' wanted to come. Sure, okay. And Nevers. And Heath, his oddball roommate, who had taken Loomis's body home and had gotten so drunk on the day of the meeting. Muncrief and his wife Imelda, and was it okay to bring their two-month old baby? Sure, fine. And Sam Lyttle? Of Guadalcanal and the Second Flying Tigers? Shit yes, come on.

Mulligan and his Wave friend; Jorge, of course, and the photographer in town, beautiful girl, a little older than Jorge.

Chapter 30

The train stopped in Vero Beach at 0813 and Leyla and Bess got off with bags and boxes. Then my thoughts were about mouths and lips, arms, kisses, words in an incomprehensible barrage, and Bess, and the luggage, oh my God, and for a time there was not a doubt in the world. This beauty, this breath-taker, my wife, come a few hours.

I was in shock and didn't even realize it. I didn't want Leyla all dressed up. I wanted her . . . plain. And it took a minute to realize that under the hat, under the clothes she was still there, only she was acting, just a little, as if she didn't know how to act.

Off we went in the chameleon, no, the Lizard, the Greeeen Lizard. I held it carefully in second and shifted. Bess looked around her and giggled.

"Is this our car, Will? Our great car?"

"The Greeeeeeeen Lizard, our *country* car."

The train had already pulled off. Leyla had left an article she wanted me to read. "Letters to a Wife," or something.

They were full of the trip. It was a troop train, they thought. Although every train was a troop train these days. And a little scary, they agreed. Two unescorted females in a sleeping compartment.

"The poor guys," Bess moaned, "they were sleeping on top of each other. It was like shipping a herd of cattle."

"Yeah, and some of the cattle were trying to get in our sleeping compartment last night, too," Leyla said.

"I didn't hear a thing," said Bess.

"Mom said, 'Don't you open that door for anyone.'"

"So, your mother knows? And what did she say?"

"Oh, Will, I think she's given up on me. I gave her your mother's phone number in New Orleans. She's going to call. My father won't speak to me. They had such plans, she said, such *plans*!"

"That's one of the better aspects of this whole scheme," said Bess, usually so quiet.

Leyla had told me once, "Don't worry about Bess. A lot's going on there." We drove out to the beach, through the lane of royal palms, which Leyla thought was wonderful. Then had to drive back to town to the jeweler's for the ring. Back out to the beach and were at the Driftwood Inn at 1000.

Clare met them both. The flowers had just arrived, the Driftwood Inn's kitchen had been turned over to us. Imelda, Muncrief's wife, whom I hardly knew, was helping full time. Their little baby—Imelda pregnant, the same time as Leyla, so long ago—was almost two months old. A little scrunched up fussy little *person*, but not bad looking.

We lugged some things to an upstairs room—the place was low and rambling and only had two floors. RM and I had to lug a big steamer trunk over to the cabin. It had all of her grandmother's stuff for us. Leyla and Bess were to change and get ready there. Clare went up with them and seemed to already be instant friends, the three of them talking and laughing.

RM had rigged up some speakers and was playing some of his jazz. He played Roy Eldredge's "After You've Gone," the wild rendition that used to cause food fights and battle royals at Pre-Flight. The manager was happy and people were rolling in and getting drunk already. Captain Sam, Lt. Farrell, Jorge, Mulligan, Hebert. I drove back to our little cabin, put on my whites, and got back just before 11. Hebert had stayed with Bess and was drinking a Tom Collins with her.

The manager found an old recording of the "Wedding March." The minister, Mr. Preston, arrived, very smiley ("Oh, I *like* him," said Leyla, "but he should have on one of those Panama hats, then it would be perfect."). He took Leyla off for a few minutes of talk. I let RM decide where the best place would be. It was pretty hot already but a good breeze swept through the breezeway and the flowers seemed to make it cooler. At the last minute, Bud Harrelson came up from Star, the radar station to the south of us, and shook hands all around.

All of us, pilots, were wearing our whites. Bess was to go first, escorted by Jorge— Mulligan was already getting raucous—then RM and Clare, last minute change, then Leyla with Hebert, who had decided to buzz the place *after* the ceremony (Fowler-Farrell, be damned), and was talked into giving the bride away.

Leyla was dressed in her grandmother's 19th century French "summer afternoon" dress of Egyptian cotton with French lace, a ribbed bodice with a lace insert, she explained to me very close to my face, whispering the words only inches away, "At the time, *in that circle*," she batted her eyes, explaining the "summer afternoon" part of the designation. "It's all hand-stitched and hand-sewn," she said, looking so beautiful she could have stood with any of those beauties back then, for sure, and taken the prize. A wide hat and veil over it, "and I don't think we're supposed to talk to each other before the ceremony . . . or even *see* each other."

We were lined up as he wanted us. He went to the spot we had desig-nated, turned around and, finally, it was all slowing down. And he was speaking about just that, about these rushed times, about the lack of cer-emony, and the need for taking time, that, "taking, even making time for some things, is so important, and pausing before certain steps, the step of holy matrimony, for example, and observing in silence, alone and together, together and alone, what we are about to do. Taking the time to wish each other well, and, particularly, today, for Leyla and Will, and, for that pur-pose, I'm asking you to observe five minutes of silence with me before we begin . . . I'll keep the time and . . . alright, may we begin?"

In the silence, heard our phone calls again, all the words that had passed between us. Plans and places: Marshall, Longview, Cambridge, passing in one standup moment towering high above both of us and then the two of us, on top like the little models on a wedding cake which, I suddenly real-ized with horror, I had not even thought about. The two of us silent in that Texas Lake in the still dark waters of the lake, the fish in the lake with us during that silent time. I felt what we were doing. Our beginnings, our time, seven children, first sight of her when she got off the school bus, her house and their side yard. And, if ever, then, I had regrets about my family and Sally, too, about Sally's children, my age, and thought about all of that. Mamoo and her wishes, her world-wishes, my sisters not here, and wanting to make peace, wanting their blessings too. No, it wasn't only playing house—apologizing in silence to RM and Clare, vowed I'd make it up to them. To Leyla and her parents for any lapse, for letting her father . . . ohh fathers, think I was stealing his daughter. The war and the damned orders that hung in some kind of balance over our heads, half hoping they'd never come in. The Flying Tigers, Sam, Captain Sam in his whites with Guadalcanal ribbons and wings, those wings that really meant some-thing . . . and that a real hero had backed down; Sam who had winked at me and grinned. And even while thinking it, a pair of midnight blue F-6s, instruments most likely, sailed over and out to sea.

Then, as if waking us from a dream, he was speaking again: "Thank you," the minister said, then the "Wedding March," the procession moved for-ward and, for now, a gentle Hebert answered "I do," to give this bride away. And Leyla and I were next to each other, facing this minister stranger.

And we each answered, and were becoming man and wife. RM gave me the ring and I was actually—as if the world's eyes were on me, my fingers fitting it to her ring finger—and these pictures popping in my mind, I took it, she held out her hand and finger, I placed it on, just a little tight, better for swimming we had decided, and this man, first reading the passage about love and, no matter what else you have it's nothing without love. The kind of thing I wanted to read slowly, over and over. Along with all the other things I hadn't read—"The War Prayer"—and the other things I hadn't done, seen, read, all of them. And, suddenly I felt my life changing a little, not my life, exactly, but the direction. The war not absolutely everything. And, suddenly, he was "pronouncing us" man and wife and telling me I could kiss the bride. Maybe one of our more conscious kisses, her soft mouth, her giving lips, more giving and ready than sexy, and in the middle of it, what is more "sexy" than giving? Her willing lips that sealed us off even from the ceremony.

The cheering section of a roaring Mulligan, Jorge the Black Beauty, Muncrief, RM, Hebert, Nevers, Heath and a few other bogey pilots, and Sam Lyttle. Then Bess and Clare and Leyla and I and RM lined up to receive the others.

Heath, Nevers' roommate, shook my hand, softly, "You crazy sonofabitch, good luck! Don't crash and burn," which was our saying, us bogey pilots, before going up at night, like "Break a leg," for actors. Full lieutenant Farrell-Fowler came up, shook my hand hard, told Leyla, " . . . This is one of the best pilots on the base," then whispered to her, " . . . maybe the *best*." Captain Sam came up, kissed the bride an awkward little kiss, shook hands, "Yeah," he said, "we'd a' made them sit up and take notice . . . sorry it fell through."

It was done. And the relief that must always follow the more formal part. Hebert had left, but, Bess said, he'd meet her back here at 1:30 or 2:00. He'd fly over, she told us.

"Is that crazy sumbitch gonna buzz us?" RM asked. "With Farrell right here?"

We looked at Bess. "He said he was coming right back."

It was a little past noon and we went in for a sit-down meal of sandwiches, hors d'oeuvres and more drinks. *And* a cake that someone had thought of. Imelda, fat and homey, had done it.

Nevers, the crazy little rat, had to tell me twice about this ensign from the amphib base and how he'd promised him a ride. Well, not just a ride but a formation flight with *us*. I told him we'd do it, the first Sunday I got back.

"Now, don't wait too long, you old married man. Don't go and get safe on us, now."

RM was grinning. Leyla was watching *and* listening. What did they want?

Farrell was still with us, sitting next to Sam. Mulligan was tapping his glass and . . . let him go, cleared his throat about three times, made his Major Hoople sounds, "Brrfssk, ahem, yes," and then actually began, after getting up on one of the folding chairs:

"I have been called upon . . . " he looked around, seriously, "to give a toast and . . . " Jorge was practically kicking the table, just watching Mulligan's preamble, "before I do, ahem, yes, I'd like to make a remark, just in passing, about the subject of these proceedings. Although he is wanted in seven states, yes, seven states, AND Cuba . . . for dangerous flight conduct, endangering the civilian population . . . on land and in the air . . . "

I sneaked a glance at Farrell-Fowler, who was grinning just as if he were one of us.

" . . . and although," he held up one finger, "He rarely passed the 'stagger' test in Daytona— " Jorge, Mulligan and RM screamed over that.

"He . . . this young and innocent *seeming* partly-clean-spoon-ready-for-soup-marine-She's-all-yours-when-you-win-your-Navy-wings-of-gold-bogey pilot," Mulligan was standing on the chair and almost fell over, "put this chair on automatic pilot . . . ahem, yes, as I was saying—"

"*Speech, speech!*" Jorge screamed. Too bad Scott Lee and Dubya D were gone.

"Somebody, please escort that bum outa here . . . well, this pilot, Lieutenant Willy B. Vairin, known in Indian circles as 'Bent-Spoon-Waiting-For-Goulash' . . . has been nominated, seconded, and unanimously elected first president of the ORIGINAL, and newly formed '*Forty-Six Degrees' Club*, and I— "

Cheers drowned him out, we looked over at Farrell, who was laughing, nothing else he could do, and Jorge and RM wouldn't let him continue.

"Speech, SPEEEEECH!" they yelled.

"Well . . . "

"SPEEEEEEEEEEEEEEEECH!"

" . . . anyhow," Mulligan staggered over to me, he'd been slugging them down since ten o'clock, "Gotta pin this decoration," and he yelled, "*This is the one and ONLY, the ORIGINAL, Forty-Six Degrees Club Medal . . . with banana leaf cluster, to Lt. Willy Vairin, USMCR!*"

"THREE CHEERS!"

Hip hip hooray!

Leyla wanted to talk to Bess, make sure she'd be okay. And at least wait till Hebert returned to be with her. Bess could stay at the Inn or else in our little cabin till we got back from Palm Beach. Her father, the admiral, had managed a flight home for her. It was either tomorrow or next day. Bess gave me a big hug and kiss right on the mouth.

Leyla, Bess, RM, Clare, Mulligan, Jorge and I and their ladies, Heath, Farrell and Captain Sam were talking, drinking when Jorge called me aside, "The orders are *in*," he said, "They're taking bogeys five at a time to go through night fighters . . . " he smacked me on the arm, "in *Corsairs*! Cleary has *seen* the orders." Jorge was grinning like a fiend.

"Yeah, but *when?*"

"Ha haaaa, soon, my friend, soon. Maybe even in May!"

I couldn't tell Leyla, and already I felt like I was betraying her, even to get excited again about the damned orders. I certainly couldn't tell her today. But a great hope was stirring in me, like embers in a fire that had almost gone out. And why today? Of all days?

Leyla caught my arm and wanted to know what *that* was all about.

"Aww, Jorge's girlfriend."

"Will, is that the truth? Something's up . . . what is it?"

"Well, he also said we might get to check out in the Corsair . . . it's the plane I've always wanted."

She looked at me a long steady look, strange amidst all the raucous shouting and people trying to grab both of us. "Well, if that's it, that's wonderful." But there was a doubt in her voice.

While we were standing there we heard something different, not just a plane passing over but a buildup, the angry hum then the roar, the shattering roar as the plane either tore the roof off the building or broke all the windows. One crescendo roar.

"JESUS CHRIST!"

"No, Evan Hebert!"

It had not crashed because it was followed by the roaring sigh and sounds of a dive-bomber climbing away.

Back he came but by this time we were out of the building on the beach looking to find him.

"Is that Evan?" Leyla asked innocently.

RM looked at her. "The only other guy it could be is standing next to you. And I don't mean myself."

It was a fearsome sight to watch that light blue beast pointed right at us, coming down at a 50 degree angle, 60 degrees, then down level and

ZOOOOMMM, right off the deck, lower than the first floor and just off the corner of the building. It struck me that *anyone* seeing it would know they're not supposed to be flown that way.

"*He got my aerial!*" The manager was screaming, and went off to check.

I watched Bess and she had that same rapt, awed gaze as when she watched Hebert tell about his crash. Farrell's face was a study in ashes.

In 45 minutes Evan was back, in whites, denying, aw shucks and, naw, I didn't come that close! And Bess loved it. Then he came over to me for a review, and, very quietly, "How was it?" Still chuckling.

"It was *low!*"

He enjoyed that. "I wanted to go through that breezeway," he said, "but the tables were in the way."

"You stopped because of a few tables?"

"I figured they might make you pay for 'em."

"*Some* day, boy!"

"Hey, did you hear about the orders? They're in! Cleary's got copies of 'em."

"Jorge just told me."

"I think they're lookin' fer a new list. The other list is screwed up, people taking their names off, more being put on."

"Well, for God's sake, if it happens while I'm gone—"

"Don't worry, you'll be on it."

It was a little sticky getting away.

Jorge and then Mulligan: "You're going nowhere! . . . NOBODY LEAVES!" . . . AWRIGHT, AWRIGHT, YOU CAN LEAVE, BUT FIRST, before you leave, three more little drinks, *then* you can go . . . Just small ones . . . YEAH, LITTLE TINY ONES . . . *I'LL* make 'em . . . No, I'll fix em . . . *Gimme* that bottle!"

Chapter 31

I dumped all of Leyla's stuff in the log cabin, except for her overnight bag—I wouldn't let her see the place till we got back—and we were headed south on old highway 1, in the Greeeeen Lizard. We yelled and hugged for the first couple of miles.

When we had quieted down I discovered I was, to face it truthfully, feeling less than joyous. And if she had suddenly popped up from my lap and asked, "Are you sure you can handle all of this?" My honest answer would have been, "No!"

'Haven't we always been honest with each other?' she once asked me. As if there could be any other way. Well, I was discovering another way. For example, I did not want her to know that the orders were in. I didn't want to spoil this time for her, or even that it might. And I didn't want her to know that second gear was sort of shot. Now, why? Surely she would discover it the first time she drove the car. I wanted the car to be perfect. Listen to that engine!

I loved it that she was not worried. I knew she wouldn't care about second gear and still I kept it from her. I worried about *her*, and the more carefree, the more I wanted to protect her. As for my world and flying: clean the windshield, pull the chocks and get out of the way. I had told her about the orders but not that I was still counting on them. At the same time, till Jorge and Evan had told me that the orders were now common knowledge, I had been ready to give it up. The war and Leyla. Leyla and the war. Well, never mind, the war was out.

The war in Europe was already lost to us. There were no marine flyers in Europe, but because the Germans were being squeezed by the Russians in the east and the soon-to-come invasion forces in the west, it looked like that part of it was almost over. The Russians "rolled" while the Americans in Italy "broke through," but the end was coming and I believe everyone except Hitler could see it. As for the Pacific, there were still great battles to be fought. About that side of my dreams Leyla understood almost nothing.

"I can see the stars from here!" She was exulting. " It's so nice feeling your legs with my head, and, GOD, just knowing we're together and I'm not going HOME, Will . . . WE'RE home! So happy feeling you drive, and the stars in their nightly course . . . that's Milton," she said, "I had this great course. A combination of scientists and poets. Galileo said, 'The galaxy is nothing other than a mass of luminous stars gathered together . . . ' And he told Milton, who was visiting Italy, and Milton wrote in *Paradise Lost*, 'The galaxy, that milky way, which nightly as a circling zone thou see'st—powder'd with stars . . . ' Isn't that nice?"

"Yeah, that's nice."

"What's wrong?"

She spun around off of me, "Will. What's wrong?"

"Ohh . . . Leyla, you've been to a real school. And you're way ahead of me."

"Will. What are you talking about?"

"I went to engineering school for a year and a half. Are you going to miss it? Those great courses you talk about? Is this going to be dull for you?"

"*Will*. Listen! You've got to *listen!* I'm exactly where I want to be. Exactly where I belong. I've never been happier in my whole life. I'm as happy as a little . . . hoot owl. Have you ever seen something when you were a little kid and wanted it and wanted it and finally got it?"

"Yeah, my first red two-wheeled bike."

"Well, you're my red two-wheeled bike. I hated leaving you this last time, at the dive-bombers. You don't know . . . I felt like it was physical, something being torn out of me. And then, no leave, and the most awful part, when you found out you weren't going overseas—I wasn't going to tell you all this—you still didn't want me to come down. Then you stopped writing for a while and, well, that was a black period."

"Darling Leyla . . . " I almost stopped the car, "I was going through, Christ I don't know what all. I didn't know what to do. It was like . . . first the war and action . . . and *then* you. So, then—"

"Where are we right now, Will?"

"About 20 miles north of Palm Beach."

"Well that's exactly where I want to be. Wherever you are . . . and wherever I am. And when we're 19 1/2 miles from Palm Beach, that'll be EXACTLY where I want to be. Now, Lieutenant-I-love-you—"

"What?"

"Will . . . maybe you don't know it, but you *need* me. Do you hear?"

She said these things and I don't know where they came from.

"You know that, do you?"

"Yes."

"How do you know?"

"I just know. You *need* me. It's almost the worst pain I've ever felt, knowing how you *need* me."

"Yes," I admitted, "I *do* need you." although I felt I was giving her the keys to the kingdom. "The question is—"

"Of *course* I need *you*. But the thing is how come I *know* it and you have to ask? How come I know it and you don't? That's the only thing in the world that's wrong. You don't know how you *need* me and you don't know how I *need* you."

She said it so simply, so clearly. I was . . . devastated . . . so devastated I wanted to cry. She was telling the truth . . . about us. Why couldn't I? And her voice. Her voice so musical I could listen to that alone and never need to know what she was saying.

"I don't know *why* I don't know. But you're making me feel like an idiot."

"And—"

"Just a second. Leyla, I know very little, okay? I know how to fly a plane and that's about all, and I'm just coming to realize how little, in all the world of things there are . . . to know, that I do know."

"Yes, RM said you were a great natural flyer, a *natural* flyer, you were born to it."

"Well, that's nice he said that—"

"And you do something else *fantastically* well. Now, as to whether you're an idiot or not, you *are*. That's from the religion course. You're an idiot and I'm an idiot, in fact we're all idiots. Now, the point is, we must find out what kind of idiots we are, in order to overcome our idiocy."

"Pheww, you *are* full of those courses."

"I wish you could have been in them with me. Well, the thing is, I wouldn't trade any of it for being right where I am."

We found the hotel. I gave my name and the man wanted to see a marriage license, which we had forgotten to get from the minister. After wrangling for half an hour, giving him the name of the minister, his approximate address, the man let us in and we went up in the tiny elevator.

We crooned and hugged and only left the table lamp on. We slept for minutes at a time, woke each other up and, at least, in this way, we were well-matched. For whole hours we had no idea where we were. We had entered the land of our real marriage again, a land, a place, a realm that we had gone to every time we made love and even before, since the lake-night out of Marshall. So, in that way it was not the first married night of our lives. This time had joined our other times alone, naked, in Eden. We were the same. The very same. I told her about the orders because I had to. Why hadn't I told her before? I didn't know. She said she understood. I was wrong about her mind. It was not something she had gained at Radcliffe. It might have been something they chose her for but what she had was something she was born with. We talked about having children. But that was for ATW (she whispered the initials). Whatever our talk amounted to she probably conceived that very night.

She had been fitted with a diaphragm and showed it to me, and explained its use. I think we used it once that night. She took it out after two hours (too soon, I think) and it felt so much better. We were back to those first times, with Leyla pleading for me to stay in and me barely able to get out in time.

The second afternoon we both caught what was almost a fever to get back to our little house by the sea.

"Leave everything to me," she said. "We're going to change that beautiful, beautiful, beautiful-little-house-cause-we're-in-it, and make it even more beautiful."

We got back and were astounded. The bed had sheets and pillows, there were a bunch of daisies on the table, pots and utensils in the kitchen, and curtains in the windows!

Leyla thought I had done it at first since I had kept her from seeing it and then forgotten that it really had nothing in the way of furnishings.

It had to be Clare, or Bess, or both.

There was a long note from Bess. She had fixed supper for Hebert here. And had only left this morning. "Evan's taking me to the airport in West Palm Beach . . . terrible about Hutchinson, I feel so bad for his sister. She was coming down in a few days."

She was talking as if we knew, as if we had been on the base all this time. Perry Hutchinson?

We drove over to RM's and Clare's. They were both home, surprised and happy to see us. As for Hutch: "Yeah, well," RM had a plaintive note in his voice, "He was coming in to the field in the afternoon, a test hop, and suddenly the plane just dove into the ground." RM shrugged his shoulders. "The only thing they can figure is that he was fooling with the automatic pilot and didn't get it turned off. They grounded all SB2Cs yesterday. Now, they're taking out all the automatic pilots."

"I remember fooling with them once," I told him, "The tiniest turn can produce a violent reaction in the controls, but how do they know that's what did it?"

"They don't; Simmons was up with him and they were talking on channel three. They had been experimenting with the automatic pilots."

"It's really ghastly," Clare added. "So sudden—"

"Coming in for a landing, it just went into a dive," RM told us again, "Steeper and steeper. West of the field . . . runway one ten."

We stayed and had supper.

As it got dark, planes were roaring over in singles, one after another. We watched outside for a while and Leyla could quickly enough tell the difference between the bell-ringing fighters and the buzzing roar of the "beast." No Corsairs went over, or not while we were there.

Claire and Leyla talked and made a big salad in the kitchen. Leyla was good at making friends. RM and I had a beer. He had a flight from 0100 till 0400 and would get out to the field around midnight. That's when he told me about the "List" the new "List."

"Now, look, Willy, they threw out the old list. People had been signing, then taking names off, others were signing on after saying they weren't going. They had 38 names and they just decided to start all over again. They threw it out. They gave us 12 hours to sign, all who were interested in night fighters. 'Now this is it,'says Spatzler. It is now in his hands, since we're all marines—"

"Got to find Spatzler."

"That's your only chance, Willy. And no one could sign for anyone else. He knows us and he still made a big thing of it. Only that person could sign."

"Did you put me down?"

"That's what I'm telling you. They threw out the other list. The one where they talked about 'those desiring.' This time, those who put their names down are going. There is no backing out. And no names to be added—"

"But didn't you guys put me down?"

"Willy, there was no way. Spatzler checked every name and ID and nobody could sign for anyone else."

"And that's it?"

"That's what he says. Spatzler oversaw the whole thing. Evan tried to sign you up and so did I. And I think Jorge tried too. No dice. Incidentally, Evan *didn't* sign up."

"And I'm not on it."

"Willy, there was no way."

"Are you on it?"

"Yeahh."

"What's going on," Leyla called over. She seemed to have a sixth sense when something was wrong.

"I've got to get hold of Spatzler."

"What is *wrong*?" Leyla came over, all sweet concern.

"That's the only way, Willy. Spatzler. See Spatzler."

"You guys, supper's ready, so, Will, what's wrong? Why so serious? Come on, let's eat."

Over supper, sitting down to what would have been a wonderful time, the conversation was almost dark. RM told Leyla about the orders, the new list, the setup with Spatzler. She looked but said nothing.

For a moment the conversation lightened up and we talked about Bess and Evan.

Leyla told us, "She likes a lot of things about Evan. His looks, his rebelliousness—"

"His sparkling wit," said RM, impatiently.

"Don't be mean, now," Clare told him, the southern belle.

RM made a disgusted noise and turned from her. "It's mindless," RM complained, "It's the *mindlessness* that irritates the (shit) out of me."

Leyla was mouthing the words, "Let's go!"

Right, but I couldn't resist RM's talk about Evan.

"Well, what do *you* want out of this? Don't you think they're shafting us?"

He looked at me, and I could tell a lot from the heat of his words, "Man, I just want to get through the program alive. I signed . . . because . . . "

Clare was looking, looking at him.

"Well, because of the Corsair and, because of this ridiculous duty, and, well, Jorge and Mulligan . . . and I thought you would be signed up as well—"

"Um hum . . . the Corsair, the Widow-maker," said Clare.

"Will . . . you said there was nothing immediate about the orders."

"Well, there wasn't, or didn't seem to be . . . actually there wasn't, until—"

"Is that what you and Jorge were talking about . . . at the wedding?"

"Yes."

Leyla was feeling uncomfortable and wanted to talk, she said. And we did leave, almost immediately. Then we were in the car for the short drive to our little cabin.

"You didn't tell me, Will!"

"No . . . It came up . . . suddenly. I didn't want to tell you, *then*. I felt like—"

"But, Will, you *have* to tell me these things. Don't hold things back from me."

Before we got out Leyla made me sit there.

I asked her if anything was wrong, anything else. She paused and then asked, "Will, I know this may sound stupid but . . . Hutchinson, the one you'all were talking about. Well, he's . . . dead, right?"

I realized then that none of us had used the word. I told her, yes, and, for the first time, felt that he was. That he had gone off and left us.

"Will . . . my darling . . . we have to talk."

Chapter 32

I carried her across the threshold and we kissed a long kiss but we did talk.

And what came out of it was my need for her. And that's what she dug in about. "Will, it's not that you don't know things. You just have to admit them sooner. Remember, about Sally, and leaving her? That time? When you were leaving her, and you were going off to work with your stepfather? It took you till then to realize how much you loved her. You see? "

I sat, spellbound and silent as she told me about myself.

"Then I told you, on the way down to Palm Beach? Remember?"

"Yes, it stunned me. That you knew . . . you *knew* that . . . I *needed* you."

"And now we have to talk about the orders . . . and the war."

"Well, I don't think that's going through. I have to get Spatzler but, so far, they are not allowing any changes to the list. So that's out. I'm not going so let's just forget it. But I *am* going to talk to him."

"Will, that's not it. Let me make it clear. It's not the orders. And it's not the war.—"

"No?? No???"

"No, and believe me, it's not."

"So, what the hell is it about?"

"Will, don't get angry . . . I just see the pain, and how you take it. And that's it, it's how you're taking it. So, it's not the orders and it's not the war, it's you, yes, *you* and how you're taking the war. It's *not* personal."

For some reason we didn't get any farther than that. And I couldn't connect with Spatzler.

For one thing we were constantly at it in bed. Then a couple of five hour flights during that week. Searchlights, they were called; on oxygen from the ground up, we flew at 15 to 18 thousand feet, from midnight till five in the morning. Four fellow target pilots and I, lights off, at staggered altitudes, were vectored out from the city, then in again for the searchlight crews to practice on. Perhaps they were being trained for a time when the Germans would attack Florida from the air. 'Yours is not to reason why, yours is but to do or die.'

Another five hour searchlight flight and, suddenly, it was over. I was coming down at dawn and happy, low on gas, a long dive from Orlando to the coast. Out to the beach to Leyla sound asleep in our little bower, I pulled off my clothes, smiling the whole time, watching her, breathing with her, hardly able to keep my hands off till I got rid of my clothes. This blessing I had, right here at my fingertips. I felt I had made the adjustment, not missing anything, not the war, not my dream, not envying anyone in the world. I sneaked into bed and hugged her. She was awake and in a second wrapped around me; I found her ear and hugged up tight, "Lucky, lucky, lucky," we whispered. Nothing else mattered.

"Ohh, yes," she said, tired, in dreams, pulling me with her. Half in and half out of dreams we made love, blessed each other and slept till noon.

In one way we were delirious with our life. Our little ugly-beautiful house from which we could be on the beach in minutes, walking in the thick sand, the tan-brown sand crystals of Red Beach, sand the size of rock salt. Over and over again we realized that outside of the flight schedule we were together to please each other and we could do anything we wanted. But, again, like a cork pulled under it came up again.

"I don't understand, Will. We're so happy—"

"Please Leyla, let's not talk about it now . . . okay? I know what you're going to say and please . . . not right now."

"You keep putting it off."

"Alright— "

"You're not flying Sunday."

"Okay. Good. Oh, wait . . . Sunday I promised Nevers and Hebert we'd fly together. Remember him, Davey Nevers? At the wedding, he was begging—"

"Ohh, Will, Will . . . "

It's just going to be an hour or two. I tell you, we'll do it when I get back from that flight, okay? First thing."

"Promise?"

"Yes, I swear, right after the flight."

"Don't swear to me, Lieutenant . . . Lieutenant-I-love-you . . . a promise will do."

"I promise!"

Chapter 33

Whenever I left Leyla and started in to the base to fly it came over me. The nice unassuming doctor begins to grow wolf fangs and thick hair on wrists and face. I drove the long straight stretch of road through the double lane of royal palms to Indian River, drove across the rickety wooden bridge, Point X-ray, over which every incoming plane had to pass before entering the traffic pattern, my blood was surging, trout were jumping in the bloodstream, even my skin felt different. My fingers played with the wheel, the gear shift, anxious for something more to do. My eyes flicked over the few instruments in the little car: speed, mileage, temperature. I stuck the left wheel on the line dividing the road, saw how close I could come to the edge. Watched oncoming cars, estimated to the second how long before we'd cross paths, or passed others, wanting it to be close between passing and getting back into the right lane in time. Judging, gauging, estimating.

The day was what some call beautiful because there were no clouds, an endless blue day. An ice cream Sunday.

I was to meet Nevers, Hebert, and Nevers' amphibious training buddy at the flight line, but first I had to find Spatzler and get it straight with him. I found him, shooting pool in the senior officers' lounge and asked him for a little private chat. His cap was pushed back on his head and I admit I had never seen him even attempting to look informal. "I hope this is not what I'm thinking it is. Cause there's gonna be no changes in that list."

"Captain Spatzler, I was on my honeymoon and— "

"I heard all about it, from at least three of your fellow madmen. I told them what I'm telling you. No, absolutely *no* changes in that list. We went through absolute hell the last time; take me off, put me on; *off*, no *on* . . . and you guys are *still*— "

"Look, Captain, *I* never once asked to be taken off—"

"Lieutenant! I'm tellin' you that's it. It's nailed down now and—"

The voice faded. I thanked him and walked away before I lost control completely and punched him in the mouth. I guess he knew how much I hated him.

When I got to the ready room they were waiting and irked.

"Well, you know these married guys! They can't get out of bed!" Nevers screamed, caaac-cac-cac and introduced me to Hal Anderson, an ensign from the amphib base ten miles south of us. Nevers was telling us we had to make it HOT, because Anderson had never been up before, he'd just seen it from the ground. And besides, "Caaac-caaac caaac, this might be my last chance to screw around in the Beast, because we start training real soon."

"You're signed up? You're going?" Hebert asked him unable to hide his disdain.

"Yeah, my good man, I'm going with the first group . . . in Corsairs." Then, for the first time, Nevers turned away from himself to question me. "Willy? You're not going? I thought sure you'd be going? Is it the wifey? Caaac caccc caaaaaac."

"I don't want to talk about it. I just saw Spatzler, that's why I was late."

I started to say more but, what the hell, nobody asked for my story. I turned and noticed Hebert watching me with a crafty look. What was he thinking? What was I thinking?

"Neither one of you guys'r going?" said Nevers, astounded.

"Look, what are we doin' today? I'm already in trouble fer down in Miami."

"Down in Miami" was shorthand for the fact that Evan had flown some papers down to the Naval Air Station in Miami, and cut out three transports in the landing pattern. "Shucks," he told us, "I was into the pattern, broke off, landed and was taxiing in . . . and almost *parked* before the first transport was in sight."

Evan was also ticked off at me because he hated to wait, and I was late.

They had already fitted Anderson into a parachute, helmet, goggles, "Don't my boy Anderson look hot? He looks like a real fly-boy, now. Right? Caaaac-cac-cac!"

Evan looked at crazy Nevers like he'd look at a bug who was between annoying and amusing. I watched Evan and laughed about him. I had never gotten the straight story about Bess from him, not that he was given to long revealing monologues. What did he think of her?

"Wellll, she's a beautiful gal, awright . . . an' if I was in the marryin' de-
partment I could do a lot worse, but, heck, what's the rush, I figger . . . I don't
know. We had a nice meal in yer log cabin out there . . . She fixed the whole
thing . . . We been writin' . . . Matter of fact I owe her a letter . . . er two."

This information was over a period of days.

Meanwhile it was Hebert who stopped us for what amounted to a briefing: "Well, look, just a dern minute. What are we doin? Goin down to
Star? Put on a show? Bud said the commander is usually off the base on
Sundays, but we'd better check with him first before we do anything. Who
wants to lead down there, Davey?"

"Naw, I wanta fly tail-end Charley. I gotta show Anderson how it looks
from back there. So, make it HOT! Caaac-cac-cac!"

Anderson, who towered over little Davey, was grinning like a big cat.

Evan caught my eye and shook his head over Nevers. The planes were
only a short walk away. Nevers went off to his plane, Evan's and mine were
next to each other.

"You wanta lead down to Star?"

"Sure, okay."

The final transformation: jungle pack and chute on the wing, stepping
up, up into the cockpit with the whole mess, in, adjusting straps, leg straps,
snapping chute straps across my chest, cockpit straps into the leather pad
across the middle, all three joining.

The plane captain was ready with his fire bottle, thumbs up. Starter motor on and winding. I could feel myself leaving the ground and a heaving
excitement inside. We no longer counted seconds; we listened to the whine
of the starter motor and at a certain note; switch on, smoke, explosion,
roar, throttle back, mixture to full-rich. I held the brakes gave the plane
captain thumbs up, he pulled the chocks and we were rolling.

Check the plane over "completely" before getting in, said Mamoo. I
didn't even *look* at the plane before taking it up. Tanks full? Windshield
clean? Let's go.

That wasn't craziness, it was economy. Take your chances happily.

About other things we were very careful. Hebert and I in those endless
test flights, day after day, would carefully note the characteristics of the
plane. If there was a level cloud cover at 7,300, we'd get right down on it,
set our electric altimeter at zero, as if the cloud cover were the ground,
climb up to 9,000, dive down to the flattened cloud cover, pull up into a
loop and make sure we came out consistently above the "ground." We did
the same with barrel rolls and slow rolls. We never hit the "ground."

It made an awesome sight when people saw us do it right off the actual ground. They were sure we would pile those heavy dive-bombers into the earth. They would shake their heads over us and sing their old refrain: "One of these days! You guys . . . *one* day, boy."

Of course, we delayed the pull-out to make it look closer than it really was. Then we added a roll after the loop. We never fell into the cloud cover. It had to be the same on the ground, "on the deck."

Bud Harrelson at Star gave us a standing invitation to come on down. So, down we went, BL, *Before Leyla*, and did our loops and rolls and generally tore up the place. It felt great to get down there as low as we could. To put a wing between the tower and the radio shack while traveling close to 300 knots.

Ever since then he'd ask us to come down Sundays.

I took off, turned south and continued my turn till the others joined on my wing. I had never flown with Davey Nevers, and had to admit he made a good joinup. Those props were chewing my wings on both sides. I could see but not hear little Davey cackling away.

I signaled with three fingers and we switched to channel three. A few minutes later and Evan was signaling, pointing at the Fort Pierce amphib base and at Davey's passenger.

I signaled with my flat hand to land at the outlying field just inland from the base, Evan shrugged and then agreed. We had flown together so long we didn't need the radio. No meat wagon or enlisted men down there, just an empty field. We were approaching the southeast runway and I gave them right wing echelon—my right fist high. I had to laugh at Davey. He was good, hanging right in there. Anderson was getting his promised ride today.

"Make it hot!" Davey's voice.

"One turn spins!" Moka, Bird-Brain Evan.

Down to 400 knots, screaming over the runway, I broke off, flaps and wheels out, cockpit open, hot air whirling in, bent straight down to the earth. I was close in and forced to make a vicious turn. Down, slowing down, curving, "I'll take the left side," I called out at the last minute, came out of my turn, hauling back, the end of the runway flashed under me, wings straight and I hit. Tail and wheels.

We got out and talked, or, rather screamed at each other on the lonely hot field of long green grasses, wild flowers—three big dive-bombers, three pilots and one tall stranger in summer flight suits and helmets—and three off-white cement runways.

Anderson was puffed up with it. "Boy, from the ground it doesn't look that close."

"You haven't seen *us* from the ground," Nevers said. Caaac cac-cac-cac.

Hebert said he'd lead us the next 15 miles to Star and Nevers could take it back to the base. We mounted our steeds again, fired up and followed Evan. "I'll be tail-end, Davey!"

He screeched something over the air, cackling, and we rolled out onto the cake-like surface. Up went the roar of Evan's then Davey's and mine, five seconds apart.

On the way down to Star, Davey had moved in so close that Evan, instead of objecting, started bouncing up and down to push him out. I pulled off to one side. Instead of taking the hint and moving out a little, Davey started doing the same thing. Up and down they were stitching the air; missing each other by a foot, less than a foot. I had a strange thought; did Davey *want* to smash into him? Did he even care?

I pulled out farther and watched. They were like two dogs fighting. And like two dogs they stopped, without any explanation. Nevers moved back in but not as close and I came in again. I remembered RM's description and thought, yes, mindless. "Mindless"? Insanity was closer to it. 300 feet high, no room to bail out, and their wings were passing each other inches apart.

We did the same hot breakup at Star and pulled off the runway to a taxi strip, cut the engines and got out. Bud Harrelson was there to greet us. Fat, jolly, good-natured, and that strange scientific-engineering kind of intelligence. He was a damned good ground-radar controller and liked working with Hebert and me. We introduced Davey to him and then Anderson, who was dazed with happiness.

"How's the old married man? Doesn't look like it's changed you much!"

We had some ice cream and made "purple cows," pouring Coke into a large cup and adding big scoops of vanilla, then stirring it into a kind of ice cream soup.

"Well, you guys gonna put on a little show?" Bud asked us. "The commander's off station today."

"I can't," Evan confessed, "I'm in trouble, I'm not even supposed to be up."

He was "on the reeport" as we said, and was forbidden to take day flights for a week.

I went up, buzzed the field, made them hit the deck, did some low turns, gained altitude and did a loop off the deck and began a roll out by the side of the field. I was almost on my back just off the ground and I felt that something was not right, it was a sniff of something, just the hint of a trap. I rolled back right side up, and came down and in, with my feet actually shivering and pattering the rudder bars in a way that I couldn't help. I know I would have killed myself if I had continued it. Just a sniff, I had gotten. Taxiing in I *did* think of Leyla, our little home, and, apologetically, all we had to live for. Was this what it did to you? I was puzzled by my thoughts.

By the time I taxied up, Davey was in his cockpit and Anderson was strapped in behind him.

I don't know whether I was warning him or having to tell someone, but I stood on his fat tire to yell something, since his engine was going and he was ready to take off, the big prop spinning only a few feet from me. I stood on his fat tire and pointed to the spot on the field where I almost creamed myself. I wiped some sweat off my brow for him and shook my head.

He threw back his head, laughing, although I couldn't hear a sound. I wasn't ten feet away before he spun it around and was tearing over the ground to the take-off spot.

"Yep," Bud was saying, "Best controllers, best station—"

"And the best pilots come down to visit," Hebert added.

"Riiight," said Bud, as if he were about to add just that.

"See that guy over there, with his wife and baby?" Hebert pointed out another ensign from the amphib base. "He was begging and pleading for a ride in Davey's back seat."

"There's one born every minute," Bud said.

We laughed, watching Anderson be jogged back and forth, like excess baggage, as Nevers cruised out to take off.

Davey roared down the runway and he must have hit the wheels "up" then *bounced* off the ground. The wheels folded in and he settled back down just inches off the ground. Ohh, hot. He had hardly lifted off when he came veering back at us, gaining speed, swept past us, one wing only a foot or so off the ground. It was horrendous looking. He couldn't wait to gain altitude so he was starting his little show immediately.

"Was I that low?" I asked Hebert.

"Ha! Your prop was cutting the tall grass out there."

Around and around he went, a continual turn and very low. Then he pulled off. We were sitting down, the three of us, still eating ice cream, and he was over by the side of the field when Hebert mentioned, almost in passing, "He's gonna roll it."

We turned to watch. I don't think Bud quite knew what it meant. It was all of a piece to Bud, the difficult and the flashy.

Nevers was on his back and Evan and I saw. Hebert knew and I knew. His nose was low, pointed right at the horizon. After that we were only hopes and wishes, but we knew.

The big heavy dive-bomber completed the roll, then dropped as it came out, then it was a streak of muffled, roaring orange across my brain.

We were on our feet. And, suddenly, Hebert was telling us: "Look, let's get the story straight. Nevers was the *only one* who went up once we got down here."

"Okay," said Bud. "Okay. I'm going to the tower to report the accident."

"I'll circle the place, you go back and fill out the report," said Evan to me.

"Do you think there's some chance? . . . "

Evan looked at me as if I'd lost my mind.

"I'll call you on channel three," I yelled to Evan who was up on his wing, into the cockpit of his beast.

The Star meat wagon was tearing out to the scene.

I walked up the wing, started it, took off and was flying the 20 miles back to base. I reported the accident over the air, was told to report to the flight office. I called Moka on three.

"I'm over it, circling," came Evan's now very deliberate voice, a voice that told me more about looking than talking, "There's a whole burnt-out area . . . not a chance he's out of it."

He? What about Anderson?

I landed and was on the way to the flight office, but already pilots were grabbing me, "What happened, Willy?"

I gave the flight office our official story, was told they might call me in again. Outside of the flight office everyone had heard the bare details, they were all asking and asking.

I found Heath at the BOQ. Heath, Nevers' roommate. Heath, the different one. He was in the room drinking. His face looked rotten. The second roommate he'd lost. Heath was a pale, freckled, pony-haired, and surprising pilot. Heath the pacifist, some said. A Buddhist, they said. And he did not help me out when I tried to explain how wild Nevers was during the whole flight.

The room had grown quiet. I didn't know what else to do. It was as if I had personally apologized to Heath and I watched him, head down, his hair a little stiff and not much longer than when we were at preflight; horse-hair, like Shep's.

"Do you know what it's like to take a body home?"

I was shocked at his words, really at anything that would come out of him because I didn't know he was thinking anything, just taking it in still. But no, he was talking and talking for me to hear him. "No, you wouldn't know . . . " And it wasn't the first statement that made me feel guilty it was the last one. That I *wouldn't* know. Because he not only meant that I hadn't ever taken a roommate's body home, that it wasn't my luck, or my "karma," but something else. It reminded me that it was Heath who had taken Loomis home ('Mother mother mother, your son is coming home . . . in a box,' we sang at parties). I knew what they thought of us—wild, unthinking.

Then Heath was looking at me. 'You wouldn't know,' was still in his eyes, somehow accusing, and still very gentle.

Time had stopped and still the cheap clock on the dresser went on in loud sticks of time.

I not only felt that I should be taking the body "home" to spare Heath that second trip, but I should be making that trip because I had killed him.

"You . . . " Heath said and stopped, "are not to blame." As if he was looking through me and talking to something or someone else.

Compounding my responsibility, so that now I was both responsible but was beyond understanding it—not what had happened and not how my hand was in it. And because I desperately did not want to hear what it was like to take a body home—we filled out forms: 'In case of accident' ("Hey, Pete, how'd you like a trip to Jersey?" Haw haw.).

I blundered on, "So awful," I told him, in the quiet room, while those tired and intelligent eyes waited on my useless words, " . . . killed *here*," I said by way of completing my thoughts.

And for the first time Heath was fully awake and seized the words, almost with the jaws of his mind, "*Here? 'Awful' here?*"

"Yes," I said, feeling suddenly that I'd fallen into a kind of trap.

He kept looking at me as if I were not only a stranger but a foreigner to the English language, "'Here'?" He said again, "Not 'awful' there?"

"I mean," I hastened to add, "without purpose . . . stateside."

"And 'over there'" Heath said, with a kind of restrained fury, "'Over-SEAS," he said, "it would *not* be awful? Is that what you're saying?"

I felt I owed him; I owed him for Nevers, I owed him for his sober, kind, clear gaze and his concern and, suddenly, I realized there was, really, something I didn't understand that a few of the others *did*. Or they understood something, that until now I didn't understand at all. RM had it. So did Leyla. Something I was missing.

Heath suddenly changed, abruptly, and dismissed it with a wave of his hand, "*You* . . . you're a *warrior*," he straightened up when he said the word, making fun of it and, at the same time, seriously, "a *warrior* . . . looking for a field of action."

"What do you mean?" I asked him.

"You and that other madman," he waved me away and stood up, moved toward Nevers' side of the room and very methodically and like an old man, began taking Nevers' stuff out of his closet and throwing it on Nevers' bed.

"He was too little to roll that big plane," Heath said, in a different voice.

I watched while the things on the bed grew into a little pile.

"Want me to help . . . get his stuff?"

"No," he said and looked at me with that vague kindness and kept on— inevitably and inexorably as if the very movement of the planet itself pushed us to continue even when our actions no longer had any meaning.

" . . . too little to roll that big plane."

I looked at the room one last time, at the habitual and similar mess all of our rooms were in, and went out to the car, feeling empty and as if I should at least have shook his hand, or, maybe should have, I don't know, given him a hug, but I didn't, of course. And was feeling both sorry and at the same time relieved, and wondered about Heath, maybe the most serious and the most complicated one of us all. And the talk about him being in trouble, about "those desiring" war and his refusal to go.

" . . . too little." I could hear him all the way to the beach. And Nevers . . . laughing.

I felt no lift even at the sight of the great ocean and the green waves rolling in to the beach as joyously as if nothing at all had happened.

Chapter 34

Leyla was running to the car before I stopped it, RM had told her, and she was in my arms as I opened the car door to get out. Not a word just kept hugging me. We went inside to the bed, laid down and she held me and held me, begged me not to say anything just hold her, and let her hold me.

"Don't talk. It's okay. Okay. Don't talk, RM already told me."

I felt myself letting go, letting go and suddenly crying, maybe the relief of not having to explain again. The longer we remained silent the more she understood. Maybe her understanding could only be marred by words. But why tears? I'm here, he's gone. Anderson, Nevers' rear-seat passenger, and the guy with wife and baby pleading to die in his place. The guy, his wife, and baby had seen it all. And after the crash they were nowhere to be seen. Just disappeared.

"It's okay. Okay."

Too little to roll that big plane. Heath had said it all.

When I came to she was still there.

"I'm okay. Do you want to talk about it now? The war and stuff?" I asked her.

"No, I don't."

"I promised you."

"It's okay."

"I talked to Spatzler," I told her after a while. She had fixed us sandwiches, great sandwiches, sloppy with big hunks of Swiss cheese and I felt like they were putting life back into me. "I'm not going. Absolutely no changes in the list."

She did not react.

She had been to town with Clare and called her parents in Marshall. Her mother and father were insisting we get a telephone. They'd pay for the installation, no matter what the cost. They also wanted Leyla home for a short visit as soon as she could arrange it. In fact they wanted the two of us to meet them in New Orleans, stay for a couple of days, get to know my mother, then proceed to Marshall for at least a week. I thought it was funny. How blithe it all was. Forget the war, just come home for a week.

"He knows we've won . . . the war," Leyla said, with a sniffling giggle.

"I talked to Spatzler . . . oh yeah, I already told you. Not going. No war for Willy."

In the days that followed I was turning it over. I still didn't think I could be killed but I did see how, *how* it could happen. And while Nevers was attempting a roll just off the deck, all that time, Leyla was in town with Clare, talking to her parents about getting a phone and having a nice visit, our two families.

Nevers' death did not add many admirers to our list, especially among the powers-that-be. In every mother's parlance, Nevers had been hanging around with the wrong kids.

In a week we had a phone. And they were insisting on the visit, the meeting of the families in New Orleans. We decided to go ahead with the short visit for Leyla. It was only a matter of when. Her father was being very correct. No more talk about annulling the marriage. How and when Leyla would travel to New Orleans and return was a tiresome topic. During the first days after Nevers we decided okay, in a month. Then it was a week. Then right away, the last of April, to do it and get it off, done with.

"I hate it, *hate* it," Leyla said, in my arms. The ten days had been whittled down to seven. Not a chance in the world I could get seven days off.

"But, I *know* . . . *how I need you.*"

It delighted Leyla: "See, Will? I know you feel a great deal. It's just admitting it."

The phone was nice and also a bother: "Why did I answer it," Leyla whispered over the cupped mouthpiece one morning the day before she was to leave.

We stayed intact while she answered like a dutiful daughter, "Yes, mom, we will . . . we are . . . yes, but he's sleeping now."

Our little Eden was not so secure from the world.

Then before we knew it I was driving Leyla down to Palm Beach to catch the flight to New Orleans. Her mother and father had already left by car. Lord only knows how the "banker" obtained the gas stamps to do it. Mamoo was very excited; the Herndons would meet the sisters and uncles, and Brucie and Arthe, possibly. I felt good about it and glad I wouldn't be there.

I was trying to understand my coldness during the final seconds before she left. I hated it, a coldness came over me at the same time I felt the awfulness of watching her go.

So she's gone. My wife is flying away. I watched her plane take off and hoped the pilot knew what he was doing. Deep inside me something was trying to say, 'I don't care, I don't care if she goes.'

The war was a muffled drumbeat, muffled heartbeat. In the Pacific the Marshall Islands had fallen, Eniwetok, after five tough days of fighting. The invasion of Europe was readying, we could feel the pressure way off in Florida, but *when*? Jorge had something up his sleeve but he wouldn't tell me. Gave me a thumbs up and a smile, but no words.

One of the bogeys, Ritchie Carle, lost it in a fog off the end of the east-west runway. He had come in, almost on instruments because of the fog, was out of position, was given a red light to go around again for another approach and went into a tree only a mile from the station. Three days later his body still hadn't been located. Hebert, walking through the heavy undergrowth, was the first to find him, but at first did not recognize the body, which was covered with dried blood the color of his flight jacket, and threw up when he realized what it was.

The schedule, our lives, and the war went on. I thought about death, about Nevers, Hutch, Carle and, oh yeah, Loomis. I was forgetting the dead. There had been other deaths, two or three navy night fighter students, but the others were known, were "us" bogey pilots.

I tried to tell Heath about what Nevers was like on that fatal day. I don't believe I got through to him. I think he figured I killed his roommate, taking him on some wild goose chase. "Too little to roll that big plane." It seems I should have told him, "No! No, Davey, you're too little!"

Other times it was all very simple. The difference was that Hebert and I had done our homework. We knew we could do those things.

I went out with Mulligan and Jorge and it was like old times. Jorge confided that he was working on something. "Hang on," he told me, "Just hang on." He wouldn't say any more.

Then he finally admitted that he was talking with Spatzler and the Fowler to have me put down in place of Nevers. He had already told Leyla, made her swear she wouldn't say anything to me. "Did you know that you and Evan have more flight hours since arriving Red Beach than anyone else? Anyhow, we start training in ten days."

Nevers had been scheduled to go in the first group with RM, Mulligan, Jorge and Woodruff, and they needed a fifth. I felt the old stirrings.

"Corsairs," Jorge intoned carefully. Evan was chilled toward the whole thing. "To hell with 'em. 'You *can* go, you *can't* go . . . ' Those desiring,'" he said in a little mincing voice. "Sounds like an invitation to high tea."

Signs were appearing all over the base, directives and new directives. The base at Red Beach was going to celebrate its fifth anniversary as a night fighter base with an air show and exhibitions. The town and the whole area was being invited. I was called in and "the Fowler" was telling me that Hebert and I had been selected to put on an exhibition in the SB2Cs. It happened the night after I had some free time and flew formation on a commercial transport with my lights off. I thought for a minute I had been reported but no, Evan and I were being 'honored,' he said, and if we could do an exhibition without breaking any flight regulations he was going to okay our part in the big air show. We had three days to pick out some planes and they would be held for us, for that day, the big show. As for Jorge's wild talk, I was happy they wanted me but I had stopped even dreaming about it. Well, a little piece of the dream, I'd still show the bastards what could be done with an old condemned dive-bomber. Maybe *this* was my war.

Leyla called from Marshall. She loved New Orleans. They had met both of my sisters, gone down to the French Quarter, to Galatoire's for lunch, to Commander's Palace for supper, had cocktails with the Barclays, Aunt Alice, Brucie and Arthe and Pearse. Uncle Willie and Tatee were in Roswell, New Mexico. Uncle Willie working on some secret project, so Leyla's parents had missed them.

"They think you're related to half of New Orleans, and I do too. God, Will! Such a beautiful city. Do you think we'll ever live there?"

"Are you talking about ATW?"

"Well, yes . . . anyhow, I miss you, RN"

"R.N.?"

"Right now."

"Oooh, *God*, I miss youuuu."

"That sounds physical."

"Wellllll, it's physical, mental, emotional . . . and I just *need* you."

"Will . . . you made me . . . *oh*, I can't wait to get back."

"What? Made you *what?*"

"I can't say right now."

"Please, please tell me."

"You make me . . . " she lowered her voice, "w-e-t."

That call was from Marshall, just after their drive from New Orleans.

One night, I had been dismissed from the controller early. It was around one. No more scheduled fighters so I was free. I climbed up to 10,000 and was nosing around, listening to the "coffee grinder" radio. I got some big band music, live. After each piece the announcer, in very mellow tones, told us ". . . you're listening to the music of Jimmy Dorsey, coming to you direct from the beautiful Squantum Lake Supper Club, just off the Black Rock Turnpike near Montauk, Long Island."

The voice conjured up a dreamy atmosphere, far far from the war, lamps at each table, evening dresses, tuxedos, dancing and dinner. I heard "Do Nothin' Till You Hear From Me," sailing along at 10,000 feet in my roaring beast, looking down at the lights of coastal towns way below me, looking at my life, wondering about Leyla, two months pregnant, then I realized where I was, and Leyla far away on this night:

". . . some kiss may cloud my memoryyyyyy, And other arms may hold a thrill . . . "

I suddenly felt a little sick. How easily could I be affected by someone else. And Leyla, so ready, so full of life. Of course we loved each other but, well, there was the Link trainer operator just two days ago, giving us a checkout for instrument ratings. I caught myself looking into the depths of her brown eyes, and realized she was looking back. What did it mean?

I flew wing on a big commercial airliner, lights off, for about 15 minutes. I was in so close I could watch the passengers put sugar in their coffee. Then I flipped down and away. I turned on my lights, rolled over and dove down in a long dive, and in to land. The 'BIG' air show was two days away. Leyla's return was four.

To Navy Commander Lewis Gresham, watching them fly stirred many things. How long had it been since he felt like that? Flown like that? Had he ever wanted to?

A dozen, fifty times, he looked up from his desk to see a dive bomber at some unflyable angle. It was a normal reaction to gasp and stand up at the sight of a plane one instant before a fatal crash. It was not just the angle, it was the angle and the speed, one or two knots above stalling in a slow spin 100 feet off the ground, and yet the crash never took place. What are they trying to do, commit suicide? "One turn spins to a landing," someone called them. Hard, slow, grinding turns too low to recover if they stalled out. Always it was one of the two.

They had been warned again and again, and "Dangerous Flight Conduct" was a charge the two of them were familiar with and it appeared on their Fitness Reports with monotonous regularity. They were hardly in line for promotion but that threat, apparently, did not worry them. And God knows what they did out of sight of the base.

Now the two stood before him. He felt he was once again among the living, too old to do any more than admire them and not allowed to show even that, an old man, well, an aging man blind from drink, unable to stop, proud and brave only afraid of blindness and going blind.

Well, they would be his eyes, his young greyhounds. And there would be friends from Fort Lauderdale and Miami up for the show: "Watch when I slip the leash on these two. Just watch."

"I hope you're pleased about your assignment tomorrow?"

"Yes sir."

"Now," he was smiling, "I don't want to tell you how to fly your planes, only keep some daylight between those wings and the field . . . and," he said, with more feeling than he'd intended, "No blood! Okay? Ahh . . . any questions?"

"No sir!"

"I think I'm going to get under cover . . . myself," said the commander, his smile bubbled over and he was laughing.

He was laughing with us and started to say something more. Instead he leaned forward from his desk and stuck out his hand. I shook it, still unbelieving. Hebert came forward and shook his hand and nodded his head.

Out of sight of the office we congratulated each other. The base commander stuck out his hand to us! How many bogeys had that happened to?

"Well, are we gonna stay out of trouble or give 'em a show?"

"What have we got to lose?"

"Only our wings."

We had worked out our takeoff and join-up at an outlying field. Instead of a two-man formation takeoff , we practiced a timed takeoff from different but intersecting runways. The plan was for Hebert to give it full throttle and straight on; I'd count to three and start down the intersecting runway. It looked as if the two planes were going to smash into each other where the runways crossed. We'd cross the intersection point with a few seconds' difference. He'd take off and turn left, into my track, and we'd be joined a few seconds after getting off the ground. We only had to make sure that the distance from where the two of us started was the same. The only other worry was whether one of the planes was underpowered. Now, if the lead plane was underpowered well, even then, three seconds should be enough.

We went up to the tower, the very heart of flight activity. "Mother" Jane

Towson was on duty and would be on duty for the air show tomorrow. We explained the plan to her and she was petrified.

"We just explained it to Commander Gresham. He said . . . 'Just be careful.'"

"Careful? That is the *zaniest* . . . do you realize the two of you have this reputation and . . . *What???* Take off . . . from two intersecting runways at slightly different times?"

"Yeah, we've done it before. It worked out."

"Not here at the base, you didn't! Not on *my* watch! Not with *me* on duty!"

"No, at an outlying field. We'll be in radio contact. Evan will start first, I'll give him . . . "

I think we talked her into it, if we would allow ten seconds before the second plane began its take-off run. She was still hesitant, "I'll have to think some more about this."

We were officers and Jane—who "mothered" us in to the field and was devastated over any crash—Seaman First Class Jane Towson, was enlisted, but the person in charge of the tower was in charge of traffic around the field. Admirals and generals were in her hands. When the tower operator told a plane to 'Take a wave-off,' that plane had to go around again and try a new approach, the rank of the pilot had nothing to do with it. When she said, "All planes circling Red Beach . . . hold your positions, we have an emergency landing," all planes in the pattern circled until cleared. The Field Commander had spoken, and it had nothing to do with the fact that "Mother" Jane was a good-looking blond, half the age of the senior pilots, and would do most anything for Woodruff, the merry duke, once she was off duty. We left a very skeptical Jane Towson and went down to the flight line to pick some planes for tomorrow.

Only two of us moving on the field under a clear morning sky of tucked-in clouds, moved through lines of planes, engines bursting and chattering, tough-bragging engines drove back the morning silence like the sun drives darkness, chased silence through blocks of planes, stones of planes under the sun a fury of light turning everything bluer whiter grayer.

". . . three eighteen permission to scramble, over."

"Three eighteen cleared."

Sun on the field again and out under it full throttle curving to straight, lock tail wheel and go. Off from three points upped wheels I held it down gathering gathering then tail-at-earth soaring up staggering up the cliff until I pushed it over to a steep climb this sluggish monster, well, life is no fairy tale and we can't go straight up.

Hebert was right behind me. We had flown together for so long we didn't need to practice the tricky takeoff. We were only checking the planes for whether either one was underpowered and how they were for acrobatics. I sat there waiting for altitude, my right leg against valves and handles 2000 feet high. The world above and below, same leg, same hands. Walk up the wing get in, straps-engine-taxi-out now climbing up over my own head.

Patched gray blues white yellow morning—over the beach deserted, located our little cabin, Leyla due in three days. Again I was asking myself, what am I doing? Is *this* my war? Is this it? Up to massive cloud architecture where the air is like sherbet, into its caves and niches up a mountain road through fragile white scarves of vapor next to mountains of gray-white, mountains of stone, then leaned into the mountain, right wing down, stick back into white darkness, blind but for cockpit instruments, hands, feet on rudders, into the heart of it rolled onto my back, saw instruments wind up, body shaking with speed, one-two-three then blue earth, white then earth brown green blue-shaded, a line perpendicular through air. How much time left? How much life?

Ten more seconds like this . . . five more

Calm earth, houses, fields, trees coming up.

One moment light-year shot across the very thread of my life and I rolled out, pulled out more, close to the ground moving up rolling, rolling in four points, dove again and rolled eight points.

"Hey, Moka, land and turn off at the first taxiway, watch me!"

"No, *you* watch this," Hebert dove past me, faster and in better position.

We were both diving for that imaginary spot that X in air 500 feet over the bridge, over which all planes entering the field traffic passed. Throttle wide open nose down and straight for it. He passed point X-ray first, both in violent opposite turns.

I fell, swinging and twisting, wings bent against straightness now leveling all power off . . . down slicing, hard at the last then wings straightening a few seconds after Evan, down and in.

Shreeeeek. I hit rolling at 60 knots and turned off at the second taxiway, engine purring, and picked up the plane captain, arms clasped overhead for wings . . . wings, I took off the safety and turned the steel piece to fold, up came the wings and changed the engine noise as it went through the triangle of folded wings.

Little specks from above and now one little speck directed me in, a speck in wrinkled blue jeans and shirt. Down looking up then up looking down.

The plane captain raised both fists at me, "Hold! You're in position."

Just a speck a minute ago, his young face was not surprised at all.

The engine wheezed out its life and I unlocked myself from three eighteen, silence but for the gyros' dying song.

Tomorrow three eighteen? It's a coin we flip. Good and fast but it shouldn't shake like that at high speed. Onto the wing and down.

Hebert met me in front of my plane: "Some day . . . Some day, boy!"

It was a joke to be alive, and not sure we weren't in trouble for zig-zagging across the landing pattern and doing it 100 miles an hour too fast.

"Did you sign us for two more? Yeah . . . Did you see where I turned off? The *first* taxiway next time! . . . Let's go . . . Right! . . . Get em up lieutenant . . . Okay, but this time not so faaaast . . . And not so lowwww! . . . You're crazy! One of those craaaazy flyers, right? Some day you're gonna skin up your ass and they'll have to put it in a sling . . . Okay, just don't crash and burn! Go get them little yellow bastards!"

Three-fifty burst into life behind me, an air-cutting bark from some monstrous dog's throat, I turned to film a huge genie of blue oil smoke. Rooooommm! Blasted apart. That instant and that instant was gone. Hebert called for his chocks and I wasn't even in the plane yet.

Up onto three-twenty-two's wing. And not blood. Not blood and not muscle but strength and waves of strength, parachute under me and no straps I started the engine and, "Chocks!" Chocks away and I hooked up while taxiing out. The plane captain gave me to the next man: Hey! Canzoneri! Riding a bike! Riding a bike fast as he could, directing me out, yelling. He understood us! Ha! Ha! Yeah! Sure! Go to hell! On on on and shot me out into the clear.

Past the first taxiway down to the end. Next-to-nothing that distance. Hebert swept onto the center of the runway picking up speed as he turned into the wind hustling to get off.

After him, past the first turn-off—we'd have to land and stop dead in order to turn off so soon, hit the end of the runway and *stick*.

Up for one dive and if the body doesn't shake it will be three-twenty-two tomorrow. At eight thousand I rolled onto my back and came down like a knife. No shaking. I leveled at 3000, held it, up into a loop came out of it level at 3600, rolled to both sides and again to the right in four points, not perfect but good; twisted rolled dove half-looped and hung it on its back. They said it couldn't fly upside down but we flew it upside down and even gained altitude with the help of the elevator trim.

"Hey Kaanga, you ready to join up? I'm south of the field over the beach at angels three."

Impossible to miss the dive-bomber moving south to north and really traveling.

"Have you in sight, Bare, I'll join on you," rolling and pushing off the sky.

"Okay, where are you?" the voice itself craned around looking for me.

On my back to keep him in sight and down out of the sun.

"Here I am!" crossed down and in front passing very close, rolled out straight to pull up again.

Back on a level I cut across Hebert's bow for him to turn inside and join up, held it steady while three-fifty pulled in on my wing and locked in place, faded blue oil-stained beast of thick wings white numbers white stars moored alongside, ten feet between cockpits, Hebert was shaking his head, a rare compliment, "I lost five years that time."

Grinning and conscious of the one thing we had learned, the one thing we did with the world's best. Now to land in a space much less than one-fourth of the runway; like landing on a carrier with no arresting hook and no wind passing over the deck to slow us down.

Over Point X-ray in a dive I held up two fingers, and we switched to tower frequency.

"Red Beach, two for pancake, over?"

"Cleared to land, one and two in the pattern," said "Mother" Jane, "runway three-six-wind-eight-knots-south-southwest," mechanically she told us about the empty field.

"The first taxiway," I said, with a last glance back, " . . . one wing and the tail wheel."

"Right," Moka answered.

"Okay, boys, don't splatter yourselves," Jane whispered.

Wings straight down we sliced a big cake of air coming into the 500 foot circle banked up like motorcycles in a closed circuit, two dogs hung-up we pulled around in the tightest turn until hooked on invisible rails, our wings straightened quick and smooth straight up the runway low fast steady.

I patted my head, kissed off and broke from that two-man projectile knifing around one glance at the tip end of runway, all power off. Wheels and flaps down and out, cockpit open, full revolutions, changing tabs check gas checked, rushing to slower, the flaps were like oars in water back-watering, dipped hard into that stream of air. Elevator tab back, back till it hit the end and the stick was loose in my hand. 80 knots and backing up, 300 feet abeam of the spot.

Into the turn nose cocked up and dropping hard, power off, a slight crosswind against me. Steeper, speed in low 70s, good control but begging for speed.

Good that I kept it in close.

It *should* drop like a brick.

Cool frenzy: haul back straighten out, flared and squashed the end of the runway almost stopped. Brakes right. Left. Right. Tapping. Tail wheel free. Right brake and turning. Tapping left, don't let it wind up.

I swung off the main river into the stream of the first taxiway in a wide sweep, tapping brakes alternately to keep it from wrapping up in a ground loop to the right.

Made it! Jesus! "Heyyyyyy," I started yelling, "How's it going Bare-Bare? Smoking brake drums and wheels through the wings but it's 'Up' for the night, heeee heeeee."

Wings to "fold" added the whine of the hydraulic actuator, up came wings and changed the engine noise beating through the tunnel of wings and body.

I saw Hebert hit hard, little puffs of smoke at each tire, the plane yawed, then straight, and swerving over into the entrance of the first turnoff, barely missing the grass beyond.

God Damn!

We were up and down. On the ground still in the air, props blasting cloud vapor off body and wings, crazy plover dodging frantically on each side, sun on hands and face, stomach to sun shining on earth facing it diving down, sun rays sent down like one of them rolling down to beach and curling waves. Flying banners hung out, I was rushing up the slot casting dead planes to the right and left and up ahead the plane captain's frantic "Slow down, Slow down!" I swung it around moved slowly between two still planes straight then forward, hit both brakes at the sign of the closed fists. The engine wheezed out its life and I flung the straps from me.

Ahh, those last moments; still curved but straightening, back on stick, back back to a crashing hard landing; brakes and throttle for control, and turn off. My whole body purged.

"How was it?" the plane captain as I came down the wing.

"Good plane! Hold this one for me for the air show tomorrow, okay?"

"You got it, Lieutenant. I'll tell Brush."

Hebert was taxiing by no helmet hair-blowing, we shook fists at each other at the world yessss *made* it, his wings rising to fold, just out of that shower of sky and still wet, three-fifty rolled between lines of dead planes, living three-fifty moved squealed protesting set into line roared once more coughed up blood and died.

Everywhere close to the field there was furious activity. Below and in front of the tower grandstands were being thrown together. Bunting strung above and around the grandstands, which were painted navy gray, battleship gray. Lemonade and soft drink stands were going up before our eyes. I felt the butterflies in my stomach. Would we show 'em tomorrow? Tomorrow's the war. What am I doing? My war? The only war I'll ever know.

We went into the line shack and confirmed our two planes for tomorrow. Brush assured us they wouldn't even be flown for tonight's flights.

I was feeling great except for a tremendous urge to call her.

Then my eye caught the little covey of brand new Corsairs, covey of seven off in their own corner of the field. What flight of birds, what flock of birds is more beautiful? Standing still they were going 100 miles an hour. With a pang in my heart I looked at them. Was that dream dead? Again it hit me, the desperate urge to call her.

The base gossip was that Heath was in big trouble. Trouble that made crashing or even being killed just a lark. He had refused to sign the list of those going. The crazy part was that pilots had signed or not signed but no one had refused to sign, until Heath.

Once again it was the words "those desiring."

When Heath pointed that out they asked him if he was *refusing* to go. He told them since it was worded "those desiring" that he was among those *not* desiring. In fact he desired it so little that . . . well, he wasn't signing.

Now *they* were upset because he had taken advantage of some loose wording.

They kept asking if he was *refusing* to sign. And, according to the report, he asked them if they had ever read Melville's story, "Bartleby the Scrivener." Then he told them he was Bartleby and, quite simply, that he preferred not to sign. They did not know what he was talking about. And Heath 'preferred not' to straighten them out.

I heard all of this in the mess-hall before I got up to call Leyla, then decided to drive to the beach to our place and call from there.

Leyla and the families had just returned from eating out and were having coffee at our house. My heart was full. It was one of those times when
we were both overflowing, happy and thankful that we had each other,
then that we were separated. Behind all of the happy talk there was the
picture of those lean and mean Corsairs. But I was telling her how beauti-
ful-perfect, the way we used to talk from mouths to hearts: " . . . so perfect,
so beautiful, every hair, every fingernail like a perfect, beautiful cat down
to perfect nostrils, perfect ears, never mind how I say it—"

"—And so Lieutenant-I-love-you, this cat, beautiful or not, is all yours
and I can't wait to have you again."

We went on but the message had been delivered. The rest was how and
when she'd be coming back. Not to worry, I'd be there and nothing could
stop me. Then I confessed about the air show and, Leyla's, "Please, be careful—" before she could stop herself.

Saying it and, then, taking it back?

"I'm *not* going to be careful!"

"Good . . . good, Will. Do it the way you know how to . . . "

"Leyla, don't *tell* me—"

"I know . . . I know . . . that's right. You're right. I'm sorry and I could
bite my tongue off. And ohh, I love you hugely—"

We broke the connection and I was left in that little cabin by the sea,
and Leyla in New Orleans. Telling me that! Did she have a premonition?

I was tempted to go and see RM and Clare but thought of them maybe
in bed and I could not move. RM was scheduled to fly in the big flyover of
all the bogey pilots, minus Evan and myself. Instead I tried to sleep and
only half succeeded, going over every maneuver . . . to come across on my
back? Four point roll out of a loop?

Chapter 36

At the field I found Hebert walking off the distances between the takeoff
spots of the two runways, up to where they met. And the tower wasn't
happy about it, periodically flashing red lights at him. He had been out to
the field at 6:30, walking off the distance from the take-off end to the intersection. "His" runway 12-Easy (120 degrees East) was four or five of his

paces longer than "my" runway, Seven-Easy. We agreed on three and a half seconds delay. At the "Go!" He'd jam throttle to the firewall, I'd count three seconds and do the same, cross at the intersection. He'd takeoff and climb in a left turn, we'd be joined at 200 or 300 feet. We'd climb and then dive on the field a few seconds apart.

The planes had been spotted for takeoff in order. We placed parachutes in the cockpits, warmed them up, and went back for a briefing, then decided to hell with it and went off for our breakfast of hot fudge sundaes. Mulligan almost threw up when he heard about it. His breakfast was four cupsacawfee and white toast. I didn't see much difference. When we returned, the public address system, after squeaking and blaring, was welcoming the crowd on this beautiful day. He could have barked over it, but the fact of the address system made people settle down.

Commander Gresham presented a Silver Star and two Distinguished Flying Crosses with oak leaf clusters to three brand new heroes along with their letters of commendation, calling each in turn forward to have the medals pinned to their uniforms, all in whites, and each presentation ending with the worn but still exciting phrase, "Above and beyond the call of duty," and signed with Roosevelt's own hand.

Commander Gresham made the presentations for the navy: more DFCs, oak leaf clusters and a Navy Cross for "Extraordinary courage and intrepidity while under fire, having landed his plane on _____" name of airstrip and island withheld—"an enemy held airstrip . . . remained in his plane, locked one brake, revved up his engine, raised the tail and strafed enemy positions, inflicting heavy damage including: 15 planes destroyed, two gun positions put out of action, killing or wounding from 50 to 100 men. And returned with no damage to his plane."

And the hero's name? Not Scott, O'Brien or Schwartzenstein, no, it was *Keggs*. Lt. J.G. Sidney Keggs.

The commander announced that Keggs would participate in the glide bombing exhibition, the target a 'battleship' outlined in white chalk on the center of the field. A 25 dollar war bond would be awarded for the best bombing.

The commander's voice had changed at the mention of the prize. A speech! 'Give' to the war effort, to support those other heroes, ". . . Who this very minute, *over there* . . . giving their *all* . . . while we here today . . . over your heads . . . over *there* . . . over here . . . until . . . driven back to Tokyo and beyond—"

"Where else can they drive 'em?" Mulligan asked the five of us lying on the greensward.

"Shut up, Mulligan!"

The low-flying formation of F6F's hardly drowned him out. Twice more they came back, flying at 2000 feet in a fairly nice V, before the first formation of five came by. The commander had finished and handed the microphone over to the M.C.

Mulligan kept piping away, "Commander, these boys over here, have also made the supreme sacrifice. More than a few have died in the battle of the Florida Straits and Coral Gables . . . and I am hereby authorized to award the Distinguished Sympathy Cross, with Purple Finger Dangling, to Ensign Iron-Nuts Benson, up Biscayne Boulevard on his back at 50 feet when the light changed—"

I turned away from Mulligan just as the call for all dive-bomber pilots boomed out and the group began moving off, except for Evan and me.

"Don't crash and burn," they yelled.

There was a mask over the field and we had to look hard in order to remember what it had been. The grandstand was filled: noise, kids, and everyone eating. A light schedule of flights for the evening and a big party tonight, Jorge was insisting: *"Evvvvrryyyyybodyyyyyy goes! Tonight!"*

Mechanics were off and hangars cleaned up for visitors. Children screeching, sandwiches and drinks everywhere. We had long been brainwashed to see civilians as know-nothing, as bumbling, as blind, and yet the whole show was for them: The mass, the crowd, the 'country,' the people back home. The ones "we" were fighting for.

Flags and bunting hung on the sides and back of the grandstand, ringing the central hangar, hanging between them, the long space where most of the spectators would pass, up the tower itself a giant barber pole/May pole, fairly shouting, "Free Shave, Today Only!."

I noted distances and obstacles. Antennae near the tower and the height of grandstand next to tower, if I come over there what would I hit?

I saw it all through a veil. All morning I had felt fear, and it was not going away. How much would I dare? I gave up and tried to listen. Hebert, the silent ("it's the mindlessness," said RM), had spoken more in the last hour than in the last week. Religion, marriage, and even mentioned Bess. It was eerie. Hebert was an animal made for movement not talk. Was he about to be killed?

Some F6s took off but hadn't been heard from. Then, at last, back they came, two two-man sections; they came over at 200 feet and simply flew past us. I was embarrassed and ashamed. This was the beginning of the big show?

"Are we gonna stay above 200 feet?" Hebert asked, grinning mischievously.

"What??" I told him, "I distinctly heard them say, 'Not *above* 200 feet!'"

Hebert fell back in the grass laughing. Mulligan warned us about more trouble and RM gave me a glance full of wives and duty. Then they left, last call for the bogey pilots.

The SB2C pilots; Mulligan, RM, Jorge and the others were in their planes and soon enough the backfiring, blasting, coughing engines changed to the sound of some thirty dive-bombers, engines turning over, it was like the very earth machinery.

Five black dots came from inland just over the trees five black flies growing. The upright oval of the engines, black slivers of wings longer and taking on color and shape very rapidly until planes purple-blue with white numbers, white stars on fuselage and wings, roaring ringing in line one after another pulled up steeply barrel-rolling into the sky.

Quickly the planes were specks again, color gone to black, wings to sticks to slivers to points in the sky. Excitement at all the ringing, wings flashing, but the rolls were the very safest and none had begun his roll lower than 50 feet.

Back they came and rolled again—a travesty, the absolute safety of it. Only the sound of those fast-ringing engines . . . the rest was a fraud. The pilots in those sleek, beautiful planes—next to the Zero the most maneuverable of the world's fighter planes—had chosen to give us nothing.

Then they came back in echelon, ready for their first run on the "battleship." They took their intervals on each other, made a dummy run, pulled up, and the competition was under way.

Such a splendid prize for the arrow striking closest to the center of the target. And for acrobatics in an old dive-bomber? A mounted golden archer with emeralds for eyes! A keg of ale! A skin of fair October brew! And a golden banana in a cluster of pine needles.

The field carrier landing group were going for their planes, the jeep carrying the landing signal officers in their bright red phosphorescent-lined flight suits was already streaking to a far side of the field where the lines of a carrier's flight deck had been painted in whitewash. Another 25 dollar bond for the best series of landings. These five, too, were fresh from overseas duty on carriers.

Then the electrifying announcement: "Lieutenants Vairin and Hebert report to Lt. Cleary in the utility shack, immediately!"

Mad dogs and Englishmen go out in the noonday sun. Over the low fence to the shack when Cleary popped out, "Now this is what the colonel just said, all acrobatics are to be completed *not lower than 200 feet!*"

"Yes sir, yes sir, Lieutenant Cleary, sir, yes sir." Cleary was annoyed and turned away.

As we were going to sign for the planes, up comes the colonel with a sheaf of papers, his grave, serious voice, harrumph, "Alright, you two, put on a good show but be careful."

We nodded agreement (salute? No helmet) and continued to the line shack to sign. And right then it was all getting unreal. Inside and outside were touching. Only one thing for sure, all of this display, so stingy, so cheap, no food for the soul, no risk. No one else seemed to know we had to get up there and *do* something. God was sitting in that grandstand, Alright, you guys! Show Me Something. Meanwhile all the doors were coming off all the hinges and everyone talking Chinese BOOM out comes Brush from the shack, handing me the yellow sheet for three-twenty-two and 'WOODRUFF' scrawled across it ten times too big.

"What? That sonofabitch isn't even supposed to be flying today!"

"I'm sorry, Mister Vairin, he said he's part of the flyover. I told 'em to hold it for you but I was out when he took it. Maybe still catch him?"

"My chute's in that plane!"

"He left his by the shack."

"The hell with it—"

"Here's a list of other available planes."

"Pick me a good one."

"How about three-eighteen? You gave it a check yesterday, Mr. Vairin."

I signed the sheet and ran after Hebert. A side glance at the grandstands full of people who knew nothing of Hebert and Vairin, below and underneath the call of duty, two boys from "over here."

My stomach quaked, and not about RB-318. That was settled. And maybe even better. Treacherous 318 shakes in a dive, but I'll make them stop sucking their bottles; stop eating hot dogs, for a minute or two anyway.

The sky overhead was a washed looking sky. The clouds were jagged and very white at the tips, and the blue was very blue.

The dive-bombers were taxiing out and Woodruff, the merry duke, waved a wild wave from 322. Blew kisses. Okay. Okay. The plan was for them, the 30 or so, to take off, rendezvous and make a number of passes over the field. Hebert and I were to wait till after their second pass, break-up, and landing. When the field was cleared we would be called and given the command "Charley" for cleared. Then we could dive and do our routine.

I remembered the fighters coming in, Zoom, barrel-rolling into the sky one after another pointed up at such a ridiculous angle, safety first, moving fast, oh yes, with a nice whine and breath-of-a-waterfall-roaring one two three four five going up that fast and rolling, up at seventy degrees and scooping out. But the crowd loved the noise and the planes coming up on them suddenly, rolling up into the air and black specks again. Niggardly rolls and puny bad bombing of a target that sat still and did not fire back.

"Put on a good show . . . Good show . . . but not too low."

On to 318 and suddenly it was fine, everything great! Happy eyes to right and left above and below the plane to plane captain up to cockpit and beloved instruments to straps and buckles to my own wonderful hands and fingers that know everything they touch, to rudder bars and dials and numbers, the smell of leather and straps gas and oil and the sounds that feed my ears the wind that comes over the cockpit.

Chocks pulled and moving. The sun in and out again but the sky above—I goggled straight up at it—a clear washed blue. The throttle answered fingers mightily and we were moving out of the slot.

All of the planes had taken off from the west end of 12-E, Hebert was already making for that end and when I turned left to go to the end of 7, got the red light from the tower and a call, "Uncle 58, the take-off runway is 12—"

"Moka, channel three—"

They were still saying something when I switched off and picked up Hebert, down at the end of his runway, ready.

I wound it up, swung into the wind and told him, "Go!" and he went. The red light from the tower was held on me steadily.

A thousand one, a thousand two, a thousand three; throttle to the fire-wall and off, watching Hebert out of one corner of my eye and the big red light from the tower with another.

God knows what they were yelling over the tower channel, but I was still getting that red light.

Our two planes flashed across the intersection, one-two, we missed by twenty feet, and that was worth a chuckle, close enough to feel his prop-wash.

I was almost off the ground when I checked over. Hebert's wheels were tucking in, beginning a slow turn into me. Then I was off, wheels up and joined on his wing 200 feet and just beyond the field. Now, by Jesus, that was better than they'd seen all morning long.

We grinned and climbed, Hebert was constantly throwing back his head laughing. We climbed and waited for the call, turning to the left and remaining over the field. How short the wings seemed. And the field, smaller and smaller. The grandstand a small batch of color. We climbed and left the earth behind us, below us. Then we were circling at 7000 and waiting. At last came the call.

"You are Charley," came the voice from the tower, "Lieutenants Vairin and Hebert, Uncle 58 and 59, you are Charley, the field is cleared."

Hebert kissed off and started his dive.

I waited and climbed to 9000, I don't know why, and that's when the strange thing began, something outside of me watching the other, the flyer, gauging, getting ready.

Coldly watched the other go down in his steep dive. Began a flat dive, picking up speed but waiting, circled the field waiting. The blue of the sky was like a strange metal and the sea was copper, the sun's rays stabbing, changing, brilliant spears, and the shaft of air like earth his cheek-bone his nose eyes emeralds stars diamonds planets and suns of suns ready to come down take it all with him from a shallow circle at seven, eyeing that patch of field. Well, they'd see him, this fragment of the world anyway. "Show-off, egoist, hot-shot," get 'em off your chest because he'll take on all of them, onto his back to begin.

He rolled tab forward and hard left rudder, let the nose have its way, just let it drop. Down. Down. Now there was no fear. Out of the sun's eye with all the brave colors: yellow sand, forest green, royal purple, ice blue water and yellow-white sunlight. Out of the sun's eye like an angry god a long ribbon unwinding, faster body shaking, terrible engine explosions, pointed down just in front of the little grandstand taking shape past the red line at 360 and 3000 feet. 2200, down unwinding fast a broken needle. Ahh, generosity's the thing. Don't be stingy. The thin line. Walk the strait and narrow.

Fifteen hundred, twelve. Eyes saw perfectly, nerveless hands held the stick loosely, head up a notch to face the earth saw the whole spread over his face that had nothing to do with him driving at the earth.

In the last possible instant, using tab and a steel arm he pulled it out, below the grand-stand, kissed the earth and gone in an instant—eyes-clawing dive that ripped their eyes out to follow wrenched their necks to see, straight up, up, up, over onto his back—speed just now below 300 knots, looked out and down he gauged it again and out of the long loop began at the top of it a four point roll within the last half of the loop—lose count now and lose the ball game—four, straight down and rolling in, pull out but close, propeller cutting the grass in front of the stands—level—curled around the tower a climbing hard turn to dive down again, down to the grass below the stands and directly at it, rolled onto his back and climbed up, wheeled elevator trim forward and climbed up the stadium on his back, beyond he rolled it out, one hand on stick his throttle hand on elevator trim, then out of it to come around over the duty runway to tuck it away, snapped the wing hard over, drop wheels, flaps, open canopy—the tromp and squeak of wheels stiff against wind, shudder as they locked into place—he hummed up the revolutions reached out giant fingers to the ground body still 300 feet of air he pivoted around, a demon in him to cut it down set it down short, hard, to *break* the flight, stop it, hit and stuck and he turned off very short, braking the plane to roll slowly.

He was coming back, realizing, feet pattering, shaking on the rudders in a way I couldn't stop. Not fear, not relief, but the overwhelming catch-up from the last minute or two.

Heath's critical eye had not found a flaw; as low as the plane could go, so he had pulled out just when he wanted to, when he had to, and not a split second's hesitation over what instant to begin. A four point roll inside of the last part of a loop off the ground. An upside-down buzz job barely missing the grandstand and then, finally, the finish and still part of the same performance, impossible short snapped off landing so sudden and still so slow, hard-curving not even flown but slow spin, hitting the very end not heavily but solid. Was it the same plane? Down and taxiing so slowly into place?

Heath turned to Jorge and laughed. Not a word. It was not a war bond rally, not an air show and not Will Vairin who had just flown but Ilmarin and the Stormwind that snatched him from the fir trees carried him off to a woodland far from here, passing hunters and watch dogs that neither saw him nor got his scent to Louhi, toothless and ancient dame of the northland, 'Who are you, of all the host of heroes? And by what magic do you come on the path of the air, carried by the Stormwind to my very door not scented by my watch-dogs?'

And these the celebrated funeral games at last, and like his performance nothing to do with the crowd, what he did in war, no connection to the war of newspapers, the war in *these* minds, the war in minds all over world, only war-movement, war-action, movement actions called war.

"Great God Almighty, look at the colonel," said Jorge.

I walked it forward, braked, revved it up, felt the chocks, brakes off, mixture up, throttle to the firewall choking it. The prop quit swinging around, coughed once, started back a quarter, and died like a good bull.

Out of the plane, down the wing, chute in hand. The mechanic met me pop-eyed.

Words bubbled out of him.

"The plane's okay," and ran for the shack, stopped, asked the plane captain to check it in, noticed dried blood in two places on the knuckles of my left hand, no idea how or what.

Caught Hebert at the shack, "Man!" he yelled.

No time, "Come on, quick!"

"Wait!" Hebert yelled, "Are you crazy? How many rivets are left in those wings?"

"Let's go!"

"Where?"

"To the beach, follow me. Hurry, you sonofabitch, I'm in trouble."

The fighters were coming over in strafing attacks, two-man sections ringing past, skimming the tower, but like row-boats in the air they went by so peacefully.

Slammed lockers and out the door.

As we pulled out in two cars I saw Jorge waving frantically, afraid to stop we roared off and off the base to the cabin. I had promised Hebert I'd help him wash his car.

We parked next to the cabin and I felt a pang, Leyla, Leyla.

Hebert was out of the car, laughing. "Did you look for rivets?"

"No, maybe I popped a few, eh?"

"A few hundred."

He kept looking over while I collected what looked like rags, and a bucket for water. Looking over, laughing, shaking his head, a laugh he was trying his best to hold back but kept bursting out with.

I felt drained. Eyes heavy, arms a dead weight from shoulders. And scared, now, of official trouble. Like lifting hundreds of pounds I asked Hebert, "Where did you go?"

"I did my dive and loop and roll and got out of there. I had just landed when you came over the first time."

"I've got to lie down for a minute. Be right back."

I lay down on our bed, wishing it was a closet and I could lock the door, or that I was in Leyla's arms and she was chuckling, rocking me, holding me tight.

From a dreamless drugged sleep I woke up to Jorge squatting by the side of the bed. It was getting dark.

I was wide awake and back to the flight in the most vivid detail.

Jorge sat there chuckling away, like Hebert earlier. But there was something else in his eyes. The tax collector come for money long overdue. "Boy, you were the show," he said it sentimentally, like Wilson, only Jorge could get away with it.

"It was great," he said, and even repeated it.

"What did the colonel say?"

"Man, they're just shaking their heads," he laughed still death in the eyes, yes, somehow, cool death hung all about him. Jorge . . . so kind, so thoughtful. Old dad. What did it mean?

Jorge walked to the window and slowly turned from where the sun had set with a voice from some duty, a voice laid on him, a voice in three, five layers all coming at me, "Look, Willy, I've got the colonel's okay. You can go in the first group. To make the five. In place of Nevers. You, me, Mulligan, RM and Woodruff the duke. We begin training in seven days. I *told* you—"

Somehow I knew it, even before the words reached me, before they had left Jorge's mouth. Not death saying, 'Follow me,' ohhh no, much more complicated.

I had known it and still a shock. Slept to no dreaming, waked to a dream and knew I'd go, I'd refuse and still knew I'd go, this time and forever.

"Jorge, I asked and begged em . . . for six months, and now the hell with it. I was ready to go, ready to renounce and go with the Chinese. Now, I'm here, and Leyla . . . I tried to get on the list and now, fuck em."

Only this time they'd crept up to my secret hide-away, and found me lying there, waiting.

"Well, Willy, you know, I told you six months ago when we first got here.

I told you, remember, I said *we* are going . . . *we*. And so now . . . here it is. I can't argue with you but, to them, we're just numbers. Ten billion times over the world. They don't care who you are, how good you are . . . .How many people could do what you did today? And walk away from the plane? An old rotten heavy dive-bomber? How many could do it in a fighter? But they don't care! They're just filling quotas. Any old name . . . just numbers. Until we get overseas. Or even after. But I'm telling you, you can still go, in the first group . . . with us . . . and *Corsairs* . . . did you forget that—?"

All the time I knew.

"When did you ask the colonel?"

"Corsairs, Willy—"

"When did he say—"

"I asked him two weeks ago, right after Nevers, but he told me this morning, 'Okay,' he said. 'I'll have him put on the list.'"

"And Willy," he added; "did you forget? South China Seas, Palau, Mindanao, Bougainville, Kolombangara, Borneo. . . . In Corsairs??? I told you, when we first got here, I told you we're going, I felt it in my bones!"

So? Not 'those desiring,' not a choice, no plea: 'Come save us, oh secret weapon, angel of destruction! The Jap dragon is loose! Come, sift the skies and knock 'em down! Cut 'em off! Back to your tents, it's okay, *I'm* flying.' Instead, one friend asking.

"Well, then, I guess . . . we're going!"

"Yeah!?!"

"Yeah. Fair enough??"

"Fair enough, Lieutenant!" Old-young Jorge's face, beaming, without a beam for lo these many weeks. We shook hands. On-on-on to Kolombangara.

"Who else?"

"Woodruff, Balt, RM, Mulligan and the two of us . . . the Solomons, the South China Seas, Mindanao, the Marianas, Dutch East Indies, Java. All those names you talked about."

"Jorge, what the shit have you got me into?"

Jorge laughed, shrugging his shoulders. He didn't know, I didn't know.

"Shit yeah, let's go. But . . . what about today? The colonel said, 'Not under 200 feet.'"

"Listen, the colonel would slit his throat before he changed his mind."

Jorge left for his "little date," warning me I had to be there tonight. "Evrybody'll be there."

I was dizzy with the news. Leyla? Begin training in seven days? Overseas in eight weeks? I had just switched tracks, and it was with a clutch of fear and jubilation that I looked out the window and discovered Hebert was gone. I reached into the closet under a pile of clothes and brought out the midnight blue gull-winged miniature, the little Corsair not more than four inches long. I could hear Benny Goodman, *The World is Waiting for the Sunrise*, and felt it, yeahh, the world's sunrise, sunrise of the long day.

The low, wide lamp cast yellow-orange light over most of the table. I lit the cigar, stale but good and smoky; plane, paper and pen on the table under the light, through the light into darkness the words rising around me, hypnotic names calling Empress Augusta Bay, South China seas. The table was the world, the orange lamp the sun, the dark wall was sky itself, and the plane flew against it. "The heavens and earth are not grown equal to one half of me: have I not drunk of soma juice? I, greatest of the mighty ones am lifted to the firmament. I in my grandeur surpass the heavens and all this spacious earth: Have I not drunk of soma juice?"

I could feel it, drunk on high fine air, the dive and down out of the eye of the world, to kiss the earth and shoot back up my heart bursting open with the sea and all the earth under my wings.

Oh my God, Leyla? Write to her? No, she's on the way. How will I tell her? Yes, a note. And couldn't get past the first words, how and why when I didn't know myself, giving up to draw on the cigar, take up the little plane, move it toward my eyes, an angle accenting the long sleek nose. Fingers changed the blue plane with the white stars—for this was the war of the red suns against the white stars—to climbing up still partly on its back, climbing up against the orange-yellow wall of light then changed again deftly, firmly made the body execute a roll, slowly and perfectly the little dark-blue plane turned against the dark sky still in yellow-orange light, then down to the table and resting on its wings swooping down and out from the body, inverted gull-wings, the only one in the world like it. And once you get what you want, what else is there? The girl, the love, the plane, and even children.

One hand went to matches, the other to the long brown cigar, smoke-less again. There two hands worked together as gracefully as rolling a plane, the hands knowing all movement is a dance, the fingers drew match, rasped it against the box, lit the tip of the cigar, drew in smoke and flame, still in the music-less dance, then a cloud of smoke, shook out flame, match thrown away dead, drew cigar from mouth open to even white teeth and a haze of purple smoke, clear almost colorless grey eyes squinting at the heavy cigar smoke, not the first or second but neither the 100th or even 50th, and looked for a long time staring beyond the orange-yellow light to a bay whose Lincoln-green arms were outstretched for him.

Going, I said to myself . . . going . . . all the way.

Chapter 37

I drove to RM's. Jorge had already been there, although RM knew it was in the works, and he pounded me on the back, that we were part of a great group, and actually happy Hebert was *not* going although he didn't understand it. We were off to Milton's Oceanside, known to the Bogey's as The Place. RM and Clare would bring me back, leave your car here.

We parked facing the sea against a log barrier that separated road from beach, and another 30 feet of beach to rough ocean itself with rollers coming straight in pounding the beach and drifting back combing through the heavy sand. Despite that roar the rumble could be heard from where we parked. It sounded like a gang war although once inside The Place was like a stage setting. People were drunk or acting drunk. I was greeted as if I'd come back from the dead. How different my life since Leyla had left. The routine was fly three to five hours a night, back to the cabin, checking the signs of new life in Leyla, mildly nauseous but no big changes. "She was born to have children," said the pleasant doctor in town, Dr. Twitchell, who claimed to have brought over 200 children into the world. Never mind, I was convinced he was in love with Leyla and how could I blame him? I secretly thought everyone who saw her fell in love with her. Did RM feel the same way about Clare? I could see that too. I wasn't in love with Clare but in love with something about her. About us. All of us. Jorge and the new group of us. In love with the Corsair and how it would bind us together, in love with the war, no matter what they said, flying, war, Leyla, our child. A certain madness was coming on me. And my dreams? Great deeds ahead?

And there in the middle of The Place amid back-slapping congratulations about 'the show' and drinks thrust at me, tears were welling out of my eyes at the thought of Leyla and how would she take all of this, our new child, new orders being cut this minute, new program. It was overwhelming and no time to digest it. There was even a date, an appointed time and schedule for our participation in the great doings beyond the horizon.

Wilson, corn-fed Wilson of the horse teeth and sentimental overkill, had his arm around me, " . . . a four point roll in the last half of a loop just off the ground," he was screaming as if he had to explain to me, "an up-side-down buzz job, *on his back*," introducing me to others, yelling the same thing. It hardly made a difference while the juke-box barely audible played some sweet song. Waylie finally stopped him, "Get drunk about it, but shut up. 'An upside down buzz job on yer back would make it right-side up again."

Wilson's hurt silence didn't lower the noise level even for a second.

Something about " . . . the limitations of a Curtiss dive-bomber," Woodruff, the merry duke and now flying buddy come a week or so, speaking as if he was the only one in the room, "and the colonel's patience, Ha! Ha! Ha! . . . " and over backwards in a wild crashing fall with his chair and out of sight. He had stolen my assigned plane but all was forgiven. "I knew you didn't want that plane, it's a real clunker."

Even Heath, "Stop drinking, 'za toast . . ." bang bang, his glass against the wood table, then held it up. There were six bogey pilots within hearing, all while the jukebox played on, couples danced, screams for drinks at the bar, waitresses rushing—"I said a *toast* . . . the man who stole a three hour air show in forty-five seconds!"

He had to be drunk. Good and drunk. Said it all in a leaden straight-ahead voice with no hint of sarcasm. They cheered, smacked me on the back, God, Wilson's big horse-face right in my face and despite the other noise realized he was screaming and I couldn't distinguish his from the other noise. Was I? Was I going to get drunk? Woodruff grabbed me by the shoulders, "Man! . . . Man!" As if I couldn't hear his opening line, screaming five times, so glad I was going with them in the first group. And that's when it struck me again. Yes, I was. Yes, we are, going. And that music, *that* music again, I believe it was right then, music not since Memphis, or dive-bombers. Leyla had to know. Had to understand.

Keggs was there! And explained about the medal, how he'd been lost and had no idea about the field he was landing on. He was low on gas, saw the field, and landed. Scared shitless when he realized where he was. Did the only thing he could do. So, he explained to us, essentially the only reason he'd been awarded the medals was because he landed by mistake on a Jap airfield then had to shoot his way out of it. I think our hearts went out to him for that. Not Superman, let the ones who wrote commendations talk like that. He was just trying to get home alive.

"I got to go . . . I *can't* stay and get drunk here."

"What? *WHAT!?!*"

"Whadayamean . . . CAN'T?" Jorge *and* Woodruff, then Mulligan, screeching.

I hadn't been out with them since, God, since . . . Jorge was so pleased and it brought me back, the night he loaned me the car for Leyla's visit. Six people wanted to buy drinks. Okay, okay. The cheapest drunk I'd ever been on.

Around midnight, one of the bogeys, "Mad Dog," chewed "Wild Bill's" tie off. Then "Wild Bill" chewed "Mad Dog's" tie off. They turned on others and, like a pyramid club, everyone was grabbing some one who still had a whole tie and was busy gnawing at it. Around midnight the colonel came in, and Wilson, maybe the highlight of his life, grabbed the colonel's tie in his mouth, bit down on it, while the colonel slapped him practically across the room but Wilson, like a good pit-bull, had fastened his horse-teeth on the man's tie and sure enough, well-slapped, red-faced, and still grinning, came away with half the colonel's tie and walked around teeth clenched talking, drinking, with half a tie hanging out of his mouth for the next hour, "Z's jee kernel'zz die?" pointing at it.

When the colonel realized everyone was in the same boat, he joined in and, I was told, even shook hands with Wilson, although that might have been someone's fond dream.

I got back around two or some time, walked from RM's, left the car there, flopped in bed half dressed or half undressed wondering which it was.

Chapter 38

Driving to Palm Beach to pick her up and sweating, sweating what to say, how to say it. If only I could have gotten in touch and told her right away. Now it was strange, and stranger. Going, not going, going. These worries side by side with driving down to her. The feeling was on me, the thing of missing and not being able to miss someone, but now less, less than ever. Maybe I was growing up. And she'd met my New Orleans side: Mamoo,

Sally, Arthe and Brucie, home of the Corpuscles—all over the world now, with hearts and minds on New Orleans. All out there, minus, well, Cacksy Jack and Wonderful Bob.

At least I could talk to her now on the phone and feel it. The confidence that she was there, the ache that she wasn't, the almost certainty that she would be.

Then she was in my arms, and I was filled with gratefulness for anyone who had anything to do with returning her to me: pilots, baggage handlers, stewardesses, the lot.

"Never again, never again, never leaving you . . . "

It was a blur of kisses, hugs. I couldn't see anything around me, hear anything else, there was a frame around her and beyond it a blur. We . . . we . . . us. Our bags, our words, our world. Into our very own Green Lizard at the sight of which Leyla began crying. It was our tequila night, our first night, and hardly able to get into the car. If I hadn't been afraid I would break open and fly into a thousand pieces we'd have done it there in the backseat, instead it was looking, touching, kissing cheeks, eyes and making sure, absolutely sure she was here.

"How could I have let you go?"

"I don't know, you beast. But you did. And it won't happen again, don't worry about it."

We were gathering pieces. Yes, a kind of gathering. After first hugs and kisses, questions, tentative touches, a kind of gathering until she came over to me and put her mouth to my ear.

"You still need me . . . Will?" she whispered into my very brain.

"Oh, my God, where is that cocky bride who tells me how much I need her? Yes. I missed, missed, missed you, and don't know how I did it."

"'Need,' I said, "'*Need*'!?!"

I was exploding, "You'll never know. You're my very arms, Leyla, the light in my eyes and I'm blind without you. But how come you don't know that?"

"Hey, I do. I do. I just wanted you to admit it. . . . Now about this other thing. This 'light' in your eyes. How do you fly without sight, is that what they call flying blind?"

"No, I just put it on automatic pilot till you got back. Besides, there's 'light' and 'sight,' I've got the sight without the light."

Miles down the road we were calming down.

"I've got so much news. Mamoo . . . *ohhh*! And *both* your sisters, Will . . . and *Sally*!"

I had to touch her. And maybe the very best of us. What felt good to me was good to her. When it felt great to her I felt it too, I didn't need to ask. And all the way from Palm Beach she was turned up against me, back to the road, head on my chest. Happy. I knew she was because I was.

We drove along the beach road, with occasional glimpses of the great Atlantic.

"Have you been good? I've got presents for you. Pralines and Sally's fudge."

"Whaaaat? You met Sally?"

"Well, of course!"

"Ohhh, Leyla, you angel tiger. You *actually met Sally*!"

"Oh, yes. And I had to promise her, three or four times, I'd take good care of you. I mean, Will, she *meant* it. 'Now, you gots to promise, to take care of mah boy.' Oh Will, what a blessing! What a blessing! She gave me a hug, and a big hug for you."

The idea of Leyla imitating *Sally*! . . . Flying and New Orleans tied up in a few words.

So, I knew I'd have to stop and tell her. Had to.

"Okay, Leyla, my angel, there's something I've got to tell you—"

"I bet I know what it is! You're *going*!"

"What? Whaaaat?"

"You're going, with the first group."

"God! How . . . how did you know that?"

"Well, it's quite a story. Jorge told RM he was working on it, and it was looking good. Now wait! RM told Clare under the greatest secrecy. And Clare told me, after making me take a blood oath. Am I right? Is that what it is?"

"Yes, soooo, you know—"

"Ohh, Will! We're *in* this . . . oohh, together. It's me and you anywhere in the world." The traffic sped by and we were hugging, hugging, rocking together, yes, the three of us and the next minutes were a flood of relief of tears and laughter.

We got to our little cabin and it was like a Cambridge night, only it was with fighters and dive-bombers taking off in two hour flurries, roaring by and out to sea, then between flights in singles or high up, at altitude, farther away our umbrella, our sky.

"So, you're taking . . . Nevers' place? Ohhhhh Will . . . I knew it. I knew you'd go if there was any chance." It was a voice of knowing and sadness too. "Yes, I knew it. I knew it."

"Well, Jorge . . . Jorge was the one. In fact I had given up on it, the war, being here. Our baby. . . . Do you hate . . . do you hate it? Do you hate me?"

"Ohh, Will, Will, sometimes I don't think you understand me at all. How could I hate you? I knew, all along you'd go, you'd be going, somehow—"

"And you knew. I wasn't sure myself! Jorge told me just yesterday, day before, sort of talked me into it. I was okay, ready to give it up, the war, my crazy ideas—"

"Jorge talked you into it? Ohh, I love it. Will, my darling, so . . . Jorge's to blame, ohh, too much!"

Sometimes she seemed light years ahead of me.

All of it was left like that, for now. She was lying next to me in the green light of our new bedside lamp, "An antique . . . your sister, Brucie, gave to us." Eating Sally's fudge, her 'furridge' as Sally called it.

I was hugging hair, lips, neck, ears, anything, then I untangled us, pushed her back on the bed and put my head down on her little mound, her legs were relaxed and slightly apart, my ear at the juncture, the "holy forbidden" warm and slightly moist and smelling of soap. I wanted to show her . . . not in words, but in some new way. I turned my head and she gasped, trembling, fearful, excited. And I knew I'd do it. I had no idea how, exactly, just gently, coming to know it with my mouth, my tongue.

"Wi-ill, Wi-ill, ohh," it was a soft cry, as if I'd gently broken her wing, and she was fluttering to the ground. Then a breathless, waiting silence from her, as unsure as I was. "But, Leyla, darling, please, darling, relax, I won't do anything sudden, just try and relax."

"Wi-ill . . . oh, do you want? Oh Wi-ill, I don't knowwwwww."

I was close to it, ducked away, saw my sweet, sweet, sweetheart's beautiful puss, so alive, then came up to it and kissed a soft kiss against the flesh. Leyla caved in, clasped my head in her legs, rolled over moaning.

"I don't know, Will . . . I love what you're doing but it's too much and I . . . Just. Can't. Stand. It."

"Okay, okay."

"Just hold me."

"No, I want to do this."

"Well, hold me first."

I pushed her back on the bed and her eyes were seeking mine, asking, wondering. It was like discovering new worlds. Maybe we were both more virginal than our Cambridge time.

I placed my head there, my face to the side. Her hands like gentle wings came down to my head and face, only touching, no pressure.

"Do you love me?"

"Will, don't ask me . . . now. I don't even know my name."

"You Leyla, me Will . . . Will love Leyla!"

Ah, I felt like Balboa, up over the rise, and first glance at the Pacific.

I was turning my head and the moaning started. I put my mouth over her curly light red patch of hair and held very still. Her hands were at the back of my head, uncertain as to what to do, only touching lightly.

"It's too much. I-can't-stand-it."

I moved my head back, opened my mouth, and touched my tongue to the very meat of her, and held it still. Leyla's long sighing moan became a crooning surrender.

She was so ready, so open, so helpless. Helpless sweet this living jewel.

I applied just the slightest suction, not even sure what I was doing, but as if I were kissing her mouth, sucking for her tongue and she was like a horse being broken in; holding my head to keep still, unable to control her body, quivering, moaning, squeezing me to her crying, and then really crying out," . . . oh God, Will, I can't stand it any more. It's like a raging fire, stop it, put it out. Oh God, give me, give, give me Will. Ohh, you're making me come, come and I can't stop."

While we did it she was holding me bucking me up from underneath, talking in tongues and long after I had come in her, we lay there for God knows, knocked over the head, before I got up, went to the bathroom, came back with a warm washrag and wiped her, bathed her, and deep in my heart singing to her, and the whole time she didn't stir.

Did *I* do that to her, or did she do that to herself?

Ohh, Leyla, whom I love so much; Leyla so fierce, so strong, so powerful. What is going to happen to us out there in the world? Will I sail straight off the planet and never come back? And then what? Me without you? You without me?

I sat on the bed while she slept; Leyla back home and lying next to me, my hand on her to keep her from flying off again. She still didn't know *when*. Less than a week. And I was torn right down the middle. Stirred and excited about the Corsair. Agonized at the thought, unable to imagine leaving her.

Chapter 39

'Spider' Maxwell, Lt. Commander, entered the room and we stood at attention.

Long thin yellow-faced, with eyes that dreamed mostly, flickered to life a moment, "Sit down."

With his first words he had thrown a cloak over us all, not come to us from far away but drawn us away with him, one of that small tribe still standing, young/old men, living dead men, yellow diseased rough talking heroes who had taken the first awful shock of the war, hit in the middle of their backs by it,

"I'm scheduled to tell you about the Corsair—"

Who could also be like mother hens, and on a different impulse

"You young bastards will know I have flown—"

In the same tone of voice he would begin on the English language if we didn't know one word of it, ". . . every single-engined plane the navy has put out, from R3Cs to F2As , F3Fs, even the SBC-4, the first Helldiver, F4Fs, F6s and what they've got now, but I want to tell you something about this one. This one is different . . . "

He took a deep breath that seemed to rack his long frame, to breathe in despair, burnt wood, papers, coal, and flame. "You see me? All wrinkled and yellow? Well, the Corsair's a pilot's airplane, and it'll kill you if you don't treat it right," the eyes died dreaming,

"Killed! Got that? Then you won't grow up to be old, yellow, and malaria-ridden like me . . . it'll kill you and then you'll be dead, dead, dead . . . "

Almost dreamily he struck the note three times, then the eyes flickered to life again, "You understand? . . . Dead!"

Walked to the window, "old" and malaria-ridden yellow lean-hipped crew cut lined-face gray smoke-eyed one, looked out at the runways and seven F4U-1D Corsairs right out of the box, with the new plexiglass domes encasing the cockpits—thumbs hooked in his belt, turned again to continue and with a new racking breath, "Well, laugh if you want to," to not a smile in the room, "But it can happen. Yes, even to *you*," pointing to no one, looking fiercely over the room, guarding us, his hawk nose and entire face like a bird's, a metal bird who talked like a man, muttering to himself now, eyes wavering like coals under a bellows.

His arms slumped and he walked over to the desk and sat down on the edge of it as if he had just given us up.

Not one among us would have guessed that this old-young commander, the "Spider," who had seen action in dive-bombers on and off carriers at Pearl Harbor and every campaign from Wake and Midway to Guadalcanal was giving his last lecture.

He sat on the edge of the desk and looked out at us, hopelessly.

The room was totally silent and we stared back from lowered eyes. This was the first of 186 steps, six a day, weather permitting.

Suddenly he was on his feet, his face seemed less yellow and wrinkled, only his eyes were farther away.

"In a fighter cockpit, specifically, the F4U-1D Corsair, in a place large enough for a man and a little larger, has been fitted 50 or more gadgets; not including eight engine instruments and six flight instruments.

"Under the bucket-seat, to the side of it, back of it, on the floor between the pilot's legs, attached to the stick, to the throttle, to the right and left of him are rows and banks of buttons, levers, wheels, nuts, handles, knobs, tabs. Forward to the left, forward to the right, are more, under those are still more.

"All must be known intimately, more so for night work, but never, day or night, should you have to look for the required button, knob, or lever. You need to wink the port wing running light? The hand should go to the bank of lights immediately and have the toggle working in a second: up for *bright*, center for *off*, down for *dim*.

"A blindfold cockpit checkout will be the first and most thorough check. For that you will not leave the ground until you have spent four to seven hours in the cockpit, until you know every one of them in your sleep. Otherwise they are just so many obstacles. Pull the wrong one, turn one too far, or aid the hand with eyes that should be looking out and there's trouble.

"You enter the cockpit; how many do you touch before starting? Somebody count 'em for me: you raise or lower *the seat*, hook up *safety belt* and *shoulder straps*, adjust *rudder pedals*. Check for *pitot tube* and the *cover*—off. If it's altitude check *oxygen supply* and hook up. *Jungle pack* to *parachute harness*. Gas and gas gauge, and *switch*—take-off on main. If it's gunnery check your *gun-sight*. How many gadgets? *Ten*."

Whoever was counting had a different number; the "Spider" rolled over him and went on.

"You're ready to begin: *battery* and *generator* switches on. Gas tank *switch* on *main*; *primer on, electric fuel pump on. Throttle* cracked one half to an inch, *mixture* back, energize, engage the *starter motor.* Alright you're started, *cowl flaps* open. How many gadgets? *Twelve.*" He could have said 20 or 30, the number didn't matter.

At this point he stood up, with a great weariness: "The rest you know. Brakes, stick, ailerons, rudder, trim tabs, engine check—"

"Uh, Commander Maxwell," Balt began, with some trepidation, "fifty gadgets?"

"No," the 'Spider,' answered him, with a slur, "actually, according to the manual there are 67, but I didn't want to frighten you."

"Thanks," said Balt, "Thank you, sir."

"Any questions?"

Five or six hands went up. He looked them over slowly. Those eyes breathed in and out. "No?"

Did he even see them? "Flip out the lights, Herb, let's have the movie," and the hands went down in darkness, and a few snickers.

"The Corsair? Commander Maxwell?" came the voice behind the projector.

"No, Herb," he said, long, drawn-out, bitter, "the new diesel freight train!"

There were twelve of us in the new squadron, new and newly thrown together. Half navy and half marines. 186 steps they had told us. After the first few we hardly kept count, we twelve, and of that number, six bogey pilots turned night fighters: Mulligan who had bought or bribed his way into our group, Jorge, RM, Balt, myself and Wilson. We were the marine half of the squadron. The other half were navy.

How did Wilson come into the picture?

Wilson . . . whoeeee, what we wouldn't have done to get rid of him but there he was, Iowa's offering, corn-fed and more loyal than a golden retriever, "yeah," said Balt, "and more slobbery." Anyhow, three of us all the way from Memphis and Jorge from dive-bombers, the big four.

And Woodruff? The merry duke? First there was a series of tests. Something about his blood. He grinned about it but had to go back for more tests. Then to Jacksonville for still more. By the time he returned from Jax the smiles were gone. Woodruff had leukemia. He was out. Out of the group, out of the war, and headed home. What to say? What to do? Balt, stocky, grinning partygoer had been with Woodruff since preflight school and I saw him serious for days in a row. He helped Woodruff pack, we all got drunk and saw him off on a train to Chicago. Strange smiles, strange handshakes, his war over and done with, but still in uniform. He'd write. We'd all stay in touch. Sure.

And so Wilson, first to go in the next group, was bumped ahead into ours.

Well, those were our dues for RM, Mulligan, and Jorge. Balt was one of us. But Wilson?

Balt, Oklahoma's son, high school football star and definitely more at home on the ground than in the air was, despite that, a good flyer. Once we had been testing planes when he called for me to fly in tight off of his left wing. When I did, I saw him point at the root of the wing and there out of a nightmare was the little white metal flag, sign that the wings were not locked in place, the little flag that was supposed to disappear into the wing when the wings were locked. Either his wing was not locked, and the wing could fold at any second, or someone had stepped on the little flag and bent it, preventing it from disappearing into the wing. Balt's ruddy face had turned pale. I called in and escorted him to the field for a straight-in emergency landing.

"That'll net you a double martini, at The Place . . . to*night*," he told me, after he was rolling along on the ground at taxi speed.

Even from the beginning, the fear-of-God talk on the Widow-maker and our cockpit checkouts, it was happening to us, the call to our blood, and, yes, we did spend at least six hours in the cockpit, loving the great Corsair, fastest in the world. For once I didn't duck out of something I was told to do. In fact, I went a little overboard.

I found that the whole thing was affecting me and Leyla in a strange way. For a while I thought I had it all. She didn't try to curb any excesses even though she knew she was pregnant. But that was not it. And impossible to say any longer. The air show had been a piece of it. But that was not it either. The air show had been to prove . . . something. If the war was out of reach, then *that'll be* my war. Now, it was different. We were going, and nothing to stop us this time. Going and going in the best and the fastest.

But with Leyla I didn't any longer know what to do.

"Has anything changed? Will?" she asked one day after movies, lectures, flights, intelligence briefings, the twelve of us, our six and the navy six because, I think, the fever was coming on and no matter what we did each day, how many flights, lectures, ship and plane recognition classes, briefings, it was not that, it was the other; marriage and children was for after, after . . .

"You seem . . ." and for once I caught a whiff of something new in her voice. Leyla worrying. "You seem . . . I don't know. Like I'm losing you . . . just a little bit."

I could hardly talk to her because we were scheduled for a flight at sundown and I could feel it already. There wasn't time to slow down. Could hardly listen to stay still to listen. And I knew she was picking up on that.

"And, Will, you haven't . . . we haven't . . . still haven't talked about the whole thing—"

"I know, I know, I can't help it—"

"No, Will, this isn't about you, just you, it's us, and . . . the baby."

As distracted as I was it did stop me, "Nothing's changed," I lied, but uncertain as to exactly how and what.

"Ohh, God, Will . . . I feel like. . . . We have to . . . we have to really talk."

RM was honking. We kissed and I left, wondering. Her fingers were in my hands for miles.

RM was feeling the same thing, it was the feeling we had back in dive-bombers. We hardly spoke all the way to the field. We were like hunting dogs pointing at the sky.

"Leyla's pregnant," I told him; I almost laughed out loud about how un-sure we were, of everything, only that the music was playing my blood.

"Yeah," he said, hunched over—the flight, the flight in us, over us. "She mentioned it to Clare. You happy? You know they're planning a late sup-per, the four of us."

"Yeah."

"Supper around ten thirty or eleven. Nice . . . ahhh, you know, we al-ways knew we'd . . . have kids."

Over the bridge at Point X-ray, the sun just going down behind the trees, we were due on station at 7:30. I wondered just what was happening to me. I had hardly reacted to her news, the first of seven? The thing is I was already full to the brim.

At the field, in the ready room, we welcomed each other, even the navy half of our squadron: "Ayy, tell me again, what do you fly? . . . Well, Skin-head, I fly the Coarse Hair . . . You mean the ffffffffffewwwwww!"

Balt came over and showed me Mulligan's hair tonic, "CORRECT, THAT IS, C-O-R-R-E-C-T, CORRECT HAIR TONIC, put out by the—"

Mulligan was wrestling Balt to get his bottle back, Balt continued, holding the bottle away with no problem although Mulligan's long arms nearly had it.

"Hey, wait! Gotta tell'em, it's . . . it's . . . put out by the RASSLER HAIR HYGIENE—"

He threw it to me, I handed it to Jorge, Mulligan was after it, only a few steps too late, then Balt was sprinkling the stuff, slopping it all over. The bottle was empty by the time Mulligan got it back. No problem. Here it is, old sport! And the whole place reeked of it.

"You jerks! That's expensive shit!"

The colonel came in, Colonel Marvin Hartigan, "Marvelous Marv," we called him behind his back, our squadron commanding officer, but exactly how that happened was another mystery. He had transferred into our night fighter group from transports. As a matter of fact, he *flew* like a transport pilot but that was another of the imponderables. And full Lieutenant Jarvis Willetts, good old North Carolina boy, briefed the colonel—just another student—along with the rest of us on what we bogey pilots had been on the other end of for six long months. The give and take and constant chatter between the ground radar station and our airborne radar.

The navy six, including the colonel, would be driven out to the ground radar stations and the rest of us, ex-bogeys, would demonstrate our skill in intercepting the bogeys and shooting them down. They would thus learn voice procedure, the constant chatter between the ground controllers and night fighters. When we got down we were supposed to switch but we begged off since we were so familiar with the procedure.

We were still getting used to the Corsairs and had not flown more than a couple of night hours but what a difference in power. To push the throttle all the way forward was like being strapped to a hurricane.

"Tare Four for scramble, over?"

"Granted, Tare Four, or is it Uncle 58?"

"Give me a break, Mother, the beast is history."

"Alright, you fighter pilot, go get 'em."

It was a medium dark night and my radar was working well. I picked up the target and closed and identified the big beast from 200 yards and, finally, it was me calling out, "Splash, one bogey, Tare four . . . "

"Good work, Tare four, your new heading . . . "

He released me at 2100 hours, after 30 interceptions, and I beat it back to the field, thrilled by the beauty and the handling of this fine steed through blackness, calling in just before Point X-ray and the answer: "Roger, Tare Four, cleared to enter pattern, take your interval, there are three in the pattern. Runway one eight, wind four knots south southeast."

As I curved into the final leg it occurred to me: I'll be a father! *Our* child.

I socked it down, tail wheel just slightly before front wheels and kept it straight down the runway and the long lane of flarepots, unlocked the tail wheel, picked up the plane captain, and followed slowly, folded wings, and walked it into place.

RM took another 15 minutes but we were on the road by 9:20.

The girls made a big to-do when we walked in. Leyla wanted to smell the flying, hugging and sniffing me, "I smell it, flying and the flyer, yeah!" I put up with it, smiling and blushing at Leyla's zany ways and the notions she came up with.

They had fixed martinis in a pitcher and it was obvious they had the whole thing planned out. A tray of cucumber sandwiches on little squares of bread, with cayenne pepper sprinkled on top. Leyla said she learned it in New Orleans. They had confided, conspired, and we were the beneficiaries. They sat us down, served us martinis, took our shoes off, passed the little sandwiches, and were back and forth between the kitchen and us.

"I do believe these girls are on the make," RM opined.

"Yep, tonight we're geisha girls, and you guys are the masters . . . or whatever—"

"The customers," said Clare.

"Right," Leyla agreed.

Oh, God, this very beauty, talking like that, and mine . . . mine. It was like truly having it all. And for a second I was back in the cockpit of the Corsair, curving in to the field, loving her from 500 feet. Time. Minutes. Seconds, while the war hovered way out there.

I don't know when it started or who asked it first but suddenly it was the program and rumors. Clare mentioned it, and Leyla picked it up.

"So? What's this about Pensacola and the carrier?"

They had obtained the news almost as soon as we had.

We told them about the furious daytime flying schedule; more and more field carriers to get us ready for the carrier checkout. Two or three field carrier flights every day till we had all qualified.

"Should be . . . around July 10th, ten days or so. We'll be gone for two days. One day there, overnight, the carrier, and then back here."

"You know," Leyla announced, "you know, I don't think the whole thing, even in the Pacific, is going to last too long. I mean, the invasion of Europe going so well—"

"Ohh, no . . ." Clare moaned, "can we go one night without talking about the whole thing?"

I was going to let it go, knowing it was her fond wish.

Later Leyla told me she could have bitten her tongue off for starting it. Then it was the war, and risks, Nevers, other deaths. Most recently a night fighter student had bailed out. His chute never opened. Our photographer buddy had pictures of the indentation where his body hit. The photo was restricted, not to be shown to pilots—as he showed us the spot in the ground. Most recently, two F-6 pilots and planes had disappeared south of Lake Okeechobee and not been heard of since.

RM was putting some music on, the King Cole Trio, which brought back dive-bombers and the whole thing, dreams, war, great deeds. Then, despite Clare, he started in about the latest group, and Kamikaze attacks on their ships. "The wounded are lying on deck," he said, "and suddenly here comes another wave—"

"Let's not talk about this, *please*," said Clare, as if it was spoiling the whole evening.

"Well, Willy," RM was after it, "you talked to those marine pilots back from Guadalcanal. What did they say about it? About the whole thing?"

"They said it was tough."

"Ohhh, no! Ohhh, no they didn't! They said it was SHIT! That's the word they used."

"They said—"

"No, no, no, they said war was 'shit.' Willy, the word is '*shit*'!"

Clare was glaring at RM but he was burning to prove something, and the three of them were a conspiracy. I was the lone deviant. I was no longer defending the war, in fact it was changing even as I thought of it.

The monster had suddenly appeared before me, naked, no bugles, no flags. To shoot someone down? What did it mean? Could the enemy be 'brave'? The question was too ridiculous. Of course there was bravery on both sides . . . well, that might be the string that . . . God knows.

Only there was something else. And it was coming up, as if my entire childhood rose up before me. Singing On-On-On to Burgundee with Aunt Alice, Lindbergh landing one field over from where he was supposed to land and all of us running, with our little American flags, running to see the hero. To touch the plane? To touch . . . him? Touch glory? Had it all begun back then?

The war in the Pacific, RM told Leyla, could last for a long time and told her how the Japs were dug in on islands all the way to the mainland of Japan.

"Well," she said, defensively, "maybe not long enough for you two to get into it."

"Meantime, Willy, about taking chances—"

To draw attention away from that, I mentioned the British major who had come over to learn American night fighter tactics and was last contacted 10 or 15 miles out to sea and, "Oi cawn't make the coast." No sign of him or his plane.

Then, like a bulldog, RM was back at it, "My thing is, Willy, why take un*necessary* risks? People get bumped off all the time, not even trying! In fact there's going to be a congressional investigation here at Red Beach, because of all the people who have been killed . . . .here!"

Actually, I knew for all of us, it was titillating, survivors in a dangerous trade.

But I was getting some strange looks from Leyla and so I told them the kind of thing I knew they'd like, "I realize . . . for a long time, war has been a very romantic notion with me, and—"

"What??? *What????*" RM was up, staggering around, "Am I hearing right???" He clapped his hand to his head. "Wait a damned minute." The others were laughing, as if it was part of a secret agreement between the three of them. But RM wouldn't stop. "Now that calls for a celebration. Crack open the champagne. I mean, Leyla, don't you have some 100 year old wine back at the cabin? A cask of Amontillado? Some Old Calvados? This boy is showing signs of growth. Either that or he's coming down with something. Take his temperature, quick!"

He went on and on and the girls were hanging on to each other laughing. I didn't know how much was at RM's antics or because the whole group had long ago agreed with RM about me and the war.

RM couldn't stop, about the latest group going through and their experiences. Lying on the deck of a carrier, wounded, under attack by Jap divebombers and how the Japs were trying to plunge their planes into the ships. The wounded were pleading, begging for someone to kill them. "Giving the medics their 45s and pleading to be killed."

"Do we *have* to—" Clare was saying.

RM stood up, paused for a second, "I'm sorry, to talk about this, Leyla . . . and Clare, but . . . well, it's in a good cause. A couple of pilots' hair turned white, in eight hours. Within an eight hour period. Dark brown to white."

"Okay, RM, but I don't know what that has to do with me. I admitted I've had some romantic notions—"

"Well, that's progress, Will—" said Clare.

I was looking for help from Leyla, not much but something. Instead she seemed to be waiting. I stumbled on, "Well, I admit I don't understand it about the war, exactly, but RM just for starters, what the hell did you sign up for? You're happy here, so? And so am I, but—"

"Because, Will . . . *and* Clare . . . I think it would be better than being targets in these clunkers for the duration of the war."

"It doesn't bother you that you're better than nine-tenths of the pilots who're shooting you down, 20 or 30 times a night?"

"Ooohh, Will," Leyla moaned, "Now that *is*—"

"No, Willy, I don't see it as a game, or competition. I don't think about it like that."

"I did. A couple of times a night I'd whip around, get on their tails and yell out, 'Splash! One more Yonkee down, for the greater glory of the Rising Sun!"

"Will, you're just nuts!"

"Come here, my hero!"

"Crazy as a bat!"

"No, *clazy as a bat!*"

And for a while the tension eased. Then RM was talking and I felt I was being pinned to the wall, as much by RM as by Clare and even Leyla. RM was suddenly talking like the enemy.   "Willy," he said, as if giving me one more chance to join the human race, "If *we* do it it's bravery. If the Japs do it it's because they don't care about life. On Guadalcanal we called their tactics 'insane,' 'suicidal,' 'fanatical,' but *our* defense was brave, heroic, above and beyond the call of duty—"

"Why are you praising the Japs?"

"Ahhh, Willy!"

"Are you saying these guys, the Americans who fought on Guadalcanal, that they're not *brave? They weren't*—"

"Willeeee," RM was turning away, disgusted, " . . . just grow up."

"What . . . the hell do you mean?"

"WILLEEEE . . . " his voice was a growl of frustration, of disbelief. My name like that meant an essay so long he might not get through it in one night.

I heard it all in his voice and felt inadequate. I didn't know what he was talking about. I wanted Leyla to jump in on my side but no, there she sat, composed, only a little agitated.

And Clare? From the looks of it she understood RM very well. I should "grow up."

The heat was rising to dangerous levels. Defend myself? We were seconds away from a fight, the hell with the cost.

"God damnit, I don't understand you at all."

"Willy, calm down. It's not the Japs or anyone else. Here, let me read something that might clear the air." And he was gone to the next room to get it. And while he was gone I received one soul-look from Leyla, before she joined Clare in the kitchen for coffee and beer.

RM was back and was suddenly reading, in the blink of an eye, "Willy, this is from *The Book of the Damned*, by Charles Fort, an unusual book, and here is what it says about him: 'Fort introduced into science . . . a defiant refusal to play at a game where everybody else cheats, a furious insistence that there is something else. A huge effort, not so much, perhaps, to grasp reality in its entirety, as to prevent reality being conceived in a falsely coherent way.'"

I felt a huge block, no, I *was* a huge block . . . of ignorance. Maybe because of the anger but I didn't have any idea what he was talking about.

"Did you get that, Willy?"

"I heard you . . . I hear you knockin'," a blues line we joked about only no humor now.

Leyla began explaining, repeating part of it, ". . . very interesting . . . to prevent reality—"

I was reduced to nothing. Leyla understood it. He did. Clare did. I was the dummy. "No," I said, as if revealing my own terrors about not understanding. Of the difference between me and, maybe, the rest of the world. Leyla understood, of course. She'd been to school but her lover, her husband hadn't. No, I had been doing engineering problems. And 500 knee bends. "No, I don't understand it and don't see what it has to do with the conversation."

"Okay, Willy. Look, you've got this notion about the war and while nobody, nobody has the whole handle on reality, in its entirety, as he says, what he's trying to do is prevent people from conceiving reality in a false way . . . coherent maybe, but false. And I think you have a false view of this war you're . . . *we're* going into."

Clare chipped in, Leyla trying to explain further but it was all at me for what I didn't understand about the damned war. Then RM again, whose show it was, "Willy . . . just wait . . . you told me about conversations you had with some of the Guadalcanal pilots—"

"Yes. The *real* heroes—"

"—So, Willy, I'm not praising the Japs and I'm not knocking our returning heroes—"

"So, what *are* you doing?"

"I'm just . . . wait . . . Willy, you told me about those conversations you had with them—"

"Yes, the heroes, the heroes who have gone through hell, who have come *back*—"

I was being reduced. I was dumb, didn't understand anything.

Then it was just coming out of me, just coming up out of me.

"Okay, you guys. Let me try and explain. I'm . . . .well, I've had an easy life, everything came to me . . . .all the privileges . . . only my father killing himself. I never understood that . . . but that's there too, except for that it was all easy . . . I got whatever I wanted, all the privileges, and so the last thing . . . war, despite everything that's been said . . . tonight, I want . . . I wanted, to be in . . . the thick middle of it! Yes, even . . . the *hell* of it. This pirate book when I was a kid, NC Wyeth drawings, pirates . . . see, it wasn't the treasure, not the gold, not pieces of eight; it was . . . being out there, really out there, for once in my life, no family to save me, get me out of scrapes . . . outside of the law . . . daring everyone, well, there was this picture, lone pirate on the deck of his ship, a hurricane . . . no one to call on, green waves towering over the ship, he'll get himself out or go down with it, one man on deck . . . battling the elements . . . see these pirates have already said the hell with law, to hell with countries and governments, to hell with order, bring on chaos. It's us alone in the world, no barriers between us and the world . . . and hung if we get caught . . . and those marine pilots on Guadalcanal felt that. Playing poker three days straight, paydays two months ahead. Betting the farm. Betting their lives. Like . . . the ultimate . . . nothing matters because they know . . . they *know* . . . They've walked into the lion's mouth and danced on his teeth. The lion closed his jaws and somehow they got out. Back from the dead. They lost three fourths of their original group of pilots, maybe more. Gone. Okay, they know war is *shit*. The Japs are *great* pilots. We've all been lied to, again and again. But they've run into it, the great lie itself. They've eaten it, then . . . spit out by it! Their bodies say it, their very walk says it. We have been lied to so deeply, so profoundly we can't even get our minds around it. Lied to about life. About sex. About the joys of civilization. They know they've been deceived. It's all a huge joke. Lied to about the enemy. *They* said this, all of it. Lied to about what we're fighting for—Pearl Harbor? Or control of the Pacific?—lied to about 'glory' about fighting for a country. *Dying!* They told me this, RM. They were laughing, 'You don't die for a country . . . you die because your plane got shot out from under you, or a 50 caliber bullet hit you in the head.' They come back to flag-waving and speeches. But there's no one to talk to. No one else to understand. People are looking at them with tears in their eyes, worshiping them, and so they play along. They play the game because there was no one else to talk to. Because no one else has gone through it. And unless you've gone through it you'll not understand. And no one *else* has. *They* understand. And maybe no one else. They talked to us and I got a sniff of it. They've been screwed, screwed out of a normal life. So have we bogeys. Only they've been screwed to the *wall*. They bet money three paychecks away. What the hell's it matter. They're back from the dead! No-after-the-war-for-a-fighter-pilot. Well, somehow, they died and made it back . . . they're literally and figuratively back from the dead. And they come back to banners and flags and people who want to cheer 'em and pat 'em on the back and understand nothing. How do they tell *those* people that war is shit? They're heroes! And heroes don't talk like that! They get into these poker games as if they're looking for something, anything, maybe for meaning itself! They're betting acres of farms back home! What does it matter? What does anything matter? Only the game. Only right now. After what they've been through nothing else matters.

"What does that say? The pirate on the deck of the ship in the hurricane. What's important? Not money, not tomorrow, not *saving*, for God's sake, not yesterday, and not the country. *Now!* The next card, the next roll of the dice. *Now*, with this ship under my feet and here comes the next wave . . . but I'm alive this second so bring it on! Battle with the elements; with God! They're saying something like that. And I want to taste that. To see what they saw . . . all the way . . . *all the way* . . . and I don't want to take anyone's word for . . . ANYTHING . . . THESE eyes . . . I want to see it for me, for myself! And I won't take anyone's word. I want to throw myself into it all the way, nothing held back, without fear, there! No fear! To at last do something totally! And totally fearlessly. To see for myself. Not to hear it from anyone else! Totally! And don't tell me about logic and making sense . . . It's *beyond* making sense . . . *I know it doesn't make sense.*"

I was crying at that point. Ashamed and talking about things I couldn't explain.

They were up, hands on my arms, Leyla at my ear, words of love, her hero, or something, over and over again. Clare abashed. RM his arm around me patting me on the back.

And when I'd recovered, laughing again, RM was saying, "I think you're crazy, Willy, but I love you . . . not to sleep with, you know . . . I've got that," laughs all around, "and, maybe . . . as long as we're going. Well, maybe it's the only way."

Even Clare, looking how? Strangely? I was crazy but she was laughing.

We left. Back at the cabin Leyla tried to make me laugh and ended by irritating me. She would take my face and gaze into my eyes, looking, she said, and just loving me. That's what she was doing. And, no, she wasn't trying to talk me out of anything. But she was strangely quiet.

"Yeah? And what do you really think?"

"I love you . . . and . . . I want to understand all of that, all that you—"

"But, Leyla, I'm the one who doesn't understand! All of that talk, to-night, it's about what *I* don't understand. Why is it I feel this tremendous urge to be out there, alone, against this *force*? Me and my plane . . . the dragon's head . . . .the hero, it's all craziness, right?"

"I didn't say that—"

"Heath, Nevers' roommate, called me a 'warrior . . . a warrior looking for a field of action.' And . . . he never blamed me for Nevers' death. I know that. But *I* blame me for it."

"Will, darling, you can't. Can't blame yourself. Nevers did what he did. And Heath didn't blame you because you were not to blame."

"So . . . what do you really think? About tonight, and what I was trying to say?"

She sat up in bed, looking off, and holding her knees. We were in bed together but she was quite separated from me. For a while I thought I had lost her, maybe forever.

"I'd like a cigarette," she said.

"What? Leyla . . . you smoke?"

"I did . . . some . . . at school . . . around exams."

"So? You were about to say—"

She was speaking, in a voice I'd never heard her use before. "I was going to say . . . " she said very slowly and carefully, "I have a rival . . . I've got a rival . . . and I'm just realizing it. Only *I'm* pregnant with this hero's child . . . because . . . you see . . . *I* get to sleep with him . . . And . . . my rival can't do that."

Chapter 40

During the first part of the program we had been flying one hop in the morning and one at night, plus movies, lectures, briefings. Then time was closing down on us and there was the wild attempt to fit the paper plan over actual days—mornings of rain, nights of fog when flying was next to impossible. Nights and mornings that cared nothing for such programs or even the war. Finally it was admitted that certain things could be done away with, that we might be able to fight the war without seeing "Democratization of South Pacific Natives," and "The Care and Handling of the M-1 Rifle."

Full Lieutenant Jarvis Willetts, from the mountains of North Carolina, led the six of us up, over, around, through white cloud mountains over Florida.

"Wilson! If you kill me I'm gonna kick the shit out of you."

"Alright, knock off all unnecessary chatter."

"Jarvis, believe me, that was necessary."

"Knock it *off!*"

Balt at his cockiest, scraped a wing taxiing back. Decision: Three day's restriction to the base and a twenty pound wing tip as his constant companion.

May 26. Allied offensive toward Rome slows down before mountainous terrain and stiff German resistance.

May 28. The Chinese Seventy-first Army is committed to the battle for Burma, south of the Salween River.

Step 67 Red Beach. Ship and plane Identification

"Eyes front. I will now raise the curtain. Tell me when you can see something."

"I seeee . . . a train tunnel."

"A big pile of mud!"

"You know," said the unknown instructor, another j.g.; "this squadron, *already* has a reputation . . . so, perhaps—" it was an uncompleted warning.

"Ummm, as a superior group?" Balt asked him.

"Not exactly," said the instructor.

Finally, slowly, like a rheostat being turned up—chairs, other people in the dark theater—and up ahead on the screen: small, vague, jagged shapes were beginning to appear.

"A bunch of ships!"

"Don't be vulgar!"

"Alright, how many see ships?"

Slowly . . . Jap cruisers, destroyers, battleships, two carriers and some merchant ships.

After discussing the different classes of ships we got the lecture.

"On a starlit night there may be one-hundredth as much available light as with bright moonlight . . . pilots shall wear red goggles for half an hour before night flying . . . avoid bright light one hour before . . . never stare . . . . eat lots of raw carrots . . . keep windshield and goggles clean . . . no drinking four hours before night flying . . . cockpit lights on dim . . . and never look directly, with the center of the eyes, look indirectly, from the sides of the eyes . . . "

We nodded at the intent instructor, only there were no red goggles, no raw carrots, and we, the six ex-bogeys used only earphones, no goggles, and turned down our cockpit lights automatically. As for drinking and the four hour curfew, well, ya can't win 'em all.

Balt frowned, pretended to be taking notes and looked around with a crafty smile on his broad face. Mulligan was looking "indirectly" at everyone. Jorge passed a sheet around, desk to desk, a long thin pilot in the form of Bugs Bunny was gnawing on a huge carrot, wearing thick dark glasses; behind them he looked indirectly at a passing woman.

May 31. Intensive allied bombing of French and German rail and transportation facilities. The tough, big P-47 led the way.

Step 97. Red Beach. Field Carriers.

"This may be your last daytime field carrier landings before night field carriers. After that we fly cross-country to Pensacola and check out on the carrier. Make it good."

I stretched back for shoulder straps and locked in—we were the same through locking ourselves to planes, pressing buttons, levers, directing raw aviation gas to carburetors, the very blood of us, the glue that bound us.

I felt like a tiger, relaxed in strength and readiness. Cockpit closed, wheels up, cowl flaps, cleaning the air lines of my beauty, black shapes turning into planes ahead curving inside and closing on each other, pointed the nose ahead of that first black dot, right hand light on the stick, left hand adjusting tabs, feet against rudder, eyes gauging steadily and swiftly, changing as I pulled into place, backed throttle then moved in like a filing drawn to the magnet. A boat of three planes. Four. Five. The boat was being constructed. There's the bow, I'm part of the port quarter. Six. Seven bent-winged Corsairs. A gentle turn to sea. The phalanx crossed the line of green water—white wash, beach—green land.

South in a gentle dive, then steeper to a jagged rush parting the still blue air, seven harsh-talking bent-wing machine birds in a dream turn over three runways in a neat "4" enclosing a tetrahedron in its triangle, down through that blue air turning green for sky bending trees reaching up came straight up a black runway over Torgerson who ran from his jeep with bright nylon paddles tucked under arm.

Right echelon and the wheels-down signal from Jarvis.

"Clear for Tare flight, clear, clear to land, Clear. You are Charley, Tare Flight," Torgerson's Georgia twang, from the jeep radio below us.

Right echelon for seven, Jarvis churns his arm for wheels. Churns and churns.

Head down—execute!

Rocking and sliding off and down away from us. Wheels were coming out and the echelon was bouncing.

I rocked off, leaving RM, turning back toward the runway, cockpit open to a wild wind, I readied my house, slowing, trim tabs, flaps, prop, trimming again as it slowed down. The others were landing and taxiing forward slowly and I got the "Land and Stay Down" from Torgerson (a side churning signal) then he picked me up; I kept it slow and wanted a constant turn, nose cocked up losing altitude slowly steadily as I approached the flags and the little group standing behind Torgerson and his paddles, observing.

At the last instant he gave me a slow-dip then a cut-gun.

I gave a burst of power for the "slow dip" then throttle off, stick forward and, just as the plane was obeying, stick back and hold, dumped it in on its tail-wheel it stuck and rolled, under control. At the turnoff I looked back and saw the last three Corsairs rolling along at taxi speed.

We left the seven beauties in a line, ran to the group, collecting at Torgerson.

To see each other after flight was a party, "Why, you sonofabitch!" Meant, "What? You still alive?"

Top called it as it stood, "Willy V, you need six more landings . . . Woodruff? Not here?"

Balt explained to him while Wilson held up a hand and stuttered about taking Woodruff's place. Balt glared at him but kept his mouth shut.

". . . Webster you need seven more landings . . . Nick, seven . . . Jorge, eight . . . RM eight, make it nine . . . (you're high, get it down a little) . . . Mulligan, make it ten . . . Balt . . . ten . . . " He went on down the list till he got to the colonel—'Marvelous,' we muttered behind his back—"Colonel," he paused and looked over patiently-impatiently, "SOS—"

"What?" said the colonel.

"'Same Old Shit'. High, erratic turns . . . .Smooth it out, *smooth* . . . "

The colonel nodded and there were a few smirks, mainly the navy half of the squadron, since he flew with them, thank God.

He went on, then assigned planes. "Nick and Willy observe first . . . Colonel, I want you to observe a couple landings then I want you to take Snuffy's plane. Snuff? Two landings, got it?"

"Alright," he announced, "Nick and Willy are down; Horney, Jorge and RM, you're down to observe; the rest are flying. Take the planes as they stand. Taxi by me so I can get your number and order, keep a good interval, clear the runway as soon as you're off the ground. Okay, go get 'em!"

The outlying field with its high grass was quiet except for voices, then an engine fired, and the first Corsair rolled toward them lean and wind-hungry.

Torgerson, his paddles under his arm again, dictated names and numbers to Nick as they taxied past, and blew his nose with a dirty green handkerchief, which was nearly blown out of his hand as the planes revved up and took off.

"Tare six in Fox seventeen," said the jeep radio, broadcasting from the big fighter not more than ten feet away. The plane jumped like a horse and moved away roaring, gathering force, rudder swishing to keep it straight.

Tare eight moved up, looked over, then down the runway, roaring. Tare Two, Tare Five, Tare Eleven. The seventh plane was not airborne before the first emergency, and the second.

A simple thing that all of us waited for after two interruptions of engine power, two little gifts of silence in the midst of otherwise constant thunder.

". . . sssssssss Tare Six . . . .emergency . . . engine-cutting-out-on-takeoff."

Torgie grabbed the hand mike from the jeep, "Roger, six—"

"Tare Five, returning to base, hydraulic failure—"

"Roger Tare Five and Tare Six," Torgerson was extra calm, "all planes hold your positions. Tare Six the field is open, take any runway . . . Tare Five return to Red Base, call in emergency, use your hand pump for brakes, Lizard, over?"

"Roger, Tare Six."

"Tare Five returning to base, out."

"Crash truck and fire engine standby, emergency!"

The fire crew ran for their gear piled on top of the truck, looked through their tremendous hoods, like jousting helmets, off they went.

Around swung the plane, Tare Six, aka Snuffy Smith, in a low and erratic turn. The fire truck pulled away, uncertain about which runway, the men hanging to the rails, swinging with the turn. Off the grass it picked up speed, the engine noise hooded and very different from the powerful flying engines. When the driver double-shifted the men swung forward and back slowly, like plants underwater. Tare Six had gained a little altitude and decided on the runway in use.

The fire truck was halfway down the runway to the side, the Bloody Mary was racing to catch up. All eyes on the plane. Tare Six was coming in with plenty of room, power on, settling and coasting in.

The Corsair shot past the two trucks that raced after it, staying as close as possible then, seeing everything was okay, slowed down and swung back toward us. Already the men were slapping their gear back on the truck. Tare Six continued down to the end of the runway, luxuriating, a joy ride down the boulevard. We could feel his relief from where we stood.

Overhead five planes circled while Tare Six taxied back to us without a break in the engine rhythm. He pulled up and wheeled it around and looked a little sheepish for still being alive. Bill "Stoney" Stone, the navy half's instructor signaled, went up on the wing when Tare Six dropped the flaps, Stoney's long hair blowing wildly in the wind from the prop, and bent in to the cockpit to talk, then jumped down and rejoined us.

"I think it was just the mixture," Stoney told us, but God knows what he thought.

Snuffy, Tare Six, raced the engine, leaned out the mixture, let it run a minute or so then he was off. Torgerson gave the circling planes the all-clear and the landings began.

At the end of that session we were informed there would be at least one more field carrier session before Pensacola.

June 1. Allied forces take the offensive south of Rome to knock out the German Fourteenth Army and encounter heavy German resistance. Intensive Allied bombing of Nazi-occupied France and the Low Countries in readiness for the coming invasion. Month's toll: 900 locomotives and 16,000 freight cars destroyed.

Step 130. Red Beach. Plane Identification, Friend or Foe.

Again the dark room and time for focusing. Pencils and paper for each of us.

"These will be at one 100th of a second. You cannot afford to make a mistake. Not *one*. Passing grade is 90%. It should be perfect, but . . . Okay, Herb, give us thirty seconds."

A flicker of light but by now we were used to it:

Click. In the first flash of light heads turned from the screen and only the scratching of pencils could be heard.

P-47, fat and heavy. Very fast . . . at altitude.

Click.

Spitfire, like a little sleek glider.

Click, click, click.

Hawker Hurricane, slightly beefed up Spitfire.

ME 109, big spinner, rounder-bodied than Spitfire but square wingtips. Sits on wing.

P-38, twin booms.

"Boing!" Balt yelled out. The army's Dick Bong had just shot down his twenty-first Jap plane, and everyone knew he flew P-38's.

"*Silence!*" yelled the instructor.

"Ahh, shut up," RM whispered. The P-38 could be spotted at one-eight thousandth of a second.

Tony, one of the Jap Zeros, cross between an ME 109 and a Hurricane.

F6F, Hellcat, so familiar to all of us, stubby, square wing-tips.

Betty, twin engine bomber, flying cigar, slightly larger than the B-26.

Zero, Mitsubishi, clipped wing, "Jack"?

P-51, Mustang, the one, the one other airplane I would have been happy with.

I think I missed one of twenty. Not "Jack" it was a "Zeke."

We were up, signed papers and compared notes.

"Did you hear about the guy up in the Aleutians? He shot down three planes; two PBY's and another F6F."

"Two more and he's an ace!"

Tonight was "Low Level Interceptions."

Chapter 41

So much had changed since the night at RM's and Clare's and the talk of war. Leyla was very definitely pregnant according to the base doctor, and was feeling nauseous and a little dizzy, especially in the mornings. "Exceptionally healthy . . . born to have children," he said for the eighth time.

Meantime, we were faced with a heavy schedule. Everything for us was 'serious' as in 'serious' drinking, so it was a 'serious' schedule.

Early morning and into the nights. Flying at 0800 for air-to-air gunnery—high side and low side runs firing at a cloth sleeve—or strafing a fixed target, usually a smoke bomb out at sea; films, intelligence briefings, gunnery flights, navigation, instruments, lectures, more films, the last of field carriers, and the frantic call to get ready for Pensacola and the "serious" carrier. More talk that we would be carrier-based. And beyond the carrier? "Serious" action.

RM and I juggled cars so the girls also had a car. The others lived on the base, except for Balt and Jorge who lived out at the "Castle" with Heath and other bogeys. And because of the program and changes throughout the day we were constantly calling, canceling supper, telling them it was "on" again and when we'd be back.

"Can't they make up their minds?" It was mainly Clare who complained. I think she had never rightly understood why RM was going, after all the war talk. And I can't say I did either.

"Clare, Sweety, things change. We're telling you as soon as we get the word."

Occasionally she sulked, sometimes quietly, sometimes out loud. I don't know what the two of them talked of when they spoke about it, I'm only sure it was different in front of us.

I felt uneasy and uncomfortable the first month of her pregnancy. I was at a peak and felt that I had to hide it. But that was with me, and I can't blame it on Leyla who was totally with me, "I don't even know what I'm saying, but it all just sort of breaks my heart it's so perfect, even that you're going . . . "

I didn't know what she was talking about and yet I knew. The endless strength, not just energy, the chance for doing, for knowing we were perfect; so quick, so ready for the whole thing coming at us, for the perfect meeting, perfect war, perfect shatteringly beautiful water—to fly those islands, coral and sand, coconut trees in the ever-cooling winds and the east, the east of sarongs, pearl divers, Malaysian pirates, and the perfect buck-toothed grinning enemy.

Sometimes I went to the bathroom, closed the door behind me and just stood there, a split second away from a wild dance, my face against the wall, listening to the wall, and how wonderful. How wonderful, just how wonderful. The Corsair in my hands, my heart, my eyes, and love love love all around us and sometimes so strongly just the perfection she was talking about that I wanted to scream it to the very skies just turn up my head and scream! How the earth feels in its turnings around the sun; how in the midst of its own special work how the earth feels spring and out comes green.

Other times approaching the plane, looking at it after all those dreams, the cockpit set right in the middle behind that long nose containing 2000 horses, the body itself narrowing from prop to tail, an almost invisible curve, the simple speed shape.

They were not religious those feelings, not to God up there, but to me. The worship of the exactness in my fingers, my own great reflexes, my own great eyes to shout for this wonderful chance to use it all. "Come on, you wanta live forever?" only I'd never tell them that, not even RM—the marine lieutenant to his men; get up and charge. That was part of it, the sudden fierce urges to get up there again, to fly closer, closer in formation, closer to the waves, to put that little five pounder in the center of the center of the center of the target.

It was hard not to exult out loud and yet there were no words only my skin shouted while we stood and listened to instructions by Jarvis or Stoney, the calm pre-flight drone:

"You'll take off in ten minutes . . . rendezvous around the field between 3 and 4000 feet . . . nice formation . . . the target should be circling the area . . . start your runs from 10,000!"

Take off? You mean FLY??? Take it OFF?? Yank that beauty off the ground? Fly it? I mean, man, to FLYYYYY???

And . . . "nice formation"?

As in perfect? Jarhead, do you mean perfect formation?

Was that what Leyla was talking about? "I mean, all of you together . . . it's perfect. You've talked about them, RM, Jorge, Mulligan, Hebert, and now to see them . . . in the flesh . . . do you know what I'm saying? To be here when you come down from flying to catch you after it?"

"Yeaahhh," and turned my attention to this red-haired beauty, with a little tummy— actually flat—and dug my fingers into that nest of hair, and in the same instant she was reaching for me, "Youuuuu, what were you thinking about? It wasn't US . . . was it?"

"Yeahh, I was listening to you and . . . sort of dreaming of us, and the sea and flying, sure I know what you mean about the whole thing, the squadron, us, you and Clare, all part of it."

We hugged, maybe each with our own visions. Actually I was proud of Leyla's feeling about flying, and know that Clare, as much as she loved RM, was different about it. No, she didn't worry constantly as she had told me that day before Leyla came down, but she was more of an anchor.

Leyla flew with me. Even pregnant she flew with me. And I know she was going through things with the baby and the adjustment and it was not all peaches and cream and sometime, somehow, I would make it up to her.

On the day before we left for Pensacola we were briefed about the trip. Report to the ready room at 0730. Colonel Marv Hartigan would fly half the squadron, the bogeys, in the DC-3. The navy half and Stoney would fly seven planes to Pensacola. We would arrive around 1200, have lunch and be in the planes at two, "*In* the planes turning over at two," Jarvis informed us. "From there you will proceed to an outlying field and one last field carrier landing practice—"

Balt was whispering something to me but I hardly caught it, "The colonel . . . "

"Balt, do you have a question?"

"Not even one tiny little question, Jarvis. Please proceed."

Jarvis glowered at him but Balt just smiled a big cat's smile.

Torgerson took over and told us, "There are some of you who still are not ready for the carrier. We'll stay out at that outlying field till the sun goes down or until you get it straight. Everybody will get in at least one landing, just to keep your hand in."

The colonel, Marvelous, was still coming in high and fast and angling in a strange way. As far as I could see he would never make it. I don't know what Torgerson thought. I only hoped the colonel wouldn't hold us back.

We had a morning of movies and were off that afternoon.

The last of three movies was *HP*, for Hot Pilot, *Showoff*. Even though we had seen it before, we always laughed at it. It was an Air Safety film and 'serious!' Definitely "Not funny!" The flying playboy had a hot little plane and was always looking for trouble. He was fond of buzzing his girl's house on his back. The main character ran away with the movie and the moral in his speedy bi-winged sport plane, although he ended up in flames stuck halfway through his girl's barn.

"There, Willy," Jorge called out from in back of me, "that's as low as you can get!"

There was not a serious face in the semi-dark room. Maybe the bad photography, or the faked burning plane, or restlessness at the third movie in a row. Still, we had taken three more steps, like the pile of pamphlets we had to read and sign our names to: Purification of Salt Water, Shark Sense, Surf Swimming, Downed in Enemy Territory, Coast Watchers, Water Landings. A pile of pamphlets that stood in our way like Pensacola, like flights, like lectures.

We had an evening at home, rare that we didn't check in with RM and Clare; Leyla fixed potato salad, and kept saying that the potatoes weren't quite done, I know she wanted it to be perfect. She ironed two khaki shirts for me, demanded to iron them and got sentimental about ironing my shirts for the carrier. I told her I'd be wearing a flight suit and it was already packed away. She got it out, washed it over my objections, hung it out in the stiff, hot breeze of late afternoon, and ironed it in the last stages of drying.

"It's what I can do, Will, my dearest Lieutenant I-love-you. And I'm gonna do it. And it's going to bring you luck."

Chapter 42

The girls drove us to the flight line and we were about five minutes late. Fierce kisses and we were waving goodbye to them and it was a little desperate. As far as Leyla was concerned this was our first separation. Well, our first enforced separation, and she felt it as if she were seeing me off to war. Standing next to that poor beat-on automobile of a faded green hue, standing next to that wreck of a car and to say the two of them did not go together is to say it all. The base doctor had confirmed it again, and pronounced her "Born to produce children, in fact . . . born to produce a mighty race." I wasn't sure about that doctor; he'd undoubtedly fallen madly in love with Leyla.

Well, time was coming down between us and I would have to give her up, like it or not. We waved a last time and into the ready room, empty except for the six of us.

The sun rose up and the sweat poured down us, and after an hour and 20 minutes the colonel was suddenly in our midst, with Jarvis and Torgerson, explaining something far removed from the immediate flight; he looked us over and nodded with gear in his hand and we were walking out toward the big DC-3.

"Good morning to *you*, Marvy," said Balt, safely out of earshot, as we trailed after him to the big box of a transport, and he and RM saluted his retreating form with both hands and one leg.

Who wants to strap himself to a transport plane with *anyone* flying it? But with the colonel? With Marvelous Marvin? Well, it was our sentence. And at least this was a plane he had been trained in.

Wilson had his deck of cards and he and Mulligan, Balt, and RM were already involved in a poker game with promises to continue on the plane. I was going to sleep on something, somewhere. Jorge was joshing me about "giving it a rest," as we all piled into the same door. The colonel and Jarvis disappeared behind the cockpit compartment.

The navy half, with our seven Corsairs, had already left for Pensacola. We would fly the planes back. That was a promise. The colonel, who had never checked out on a carrier, had been given three private practice sessions with Torgerson and we were delighted to hear Torgy admit that the colonel was "Not exactly what you would call a born fighter pilot."

At the end of the runway we sat for a few years until the war was over and a few more had started up, treaties were made, signed, and broken. Finally we rolled into take-off position.

"He walks up to the plane like he was gonna take off on the taxi strip."

"Don't go off half-cocked, Marvelous!"

Slowly the power mounted. The whole plane shook.

"Jesus Christ," said Balt, petrified. "This is serious!"

The brakes were released and like a chill leaving the body, the ground was moving back. We were off. And, with a pang, it hit me. Leyla's pregnant. My wife's pregnant. And for whole moments it seemed to me that all the rest of it was an inconsequential game. And I felt a gratefulness to her, because she, much better than I did, kept her mind on the important things and would not be moved off.

The others had picked up their poker game, an upside down jungle pack and parachute served for a table and I watched them, with Mulligan complaining about sleep and the rest pushing and shoving him awake.

Jorge came over, my devil and 'going' friend, "What's eating you?"

"Nothing . . . well, she's pregnant, you know?"

"Yeah, I heard. Sooo, you've got a little pilot on the way."

I laughed at that, "Yeah, one anyway. I hear you have a whole gang you don't even know about."

"Filthy rumors," Jorge said darkly, "My detractors stop at nothing."

"Neither will *their* detractor."

"Don't you go joining them. Remember who got you into all of this!"

"Yeah . . . right!"

"Look at Wilson," Jorge confided. And we did. You could almost see his mind working from outside.

Only, as it turned out, Wilson with no face but his own beat the shrewder players.

Mulligan left, made himself a bed out of harnesses, canvas bags and parachutes and some old tarp from in back of the plane and was asleep one minute after he lay down.

"No conscience, that boy," said Balt and the three of them continued some kind of three-handed game.

The tail of the plane was pointed at the base and underneath us the little lakes were going back and new ones kept taking their place, smooth and dark and bordered with green.

The propellers were an out-of-sight gray wraith in front of each engine squeezed tight in their silver jackets, and the shiny bright spinners in front were spinning silver. Over and under the engines the flat shark-mouthed intakes sipped the morning air. The propellers' constant gray shine was like the very pull of life itself, drawing events and the war north-northwest to Pensacola, the carrier, and beyond, as if we were at the huge table of events and it was moving toward us, all of it; carrier, west coast, Pacific ocean and war. And all we did was jump in cockpits, fly a few hours and come back.

Only now we weren't flying, we were simply going through the air on the colonel's hesitant wings. Still we were leaving everything behind. The first flight in a long time in one straight line, actually going somewhere. The spinner on the port engine cleaved farms, lakes, barns, fences. We were back here, with no control over any of it.

I slept, Mulligan slept, the card game went on. June 18th, 1944.

Tallahassee passed under the plane, or else the plane passed over Tallahassee. It was hard to say which. I was busy dreaming of pulling Pensacola toward us or being pulled toward Pensacola even arguing about it when I was awakened either to a crash or a landing.

Hyoi, hyoi, hyoi, the wheels said, then the Ys and Hs changed to Rs and we were taxiing. Pensacola. Three hours closer to the whole show.

We taxied up to the Corsairs parked near the tower, and there they were, the other half of the squadron lying around on their parachutes, underneath wings, as though they had camped there for weeks.

We waited. Oh yes, Marvelous had not yet opened the pilot compartment door and we'd wait for him. Balt couldn't wait to yipe over the colonel.

Out he came, apologizing and a littler sheepish to Jarvis (who had been asleep) for the landing, because flying—like death, elimination and nakedness—strips away rank and titles.

I didn't envy him, seven critical pilots sitting in judgment on the landing of the eighth.

We walked over and greeted the others, the lucky ones who had flown the Corsairs over: Ohh, yeah, Hi man? . . . Whatappened? . . . Where-you-guys-been? . . . Did the colonel pass his cross-country flight check? . . . SOS!

The subject of most of the remarks went in to close out his flight plan. We were to wait right here, and Jarvis pulled out a muster sheet and started in to torture himself:

"Answer'r yer names—"

"Here!"

"Cut it out!"

"Here!"

"Alright!"

"Here!"

"*Cut out the shit!*"

" . . . here."

"Balt?"

"Here."

"Baumgardner?"

After the muster Jarvis told us we'd have to stick together because we'd have one more flight this afternoon, *maybe* . . . .it depends—"

"Everything depends."

"Shut up!"

"We're shooting for three o'clock, if we can get a field. We'll have a meeting after it, the carrier is scheduled for early tomorrow morning; no drinking or horsing around, and the colonel will be back for further instructions."

"FURther in-STRUCtions?" Baumgardner, 'the Lizard,' said as if his voice was rolling over his Adam's apple. Everyone was laughing, even Jarvis and Torgerson. It was a great reliever, if there was any tension. The colonel came back, told us where to go for lunch and what to say to get in. Now, HE would be staying in the Senior Officer's quarters and WE would be staying in the Junior Visiting Officer's quarters. The two were across the base from each other but he was trying to get a jeep for us, because the base was as big as a mid-sized city.

After lunch we would be standing by. There would be a meeting before and after the flight and another meeting this evening about the carrier.

"Lotsa meetings," Jorge told us.

Despite all of the meetings it would be tomorrow and the carrier, and even that would pass, and all the rest of the meetings and then five days left at Red Beach.

The ponderousness of the whole big base hit us, at last, and Mulligan and RM couldn't get over it: "Hangar 86-B?" Red Beach was like a skeleton in a wild dance. Here the movement of a hundred planes was hardly noticeable.

At three we were back at the tower getting instructions. Three landings apiece and from that point whoever needed more. There were only five planes available, two of the Corsairs were having their tail hooks checked and so the colonel would lead five marines, the rest would go in the DC-3.

We flipped a coin and Balt lost. Bye bye, keep those navy bastards in line, okay? Balt drove the jeep back to the DC-3 and we walked to our planes inside of the huge hangar.

Had I forgotten everything? Could I still fly?

The tremendous bursting explosion of the engine inside of the big tin hangar and it was back. Again we were waiting on the colonel, Tare One. He called and we moved out of the hangar almost parallel and were into the sunshine, and turning in line.

"Tare One, spread your wings!"

Wings went out straight and the sky was over us.

"Take off in order of taxiing."

"Okay, Green Hornet," someone muttered, the colonel didn't respond.

The tower directed us, then okayed the takeoff and we sailed out onto that smooth wide sea and took off in twos.

We objected to Jarvis, of course, but where was he? Why was the colonel leading us out to field carriers?

Never mind, we were out to fly in daylight. Someone had found a strange droopy crow for a squadron insignia, and the longer we looked the more we liked it.

We flew and changed around for the navy to fly and watched them go through it. The colonel flew both halves. I got a cut and "remain down" just before I went crazy: Earth. Sun. Sky. Wings. Flight. Walk. I stood over Snuffy Smith as he got in my plane, helped him in, "It's a good one . . . all trimmed up for flight . . . leave it on main," he looked up uncertain, did his straps, held the brakes, dropped flaps for me to get off and I was down.

When that half was finished the navy boys took the planes back to mainside and we got in the DC-3 with the colonel at the controls. Jarvis would fly copilot. Top went with them and they closed the pilot compartment door behind them. What was to be done about Marvelous? Time was up, no more field carriers, and he was still SOS, Same old Shit, angling and fast.

We had played that low-sky-earth game until it was all the same—up is down, down is up. Flying at 1000 feet, or 700 what's it matter? We had strapped ourselves to the colonel's hesitant wings and the very air around us was zinging, popping. What mattered? Now listen, this is it! One by one we slipped to the back of the plane, to the tail of the big hollowed out transport. Then at a signal we charged forward, making the plane head down dangerously. Who started it? It started itself. We lay in a heap next to the pilot compartment door. We were sick from laughing. "Okay, when I say three, we race to the back!"

Then we were running, charging through the plane to the tail, making the plane zoom into the air. For a minute we crouched together in the tail, screeching with laughter. Then when the plane had been steadied for the mysterious weight in the tail we charged forward and smashed into the pilot compartment door laughing bodies, a big football pile-up at the center of the line. Wonderful! And if we smashed into the ground? Up, down, life, death, for that whole time not one of us cared in the least.

Ah, Japan, country of contrasts, of Samurai and flower-arrangers, this is what you will meet, this is what will meet you.

The pilot compartment door was being pushed open, vigorously, frantically—held shut by the lifeless, wheezing bodies against it. Jarvis's head appeared through the opening, white with fear, red with anger, purple with amazement, "*God damnit*," the head roared, "*You all gone crazy?? You're all on report! We almost stalled out!* "

He filled us in later. Top was being checked out and had never flown the DC-3 before.

The Colonel, Marvelous, was embarrassed, just embarrassed. Top was pissed off, Jarvis was screaming mad and should have saved some of it for later.

There was a party brewing and we all knew it.

We ate at the Junior Officer's mess and didn't smile at Top and Jarvis, who sat two tables over from us, but there were some snickers no one else heard, and that afternoon we decided on our crow. Jorge and Mulligan got it blown up, a big and perfect reproduction, our squadron insignia. Not a red lion on a white field, not an eagle, not a hawk, a lonely, skinny black crow on brown and gray brambles. Sad and hungry crow, loony bedraggled midnight blue-black like our Corsairs. The goofy eyes head down wings hanging drunk or tired, long beak almost touching the weak half-dead twig his claws held, framed by a setting moon but even half-dead skinny, hungry and long beaked there was something—skinny-hungry-exhausted still a wild and despair/fling readiness, ninth inning-two-outs-scream-blasting-unreasoning-uncalculating-thank-Jesus effort. We would copy our crow on the left side of every Corsair fuselage coming up, yes, The Hungry Crows! That's us!

Good! Great! Agreed! Resolved!

Torgerson talked to the twelve of us briefly and told us the Colonel was planning the next meeting tonight at eight, "Just some last words before the carrier tomorrow morning."

Yes, sure, although why he couldn't have given us some 'last words' right then was a mystery that would remain so. Till eight.

The colonel, with other means of getting around, gave us his jeep. Perhaps that was a mistake. Eight of us got in and, first off, managed to knock over a hedge in front of our BOQ because Jorge insisted on bringing us "right up to the door." In half an hour we were headed for the officer's club and our first drinks. And bottles. Well, we went ahead and bought bottles "to take back." Of course.

"I wouldn't drink the night before the carrier, would you?"

"Hell, no, would you?"

"No siree, would you?"

"I told you I wouldn't."

"Tell me again."

"Is he snickering? I believe he's snickering."

"Isn't he?"

"Yeah, he's a snickerer."

"I'm not snickering, *you're* snickering."

"Get serious, will you guys!? And furthermore what time is it?"

"I'm glad you asked that."

The club was the same old fortress where Tony and I had entertained Martha and Faye but what a difference. Now a museum of sorts, renovated with mahogany, tile, brass and long windows overlooking Pensacola Bay.

Balt discovered the crazy running rendition of "After You're Gone," with Roy Eldredge's high racing trumpet solo that used to set everyone screaming at preflight and played it four times. Mulligan and I wandered over to a wall display of knight's armor, helmets and daggers from the 10th century to the 19th: Italian, French and German but also pictures of Japanese ceremonial arrowheads with tiny perfect squirrels cavorting in leafy trees— framed by the arrowhead itself. These arrowheads, said the caption, were used to open hostilities between opposing armies, "sent into the air with pierced wooden turnips attached to give forth a whistling noise in flight."

Now that was more like it. Ah, 300 years ago they knew what it was all about. The Italian, French and German armor and helmets! So many angels, flowers, fancy leaves, prancing horses, voluptuous women on shields, dragons, tendrils, vines, grapes and spears, sheaths of arrows. Leaves and flowers so fancy they never existed, and battle cries! "Montjoie," the French cried, and into battle.

Joyous shout as he flings himself at the enemy! Oh my heart ached for those times.

Into it, all the way, "Montjoie!" You wanta live forever? I didn't want to regret anything but when I looked at that sword, those arrowheads, that cry of joy and into battle, well . . .

"You guys comin' to eat or what?" Balt yelled, exasperated, as if he'd been all over looking for us.

Oh well, the next war might be all machines, as Heath pointed out. And the heroes will be the highest taxpayers. I turned from archers and mounted knights to that screeching trumpet once again in the air. So? Don't we have the Corsair?—screeching trumpet, flying notes— the most beautiful? And its wind lines? The others are earth-bound while we go with the wind. We won't die of old age. So, if it ends quicker more suddenly for our brains— those stomachs for impressions—then we must feed them better, leaner, happier impressions. Until then every meal is the last.

A linen table cloth and lamp in the center.

"Well, this is more like it," Jorge was smiling to himself, looking back on life with his old father, "He's kind of a contractor," he used to tell us, with the same rueful smile.

Wilson didn't know what to do with the unexpected luxury. He had been ready to act normal while the rest of us were already snickering.

Balt leaned back, watching Wilson for a long moment then, "Poor Woodruff," he said, "he's gonna miss getting his ass shot full of holes . . . oh well" and he turned to the next table where a full commander and his wife were eating, watching the wife so openly and frankly that the commander's face changed from happy to insulted and was at the point of coming over.

The wife was a lovely thing in a high-necked dress which clung to those two appendages, loving them, whether false or real.

"I say they're not . . . not real," RM told Balt. "In any case you better keep your voice down."

"By God, yes they are," said Balt, "I'm an old tit man and I should know."

"Yes, you *should*."

The commander studied us coldly. Then the meal was served.

"Damn' good eatin'," Jorge started it.

"Good chow, boy!"

"Dig in, man!"

Eating low to our plates, growling over the food, slurping it up for the commander's benefit, exclaiming and clashing knives and forks we stowed it away, staring around, tearing the bread angrily, all in it together, "serious" except for Wilson whose frank peasant face was red from laughing.

Maybe Mulligan saved us from trouble. "Jesus Christ," he shouted, "It's eight o'clock!"

We jumped up, grabbed the bottles, stowed the two cases of beer and into the jeep, Mulligan at the controls. He jerked us from nothing to 60 in a few seconds and for five minutes we raced along the base road.

"Hey, Mulligan, old man, you know where you're goin'?"

"Not really . . . anybody have some ideas?"

At 8:30 the six of us entered the building. Top, Jarvis, the navy half of the squadron were all there; the colonel didn't even pause:

". . . So, I'd like everybody in bed by *ten*. I want you men to look sharp tomorrow . . . the money's on the table and the chips are down . . . and, they're playing for keeps out there . . . that's a long drink of green if you miss it . . . watch Torgerson, uhh Top, but remember, he can't fly the plane for you . . . that's *your* baby, and the chips are really down . . . this is the big one . . . come in too low and hit that fantail . . . hit that fantail and it won't budge an inch when you hit it . . . Lower, and you land in the spud locker . . . and it's happened before. So, let's do it right . . . the chips are really down and that's the only reason I'm speaking to you like this. That's why I want you in bed early. I'll be in bed myself by nine or ten, and I'd like you men to do the same because they're really playin' for keeps out there!"

The colonel went on and on, repeating everything he'd just said. Perhaps he even sensed it but he couldn't stop.

Who was going first tomorrow? Navy or marines? They didn't know. Everybody up, ready to go by 0700.

"Up at seven? We're supposed to be in bed by nine!!! When do we sleep?"

"Balt, don't be such an idiot. Go to sleep now and you'll get eight or nine hours."

"Oh, he meant *tonight???* Ten *tonight???*"

Jarvis was beginning to hate Balt, or maybe he was well into the middle of his hate.

Jarvis and Top were staying two buildings over, the colonel would be about a mile away. The door had hardly slammed on their departure when it started.

"Okay, you guys, the chips are down!"

"That fantail won't budge—" And so on.

The first case of beer was hauled from the jeep. Bottles from overnight bags.

"I need a long drink of green . . . pour me one, I'm playing for keeps . . . I'm up for a nightcap."

"Nightcap? You can't have a nightcap till you've had a coupla *day caps*."

"I wouldn't cross you for anything, not even for a long drink of green."

Mulligan was measuring the front doors, a double door arrangement, "Hey, if we open these double doors it might just fit."

"Yeah," Balt picked it up, "then we wouldn't have to carry beer from the jeep."

The jeep could hardly fit in the corridor but it was quite maneuverable in the lobby, and the little engine made a fine noise in the wooden building.

The game was to hit a runner before he got behind one of those columns and, of course, one of the columns was hit, gouged up like a rhinoceros had hit it. The jeep was okay but it sobered us up enough to drive the jeep out of the building, down the front steps and off to the base movie. "Gotta go! There's a flying picture and an African movie."

Into the movie talking and laughing and the first warning by the Shore Patrol.

"Look," Balt told the SP, "we just got back from overseas and we're a little, you know, uneven."

"Yessir, well just hold it down . . . sir."

The African movie was on. The western scientists were looking for a drug to cure sleeping sickness and they had to test it out on the animals— black panthers, lions, leopards, in cages—in the village of the friendly natives. But the friendly natives were getting impatient with the "scientific method," besides the chief's son had caught sleeping sickness. Sandra, the chief scientist's daughter had smuggled herself along on the expedition and everyone except Harold thought it was a big mistake. Harold was the young scientist—with new ideas about science and other ideas about Sandra. Sandra's father didn't like any of them (ideas, Harold). Then there was a bad white man, rum, and a loyal black man who was bound to get killed saving them all. Harold wanted to go to the only known place where the plant for the cure can be found. Zambuli country.

"Too dangerous," says Sandra's father.

"We can make it! I *know* we can!"

"*Sure you can, Harry!*" Balt yelled. The shore patrol warned us again.

Harry is going to the Zambulis with a small expedition. Sandra shouldn't have gone but she can't help it. She had to.

Huge spiders. A python crawls down a tree. Sandra sobs against his shirt. Alligators push off from the banks. The bearers won't cross the river. Batumba on other side.

Next morning they are deserted. The bearers are gone. The hell with it, they'll cross anyway. Eyes peering through leaves. Painted faces. Captured. Tied up. Sandra's breasts almost pop the buttons on her gleaming white shirt.

"Batumbaaa!" Jorge yelled out. People laughed all around us.

"That's your last warning," said the shore patrol.

Just before being killed Harry pulls a thorn out of the foot of the chief's son. Boy recovers. Heroes. The Batumba chief helps them collect the juice of the goola goola bush. Tribal peace. Happy safari.

But back at the original camp the old scientist, Sandra's father, has caught the fever, the chief is dying. And . . . the animals are getting restless.

Spontaneous chorus: "THE ANIMALS . . . ARE GETTING REST-LESS!"

All's well, despite the fact that the scientists have burned down half the village, caused the deaths of about 30 natives when the animals got loose during the fire. Harold returns with the needed cure. Everyone left recovers. Harold and Sandra embrace in the African moonlight, as we were being escorted out by three baton wielding Shore Patrol seamen.

The next film was coming on and we realized we'd already seen it. It was the flight program in caricature. Tom Bailey, his heart in the skies, joins the Naval Air Corps. Just before we left we saw Tom Bailey knocked down in boxing. He "discovers" his ability to take punishment. He gets up, "Say, this is okay!" Tom Bailey can take it.

Just as well, we'd never have lasted through that one.

Mulligan and Jorge wanted to break into a huge mess hall, which we passed on the way back to the BOQ but were talked out of it.

"What time is it?" Balt asked.

"I'm glad you asked that," said Mulligan.

"Listen, Colonel, I don't need to sleep . . . I can TAKE IT!"

"Yeahhh, this is OKAYYYY!"

"Heyy, baby, the chips are down! Tom Bailey told me allll about it."

At the BOQ the navy half were on the floor of my room shooting craps. There were apples, gin, beer, vodka and a lock-jaw intensity.

"The chips are down, now *shoot* . . . Raise you half a buck . . . It's the spud locker for me. . . . Listen, the colonel could sleep for a week and still he'd fuck up . . . Speakin of that, how we gonna get to bed by 10 when takeoff's at 9:30 . . . He meant tomorrow night . . . Hey, that's a long chip of green you're drinkin . . . Gin and apples man, that'll budge you alright . . . Batumba, I lost again . . . So Harold said, Come on Sandra, let's fuck, your old man don't care . . . "

I lost three dollars to Snuffy and was out of the game. Wilson, Jorge, Balt, Snuffy Smith, Baumgardner and Kerry rolled the dice up against the door. Wilson, old Puddinhead, played like he'd done it all his life. Mulligan stood over them watching. Where was RM?

I went out in the hall and caught him walking to his room. "Where you been?"

"Talkin to the little lady."

"Oh God, you think it's too late for me to call? What time is it?"

"I'm glad you asked that—"

"No, really . . ."

"Well, it's after midnight."

Back in the room I wondered about us. This big test tomorrow, well, today, the carrier coming up and everyone drunk and on the prowl. How had we gotten into this?

A thousand lives and we could only live out one; still trying . . . pick up a string here, drop it, another, turning, turning. And I picked up one that led to Leyla. Call her in the morning, okay.

"I got a quarter of it . . . Craps you lose . . . Ahaa, gimme a quarter . . . Five and a two . . . well fuck . . . That's the way we go . . . Alright, roll the quarters . . . Now! . . . I need more beer . . . Bastard, you're comin up . . . I need a beer for luck . . . Okay, bring me one too, Snuff . . . Here, have a swigga this . . . I'll cover the buck . . . Hey, let's *do* something . . . Alright then TWO . . . Okay, whatta we got down there . . . Keep the three and get a four . . . SEVEN! . . . Wilson, you no-good Ovary, you fuckin-near-killed-me! . . . Come on . . . Never do it . . . I said, god damnit, who's fer the O'Club, that jeeps just sittin out there doin no harm to nobody . . . That's a disgrace . . . Oh Oh, fresh meat . . . What are you guys playin here? . . . It's a game called craps . . . No, it's mine, I got it covered . . . Here's one says he don't make it . . . Gotcha . . . Out comes the paper . . . Oh, I see, you just add up those little points . . . Yeah you just add up the pricks . . . There're seven in the game now . . . Ohh, Sandra, that hurt! . . . Oh Ho, Batumba, look out! . . . Whoop, almost. Five and three's eight . . . *Right* now! . . . Eight's the point. . . . Alright, *right* now! . . . Six . . . Eight . . . Six, couple more, couple more . . . Okay, you lose . . . alright, let the two and a half stay . . . Watch it! The animals are getting restless! Shit! Just like that. . . . Alright! Let the four ride . . . Ohhh, three fours in a row . . . Jesus Christ . . . You lucky sonofabitch . . . That does me! . . . I tell you it's when the drums *stop* beating, Harry . . . "

There was no end to it and since the game was in my room, mine and Balt's, I went with Jorge, Balt, Mulligan and Snuffy Smith in the jeep to the O'Club. It was supposed to close at one and we got there for the last twenty minutes. The four of us pooled twelve dollars and decided to break the quarter slot machine. We had a couple more drinks and the money lasted about fifteen minutes. "Last call!" said the bartender.

We beat on the machine and rocked it back and forth, then we got around it and decided to steal it. People just parted before us and we walked out the door with it.

We were almost to the jeep before the Officer of the Day and the bartender came running out to get us. The OD flashed his light in our faces and ordered us back with it, but he was so . . . funny . . . nothin' in the books about stealin' the slot . . . the thing was really heavy, dancing around with it, laughing and cursing. That OD with his flashlight in one hand and a .45 in the other, brandishing it.

"Man, don't you know better'n point a gun—"

"That's how you *kill* people—"

"I hope it's loaded, 'cause those unloaded guns—"

"Shoot me, god damnit I dare you—"

"Dear Madam, regret to inform you—"

"Stick that water pistol up your ass—"

"Killed in action, stealin a—"

"YOU GUYS!!!" said the OD, "craziest thing I ever saw—" His face was white and he looked at us and looked at us . . . I mean what good was his gun if we didn't understand . . .

"Awww, it was only a joke," Balt told him.

"You're lucky *I'm* on duty!" said the OD.

"Call that luck? Ten more feet and we'd a been gone."

"Lissen OD I'll take all the blame. My name's Tom Bailey . . . Shut up Balt, maybe he saw the movie . . . .That's right, I mean Jim Bailey . . . I'm Harold Bailey . . . Joe Bailey . . . I'm Sandra."

Maybe it was the bartender who spoke up for us at one point, after we struggled the big heavy machine back to its place, anyhow we were suddenly tearing along some road, Jorge at the wheel, as drunk as anyone. A tremendous crashing accident is what we needed. We hung out from all angles, crawled across the canvas top of the jeep, across and in at the other side.

Up onto the grass and the walkway. The jeep stopped on the third step of the BOQ. We pushed and hauled it in, looking for somebody sleeping—disobeying the colonel's orders.

"Nobody sleeps . . . Nobody sleeps till the drums stop beating . . . For sleeping sickness . . . "

It was slow going down the hall—couple of door knobs and the side mirror of the jeep—honking the horn, racing the engine.

"Sandra, we can't go on like this!"

Somehow, Jarvis was there and it was strange, one un-laughing face. He wasn't un-yelling though, "It's three o'clock! And the colonel said to be in bed by 10:00!"

"Ooh, he meant to*night?*"

"*Mulligan, I'm warning you,*" Jarvis said with an amazing new voice, "I'm getting reports from all over the base! Disturbances at the theater, something about stealing slot machines from the O' club . . . riding on top of the jeep!" He wasn't snickering either.

"I'm not snickering! Are you snickering?"

"I'm not."

"Don't snicker at orders, boy!"

"*LISTEN!!!*" Jarvis shouted. Now *he* was red in the face. "I'm giving you guys 10 minutes . . . get this thing, this jeep, outa here, and be in bed!!" He walked out of the building, as if he was stomping on our heads.

"Was he serious?"

"That man wasn't snickering!"

"Did he snicker?"

"Nope, left without a snicker."

There was a little singing, last drinks, but it was over. We got the jeep out and it was quiet within 15 minutes.

Chapter 43

At seven, Jarvis, with a vengeance, was going through the building, rapping on doors, everyone up for breakfast. The rumors were that the navy half would go first, but nobody knew for sure. Confirmed at breakfast. Our half would fly the afternoon flight.

"In bed by 10," said Jorge, the first snicker of the day.

Why, why that ridiculous party last night? We talked at breakfast and no one seemed to know how it had started and why we kept at it for so long. In a way, as if we had been daring each other. I called Leyla and she told me that RM had called Clare last night. Yes, she had expected a call. Hadn't we been together? I told her a little about the festivities.

"But, Will! Isn't this a big test? The carrier? Isn't it pretty dangerous?"

"No. But I don't know why we had this crazy party."

'It's not dangerous? The first time on a carrier?"

"Well, a little. It'll be fine."

"Well, of course, my Lieutenant . . . Lieutenant-I-love-you!"

"You angel! How are you . . . you and little Philodendron?"

"We're waiting for you. Both of us are."

"You're so . . . sunny."

"Are you cloudy?"

"A little."

And so on. Suddenly last night seemed insane. Never mind, I knew, even walking back to the building, that sleep was out of the question. I sat on the edge of the bed wondering about "normalcy." Balt without another word was in the sack and turned off. Hebert would have been asleep 5 minutes ago.

I felt the excitement in my body. It was a concentration point, a small blood clot, a brain clot maybe, but the minutes were crawling by. I walked down to the hangar. It was an unusual sky—white clouds against blue slate in all the corners—a hazy sun overhead, a nipping little breeze that might be a spanking good breeze over the carrier deck. Suddenly I felt desperate and weak-kneed, confident, nervous, crazy and haunted, hot and cold. Waiting. Waiting. All my life, waiting. I wanted to tear hours out of my brain.

In the big hangar, 86-B, I spotted Wilson, also looking lost and just standing around.

We found some visiting army P-51s and crawled over them. Such a simple airplane, almost sweet, a baby whose designer just walked up to women and said 'now I need sex' and got it. P-51, that little beauty, and shook our heads over the "Turkeys" the big torpedo bombers. "I checked out in one," I told Wilson. "It flies like it's on tracks. Safe, slow and solid."

We walked up to the tower, out to watch take-offs and landings; through time, keep moving. At 11:30 we went back to our building and woke up the others for lunch. The planes had not returned when we left the hangar and it wasn't till we were eating that, at last, in came the conquering heroes.

"Heyyyy, how was it?"

Yelps and screams from the flushed new conquerors ten feet tall, telling and telling:

"Big? It's like a postage stamp, then you land and it's two city blocks long . . . It's like, wait, I'll tell you . . . You're comin up to this big flat space . . . Wait! Yer jumpin a fence, see, and suddenly yer pants are caught . . . And there's nobody, nothin, then . . . yer pants are snagged and you're stopped . . . You hit and stopped and from nothin, nothing and no one, suddenly a million different colored shirts are runnin at you . . . In mid-air, mid-air,

you're snagged . . . Like pirates, blue, red, yellow, green, orange shirts . . .
You're shootin down the deck and you're *off* . . . Much easier than field
carriers . . . What? It's twice as hard."

"How did the colonel do?"

"Lousy! Two thicker-than-owl-shits but he made it."

"Tell em what happened, Batch!"

Batch, Skinhead, Satchmo Bachelder put on his woebegone expression
and began:

"Well, I knew I was doing lousy, a couple of wave-offs and some frantic
signals from Torgerson . . . .well, I came in real hard, banged it in, blew a
tire, which I didn't know about at the time, well, all these guys come running at me, the admiral was screaming over the bullhorn, whistles and
everything. I was near the port side and they got under my inboard wing
and pushed it up, they *raised* it! See, I didn't know I had a flat, and I thought
they were going to throw me overboard for doin' so terrible, I swear to
God!" Batch sat there, slumped over, despondent, reliving it but eating it
up, how we laughed at him, even added to it, "I didn't blame em," he said
sadly, "I *wanted* em to! Instead they changed my tire, right there, in half a
minute, and I was off again—"

"That settles it, me not make like bird in Batumba country . . . Batumba
wa-wa get thunderbird wet . . . Bwana colonel him say chips are green and
money on table . . . Yeah, and marine be in thunderbird when sun say one
o'clock."

The planes were gassed and ready and Jarvis collected us in front of the
hangar.

He was silent for as long as he dared. "You are the fourth group I've
taken through and I'm not going to say any more about last night—and
this morning . . . *Balt, do you have anything to say?*"

"No, Jarvis, not even one little word!"

"Well, shut up for once! I'm not going to talk about last night no more'n
to say that you're good pilots but more god damn trouble than I ever imagined. Just . . . don't fuck up out there. This is it! Go to your planes."

Baaarrrrrooooommmmmm another plane had started two over. I
jumped the throttle up half an inch and felt it surge, ducked down to wring
out the pleasure, hiding, pleased about such a simple thing. I looked over
at Jorge, behind and to my right, and we shrugged our shoulders at each
other in newborn ignorance.

Jarvis was moving out! I looked frantically for the mech and then felt the other chock pulled free, he danced away and I was rolling. The world was not so young, not in its dawning, but not so old we couldn't still smell the newness.

And it was engines under wings and hangar, then engine under wings and sky, and then wings unfolding, stretching out, engine under sky. The seat pack had slipped forward and the inflation tubes from the mae-west were sticking my chin when we turned, and we turned and turned—swing nose to the right, look out to the left, swing to left, look out to right, S-turning in line and more necessary for the Corsairs' long nose. Then we were stopped. Braked. The sky had changed. The haze had burned off, only there was slate gray in all the corners. I pushed the throttle forward and bent to the instruments, but what was the use of checking the engine? I wouldn't take it back even if the engine fell out.

Then we were moving up, like bullets in a chamber, and the runway was the barrel we were shot from, and the next time we rolled, the next time those wheels came out would be . . .

Out to sea we headed, crossing the beach and still joining up. The colonel would have circled the field three times but not Jarvis. Jarvis circled once and struck out, devil take the hindmost. For the moment the sun was in, and the breaking waves looked extremely white and the water dark green. Then we were beyond, heading straight away from the beach over darker water. Goodbye land. I let it go. These wings are my arms, my own arms, and I'll sail over oceans on them.

When the sun came out again the water was not quite a clear indigo blue. Jarvis was smiling across at me, 12, 15 feet away nodding, pointing and smiling.

In two quick glances I picked up the tiny carrier so far below us. It was in sunlight but soon would be in shade for the huge cloud bank shadow was coming closer to it.

The formation had tightened up and I closed on Jarvis's wing. Yes, I was in love. No help for it. The sea, the carrier, the formation, the Corsair with me in it.

"Hello, dealer, hello dealer, this is Red Fox One, seven cards at your disposal, over?"

A crisp chattery voice answered Jarvis, "This is dealer, understand seven cards. Your angels five, will advise, out."

Jarvis put us in a gentle dive to 5,000 and we began circling, forging a chain of ovals ahead of the carrier's course. 5,000 feet below us the carrier was changing its course, a little postage stamp heading into the wind and readying its deck to receive us.

It was the fifth or sixth oval when we got the call from some hidden quarter inside the small toy down there. We were "Charley," cleared to commence landings.

In a gentle dive going ahead of the carrier we flattened the sea and turned downwind just before hitting the 500 foot circle. Into right echelon on the downwind leg. Jarvis gave us the clenched fist for wheels and we passed it back, not looking. Waited. Waited. Execute! And our wheels were out in the air and locking in place.

The straightaway was a long one, very safe. Now, over the carrier. Now in front. Jarvis rocked his wings and broke off and down. I was leading.

Waited. Began counting the prescribed thirteen, gave up counting, turned to see Jarvis's position, started counting again, dropped it, signaled to RM, who nodded back seriously, rocked off, simply sliding off the formation. I dropped flaps to thirty degrees, looked all over the vast field of ocean, checked the tail hook down and craned around for the carrier, then for Jarvis's plane, a dark and fragile little thing against the sea. Abeam of the bow I popped full flaps and began the pattern. Altitude two hundred feet, speed eighty-five, and the damned inflation tubes sticking me in the neck. At ninety degrees I was slightly astern the ship and, like a flash, saw Jarvis's wing go up in a strange awkward maneuver. Wave-off.

I'd have to slow down more, eased off power and picked up the flags standing straight out. Thinking water deep blue and the long whitish wake behind the ship. For the first time the undulations of the ocean which before was a smooth unbroken mass; men along the sides of the empty, lonely deck, waiting, saw the light trail of smoke from the stack, the heavy movement of the ship through water, while curving in and cocked up.

Suddenly a low dip. I pulled the nose up, added power. No good, got a prolonged "low." More power. The attitude was right and the nose coming up slowly, but so slowly, right up on the carrier's stern, staring at Top's flags—adjusting by feel to something I'd never seen before.

Beginning to straighten the turn, broad deck ahead and fast. Torgerson's flags to Cut Gun. Not knowing, only responding, yanked power off, dumped nose, hauled back stick and hit the deck, hitting and rushing at a furious speed forward then hung suspended. Yes, I had snagged my pants. In the next instant the smoothness and flatness of the carrier deck exploded— red shirts, green, luminous yellow charging at me then sliding underneath the plane. The deck officer giving me a "hold brakes" and "wind it up" then flagged me ahead, like a flag at Indianapolis, go go go. I took off brakes, picked up speed and pushed the ship behind me.

The fierceness was on me. The world was in my hands and happy fingers while I sailed over the water cocked up. Around again. Top's flags stood straight out with never a motion. He was locked there. At the cut I saw his smile.

It was a hypnosis of curves and straights of quick glances at instruments then even that was gone, no instruments, only flying, only feeling, from my ass to every extension of the plane and that peculiar sensation I was the plane and it was me adding or taking off power, judging, watching, sending signals to arms and legs, cut, the flag across his throat, stick forward then back in my lap and crashing to the deck, snagged, wind it up, let go brakes and off again. What a game! What a game!!!

On the sixth landing I got a "Land and stay down!"

After the pirates had unhooked the wire, a yellow-shirted plane captain in a leather cap strapped under his chin was flashing signals faster than I'd ever seen. Forward, forward, forward, fold wings, forward, pull up tail hook, forward, forward. He had taken over, no time to question. I knew I was re-acting slowly but it was all so new (I'm down! Down on the carrier!), different style and the frantic plane captain, "git 'em out of the way, there's more comin aboard," and now over to the very edge of the deck, so close to the edge I could look straight down to the sea-green water rushing by. Then straight, and hold! Cut gun—the plane captain's finger across his throat.

I released the brakes only after the prop had completely stopped turning. Switched off.

The silence was taken over by the distant planes in their circles and by a strange throbbing. The ship's engines! Then it hit me. I'm down! Did it! I did it! Kissed my own elbow! Jumped over my knees! Left my shadow behind. Rearranged stars. The world on one finger. Way down there to my right the sea had changed to green and ruffled, tearing, washing by us. Stopped on a moving vehicle—ocean, sky, ship, sun.

Suddenly Brush was running up and I dropped the flaps for him to climb up. "How goes it, lieutenant?" He screamed, his hand on my shoulder, "*We been out here two days now. This is the life!*"

Yes, yes, "It's great!" while I hefted out of the cockpit, sorry to leave the magic. Clouds, ship moving, Brush out here, onto the wing, all the motion I'd just left and still going?

"God al*mighty*!"

Brush was laughing and took the chute from me. "You have to leave the chute in the plane, he said, "I'll take care of that."

He was laughing, I was laughing and no need to explain.

I jumped off the wing onto the flat deck of wood, watched the green sea rush by, heard the muffled rumbling of the carrier's heavy engines, as if it was my own heartbeat.

"God al*mighty*!" Whooped and laughed and went to find the others. Amazement with all of us. Balt was both proud and shocked—if he let himself go he might find himself in the landing pattern again, cocked up slow, dragging the water with the hands of his heart outside patting the ocean's surface measuring "the distance from the highest wave to my big ass." RM's cheeks were stretched and we smacked hands together. Jorge was growling how we made it. Mulligan was debonaire. The word was we would sleep on the carrier, get a catapult "shot" (take-off) in the morning and fly back to base. For now flying was "secured" for the day, the sky had turned and a thin subconscious rain was stinging across the deck.

Down to one of the ready-rooms to meet with Torgerson. We'd done fine, only three wave-offs, everyone was checked out. Jarvis was proud of us and told us, once again, "the word" was that we'd get carrier duty, leaving from the west coast.

Torgerson showed me my grades, five okays, with only a "low dip" on the first landing, and one "AEGOY," he laughed.

"AEGOY?"

"All Eyes Glued On You," he said and gave me a thumbs up.

RM and I had a tiny cubicle with upper and lower bunk, a neat little washstand, and a head down the hallway. Everything was painted steel. The mattress was straps of tough canvas.

"All-weather fighters off of a carrier, that oughta please you, lieutenant!" RM said, with a satisfied air. "I gotta lie down and think about that. . . . Dinner at 1900, that's 7 o'clock to you!"

Our quarters were just below the flight deck where we had been banging them in all afternoon. Through the catacombs and up a ladder then out into the wind and rain and a dark flight deck. The stinging rain was not coming down, it flew horizontally. Ahead into it, my feet barely touching the deck, one hand into a pocket clutching some pieces of money. Walking toward the bow I went over it again—not fate but somehow, somewhere there had been a choice (maybe only a birthmark), maybe a remark during the conceptual embrace lodged with the seed, some terrible determination into a childish oath now grown up. A determination or oath irrevocable not because I had sworn it or because it had sworn to me, not sad, not evil. And both Heath, who thought war was ridiculous, and Balt, who just shrugged his shoulders, were ahead of me.

I walked forward to the bow, stopped by a slicker-covered marine with a rifle slung over his shoulder, was halted and allowed to pass. Looked out on our dark heading, feeling this huge ship moving up and down slowly, majestically, with the sea itself, then turned back, was almost blown back, down to our little room, closing the hatch and, miraculously shutting out the night, discovered that I was still holding the coins in my pocket, like pieces of earth. All a memory, the starless sky and pin-pricking rain. RM was lying across the lower bunk with his mouth open and his field shoes still on.

After dinner, the 3,000th meal served, we went to the movie on the second hangar deck. It made a cavernous theater. About 60 percent of the carrier personnel attended; deck men (the pirates), plane handlers, mechanics, crew chiefs, crash-crews, stewards, cooks, messmen, gunners, seamen, pilots and ship's officers. We sat in the "Men", "NCO ", "Officers" sections. Behind us, on a raised platform behind a low canvas-covered railing, sat the senior officers. In the center was a dais of five chairs, the middle one a grand leather throne. A murmur ran around the crowded hangar deck when the chair was filled. The lights went out and the movie started.

"That little roly-poly guy up there was plenty lucky," Jorge told us, "he got here just in time for the movie."

"That's the admiral, you dumb sonofabitch!"

Jorge snickered.

After the movie we were headed direct to our quarters. On the way, Jorge wouldn't stop; "There's this flat carrier and that's it, like a big plank out on the ocean. But underneath that flat plank is an ant's nest with thousands of catacombs and ants everywhere."

"Yeah, and I want to tell you, this ant is going to hit the sack. Now."

Morning was the thrust of the big ship into the wind-blue waves, so different from breakfast below decks, on tables padded with linen, where the confidence and pride of the messmen that this ship and the heavy silver and metal coffee pots were forever, forever, forever. And the lukewarm scrambled eggs and boiling hot coffee did put courage into us all.

"Pilots man your planes! Pilots man your planes!"

The voice shot straight into the bloodstream.

We were leaping up and running, mouths full, coffee sloshing.

The wind was coming across the deck. The planes were in position, engines turning over. I found my plane, the plane captain throttled back, dropped flaps, gave it over to me, chocked but already turning over.

The huge pistons of the catapult recoiled hissing as they drew breath for the next plane, like a living giant slingshot firing us into the air. The planes waddled up then waited, engines churning the moist air dancing back, brakes held then waddled forward one plane length, the signalman gave us come ahead one, lined up the next on the catapult ramp, pilot ready fingers looking, looking, braced against the crash pad, handlers charging back and away from the plane locked in, cocked back, then stick hitting my leg for someone to climb up, then a seaman jamming a piece of paper in my mouth, directions to base, off the wing, full throttle thunder, held and notched back straining—the arrow and the string tight stretched—flat hand up to face and down, a split second then shot out, freed whoooooossssshhh out off the deck and on air, wing bending to the right and up, the piston a vast sigh and lungs collapsed only to inhale and collect itself for the next one, all on the ship churning straight into the wind of a new day.

The piece of paper said "335 degrees, 15 miles."

Chapter 44

It was winding up, happy crazy turning faster, faster, turning to finally snap some main spring. Leyla and bedtime and clinging each to each and breaking away with her still on me, in her, to eyes on a dark ocean where stars sprang up and up and up, some mystical union gathering, harvesting energy, wild with energy by the time dawn came. We had flown back but it was ratcheting up higher, higher.

More furious and immune to everything that didn't lie in my path, among lepers or in the middle of the worst plague immune—jealous disease, immunization from all others. Lectures and days, three more and that's it—lectures, days, flights and training films—and no more talk of the world; we'd go against the Japanese for it was Jap shipping, Jap planes and the rest was only news—the war in Europe, in the Pacific on the China mainland and "straight" propaganda "what we're fighting for." Caricatures so grotesque that our audience of 12 could afford to hiss the villains and cheer and laugh at an American stalking through underbrush: "Maybe he's from Mississippi, maybe he's from Vermont . . . " cartridge belts crisscrossed, hand grenades like leeches hanging all over him, two pistols and a sub-machine gun at his hip, "But wherever he's from, he wants only one thing . . . *peace!*"

"Oh boy!"

"Piece? That's . . . hey, I'll settle for piece!" Balt yelled out, and no one stopped him.

Then fast over earth, wings layover with just a touch on the stick to curve over beach and still banking until over ocean over deep water and down, down on blue water, blue-green with foam tracks, nip the waves, pull up curve back toward beach, everything meets— Sky meet earth. Earth, meet ocean. Ocean, meet Sky.

All to the song—going going going. And it was truly when we got up in the morning and stretched, drove to the field still yawning for day instruments under the hood, escorted by an "eye" then trading around, an "eye" for the other, we had been dead for a four, five, six hour stretch. Breakfast, kiss kiss, drive in, sign for plane and walk up to it were delays till we were alive again in cockpits with the vicious air rushing past us.

Gunnery? The armory crew folded long belts of slim steel 50 calibers into the wing cartridge boxes. Slammed the wing boxes shut, jumped down off the wing, "You've got purple, lieutenant, your color's purple!" Those slim 50 calibers dipped in purple paint.

"Right, we'll shoot em down with purple today."

Taxi out in order, join up and out to sea, weaving over the tow plane and climbing. Ten miles out to sea the tow plane takes his assigned direction.

Long echelon of sleek-nosed Corsairs ready to break. Like a long jagged stick in the sky. The first up and over, gone; the second, vapor trails and down after the sleeve.

Now, tight and delicious, vapors stream back, around and down on the white target sleeve, yellow lines of gun sight imposed faintly on sea, sky, target; gauge, close, trim, center, lead it and fire—wings bucking, bright yellow pencils pierce the white sleeve—break off, full throttle, pull up ahead on the opposite side, again, again, again, till there is nothing else in the world.

Join up. Planes slide in like checkers, tongues unstick. Around the field, breaking off, land, to the briefing: "Damn' good shooting but God what a lot of noise on the radio, you guys have *got* to observe radio discipline . . . Balt!"

Two days to go and everything stopped. Rain, solid rain, occluded front. And strange news: Spider Maxwell killed ferrying a dive-bomber, a plane he knew like the back of his yellow hand. Maxwell had entered our lives like a wraith, a flicker of time we would not forget. He had walked in the room, begun talking like that, gone to the window, come back, looked around, talked some more, signaled for the movie to begin and disappeared during it.

Killed? He had even told us about it. We didn't understand it but he did. Alright, we granted him that. We didn't question his right, either. But why did he have to go through it again? For two days we were stopped. And Leyla so happy.

"You haven't stopped since Pensacola . . . and there's so much to tell you."

"Yeah, we're stopped alright. So, tell—"

"Well, to begin with . . . Will, look at me . . . I've lost you, *lost* you—"

"What do you mean? Tell me, I'm listening."

"Well, it's about that other life. Remember? Me, the baby, you, your mother and family, Sally, me . . . and your leave—"

"Good! Tell me!"

"Oh, Will! Anyway . . . Mamoo called. We have the Barclay place on the Gulf coast, right on the beach, well the Barclay's are loaning the house to us for your leave!"

"God, really? That's great!"

"Yes, it really is. And we'll slow down and just have time together and no interruptions."

"Great! But why didn't you tell me?"

"Will . . . you've been running. Tearing off. I've hardly seen you, night flying, day flying, lectures, meals on the base. Clare is livid! She's threatening to leave for home till RM can get his leave."

"Yeah, he said something about it."

"Well, it's not been easy . . . Will."

I didn't want to talk, just lie there, holding her, holding us, just to have the time and just be there, even if we went to sleep and that's all.

But it didn't stop, even then: "It's like a fever, a fever that makes you run and run . . . so frantic it's really . . . almost frightening . . . well, drunkening, anyway."

I was hoping she had not heard the news and, as I was thinking about it, she told me, "Did you know him well? Stoney? The instructor?"

"Pretty well . . . how did you know about that?"

"Ohh, Will, we hear it all. We know it almost as soon as you guys."

I had gone over it and over it, Bill Stone, instructor for the navy half of us, good pilot, a short runway, engine failed and he went in flipped and it broke his neck. Did he pull back the supercharger instead of the prop? Tired from a 24 hour party? The supercharger was pulled all the way back. Why? Mistook it for the prop?

Normal takeoff, cockpit closing, wheels up and flying. Then what? Pulled the throttle back? The engine died. Keep it straight. Into the trees he crashed forward and crashed forever. He must have remembered . . . trees. And what more? How were the last seconds? Stoney had those last seconds and just stepped off and left us standing there. A tiny history and nobody had it. Maybe some weird scene some weird last split-seconds. Out there crying and never known. The merest detail, only a fragment. But take it out and run water over it and look again. History made up of similar unknown million, billion details, multiplied as the event grows in size and all together croak/scream-out/laugh-gargle/cough up the word—stinking history; everything's dark all is unknown.

Grounded. Socked in. Alone with Leyla and instead of happy I was feeling . . . I couldn't explain it. For it was nothing she had done. Only it was a kind of sickness. If we couldn't be flying or putting those steps behind us I wanted to get drunk and be with the others. Fly or get drunk. Very simple.

"Want to go over to RM's and Clare's? Maybe go out and eat, at The Place?"

"Good. Good!"

"I just feel so . . . I don't know, so restless. So . . . useless right now."

We got dressed, both feeling a little strange. Went over, got them. Clare looking worn out. They had been fighting.

Go out. Go out to dinner. Pass the time. We went to The Place in the Green Lizard, got a table for four. It was still early, not even dark yet. Strange not to have any planes flying over. Nothing. Only the sea, eternal sea, washing in and dragging, combing through the sand back out again, then the frightening silence between waves, as if the world was standing still.

The bar was filling up, some of the bogey pilots were singing a song we had taken for our own:

Oh some generations have been lost
And some have died at sea
But ours went faster than all the rest
In guvverment propertee!

Oh the draw was quick and many were killed
When they danced the six-shooter reel
But none went as fast as our band,
Flying guvverment steel.

The girls were looking at each other and seemed to understand something. It was something they had agreed on, Leyla nodded and Clare spoke up.

"Can't we go somewhere . . . honey chile," as she sometimes called RM, "and get away from all this . . . just for a night? Somewhere down the beach a ways and find some place . . . to get away, for God's sake?"

"Okay!" RM looked at me for agreement and within minutes we were driving south on the beach road, 1-A , to find a place, RM driving.

Even the fact that we were driving away from the base, had brought relief and the girls were chattering away without much comment from either RM or myself.

Earlier today I had gone up to the flight tower, the crab's eye, just to see the spot where all the commands emanated. I was greeted by Jane and a small and quite good-looking blond, Sweeny. I stood next to the field radio and heard two men talking over heavy static, the men speaking in the clipped jargon of radio. Sometimes it squealed when both started talking at once then was quiet again only crackling static. There were banks of equipment everywhere and the steady hum of the big radio, that tune maybe the sound of our very earth, not the engine noise, not wheels and gears but the friction of our huge ball whistling through space.

Another radio was playing tunes and then pausing for announcements.

"You don't mind, do you, Sweetie," Clare asked RM, asking me as well. "I can't wait for that leave . . . much as it means a time closer to you guys going, but I've really had it with the base, the flying, regulations, all of it. Incidentally," she interrupted herself, "Leyla, you two are going to your aunt's house, Will? On the Gulf coast?"

Leyla told her all about it and RM was wishing he could come down and see that area. He had never been to New Orleans and had always been fascinated by tales of the Crescent City.

We drove along with both of them making plans for during the leave and it seemed just flip enough to make me know it wasn't going to take place. We would have 12 days before we had to report.

"The orders are in, you know?"

"What?"

All three of us were gasping at the news. How had he found out? We still had two days of flying.

"Well, the orders are in and that'll take precedence, no matter how much more we're supposed to do."

"Well, for God's sake, what do they say?"

"Nobody's telling. Just that they're *in*."

"I also have an announcement," Clare told us, "I've been saving this and I've told no one else. So, here it is! *I am . . . we are . . . pregnant!*"

"My God!"

And we were all exploding. Clare about how hard it was not to have told Leyla. RM driving in swerving half circles down the highway.

In that mood we decided, definitely, down to Stuart and the best place we could find.

As we put miles between us and the base I began to feel we had been cut loose and really were on our own. The leave had already begun. I grabbed Leyla's hand and she moved over close. We had a secret from the whole world. It wasn't just the baby, it wasn't close friends, although that helped, it was just something we had had ever since Texas days. Ours forever, the click between us. Yes, the click. And I realize it had been hidden for a while. The program, flying, the Corsair and going, but this drive and Clare's news, the night, the leave coming up, the Pacific, those islands and that destiny magnet but all of that too, yes, even that, yes, homing slowly on that destiny magnet but also this wonderful, this wonderful woman-girl at my side, knowing about it, knowing all about it. I was close to screaming.

We found a great place in Stuart, tables overlooking the ocean, dim lamps on each table. Quiet waiters, good food, a round of martinis and, nothing scheduled till tomorrow afternoon.

That night was like coming up for air after a long swim underwater. We talked, we laughed, joshed with each other, our two babies with their babies. Maybe RM and Clare could get down to our Gulf coast house during the leave. We'd see about that. After dinner we drank brandy, paid a whopping bill, what's it matter? Drove back almost silently, but a happy silence.

I don't know what they were doing back there but it sounded like fun.

Clare and RM let us off. It was one-thirty. We were going to get in bed and just look at each other, get to know each other again, sleep late and have a big breakfast over at their place, time to be decided by phone in the morning.

For us it was like making love only, in a way, better. We were hugging and just passed out.

Then it was underwater again for the last two days.

Chapter 45

We had become resigned to continue training forever. It would go on and on: Low Altitude Night Interceptions, Night Glide Bombing, Night Navigation Problems, Air-to-Air gunnery, flight briefings before and after, Intelligence Briefings, and always the same tone of voice: world-weary, serious, manly, patriotic: "June 20: Battle of the Philippine Sea: Three Japanese carriers sunk, more than 400 Japanese planes shot down. Two U.S. carriers, two battleships and a cruiser damaged, 130 U.S. planes lost. June 21: massive raid on Berlin, 1,000 allied bombers escorted by 1,200 fighters inflicted heavy damage on Berlin. July 1: Russian troops crossed the Berezina river, captured Borizov," with maps showing the vast field of Russia and the present occupation by German troops. "July 3: intense bombardment of Iwo Jima and the Bonin Islands by U.S. naval ships and aircraft. Two Japanese transports sunk. July 7: nearly 3,000 Japanese troops made a suicidal attack on US Marine units on Saipan, inflicting heavy damages before they were stopped. July 9: Caen, in southern France, captured by Canadian and British forces . . . "

Toward the end of that two-day madness, my last flight. Sandwiched between everything was the thought of Leyla. At last I'd tell her, I'd show her how much she meant, even if she already knew: she must know, certainly, certainly she knows. Watch her swim, watch how she stands on her two feet, even with uncanny balance the feeling she's about to fly off the earth yet so long-legged so long full-legged Grecian urn earth-bound; a panic seized me at 10,000 feet on my last night interception flight. And what happens to her? Me and the child both on our way.

The station, Tarbaby, released me, "Good work Tare Four, and good luck out there! Drop us a line, over from Tarbaby."

"Roger and out, thanks, Tare Four."

"Tare Four this is Bat Twelve, returning to base. Do you wish to join up, over?"

Join up? A Corsair flying wing on a Beechcraft?

"Tare Four to Bat Twelve. I'll have coffee for you by the time you land, over?"

"Ho ho, you're that fast, eh? . . . Tare Four, Tarbaby gave us a fix, eleven miles, heading two zero zero, over?"

"Understand 11 miles at two zero zero, this is Tare Four, out."

"Hello, Tare Four—"

I snapped off the radio umbilical cord, free from Tarbaby alone with the white fresh untrod fields of snow, pushed down till I was sailing just over them, executing a good slow roll until the very last when I sank just into the cloud matter—there went Nevers.

I pulled up 100 feet above it, looked around, no lights, no planes just stars infinite blue-black deepness and below the vast Sahara desert, my own world and all the stars to see, felt a strange sadness. Practice is over, the long apprenticeship done with. Coming, ready or not.

I climbed to 9,000 then began a dive. No blood from my nose and no sound only the sensation of slicing through small hillocks zipping valleys, pulled the stick straight back dropping the cloud field instantly into blue and sprinkled star lights then hung on my back and slower let it fall through the great swinging circle let it have its head picking up speed for the suicide plunge and last glimpse of white fields, whites of beaten eggs tossed ice cream a little fly diving into the mess of it and swallowed by it an arrow piercing, arrow feeling arrowness, head burrowed in cockpit nursing needles, speed holding at 380 knots, altimeter winding down wings straight. The Japs called the Corsair 'Whistling Death,' according to our Intelligence Officer. It was whistling now, only I couldn't hear it.

The program was done with. Now orders, a nice leave, the West coast, the carrier, and west into the fray.

The last day on the base I heard Hebert was in trouble. My old Trouble Brother had come back from a flight early and it was the talk of the base.

When I got to his room he was sitting up on the bed. He was tired of the whole business. Night flights as target, shot down again and again. As usual the authorities had no idea what he was about. Bogey pilots canceled flights and told them there was "oil on the windshield" or "the engine was running rough." When the sun went down some pilots would come in early with a "rough engine." The same planes that had been okay that afternoon.

"So just once, once," Hebert told me, as Balt walked into the room, hungry for the gossip, "I came back early and told them the truth. They kept asking me if there was something wrong with the plane, and all that."

Balt was yelling and laughing at him, here was a guy who didn't get it.

"What? You mean you don't get tired just because there's a war?"

"No, ya jerk," Balt instructed him, "Tell em, 'listen, my engine's running rough but, I believe I can just make it back to base—'"

"Oh, lying!?" Hebert was actually offended.

"That way," said Balt, the wily one, "you're a hero at the same time!"

"Anyway," he went on with his story, "when they asked me *why* I just told 'em I was tired . . . and some commander was down there yelling and screaming, tellin' me, I 'had' to stay up there. I just switched over and left . . . 'there's a *war*' he's yelling. Hey, I know there's a dern war. Then the tower started in on me again. Flashing me red lights, but I just came in. Got in my car, drove back to my room and went to bed."

"Now tell about—"

"Wait a second . . . that was a couple of days ago." Suddenly Hebert turned on Balt, "Y'know, *I* didn't start the dern war," and no argument there, for the truly detached, the unconscious monk who didn't care how, when, who, what, and would just as soon have fought for Germany or Japan, if it weren't for the language difficulties, while Balt was still yelling, 'tired'? 'TIRED?'

"Anyhow, next morning about 8:30 in comes two commanders—"

"Nacherly, old Bare-Bare has no clothes on—"

"So, there are these two commanders, bein' very friendly, like they had just come to pay a friendly call. But then as I began to wake up I began thinkin' that the commander of the station and the other commander, Smart, Commander Smart I believe, and I found out later that the other one he's one of those head doctors, you know for guys who are nuts, so I figured these two have more to do than come around payin' me visits—"

"You're a smart boy, Hebert!"

"Shut up, wise guy . . . so they start asking, 'How're ya feeling son?' And all kinds of crazy things like that. Well, I felt alright, and so the station commander starts in, 'Evan,' he says, 'this is doctor Smart,' I heard he was the head doctor, that Heath was goin' to." Hebert was laughing, trying to get us to see, wasn't it crazy, the *nut* doctor; to see *him?*

Balt and I were laughing at Hebert for all kinds of reasons.

"Then they finally got around to it, 'Why did you do it, son?'

"Because I was tired, I told them. But they kept asking me what was *really* wrong! It went on that way, they were really acting crazy. For a second there I wanted to ask them if they understood the English language. Finally the commander, the station commander, says, 'Well, listen, son, promise me you won't do that other thing again, alright?' Then he says, if I was feeling bad to go to the doctor and get myself grounded, 'But don't do that other thing again, alright?' 'Alright,' I told him, and then they shook hands with me and left. That's all."

Balt was whooping away. Only Hebert could have gotten away with it.

Well, I knew they had run into an honest madman and had no idea how to deal with him.

"Whatarya laughin at, Balt, that's the first hop I ever got out of!"

"I'm laughin cause you told the truth . . . man, that's unheard of."

" 'Was there oil on the windshield?' Nope."

He was imitating both of them: "'Son, is there some other reason that you're not telling us? This is wartime, you know,'" as if, for Hebert, that explanation might be necessary. "Now, this is wartime, and to leave before the flight is over is disobedience to an order. There are *serious* consequences to that, son.'"

"'Look,' I told them, 'Guys give some chicken-dung reason why they're bringing the plane back and nobody questions them. I tell the truth and there's all this trouble. I was tired so I came on back. The first time I ever cut a flight short, you can check my record. There was nothin' wrong with the plane, I was tired and fed up doin' the same thing over and over again.'

"They just left," he told us. "I don't know what they're gonna do. I'm not concerned about it. I guess you're not supposed to get tired during a war . . . ," then he turned to me with a smile, the old cocky smile, "but, heck, lieutenant, *you* can't leave the base, we still haven't flown through that danged hangar yet."

One thing was clear. If you lied you could get away with murder. Like the colonel telling me to lie about flying wing on the transport. Tell the truth and it means wings and commission stripped away and a few years in jail. Just lie and all's well. Almost everyone shook their heads over Hebert. Instead I was feeling that the world wasn't made for him, or, perhaps, for me either.

Only a few weeks ago he had brought it up again. Let's steal a couple of planes, go down to South America, smuggle stuff, diamonds er drugs. Wild takeoffs, people shooting at us. He would go on and on about it.

Instead of an answer I had a picture of the madness we were in. War. A cavernous roaring furnace a mile wide, swallowing everything: men, tanks, planes, battleships, whole cities, women, children, the aged, the crazy and the sane, no matter, into the furnace, voracious and unappeasable, sucking everything down.

Balt left, still shaking his head. Hebert and I stood there, knowing I would not see him again. I mean, of course, there was all of that impossible time after the whole thing's over, if either one of us was still standing. So, we shook hands. Goodbyes are not difficult they're impossible. What does it mean? All of this time spent with someone and then there's a parting. It should have been one last flight together, no words, because in a plane we needed no words, the two of us understood with a nod, a hand signal: "Open those hangar doors, we're comin' *through!*"

Circumstances separate us, or we let them separate us. We had never had many talks. Hebert was a Catholic and that was it. He was a good Catholic boy who would never miss Mass but would steal airplanes and skip the country if I had only said the word. Or flown for the Nazis or, after it was all over, down to South America and fly for some general in the Chilean Air Force. No theories, please, just point him at "the others" and let him go. I couldn't help but feel that I had betrayed him. Or I had betrayed the willful child in myself. And that too couldn't be helped. Hebert on his own? It would be a trail of incidents like the one he had just gone through. Too honest, too direct for this world. I was leaving my irresponsible little brother and there was nothing to be done.

"Listen, just don't get tired! Alright?" I tried to catch his eye.

"Right! I won't get tired, I'll just get oil on my windshield."

We laughed and I left him there.

RM was impatient with the story and anything that came out of Hebert's mind, "If you can call it that."

It wasn't that easy for me. Hebert and I had been together from the beginning, from CPT in Arkansas. It wasn't that he was impossible because of course he was. And much of the time I had been impossible along with him.

Time moves us or moves through us even when standing still. Suddenly everything was done. We had picked up our orders and were vacillating about one more party but the girls won out. We were packed and ready to go. Leyla had rented our little cabin, as a favor to our landlady, and nothing more held us to the base. We had sold most of the stuff to a brand new dive bomber pilot, one of the new bogeys, and his wife. They hesitated about buying the bed and I told them to just take it. I had an absolute horror at the thought of lugging it to the dump. Our bed? Selling our things? All of it was blasphemous.

"Never mind, our bed is wherever we sleep tonight . . . together," said Leyla.

That was good enough for me. And suddenly the gate was wide open and there was nothing else to be done.

We had even been paid, our last check for the month in addition to leave and travel time.

RM and Clare were packing boxes. Clare had sent a ton of stuff home and still had a ton of stuff to go through. RM was exasperated and so all four of us went to The Place and had beer and sandwiches. Then Leyla was looking at me. Go, go, let's go, said her look, akin to the look when we were on our tequila date so long ago, the look saying kiss kiss kiss me.

We stretched and left, but not before Jorge, Mulligan, and Balt came by, already half cocked, talking up the big party tonight. We're off, we're free, we're finished! Clare was stone-faced and Leyla just laughed. When they saw that we were not staying around any longer than absolutely necessary they gave up.

"Alright, well, see you in Jacksonville. Now, don't be late," said Mulligan, who would be late for his own funeral.

"Mulligan!" said Jorge, as if he was talking to a dog who kept jumping up on people.

"Don't crash and burn, Willy Babe!" Balt said, "I mean till we get over *there!*"

"Listen girls, I mean *ladies*," Jorge announced, "We'll keep an eye on these married guys out there on the West Coast, so don't worry!"

"Who could ask for a better chaperone," RM said, to Clare's sarcastic growl.

Chapter 46

With a month's pay and pay for 12 days' leave, three copies of our orders, reimbursement for various incidentals, we made out well.

RM promised to call us at my aunt's house. Clare sat me down and read the "War Prayer" out loud just before we left. I was touched by her doing it but my mind was a million miles away. That stuck with me, her reading it to me, more than the words—A's victory means B's defeat. So, tickertape parades for one side means cities, crops, and towns destroyed and parades to the cemetery for the other side. I had never had a thought about the other side, or about peace at all.

Leyla promised Clare, "I'll explain it all to him on the way home." Those two beauties laughed about "it" and me, I guess, as if it was nearly impossible for me to understand plain English.

For the last days the phone calls had been furious. Leyla was handling all of the arrangements. Mamoo was calling to find out about our schedule and when we'd be arriving. Those were the last calls on our phone at the log cabin. Leyla also imparted to me the fact that Arthe, my sister, had called with the news that Mamoo had had a "little" operation, but she was fine now and would tell me all about it when I got home. When I heard that I called to find out about her "little" operation. The removal of her left breast. But that was a mere nothing she said. The big news was the leave and the Barclay's house, which they were so nice to lend to us for this leave. And Arthe *was* going to be there. And both so excited! The kids were fine, little Arthe and little Carl, and another one on the way.

One last call to Mamoo who was "thrilled, just thrilled and delighted and can't wait to see you both." And said she was feeling fine and had recovered completely.

"You sure there's room for us all?"

"My darling, of course there's room. There are rooms to spare . . . and even if there weren't!" Together . . . we'll all be together, what else matters?

Goodbye to RM and Clare, our little log cabin, to Hebert, Mulligan, Jorge, and were on the way home. And Hebert? I felt a sudden chill in my heart. And Heath, I wanted to see him, wish him luck. I was a "warrior" and so what was he? A warrior battling against war itself?

Leyla had been wanting to tell me, for a long time, she said, once we were settled into our drive, into our coming-up time: whole, alive and having each other. So blessedly thankful for this leave, and whole days without flying.

We drove north, then crossed the big state of Florida, east to west.

"Now . . . " Leyla said, "a new chapter begins! Lieutenant I-L-Y!" She looked a long time at me as we drove away from the base, and then, "I think I'm going to have trouble saying goodbye to that kind of life together, our place, you flying and coming back to me at the end of each day." And she looked so long that it made *me* sad.

"It was heartbreaking," she said. "Just heartbreaking."

I was stunned. "Not happy? You just said it was a happy time?"

"Heartbreaking," she said again, with tears rolling down her cheeks. "Just heartbreaking."

"Can you explain that? Try and tell me?"

"No. You'll never understand . . . *heart*breaking."

She would not go any farther, only to turn her back to the road and hug me, the way we used to drive together in Texas.

Leyla began telling me of her father and how long she'd known about his drinking problem, and how she loved him regardless. And that he was getting treatment for it. I told her about Pearse and how much he had helped me, still that other side of him was frightening.

We stayed over in a motel in some quiet, oak grove town in northern Florida, away from others, fell in love again again again, talked about this new new beginning, whether she'd take courses while I was gone, or be home in Marshall with the baby. Leyla could hardly mention the word without going into a fit over it. "Just think, Will. We're bringing in the beginning of the new generation. The absolutely NEW generation!"

A thousand things were on my mind and all the time we were rushing to my childhood: New Orleans, the Gulf coast: the family, Sally, Uncle Willie, Mamoo, the sisters, *my* sisters. For whole moments I seemed to understand . . . to under*stand* . . .

"Leyla . . . my darling . . . I can hardly say your name without everything I feel about you—"

"And his wife," Leyla said, hugging my arm. "I love sitting like this, the way I used to sit with you driving and me . . . like this . . . up against you."

"What I was about to say . . . something I've been thinking about . . . do we have that book? The Mark Twain . . . The War Prayer?"

"Yes, it's right here . . . in the back seat . . . don't tell me you've been *thinking?*"

"God, all kinds of things are happening. The War Prayer, such a new thing—"

"To *you*—"

"Yes, well," I felt the heat of stupidity enveloping me. "Yes, of course, to me—"

I was burning up, "Leyla . . . *don't*, don't make me feel stupid. Any more stupid than I'm feeling right now—"

"Will, I could never feel that, but go on, I want to hear."

"Despite never having heard of 'The War Prayer,' have you ever felt that you suddenly understand . . . everything? Everything in the world? I know that sounds crazy, but I had that feeling, suddenly. That I understand—"

"From feeling stupid to understanding everything? So, how does 'The War Prayer' fit in?"

"To pray for one side . . . means . . . I've got to read it again."

Next day we made it through Mobile and the Gulf coast. I watched Leyla drive and she became very self-conscious.

"You'd make a great pilot, my angel . . . "

"You want me to smash into a tree, keep talking like that."

Shortly after that we shifted around. Leyla said she couldn't do it, I was watching her.

I drove to Gulfport and we ate an early supper in the huge dining room of one of the sea side hotels with a bunch of soldiers, walked on the seawall afterwards, and were both so excited that we decided to stay over, one more night absolutely by ourselves. We took a deep breath and decided against it, to go on to the Barclays and meet everyone. With joy and hesitation we decided to go on. I had told Mamoo we'd be there today and already it was late.

It was the fifteenth beach house toward New Orleans after the little town of Pass Christian. All had spacious grounds and were set back off the beach road.

I suddenly recognized it and we pulled in and stopped at the white gate and honked. I got out and Brucie was running with Mamoo right behind her, down the steps and across the sandy grass.

My mother hadn't stopped exclaiming even for a second, "Oh boy oh boy, so happy I am!"

Brucie flew into Leyla's arms, then mine, her whole face smiling wide. Mamoo with her arms around both Leyla and me, Brucie on Leyla's side.

Sally was standing on the porch beaming. The big black bird and my mother the little wren were so funny together, only it brought a catch to my throat.

When I had my first turn alone with Sally in the big spacious kitchen, she just couldn't get over Leyla, "Oh, my boy, ah declare!! She de pretties' thing I *evah* done seen! An' *Will*, she gave me the nicest welcome, yeahh, she did. But she is *so* pretty . . . so very pretty!"

"Don't let Brucie or Arthe hear you talk like that, Sal."

Sally whooped.

Arthe would be here first thing in the morning and, of course, couldn't wait to see us.

Arthe was so full of promises, dashed hopes, screeches, impulsive decisions, and still her life was so full of wanting, wanting to do the right thing. Everyone loved her and still everyone was exasperated with her.

Mamoo had made all the arrangements. Leyla and I would be sleeping upstairs in one of the two front rooms, overlooking the tall oak trees with a view of the gulf. I saw her look at Leyla for approval. She spoke to Leyla woman to woman, the way she did things, so matter of fact, so ready to change and accede. She had thought about it but wanted Leyla's approval. So New Orleans. Leyla was a captive. Mamoo had described it to her and showed her and waited for Leyla to agree. So flattering, superficial and truly gracious at once. So very New Orleans.

"Are you'all hungry?"

"I'm fine, Mamoo," Leyla said with a great handsome smile that I loved her for.

"Well, we have some wonderful red bean soup that we brought with us from New Orleans."

"How about saving that for tomorrow," I said. "On second thought—" and they both laughed.

Brucie was helping Leyla unpack and I was going downstairs when Leyla called me back, "Just a damned minute, Lieutenant!" I went over for a kiss and Leyla's whispered, "I'm so glad we're home."

I went down the broad staircase and into the huge kitchen with Mamoo. Sally was happy and hurried to make it ready. Mamoo sliced a lemon and got out some sherry and we had a little cream sherry.

Sally had some hard-boiled eggs in waxed paper she had brought from New Orleans and took a fork and chopped those eggs into bits.

"Hey," Sally said, "de GENERAL' home, an' de troop' got ta pay 'tension!"

Brucie came in and wanted some.

"You ask de GENERAL, Brucie! Only he give permission den you can have some."

"Oh, really! Well, GENERAL WILL! Can I have a little soup?"

"Give the kid some soup, ol' gal."

"Yes suh!" And Sally did a movie version of a salute.

It was all too much. Home. Home with Leyla, Sally, Mamoo, Brucie, and Arthe coming tomorrow. Then it was raining; safe home, nowhere to go and the rain coming down. It made me realize we were in the embrace of those two great arms, the arms of Florida and Texas-Mexico, the area which corralled those storms and herded them to us, rain, weather, greenery, New Orleans and the Gulf coast. Those oaks were taking a shower, those tough limbs and hard green leaves were soaking it up. Dark, enfolding, and the rain was cooling the July heat. The rain had cut us off from back there, from everything, the trip, the base, orders, even the war up ahead.

The soup was great. We were careful to sprinkle the chopped egg, squeeze lemon juice, add two dashes of *dry* sherry, about six drops of Tabasco and . . . magic!

"Ohh, Sally! I'm home and no joke about it!"

"Ha haaaa, nothin too good for the GENERAL!"

Mamoo would have preferred to eat it in the big dining room but this was Sally's party and Brucie and I were perfectly content right there at the big kitchen table.

"Have you lost weight, my darling?" Mamoo asked, "You're looking a little thin!"

"Mamoo, we flew day and night! It was quite a program."

"I'll bet you did—

"I'm still slowing down . . . when we weren't flying it was movies, briefings, lectures—"

"Well, dey gotta git you ready!" Sally explained to all of us. And Mamoo rolled her eyes.

Brucie told us that Leyla had suddenly felt very tired, and wanted to lie down.

"Well, of course she's tired," Mamoo said and we both went up to see her.

Leyla was still as a stone. Safe, here. She must feel it, even as we stood there.

Chapter 47

Next morning, after a dreamless sleep, the last of my dreamless nights while there, Arthe arrived, bright and early, telling me that I better appreciate it. She wouldn't have gotten up at six o'clock for anyone else in the world. There were the children. Blond, curious and shy. Little Arthe came over and gave me a proper hug. Carl put his hand out. I took it and grabbed him around the shoulders.

"Carl and Arthe, how original," I teased her.

"Listen, you, naming children . . . it was a battle, let me tell you. And, Will, I can only stay for half a day, unless I can get in touch with Carl and stay over. He's instructing in P-40's—"

"But, Arthe [Arthaaayyyy] you simply *must* stay over. You've hardly seen Leyla and—"

"Mamoo, I will, I probably will, but first I've got to call him. I've been away for a week—"

"But my *dear*—"

"Mamoo, will you *please*—"

It was finally settled. Arthe would call him immediately. She would explain about Will and Leyla and stay over.

We had breakfast in the big dining room and Mamoo was happy, all three of us children together. Sally fixed very light scrambled eggs and toast, with Mamoo's favorite, the little sausages, and French coffee with chicory. It was delicious. Leyla was completely recovered, she said, her little woes were gone and she ate a big breakfast.

"Remember you're eating for two!"

"Eating for TWO?" said little Arthe, in amazement. "She's *eating* for two people??" Her eyes were wide open.

We laughed, and Leyla told her, "Actually, I'm eating for three or four, this is a big baby!"

Arthe explained to her and little Arthe was furious that maybe people were laughing at her. The children went outside to play and were warned not to leave the yard. "I'm scared to death of that highway," said Arthe.

"Can we go to the seawall?" little Arthe was back a few minutes later with little Carl at her elbow.

"No, you can NOT! Don't you dare leave the front yard!"

"Arthe! God!" My rebellious sister demanding behavior of these new little rebels.

Leyla looked over, "That's the newest generation, Will! This little bundle is a candidate for."

"His little cousins! First cousins!"

"Ohh, I can't wait to see *that!*" Brucie said, Arthe was a quick second.

"Let's take our coffee out on the porch so we can watch the children," Mamoo said.

Mamoo was overcome, and had tears in her eyes. So glad to have all three of us, and Leyla . . . together. In a real way so was I. Everything behind me and everything ahead. The furious program, night flying and the new Corsair, the carrier, all of those things settling down behind me, still fluttering down, events like leaves when a car rushes through them, even though just days behind me, and everything up front. All of that; home, the leave. Sally here, the beautiful gulf in front of us, home, home *with* Leyla. Leyla with that treasure inside of her.

Brucie sat next to Leyla, ready to wait on her, ready for the first sign of discomfort. Inside I was laughing but, God, how I had missed all of this without realizing it. The battles between Mamoo and Arthe, Brucie's comforting of Leyla. Sally and her talk, her cornbread.

Arthe came back from her talk with Carl. Everything was fine. "But I've got to leave tomorrow morning early. Will, Leyla would feel the same way, I'm sure. You understand, right? Don't you? Sally is there any more cornbread?"

"You ask the GENERAL . . . can you have some mo'."

"The what??? Oh, the GENERAL! Okay, General, may I have one more little piece of cornbread, please?"

I nodded sagely. Sally gave Arthe another piece and laid the corner end on my plate and winked at me. She let me know, yes, the four corners were my favorites.

"Stand up, let's see!" Arthe was commanding Leyla to show how pregnant she was.

Leyla stood, blushing, poking her little moon belly out for us.

Arthe started laughing, "Oh, Leyla, so adorable! You hardly show at all!"

Sally was in from the kitchen, watching, a dishrag in her hand, smiling, approving, and couldn't help herself, "Das right! She hardly show at all! Why a person wouldn' know she wuz pregnant. Ain't dat right, Miz Aphra?"

"Absolutely right, Sally," said Mamoo and followed it with a plea to take our coffee onto the front porch.

"Three months," said Leyla, then looked at me because we had talked about it so often, exactly when it had happened. Three months. Three and a half.

Brucie just sat there, adoring. I knew it. She might as well have said it.

As usual, when Arthe was there we fell under her spell. We had to go shrimping and crabbing. Had to, she said. It's what one did across-the-lake. We drove into town, got some bait, found the crab nets in a locker at the end of the pier, tied the greasy hunks of meat to the nets, and dropped the nets into the greenish water.

When we went back to get oars for the dinghy and were crossing the beach highway a car honked, swerved over, doors popped open and Amoss the Mouse jumped out, we ran and grabbed hold of each other. I introduced Leyla, told him we had an heir, "Yeah, I heard! I heard! But damn, it's . . . I'm amazed to see you."

"Yeah, great! You on leave?"

We both were, as it turned out. And both headed for the West Coast and overseas. Amoss had finished up at Key West and was in Landing Crafts. Suddenly plans. I could already hear Mamoo groaning. We traded phone numbers and planned a trip into New Orleans for the coming week. The Mouse was leaving in eight days so it would have to be quick. Thursday, how about Thursday? Sailing? Okay, good, Thursday. Thursday? What's today? Saturday. Yeah, okay, Thursday. Call me. Okay. They roared off.

Within an hour we had crabs all over the crab nets and none of us knew what to do with them. It turned out that Arthe had no idea either. Besides, she hated crabs. Hated them.

"I think they're the ugliest animals, insects, fish, species, whatever they are, in the world!"

"But Arthe, you said, we've *got* to go crabbing!"

In a second we were doubled over laughing. Leyla was a little amazed, not knowing Arthe very well. Brucie knew how to pull them up and catch them, and we were about to, then decided the heck with it, let them go. Let 'em have the bait. Go on, have a feast. We were laughing at the crabs, "*Eat! Stuff yourselves!!*" we screamed into the water.

The girls decided to go into Pass Christian and shop for the fixings for some potato salad, and all the ingredients for pecan fudge. Oh yes, oh my

God, yes! It'll be so much fun! And fruit. Lots of fruit. Leyla felt fine and wanted to go. Arthe's two little ones jumped in the back seat.

Earlier, in a quick moment, Sally had asked about plans for our family. "You an' Leyla, plannin' on lots more children, Will, mah boy? Sure you are, right?"

"Absolutely, Sal. *Seven!*"

She fell out. Whooped and hollered.

Leyla came back to check on all the fuss and laughed when she found out.

"You think he can manage seven children, Sally?"

"Whaaaat? Dat boy??? He kin manage with fo'teen, ha haaa, fo'teen or fifty, whatever! No flies on dat boy! I mean to say, no flies on de GENERAL!"

"Now, that's the spirit, Sally. Well, we'll see what we can do."

"Awright, now!"

Leyla had to give her a hug.

"What a sweet thing you have done brought to this family, Will!"

They left for shopping and I stayed to talk with Mamoo.

"Ohh, I'm so happy, Will, my darling. Time, time we always seem to have so little of. . . . would you like some more coffee?"

"So, tell me about the operation? Was it painful? Is it?"

"Ohh, my dear it's nothing. It's been forever since I needed them," she laughed.

It was in the tradition, the sisters and their brave utterances.

"In the light of everything that's been happening it's the merest trifle . . ." she almost snickered, dismissed it, puffing on her long cigarette holder.

As I was sitting there, wondering what it was we would talk about, what we should talk about, on this last chance to be together . . . what really needed to be said. Just time together? Just reminding ourselves of the whole thing, life itself, what anyone means to anyone else? All the times I had disappointed her, what she so vaguely but desperately wanted from me? And here we were, rocking away like two old people, rocking away on the front porch of the country home.

"You know," she said, her eyes filling with tears even as she puffed on her long FDR cigarette holder, "I mean to say that you will never know how much it means . . . your being here . . . "

My mind had wandered to an old newspaper in a box under the stairwell this morning, an article about the Battle of The Empress Augusta Bay off of Bougainville. Nineteen forty three, already more than a year old. The Empress August Bay! That name! I was like a deer caught in the head-lights, the name had frozen me.

" . . . just to have you nearby, to know you're there. Of course, you know, I love you three equally, and it would be impossible to . . . "

The sun was hitting the small waves, and I was going way out there . . . wayyy out there.

I was thinking of the German ace who had been given a leave, someone had gotten hold of his diary and we had passed it around. The German high command had forced him to take a leave, a beach house and all the amenities forced upon him by a grateful country for two weeks: Go there, enjoy your wife, your beautiful daughter. You've earned it. In four days he'd reported back to his squadron for duty. Why? Couldn't he enjoy it back home? Commanded to enjoy the beach, his wife, and little daughter? Com-manded to stop and enjoy them? He couldn't *stand* it. In four days he was back, the fever had him and he left for the smell of high octane gas, his flying buddies, his Messerschmidt, the great game; and was killed no more than a week after he returned.

"So, Will, darling, Leyla tells me that you're scheduled to be on carriers? A carrier? Flying off carriers?"

"Yep, Mamoo, it's a wonderful life aboard a carrier. It's like a floating city."

" . . . and . . . you don't find it difficult to bring the plane . . . to fly it onto the carrier? But I suppose they train you to do that . . . exactly how to do it?" She was amused at her own ignorance.

"Ohh, yes, over and over. First we practice on a field, it's called Field Carrier Landings, then we checked out on the actual carrier, at Pensacola. It is just amazing, like some fantastic game . . ." I showed her with my hands, my right hand the ship, coming in to it was my left hand. I could feel again the explosion of pleasure at the cut gun and hitting the deck.

"My Lord," she said, "it frightens me to death just to think of it. And tell me, my boysie darling," a term I hadn't heard since boyhood days, "but tell me . . . you're not the least bit nervous? Or worried? At those times? I mean—"

"Not at all! Just total involvement, eyes, hands, feet, gauging, reacting. It is marvelous! I've never been so involved!"

She sat back, admiring. I felt as if I had to say those things and felt just the tiniest bit of a fake in doing it. Then again, it was not to worry her but because it was impossible to explain. Sitting here on this wonderful wide porch overlooking the big yard, the sparkling water, the Gulf of Mexico, with nothing to do other than what we were doing. Imagining it from here, rather than in a plane coming up on a carrier deck. Sitting here I could even imagine being frightened, thinking of all the possibilities. Doing it was totally different.

"So, my boy, tell me about the orders and exactly how much time you have here, but first I want to just say that a lot of people have sacrificed some things for us to be here. The Barclays, because July is, you know, one of the very times when everyone wants to leave New Orleans. And Sally coming here, leaving her home, and Esther, because Isaiah is, I believe, in Italy, you know. Although I know she wouldn't have missed this for the world. Brucie, who is in summer school at Newcomb, but has taken time off, to be here. And Arthe, with the children."

"I think it's amazing. I didn't expect anything like this."

"Well, it's little enough but I just wanted you to know. You must write to Bar and Maboo and thank them for giving us their place."

"I definitely will. That's a promise I will keep."

"Now, there's something else I did want to talk to you about . . . about Pearse and the hundred dollar bonds—"

"Arthe told me something— "

"Well, my dear, maybe it's best forgotten because, while I was in the hospital he . . . uh . . . got me to sign the checks, the bonds and, well, that money is gone."

The bonds were sent home automatically, taken out of my check and sent home every month. Arthe told me Mamoo had signed them and he'd spent it all. "Just drank it up," Arthe had said, totally disgusted. "Ohh, I can't *stand* to be around him," she said, and actually shuddered with hatred.

His alcoholism was a shocker. It was like living with two different people—smiling, philosophical Pearse, the one who knew all of the answers, the war veteran, the wise counsel, the one who helped me stay in college as long as I did ("plenty of Germans to go around . . .") and then the other whose smile slipped around corners, the fawning subject to the king, alcohol.

How did I feel? Mamoo was watching to see how I'd take it. But what did I feel? To tell the truth I had forgotten all about the $100 a month going home, either to be there after the war or to go to her if anything "happened" to me. I didn't resent it or think much about it. It was money I hadn't seen or counted on, like something that was not there, was never there.

Arthe's words settled into me and I could hear her pronounce them again, "I can't *stand* to be around him."

"Well," my mother went on, "the uncles found out about this, about what he has done, and have joined together to pay back all of the money he spent."

"Mamoo, I can't accept that. They had nothing to do with it."

"Too late, my darling. I have it right here in an envelope, here, let me go get it."

"No, no, don't." I was crushed, and embarrassed they'd even found out about it.

At the bank of good deeds I was completely overdrawn—no, bankrupt. I owed so much already that, in Sally's terms, I didn't belong in jail, I belonged UNDER the jail. It was truly payback time for me. Time to do something in return for everything the uncles and aunts had done for us, all of our lives, and my own fierceness would have to suffice till I was overseas.

Before I knew where she was going, Mamoo had jumped up and come back with the thick envelope. I didn't want to touch it. "Will! You *must* take it! Take it or give it to Leyla! Here!"

I took it and read the words on the outside, "We love you, old scout! And we're proud of you!"

The words baffled me. 'Proud?' for what? It was all a mystery. And now we sat there, facing the gulf waters with time together.

Sally came out to the porch smiling, wiping her hands; "Miz Aphra, what you wantin' for lunch? De girls talking 'bout some potato salad, least dat's what dey said—"

"Sally, why don't you take a rest for a few hours and we'll manage lunch . . . or, maybe the soup?"

"Miz Aphra, ahm ready to help out in anyway, ef dey jus' tell me. As fer de soup, maybe a cup for each person."

"Sally, you' just out to cause trouble." I told her, "*You* know it and I know it—"

"W'y mah boy—" she complained then started laughing.

Sally and I always knew when we were joking.

"Well, Sally, maybe leave the soup out, or warm it up."

"Awright, I be back there."

Sally left and Mamoo was talking about time, just time, she said. "Even to be able to talk together," she said, "it takes time to unwind . . . you've been on such a hectic pace . . . for so long. But, when that happens, when you settle down, if it ever happens, I'd like to hear your opinions . . . oh, about the family, your sisters, even about your mother. Your own life . . . I mean, have I badgered you too much about writing and staying in touch?"

"Let me tell you, it's been pure hell!"

"Will! Are you serious?!"

"No, Mamoo, I'm . . . God, if anything, I think I had it too easy—"

"Well, my dear, if you *did* it was because bringing up a boy, alone, I mean one parent of the other sex, can be more than a little difficult . . . but I do think, if anything, that you were given the long end of the stick . . . uh, many times."

"Oh, undoubtedly. Do you remember one night at supper. I thought somebody was getting more than I was. I'll never forget it. You paused a long time and stared at me, 'My darling boy . . . . .my darling boy . . . have you EVER . . . been left out? Of anything?'"

"Oh, I *don't* remember that at all."

"Well, *I* do . . . word for word. And you know what? You convinced me! Because you were so convinced . . . it was a boon. And a relief."

"Really? Well, maybe that's exactly what you needed—"

"It was great . . . you were convinced . . . that was good enough for me."

I think for the first time in my life I became aware of her doubts. And her power.

"Don't you see, Mamoo? How we trusted you? Whatever you said?"

"No, I don't."

"You're just fishing for compliments."

"No— oh, here come the girls. This must be continued, promise me. I wanted to talk to you about so many things. Oh, I suppose there will never be time enough. Maybe when I'm a hundred and twenty—"

They had pulled the car around to the back of the house and lugged bags and bags into the kitchen. Sally was back inspecting it all.

"Got enough food fer a week er two," said Sally, at first just commenting then beginning to laugh then came over to me, "An' when, mah boy . . . when Sal get *her* chance at you, at the GENERAL?"

Arthe heard her, "Sally, remember whenever Will got kicked out of the dining room and you two would be back in the kitchen laughing away."

"We had some times back there, me and mah boy," suddenly she could hardly stand up she was so tickled. "Brucie, please don't get mad but, Will . . . remembah Brucie's cat, that little skinny thing, well . . ." she could hardly go on.

"Which skinny thing? Every birthday she got a little kitten."

"Don't tell that story . . . it's so mean," Brucie said.

Sally could hardly stand up. I had to finish it for her.

"The cat's tail got caught in the swinging door between the kitchen and dining room and—"

"Don't even listen to this, Leyla, it's enough to make you sick—"

"An' the cat . . . the cat . . . O lord have mercy on us—" Sally couldn't breathe any longer.

"The cat was on one side of the door and a piece of the cat's tail . . . I know it's terrible—"

"Ohh, Brucie, but it *was* funny, oh God."

Sally had walked out the back door to try and stop laughing.

Arthe was laughing but commiserating with Brucie. Maybe Brucie was feeling it because we had picked on her, scared her, teased her.

Leyla was caught, a new part of the family and being brought in to one of the hundreds of scenes. Suddenly Leyla was walking quickly out of the room, calling to me.

She was sitting down in the dining room in a big chair and reaching for my hand.

"What? What is it?"

She placed my hand on her moon belly and waited. She was staring at me with great concentration and then, a little flutter under my hand, a movement across her stomach, like a little wing passing from one side of her stomach to the other.

"What is it?" Brucie asked.

"*The baby!*"

"What? What? Oh my God, Mamoo, come here quick."

We were crowded around Leyla who was almost lying down in the chair, with a heavenly look on her serene face. "They told me it would happen around three months or so but that was it, the first sign of life!"

I was so overcome at this miracle, this flight of life, this wing brushing across its world and my first contact with what we had called forth. Over and over I was feeling that wing across the world of Leyla's stomach.

"Oh, Will," Brucie was astonished, "that's so great you felt that. It's just so great!"

Arthe, the tough one, was overcome and wiping away tears. Sally was standing there in awe. Mamoo wanted to take us all out to supper to celebrate.

The talk was fierce. Through it all Leyla was the quiet one, only the smile that put everything into perspective.

"No," said Arthe, "we're making supper here. We're having Sally's soup with sherry, potato salad and artichokes with a dressing I just learned about. It's delicious. You're all going to love it! Love it!"

"Arthe weren't you supposed to leave early this morning?"

"Well, Brucie . . . We had to . . . go crabbing and everything! And shopping!"

"And feeling the baby! God!"

For the rest of the night Leyla was changed . . . in a different dimension. She tried to tell me about it. "You're pregnant, and you get used to that. But even plans for the baby are so . . . calculated. You know, we'll need this . . . and that. And then suddenly . . . you really *know*, no, that's when you . . . understand! I'm not just pregnant, I'm bringing a baby into our world . . . to be with us, the living child for us, and Will . . . " the tears were spurting out of her eyes, coursing down her cheeks, "Will, you won't be here! When she's *born*! I don't know if I can stand it . . . I'm sorry, everybody, but Will, you promise me, promise me that nothing will happen . . . you god damn it, promise me!" There, it was out in the open.

Leyla was swearing, apologizing, crying, swearing again, feeling terrible that she was losing it in front of everyone. "You know, Will! What I'm talking about!" Staring at me. Piercing me with her eyes.

Mamoo was holding her and told her, "let's go up to your room for a few minutes."

I told her we'd bring supper up to her and she clung to me, a hug so hard it hurt my neck.

"That's not it!" she said. "Do you understand, Will?? Do you??" Then she allowed Mamoo to take her upstairs.

That night was the first night of my dreams. I think they were dreams brought on by Leyla's cries for me to promise, to promise. Promise. Promise.

After supper she tried to explain to me. "It's not, it's really *not* . . . what you think, Will. I'm just remembering, the night we had the talk with RM and Clare, and you said you wanted to, '*throw* yourself . . . .' Okay? And I have had nightmares about that."

Before the supper was done we had started the fudge. With Sally officiating at every step of the way. "De secret be in de salt," she told us. "An' to let it alone!"

From laughter, to amazement, to cries of grief and worry.

I went up to see Leyla and she was wide awake and feeling terrible about her performance. "Yes, but it was not just hysteria, Will, and I do apologize for bringing them into it, but there *is* something I haven't told you, but please apologize for me, Will! . . . And come to bed now, alright?"

I went down and soon enough was back and in bed. We hugged and rocked and were so grateful for the "life" moment. She swore to me that she had not actually felt the movement, the wing brushing across her, till I felt it. We made love without the least embarrassment mouths moving head shaking affirmation, to a real coming gone religion revived, forgotten, experienced affirmed remembered and treasured.

Later in the calm pool of love all around us Leyla talked slowly, almost sleeping.

". . . and Will, I said '*she*', like I already knew it's a girl. Do you think I knew?"

"I don't put anything past you . . . now you were going to tell me something."

She sighed, exhaling a last vital breath, "I'm . . . tell you in the morning."

Suddenly I was at 10,000 feet, somewhere between a dream and a thing that had already happened—a clouded still blue storm sky and in the opening below, the ships of the fleet, the enemy, as if posing in fleet formation for their pictures, white trails from the aft ends. Vast scene of mighty sky rain clouds and below on that blue carpet the world of heaviness, world of fleet and water . . . down out of that storm rain world lay the world of quick change where geysers of flame, water and smoke erupted from steel ships and metal bits tore into planes and men—changing worlds and changing worlds and changing worlds. Another second . . . one more . . . one more.

And still like bright fish through the ocean of air, 16, 17 planes flashing through the special air, planes in royal purple, living gray-white, burning red, mottled green they whipped and turned and flashed in the newest air spinning off at the top bursting out and all the time closer, closer and yet a secret until the instant after the last instant will come as a stranger . . . spinning off . . . here comes . . . another second . . . another second.

And waked up to broad daylight, to a fresh day breeze in from the gulf a spanking morning breeze, collecting last night, our baby's life, and missed my own room, my sleeping porch at 6031, my book of heroes, Balboa looking out with rugged beard on blue Pacific. First signs of life, first view of the tremendous ocean. Then I was back to the dream, so real I didn't know if I had been dreaming or awake, and dreaming as soon as I woke up.

Arthe left that morning and the kids, whom I had hardly had time to see, gave me hugs and kisses. Such innocent kisses I had never received. She had a nice long talk with Leyla, and I felt these two are sisters. She invited Leyla to be with them in New Orleans when the baby arrives. This was a serious request, or invitation.

The Mouse called and changed the sailing date to Wednesday. Mamoo was exasperated but Leyla was all for my one last trip to New Orleans and a time with "the boys." It was decided to limit it to afternoon and evening and to return the same night. The Mouse promised Mamoo we'd be back Wednesday night.

Sweet Sid was in town, Amoss told me, just back from Italy and was on leave. The Moonfixer, still very much in training and married to a French nurse who had come over for training in the states. We'd go sailing the four of us Corpuscles and Wonderful's younger brother, Brazealle, or "Zelo", who was nominally in charge of the two-masted schooner, the *Vagabond*, in charge that is, while everyone was overseas or in training, and would be our skipper. Some others might be there: Foobar Bootsie, Little's wild young brother, and the Horse.

So, there were seven of us on the boat and a load of beer, gin, bourbon, ice, cokes. Strange crew, the younger brothers—Zelo, and the other two, Horse and Foobar Bootsie—then myself, the Mouse, Sweet Sid, who hadn't seen or heard about Cacksy Jack till he'd gotten back to the States, and the Moonfixer, almost but not yet a doc.

It reminded me of so long ago, the same boat, when Uncle Wallace and Bar had been part of the joint ownership of the Vagabond, along with Zelo's father.

On a boat there is a rain of things that need to be done: equipment to be carried on board, food and gear stored, a ton of ice, life jackets readied, unpacked, sails decided on and lugged up on deck, set the running lights, engine gassed, then heading out through the yacht basin, drinks, and the loudness of first being together. I hadn't seen the Moonfixer for half a year and Sweet Sid for over a year.

Sid had been in the tank corps under Patton. He and Jack must have been about 50 miles from each other. I had that picture of Jack's body being hauled down some Italian mountain on mule back. Oh, be gentle with that body. It was a blow thinking of the world without him.

The noise had settled down and the four of us, a year or two older than the noisy crew in the stern, had collected near the bow. Sid was talking about Italy, how he loved it, beautiful country and all, but different to see it in war-time. To trade it for New Orleans? And the Gulf coast? Blasphemy!

The Mouse was inheriting his father's marine insurance business and so, after the war, was all set. But seemed neither happy nor unhappy about it. The Pacific was staring him in the face also.

For the Fixer, another year and a half and then he'd specialize in internal medicine. And if the war was still going on would be assigned to a ship or some naval station.

I admitted I didn't know what I was going to do. Back to college, I told them. But it had a hollow ring even to me.

The Mouse had married Marque Baird, a New Orleans girl from the dances. They'd gone together in the last year before he was called up. Married in Key West.

We had taken down the sails and decided to motor slowly somewhere, nowhere.

This was my goodbye to the city. I looked off at the lights, the glow in the sky about ten miles away. I looked up at the immense sky, a basin of stars, one of those notions about the sky, immense and unfathomable *every* night but, bare of clouds and very clear gave us that feeling tonight. Our little troubles? Our wars? Look up at the stars . . . and try to realize light years. Light years of space.

Sid was talking about beliefs, and Buddhism. Strange time, Sid talking about a religion. He was much more at home telling a dirty joke. "On the trip to Italy I got hold of a book on religion. Yoga, Buddhism. Read some of that and then you're out on deck at night and see the sky. They talked about 'Desirelessness.' I can't say I understood it. But . . . you wonder."

The Mouse chipped in, ". . . you might not understand it but there's something about it . . . something that makes you want to find out more—"

He stopped and cleared his throat, was ready to grin and forget it, because it was rare when any of us talked about beliefs.

I thought of Heath, who told me that he was a 'renunciant.' That I was a 'warrior'. It was after he got back from taking Nevers' body home. I told them about Nevers' death, the suddenness, the shock of it. That orange flame across my brain.

"Our ship had a near miss," Sid told us, "a German Stuka dove on us, off of Italy, we could see the bomb headed for us. Exploded 50 feet off our fantail. I couldn't talk straight for hours afterwards. I thought maybe I'd never talk again—"

The Moonfixer laughed, "Did that worry you, Sid?"

"You better god damn believe it worried me. For the next few days I thought about my hide and what's inside of it. I thought about a soul and what it is, and if we have one, all sorts of stuff."

We laughed but we were spinning out a little farther and it seemed to us certainly farther from the good-time characters in the stern, from which we could hear laughs, exclamations, and shouts.

"The younger generation," the Mouse told us, with a look to the stern. Although they were only two or three years younger than we were.

"I worked on a guy back from the Pacific," the Fixer told us, "taking shrapnel out of his legs. He said he saw caves—on by-passed islands, you know—caves of suicide bombs, thousands of 'em, he claimed."

We were cruising out into the black waters, directly away from the city.

"So, Willy Boy, you're headed out there to see what it's like, eh? On a carrier?"

"Yeahhh!" I couldn't say any more although about a thousand words rushed to my lips. I was feeling the same old since-childhood-urge. A thing I had never expressed out loud. The fear about that well, that barrel of strength. If something or someone doesn't demand that well of energy . . .

"And what are you flying?"

"Corsairs!"

"That's a beauty of an airplane. Very fast, right? Is that the one with the bent wings?"

"Yeah, fastest in the world."

The Moonfixer mumbled something about a jet that the Germans have but I let it pass.

Shouts and laughs from the stern.

Who was steering? From the sound of it no one.

I realized that we were talking in a different way. The White Corpuscles had always been so guarded about anything we believed. As for the three in the stern, the ones who were "steering" the boat—for one thing I couldn't see Zelo without thinking of Wonderful Bob, Zelo's brother, in P-51s over Germany, in one of those "great" air battles, 10 or 15,000 feet high. Zelo and Bob, whose mother had called Washington every day till she found out through the Red Cross that he was killed—whose father, along with my three uncles, had been one of the original owners of this very boat, a man who had also proposed to my mother, and warned me, "Get out of New Orleans, soon as you can." I was feeling the incestuousness of the group; mothers and fathers, sons and daughters, the dances, everlasting ever-continuing. And Zelo's very New Orleans attitude: if we hit another boat, an explosion of laughter, "Yeahh, remember the night? Remember? . . . so drunk? Remember? We hit that watermelon barge from Mobile? Remember? The night we sank the old scow? HA Haaaaaa! The end of the *Vagabond!* Ah haaaaawww haaawwwww!"

Amoss told us how Shep discovered Buddy Lane only 200 Indian miles away but had ridden on elephant back, hitchhiked, run, bused, got there to see old Buddy, old Hank-the-tank, and how they got loaded and talked about the Napoleon House, and Maspero's, and the Camelia Grill and almost cried they missed New Orleans so much, cried in the shadow of the Taj Mahal, no doubt.

I told the Mouse, "This is to take nothing from the Taj Mahal . . . or the Napoleon House . . . both delightful places in their own ways, but most New Orleanians, after seeing the temples of India and the wonders of the Far East," I said, as we stood on the deck during that night cruise to nowhere, "tell me we are the luckiest people in the world, and as for the sights, they'd give it all up for the sight of a St. Charles Avenue streetcar."

Sid would inherit his father's funeral parlor. "I grew up with it," he said, "so I'm set right here in the old Crescent City. A lot of times I've seen the person when he was alive, you know, friends of the family. And there's the body. One day from walking around. It makes you think. The body's here but the life is gone. People, I think, mourn for the wrong thing. It's like mourning for a picture. What moves that body and face is gone."

"Sid, for Christ's sake. I tell you about Shep in India and you start talking about bodies and your old man's funeral parlor—"

I told Sid about seeing Blanchard sitting in the cockpit, in a field, a fly walking across his face. Maybe Blanchard had been frightened to death.

"What the shit are you guys talkin' about up there? Have you gone queer on us or what? We got a discussion goin' on here and we want you guys, you OLD guys, to settle it."

Eventually, we went back and joined them.

No one was watching the course of the boat and so what?

"Yeahh, fully insured, the boat, the whole lake . . . *'course* I'm watching . . . whatdaya think? W'y we'd run aground or somethin' (haawww) if we weren't steerin' a course!! Are you CRAZY?" Then the laughter, impossible not to join in, while the boat cruises slowly, blindly ahead into the darkness of the tremendous lake, maybe cruising in circles.

That was Zelo, Wonderful's young brother, Wonderful into the freezing cold of a winter night over Germany.

"Oh 'scuze me, did I knock yer drink? Lemme getchanother, sorry. What? Yer pants? Send em out, pay the costs, sorry 'bout that," guffaw—

"Zelo, just shut up and steer the boat."

"Hey! We' fully insured. Sit down, no, over here, fully ins', everything taken care of," then the barking laugh.

Goodbye New Orleans.

"—Now the peacock could tell it wasn't the alligator because haaaaw-www haaaawwww hawwwww, because haaww haawww, just a sec' . . . "

Zelo, Wonderful's young brother. Wonderful Bob and his ankle tattoo, the White Corpuscles gone: coordination, muscle, brain, books, school, flight, the beady brown eyes, round head, shot down, wiped out.

The City That Care Forgot.

Fun-loving? Uncaring?

If someone from another planet looked down and judged it?

Ahhh, let's see, New Orleans. The City That Care Forgot. Yes, and The City That Forgot To Care.

When Care left you had a fun-loving city. How else to have fun?

Get drunk and let the boat go is not to care. Care? No fun.

Give me a model city for a peaceful world!

In a world of peace and plenty, people would be like New Orleanians. Come on man, put it away. What are you drinking? WORK?? Mardi Gras is only a week away, how'ya gonna get any work done? Forget it. Lemme tell you a story: "See there was this girl, and she had the biggest knockers in the world—" or, "Look, I'm takin' you to a great place for lunch. It just opened! *Mama's!* They have the greatest Po' Boys in the world. See, they shave the beef, shave it, so it's just the *shavings* of beef. They put this wonderful sauce on it, and that's the secret, sweet and sour, hickory smoked, I can't describe it, you know, and they serve it on French bread, best French bread you ever tasted. Crisp, light and crusty, they keep the beer mugs in the freezer . . . and the beer is *very* cold! . . . "

Suddenly I remembered Pearse. Alcoholic Pearse, separated from Mamoo and living up in north Louisiana, who said it. Patriotism; the great evil. "Patriotism, my boy, terrible as it is, is not so bad in itself, but combine it with hatred and suspicion of, well, 'the other' and you've got trouble.

Combine patriotism and hatred and suspicion of 'the other' and that combination unites and gives birth to the offspring war."

And after it was all over, all, all over, New Orleans would remain, with the hierarchy and clubs and organizations and Mardi Gras and everything else that distinguished it and would go on and on.

Back at the dock we parted. The Moonfixer and Sweet Sid for home, Zelo, the Horse and Foobar Bootsie determined to stay on the boat till every bottle was empty. Every bottle on the boat.

"What about the dish-washing liquid?"

"That too!" Hawwwww Hawwwwww!

Was this "so long" to my good friends? Or goodbye?

The Moonfixer and Sid left in the Moonfixer's car after a fond handshake and best wishes. "Don't forget to come back," said the Moonfixer.

The Mouse and I were headed back across-the-lake but first he wanted to show me his aunt's house, uptown, "She's a good scout," he told me, "and always wanted to meet my friend, the flyer . . . oh yeah they're up, they keep horrendous hours."

Up the broad-paved and curbed cement walkway to the house, a raised, cut-glass, chandeliered, marble staircase to broad porch below, open-to-the-world upstairs porch for sleeping, or sitting or meals, magnolia-shaded three-tiered angel-food cake of a house, azalea-drowned raised mansion that could have gone up and out, out and back for another 14 stories for all we could tell—and if anything matters beyond this insulated, isolated, oak-strewn, oak-clogged, mossy, lawn-partying society don't tell me about it. Up the long wide marble staircase with the black cast-iron caryatids holding large gas torches gracefully, to the champagne breakfast, after luncheon much earlier, after the *Thé Dansant* followed by the supper-dance with open bar for four hours at the Court of the Two Sisters—the whole place ours for the evening for Estelle's coming-out party—followed by after-dance cocktails at the Claiborne's, and the midnight swim party (12-3) and finally to the champagne breakfast (5 to 7).

And when I finally met the "good scout," the Mouse's aunt, and she was thrilled and she caught us up on the parties just recently having taken place and I asked her, "God, how long has this been going on?" And she asked, not quite innocently, "What? Has *what* been going on?"

In one word she answered more than I could have hoped for.

No, this wasn't all of New Orleans, but a New Orleans now being inherited by Zelo, the Horse and Foobar Bootsie. And how long *would* it go on?

Till the mahogany and cut-glass doors collapse into termite dust in the air of voices long gone, done in, eaten grain by grain or niced to death: Oh, and who is this? I mean who *is* he? And your mother, my dear . . . let me see? Oh yes, she was a Livaudais, wasn't she? I knew her well.

All this a memory as the Mouse and I drove back across-the-lake at one or so in the morning. He was leaving day after tomorrow, a train to Los Angeles to pick up more orders and, he thought, to San Francisco. I'd be leaving a day later but would be on the coast sooner than he would. No idea how long we'd be in San Francisco. Maybe, maybe see each other out there.

Good to have this time together.

"How about those crazy young bastards?"

"Ahh, Will, they'll straighten out."

"Who knows?"

"Right! Well, good luck, Willy boy . . . out there, don't get hurt."

"Yep, old Amoss the Mouse. Here's to us and the Pacific."

He was off. I walked up to the house and wondered how I'd get in. Looked it over. Inside were some precious lives; one sleeping inside of my sleeping beloved.

"Will!" Came the voice from the door.

"Mamoo! You're awake?"

"I couldn't sleep, and I heard the car and saw the headlights. Did you have fun?"

"Yeah, but . . . it was a little strange."

"Well, I want to hear all about it . . . in the morning that is."

I got in bed carefully but Leyla woke up and hugged me desperately.

"Don't talk. Just hug me."

She made me chuckle, but somehow the chuckle died in my throat. I don't remember going to sleep but as clear as anything came the dream, if it was a dream.

There was even a title, with fanfare, but I don't remember it.

Leyla's gods, Sally's gods, my gods, Mamoo's gods who didn't know each other, lost and lonely sat down to past and future to now and never: High over enemy seas in the armor-plated chariot *he* flies through a hail of metal stones cast up from the floating islands of the yellow men who do not aim in this war of magicians but simply cover an arc to hit the largest percentage of flying warriors possible—heart-breaking sign of the times, vengeance against a sector, where the men who venture through it are killed by missiles not aimed at them; lost, the right-to-be-aimed-at, the right-to-be-target—not individuals, only percentages, and their plan is a good one for an arrow of metal—no feathers, lost the right to gay feathers—has pierced the life-line of *his* enchanted chariot now gasping for life—only inside this flying chariot is no number no fraction of a percent but HE, the lowest-highest common denominator.

Now the magicians who made the enchanted flying chariots thought of everything. They found a magic potion that burns rapidly when exposed to even a pin-point of fire, and they discovered a way to feed the fiery potion, little by little, to a fire-eating dragon that turns a large fan before it which in turn pulls the entire train—fan, dragon, winged chariot and rider—through the air, indeed at three and four times the speed of the hurricane winds, with the force of 2000 good horses.

Now the potion is fed to the dragon from a reservoir by a tube made of a wonderful metal being both hard and pliable, which winds over and around the moving parts of the dragon to its mouth. And yet, enchanted as they are, even they have their conditions—the fan, the dragon, and the potion. The fan must be driven, the dragon must be fire-fed, the potion must flow freely and, above all, their connections must not be broken. And each has its minor conditions, its lesser gods. The metal line that carries the potion must not be twisted too rapidly or struck by a harder metal. And, alas, it has been struck by the sharp metallic arrow and cut, so that only a small amount of the magic liquid reaches the dragon, which roars in a new way. And because of the speed and buffeting of the high cold winds the tube is about to be severed completely.

Now the warrior's enchantment depends on his skill and the continuance of the fan the dragon and the potion feeding it, that and his influence with any gods—magicians not of this planet—so in this unfortunate plight he is not only managing the chariot, which he is very skilled at doing, no, he's managing the chariot and at the same time using every incantation he can remember to all of the gods/magicians he's ever heard of: Allah, God, Zeus, Osiris, Jesus, Muhammed, Buddha, and any other Supreme Beings within earshot, their families and favorite sons and daughters and to the sun and moon and all the stars for help. Certainly if the right one hears he will be spared. If only this once, perhaps, the laws can be changed just this once so that two and two shall not equal four. Well, isn't his mission a proper one? Certain lands have been invaded by the yellow men from the far islands and he is out to punish them, to destroy them, not to be destroyed himself.

But the tube is tearing even as he prays, for the metal tube has its own god—a lesser god and, like lesser officials, more exacting—and its god has instructed it carefully that its enchantment rests on not being twisted or hit sharply, and it has eaten the fruit forbidden it. The metal tube knows but pleads in its manner, "Please, I repent, I'll never do it again." And its god, "You are forgiven." And the tube overwhelmed at this near miracle, "Oh, thank you, when will I be whole again?" And its god, "I said you are forgiven, as everyone is at the end, even if he thinks his mistakes are intentional, but shortly now your life will end."

Tube, "But you said . . . "

"Yes, you are forgiven, but if you were allowed to go on you would not understand." Tube, "But I don't want understanding . . . "

"I will teach you," said its god. "I will teach you to love understanding and remember, you are forgiven, of course."

In that instant the tube snaps. In another instant the dragon is cold and still and the fan has stopped turning. In the very instant of the warrior's most fervent prayer for more power he gets less and then none, the prayer disintegrates into mutterings farther from propriety: It's *me* God, or whoever you are, please god, damn it, it's *me*, listen! Listen!

With a certain basic courage only improperly nourished, looking and wondering at the handle in his leather-gloved hand moving over the same arc as always which always before has brought a roaring welcoming response, the same handle, which always before meant faster or slower now nothing, and as strange to him as to an ape-man placed suddenly in the seat of this chariot forced to put his hand to the black plastic grooved and cross-cut handle.

Maybe this is a dream! It crosses his mind after not the picture of his whole life but one instant of electrifying life itself—not his no more nor less than anyone's in the total procession—flashing into and through his mind with a connection-belief that the twitchings and itchings at the soles of our feet at the edge of a very high place are an age-old desire to grip with the feet, oldest expression of the urge to live just to live not die, and felt that because he was feeling everything , that he was a shaggy haired man millions of years old so what in the shit, in the name of truth, would he be doing here high over the ocean in a war going fast out of a war? For he can still hear the faint sounds of the battle off to the side. And he can see those fish-infested waters beneath him—pick out a nice soft spot of ocean—of course it's not been definitely proven that they really attack, only occasionally. Then maybe just drifting and drifting.

Unhook life raft from chute. Attach to mae west. Unhook chute straps.

Now, listen God, and listen and look, exactly where I will go down, and tell them. Please. Please. Please tell them where my life is going down.

He is sighted. The report goes in. He's lost. He is sighted again. Twice he is sighted—more than he asked for, since the god of man is different and man has thousands of second chances, in addition to getting just what he asks for. Only he is never sighted again.

For his brother warriors the report is conclusive of nothing. No understanding gleaned, not even any knowledge. Do sharks attack before death? Did his life raft overturn? Is he still drifting? Drifting. Drifting.

Chapter 48

"Well, was it fun last night? Yesterday?"

She seemed so innocent, leaning up on one elbow, hardly aware that I was still drifting . . . dreaming.

"Come here, you!"

We were hugging so that I couldn't see her any longer, only that she was in my arms. And I felt a pang about dreams. Leyla's a dream, I thought. Scenes of last night kept interrupting that dream but she wouldn't let them for long.

"Mamoo and I played Chopin on the piano in the upstairs hall, yesterday. She plays very well. We went through a lot of music, talked about all sorts of things."

"My God, Leyla, this is where I came in!"

"What?"

"The day after our first date you played the piano, you played Chopin!"

She threw back her head, laughing. "No, I played, 'I'm in the Mood For Love,' and was blushing so much I was afraid to look at you."

"After that you played Chopin, and I was thinking 'my mother used to play Chopin.' I was connecting you and her. It was like being home again. Only it was a little incestuous. Falling in love with my mother."

"Oh Will, ooohhh Will!"

"Just a second. How's that child of mine?"

Hugging, rocking, holding, glistening.

We'd have been in bed forever but there was a knock at the door and Mamoo announcing breakfast.

"Be down . . . in a minute."

And we were. Two more days. It was almost a routine and, in a strange way, it helped that Arthe was not there. Arthe kept things from falling into place, she was a juggler and ten things had to be going at the same time. Would I ever get over her? Of course not. Brucie allowed things. Would I ever get over *her*? Would I get over my mother? Sally? This family? I looked at them, all of us at the big dining room table. Brucie in a thin cotton dress because the heat had come down again, despite the ever-present breeze from the gulf. Leyla next to me, sneaking a hand over and patting my leg. Mamoo, with her hair so carefully done and her sweet and winsome face and smile, her careful look at me, speaking such usual thoughts and thinking, back behind those glasses, the kind blue eyes, thinking such thoughts, thoughts she might never confess to me. Sally had fixed something so special for breakfast, something we kids used to beg her for, the big shredded wheat bars toasted with melted butter poured over them and soft-boiled eggs on top. I knew it was from Sally, something from years ago, from 6031 Pitt Street that we could never get enough of.

"Now dis," she said, her very voice shining, as she presented the pan of shredded wheat fresh from the oven, "Dis be de general's favorite breakfast! Am I right, mah boy?" Then to herself but to everyone within a block, "Listen at me, I call him 'general' on de one hand and de very nex' breath callin' him 'boy'!" Sally began laughing and invited everyone to join her.

"Well," Mamoo interrupted, "he's the boy general! . . . And we all salute him!"

"Das right, da's for sure!" Sally sealed it up for all of us.

"Well," Mamoo said, "what's the schedule today? What's on the docket."

I watched her and it was all calm and usual but it was like a kind of terrible usualness. We would have meals and the minutes would follow each other trailing all the way to the drive to Biloxi, the army transport plane to Jacksonville and beyond. A big cloud was moving in. It was no longer a leave it was two days, and two days, and then just two days and the desperation.

I felt like I had to get up, to get up over it and take a look at the whole thing. As if I was getting up over the entire area to see the earth itself and its details to see . . . to see what, exactly I couldn't even tell, just the tremendous desire to see, to see it all.

I think I surprised everyone—and until then didn't realize they were actually waiting for me to lay out the day the way it should be—and even myself, leaving all of them out, "I want to take a walk . . . just me . . . for about an hour, then after that, whatever we feel like doing. How is the fudge, Sally? Did it ever harden?"

Well," Sally started in, with some heat, "You know yo' sister, Arthe, could never in her life wait for *nothin.*' I told her and told her it ain't ready yet—"

At one point Sally had thrown up her hands and walked away from the fudge, from the "mess" that Arthe had made of it.

"But it's *so delicious*, Sally," said Brucie, "and that's thanks to you!"

"Brucie, you' an angel," said Sally. "Ain't dat right, Miz Aphra?"

Brucie came through with these comments and it always had the effect of melting Sally, and melting her anger at anything.

"Well, it' back dere," Sally said, "done or not done."

Mamoo was shaking her head about Arthe, in total agreement with Sally. All her life, all her life it had been the same. And yet how could she stand against Arthe? Stand against life itself would be easier.

"Brucie," Leyla asked, "you're going to be married here? In this house? How marvelous."

"Yes, outside, if it's nice. Out in the side yard. And *you* better be there!"

"If it's nice!?!" I told her, "Of course it'll be nice. It *has* to be nice."

"Well, of course," Mamoo added. "And now I'm going to make some coffee and we'll take it out on the front porch where it's cool . . . if you can wait for your walk, Will, my darling."

Brucie and Leyla stayed at the table and I went back to watch Mamoo make "her" coffee. She had her own little coffee-maker, and did it by boiling the water and pouring a little at a time into the coffee grounds. "This is *slow* drip coffee," she said and did it in four or five installments, just before, *just* before the water comes to a boil, she said. I had to bite my tongue to keep from making fun of her and whether or not it made any difference. Instead I didn't say a word, watched the careful way she did it. And, instead of saying anything, I felt my love for her and her ways. It was heart-breaking, and I couldn't say why.

"Mamoo, save me some of that very coffee for a little later, okay?"

"Oh, you're going for your walk now?"

"Yes, I've been . . . feeling a real need to go . . . now."

"Well, it will be waiting for you when you get back."

There was so much more, in those seconds. She was telling me things. Not things I didn't know, that she hadn't said just those things over and over and over again. It will be waiting for you when you get back. And so will we. Endlessly.

Leyla seemed a little strange but gave me one of her sweet kisses, and even Brucie.

"Oh, your sister, too?"

"Yes, my little sister, too."

They saw me out the door across the yard and out the front gate and turned toward Pass Christian and up the first street I came across, away from the gulf. And knew that this was a special goodbye, to this time, to my time and here. Farther from the gulf the wind was only a breeze. I walked on the tarred street looking for a place to stop. Turned left, walked through pine trees and heavy foliage, over a broken-down fence into a cleared area and realized I was in back of the Barclay house. I had no idea their land extended this far back. There was the wash-house and the servants' quarters and the house itself, barely visible through vines and foliage. I sat on a big stump and knew I was facing it. And the phenomenon of the way they deferred to me. Whatever I wanted. The condemned man? And so . . . here I am, and what I have called down, and don't know if I want to figure it out. Maybe I wouldn't be here if they had said, no, we've got to play cards. Okay, cards then. But no I had insisted. By myself. Alright, then, my dear, they've allowed the condemned man . . . and now what was it he wanted? I was at the end of a very long trail. And had I gotten everything? Just as I planned? I found myself thinking of the night with the Moonfixer, talking in front of the house. When I told him I couldn't see coming back to New Orleans after the war. Couldn't see it? Couldn't see? Or, couldn't make it? . . . because I *wasn't* . . . coming back?

To 'fling myself at it?' To go into it all the way? With everything?

An absolute jumble. The dream . . .

I couldn't get it, couldn't think about it, and couldn't stop.

Did I get what I wanted? What I asked for? To grow up, great deeds in the air, glory in the air? Throw myself at it? Come back to the girl and children? Only it was a screwy kind of order. And that's what . . . that was a knot. Glory in the air, fastest plane in the world, the girl and children. Is "glory in the air" the same as throw oneself into it with everything? Everything? Then, as Leyla pointed out, everything minus everything leaves nothing.

Grow up. Fly the fastest plane. Okay, I've got it. Go overseas. Yep. Fling myself into the war. No fear. All of my strength, hopes, dreams, every bit of me. Then? Home to the girl and children? But I've got that . . . already. The girl/woman . . . and child on the way.

I went over it a hundred times. And if my wishes have come through, if they have, there's something out of line. Glory in the air, the fastest plane, *then* come home to Leyla and children. I'm not getting it. I have that already. The only thing lacking, only one thing lacking . . . fling myself into it. But that comes . . . after . . . return to peace, wife and children.

When I decided that no amount of time would take me beyond what I'd come to. No use sitting there any longer. I went back to the house, nothing resolved.

Brucie and Leyla were sitting at the big table in the dining room. They were or had been deep in conversation. And stopped when I walked in.

"Tell him, Leyla," Brucie commanded her.

It took a while but it was what she had been so upset about, the talk with RM and Clare, the night we talked about the war and pirates.

"Will," she began, painfully, "That night you said you wanted to throw yourself into it with everything . . . 'all the way,' you said. I heard those words and heard them and heard them. And . . . don't you see? Will? You're going off to . . . do that? Do you see?"

She could not go on for a while, "Don't you see? *What does it leave?*"

Brucie took it up, "Do you see what she's saying, Will?"

"Everything . . . you said, Will . . . *everything!*" From practically speechless Leyla had come to the point of not being able to stop, not able to stop thinking about it or stop talking.

"Leyla you asked me, the other night, to promise, to promise. And all I can do is promise that I will . . . I will . . . come back."

Suddenly it was revealed to me, and I couldn't tell her that. What I had prayed for,

wished for, all these years and had gained in this strange compact. The only thing left . . . the last piece of the puzzle. It had become clear, finally and ultimately, clear as a bell.

"That's what I meant. Promise. Promise, you won't give 'everything'. I told you I wouldn't interfere with the flying. Okay. Just that. Because I'm part of that . . . 'everything.'" Whatever I said now was so crucial. A truthful lie.

My little sister whom I loved and who had suddenly grown up was part of it.

Oh, how I wanted them to be sisters. To stay together. Suddenly I had the comforting feeling that they were sisters already and I had little or nothing to do with it.

"Can you answer me, Will?"

"Will you two be sisters?"

"Will . . . can you give me something, some answer?"

"Brucie, will you be with Leyla when the baby comes?"

"Is that your answer?"

"We'd love to have her," Brucie said.

"Brucie, cut it out. Will you see to it that you're with her when the baby comes?"

"No! Answer her, Will!! What can you really promise?"

"I promise . . . I promise I won't do anything stupid. Just throw myself into something needlessly. And . . ." within that "I'll come back, if it's at all possible."

"Will, do you remember that letter and the Dostoevski quote I sent to you? In a letter, about spending some time in preparation, so you could throw your whole self at the problems of the world? Will you promise me that you'll seriously think about that and come back to our life and the life of our child . . . and the . . . and the other six children we promised to have?"

"Will you take this family, Brucie, Sally, Mamoo as *your* family?"

"You're leaving yourself out, Will! See? You make me feel you're leaving, never to—"

"Of course I meant me too."

"Promise?"

"Promise. Now. I'll do it. If it's in any way possible. I'll try to do it. I'll get back, somehow."

"Just nothing . . . crazy! Nothing impossible! No flying down a Jap funnel, That kind of thing."

"You've got it. My promise."

"Come here!"

Brucie was being left out. But Leyla reached out one hand for her and Brucie seized it.

"I don't know how I can't be in Marshall for the baby, Will, but I'll come to New Orleans first thing."

"No good," I told her. "I think sometimes we have to ask unreasonable

. . . we have to *be* unreasonable. And I want you to have the baby here, in New Orleans. With us."

"Will, how can I?"

"You want to have it in Marshall? Where your parents did everything to stop us?"

"But . . . "

"Leyla, can you do that for me? Tell your folks I insisted! I don't want to go through them to get to you for news of the baby. Like it was my last wish before leaving. Tell them anything."

"Will!"

"Go home when I leave tomorrow, day after tomorrow. Spend a lot of time up till the last month with them, then come here."

"I'll try and tell them."

"Do it! Do it! Brucie'd love it, I know it! And so would Arthe, Mamoo and Sally."

That last day and a half before leaving was strange and special. Leyla seemed lifted, and was happy.

The last full day I went to see Sally. We went out on the back steps and talked.

"Mah boy, you got to take some time and see yo' gal, right? Many years as we been together."

"Right, Sal. And now's the time."

"Will, mah boy, General Will, ah got no big message for you, no more'n King Cole already come up with, to 'Straighten up and fly right.' That's no more'n I been tellin' you all along. No more'n to say dey got people what loves you back here. People what wants you to come back and make that family you been talkin' about. An' I don't know no one dat got a prettier wife to come back to . . . than you. An' old Sal can't think of two persons I'd rather be with and do for than you and Leyla. It don't do no good to tell you dat Sal love you jus' like yo' Mamoo loves you. You *got* to know dat."

"I know it Sal, and I love you back, and you know that too. I'd love to have you be with us and our little hellcat children."

After chuckling she pointed at me, "Listen, I done handled the hellcat . . . the champeen hellcat of all time. I reckon I can handle the little ones."

We talked about Brucie's little kittens and had one more laugh about that.

"Remebah, Will. We wuz back in the kitchen and Brucie had done got another poor little kitten for her birthday and you, wuz it you or me who said it first . . . "

Neither one of us could go on for laughing.

"Brucie's birthday and the cat's doomsday!"

And that was as good as goodbyes can get. We had laughed all of our lives together at one thing or another, and this was a review. We went over my friends, one by one, and I caught Sally up with them.

"Will, now tell me. What about old Porgie, Pie-Face? Remember Porgie and them steps out back, at 6031? Oh, lord, that boy like'd to kill me. Ba-bamm and down them steps he would go."

"Old Porge is in the army, somewhere. I've lost track of him."

"An' Will, now tell me, oool' Nippy, Bobby Cameron—"

"Oohh, Sal, I thought you knew that . . . he was killed over Germany!"

"Will . . . Will . . . no, I never knew dat, sorry as I am to hear it, why you never tol' me?"

"I'm sorry, I thought Mamoo might have told you."

I told her about Wonderful's family and calling Washington every day.

"Oww, Will, mah boy, I am so sorry to hear bout that, much as I had my fun about dem boys, but you know, mah boy, I never meant nothing by it. Dey was yo' friends sorta like extensions, extensions . . . .is that the word? You know what ahm sayin'?"

"What's going on out here," Mamoo opened the back screen door part way.

"We catchin' up, Miz Aphra, jus' catchin' up."

"Well, Will my dear I thought we could take a little walk on the sea wall before lunch."

"You go on mah boy, ol' Sal gots some special things for lunch that's gonna—"

"I know, 'that's gonna bust my shirt buttons'—"

Sally fell out, we got up and I went with Mamoo, intercepted by Leyla.

Arthe had called and after talking with Brucie, had Leyla on the phone and began insisting that they would all love it, then insisting that Leyla stay with us for the baby. Tell them that it was Will's last wish, last wish before leaving, to have the baby here, in New Orleans. Arthe already had a hundred plans for it. And was figuring ways to make it alright with Leyla's mother and father.

I felt a great hope. Arthe could pull it off. I was already chuckling over it. I didn't even want to be there for the details.

We went walking and Mamoo, at the end of it, was somehow relieved. We'd need till she was 120 to have enough time and decided to just enjoy what was left, with no more pressure to "get it all said."

It was strange and getting stranger. Leyla wanting to do it every chance we got, wanting to do it and not wanting to because then it would be over, God, dissolving in tears and the thought of how she could arrange to have the baby here, which she'd love to do.

She called home to Marshall and talked it over with her mother. The huge mountain was suddenly reduced to practicalities. She, Leyla's mother could come to New Orleans for the baby and stay close by. Then Mamoo was called in and with her effusive compliments how generous Leyla's mother was being, that she was sure something could be worked out. There was time and she'd take that on. And get back to Leyla's mother. Arthe's force and Mamoo's diplomacy, along with Brucie's wishes and love would manage it.

Everyone was so excited. The clouds had lifted.

RM called on that last day. Clare and he would drive to Biloxi and take the MATS transport to Jacksonville with me and meet the group in Jax. Brucie could meet them and they'd all have lunch together.

Leyla was a changed person and I'm sure the baby could feel it. She was glowing: "I feel so great, Will, my dearest, my sweet, oh God, you're so lucky. I love you, I love us to death. And I want to just say 'yes' to it all."

"Calm down now!"

"No, I mean it. I don't want to stop life, Will. I don't know quite what I'm saying but I don't want to stop life."

"What—"

"I'm saying 'yes' to children on the way."

"What about graduate school—"

"Yes to graduate school!"

"What about helping the colored?"

"Yes! Yes to that, too."

"And the world and Kolombangara, Manadalay and Tassafaronga Point?" I was becoming her cheerleader.

"Yes to Kolombangara, Manadalay, and the other one too."

"And Madagascar?"

"YES to Madagascar!"

"I get it, but—"

"Yes to that, too! Oh, Will, we heard a great tale in the religion course. It's a Sufi tale about the Mullah Nasrudin, he's the butt of the jokes. Now, the Mullah is judging who was right. He listens to the first guy's story and says, 'You are right!' Then he listens to the other party, the exact opposite point of view, and says, 'Ahh, *you* are right, too!' Then his wife says, 'But, Mullah, they can't both be right!' 'Hmmm,' he says, 'Wife, you're right, *too*!'"

"You're mad, Leyla, madder than hell."

"Yes, Will. And I'm madly in love with you and I'll need my whole life to get tired of you. I want to dance and dance with you, listen and listen and talk and talk, laugh and laugh and make you laugh and love you and love you and bed you and breakfast you and I'm only afraid we won't have the 160 years I'm gonna need to get tired of you. So, I'm saying yes to it all. Yes to New Orleans and having the baby right here, yes to our plans for where to go then, whenever we go, yes to Kolombangara, yes to children, yes to helping those mess boys, yes to peace and any wacky ideas that'll help bring it about. Yes, and yes and yes again."

"Come here . . . who's the luckiest guy in the world?"

"You are . . . ohh, Will, I'm dying. And they said 'yes' to us and the baby here and we'll just work out the details. You know, my mother always liked you, from the beginning. But . . . and I never told you about this. He, my father, saw us in the side-yard that night and it killed him. We all talked about it. Imagine, the three of us, talking about that? I told them I *wanted* you to make love to me. I insisted on it, yes, from the beginning. I told them the minute I laid eyes on you I said I'd never say 'no' to you, no matter what wild thing you asked for . . . "

"Leyla you never said—"

"Yes I did, I *told* you—"

"So plainly—"

"I told Annie that . . . I told you, in Cambridge, how can you have forgotten it? Don't drive me mad, Will!"

"I remember, but—"

"Anyhow, I'm screaming I'm so happy. And Will, when more children come well, we'll see the world with the children, alright?"

I almost choked on the special dinner, "the last supper" and after it we played cards for a little while. Mamoo wanted to do something together. They taught me the game of Hearts and we played for about an hour, then Leyla and I were in bed early. Advancing on each other as before some elaborate tango, as familiar as we were with each other.

"I don't know if I can do this . . . tonight, Will, maybe just love each other without doing it. Is that possible?"

"Let's see . . . first, put this left leg over here, and then . . . "

We slept, then sometime in the night we woke up spontaneously and went at each other without apologies

"I'm glad it worked out that way," I told her.

"Any way that's us," she said.

My packed bag was in the middle of the floor and I lugged it out to the Green Lizard.

Sally had pancakes for breakfast. She told us that Mamoo had gone out to the beach with her coffee and that I should go out there. She was waiting for me.

A big hug for Sally then we were leaving the house. "Remember," Sally said, "you remember, just *fly right!*"

"I gotcha, Sal. I love you, old gal."

"And write, mah boy!"

"Yep!"

Brucie was going with us to Biloxi and would meet RM and Clare. The girls would see the plane off and then maybe have lunch together.

"Well, Will, General Will, we better get moving. Everything's in the car."

Sally had told me Mamoo was waiting. The tide was way out and there was an onshore breeze straight in from the gulf. There sat that little figure with her coffee, only a few feet from the waves.

Yesterday, I knew, had been goodbye. Today was only the body's leaving. My mother was sitting on the beach, sitting with her back to me looking out to sea. I felt it then. Goodbye. The wind blew grains of sand around my legs and ankles and after going up to her and kissing her and saying the word, I was walking back and turned and shouted goodbye. I don't know why I said it again but the wind blew it back in my face, and the little sand stars struck my feet and ankles and the wind blew me on.